The End of Time

A Suspenseful Political Thriller

THIS BOOK INCLUDES

The Quickest Chase

The Long Way Around

The Keeper of the Lost

The Nevermore

The Strongman

The Curtain Call

Table of Contents

The Quickest Chase

Walk of Faith

CHAPTER ONE

Seditionist HQ - Los Angeles

At 12:15pm Hank was on his fourth cup of coffee and dying slowly in a tedious meeting with the auditors, but he perked up and hastily excused himself when he saw Floyd's call coming in.

"Greetings, this is Hank Bancroft, how may I assist you today?" he asked formally.

"Dad? It's me."

"I'm sorry, who is this? Do I know you?"

Groan . "You suck so bad, it's not even funny."

Floyd really *was* mad enough to scold his dad, but Hank grinned. He knew what was coming next. "Oh? And why is that, exactly?"

"Because I've been a mess all morning thinking you weren't going to let me come home until I'm old enough to retire. Why didn't you tell me? You're so mean."

"Wanted to surprise you."

Floyd grumbled. "Well, surprise, now you get to pay for dry cleaning Uncle Dav's suit because it has my snot and tears all over it. I made such a fool of myself in front of everybody."

"You're welcome, Floyd."

Hank was still grinning, although he felt bad for being so amused by the poor kid's reaction...but he couldn't help it. At least, not until there was an ugly sniffling noise through the phone; evidently said snot had not yet retreated and Hank suddenly felt a huge pang of guilt.

"So, does that mean you hate me again?"

"No. But I really wanted to like it here, and make you proud and...I'm sorry, dad. I'm almost 16 and acting like such a baby."

"No, don't say that. Missing your family is nothing to be ashamed of at any age. I *am* proud of you, Floyd, because you're a good person. Brave, kind, and smart. Don't ever forget that."

"I don't feel brave right now."

"Well, I have a feeling you'll get over it quickly. See you in about three hours. We'll have an early dinner at home and then you're going straight to bed, no complaining. Home school starts at 8am sharp."

"Yes, sir." Floyd actually sounded really happy about that, and Hank was indescribably pleased at the thought of having his boys back together again.

"I have to go back into my meeting now. Be good for Dav."

"I will, I promise. Thanks for letting me go home, dad. Love you."

Thanks for wanting to come home. "Love you too, son. Can't wait to see you."

Hank swallowed the lump in his throat, and went back to his meeting with a glowing heart.

———-

Floyd loved his Uncle Dav, but he wasn't normally the affectionate type. That's why Daven was astonished and rather honored when Floyd scrambled into the car and straight to his side, wrapping his arms around his "uncle."

"Thank you so much for coming to get me. I'm so happy to go home. Can we get some food? I haven't eaten lunch."

Of course food would be the very first thing on his mind. Dav put an arm around Floyd's shoulders and tried to accustom himself to the boy's lanky body pressed up against his own.

"Your dad said no fast food, so we'll go to a restaurant. I know you want to get home as fast as possible, but-"

"No, it's fine. Thank you."

It only took fifteen minutes to get the resort where Dav knew of a restaurant with a private dining room, but Floyd had laid down and was now sound asleep with his head on Daven's leg when they pulled up. He nodded to Lucas as the man looked back at him with a *what should we do?* expression.

"Let's just head home," Dav whispered. "He's out cold."

Lucas gently pulled the big SUV back out and onto the freeway. Daven covered Floyd up with Hank's blanket, and three hours later the teenager woke up a little disoriented and starving, but ecstatic to find himself in his own driveway. He ran inside to find Theo waiting in the living room with Shannon and Starsky and Hutch, who, gleeful upon spotting Floyd, all promptly rolled over to demand belly rubs from their favorite human.

CHAPTER TWO

The Thunderbird pulled up to the garage just as Floyd had finished greeting the dogs and Theo, and Maurice opened the door to let the contingent in the house. Hank's eyes were bleary and bloodshot as he spoke into his cell phone and held up a finger to shush his sons as they watched him come in and set everything down.

"Thanks, Rupe. I'm sure you're right. Keep me posted." He hung up, then turned to his sons. "Hey kiddos, sorry to keep you waiting. Welcome back, Floyd."

Floyd stayed by the dining room table, suddenly feeling overly anxious. He rarely, if ever, saw his dad in such a state of messy fatigue, and all of his anxiety buttons were instantly pushed.

"Yeah, dad. I'm here."

"I can see that," Hank replied wryly as he ran his fingers through his hair and put his keys on the side table. "Actually, I'm so tired that I'm seeing two of you and two of Theo here right now. And possibly three Shannons, unless you brought home a couple more goldens."

Theo shifted on his feet, as uncomfortable about Hank's appearance as his brother was. "Not today. Are you alright, dad? You were supposed to be home hours ago."

"Yeah, you know how it goes. Floyd, wait for me in my study while I change, okay? I'll be right there."

Floyd's stomach twisted into knots at that; the study had been the location of too many deeply unpleasant conversations and very few happy ones. Hank was no less perceptive when tired than he was wide awake, and he caught the aggrieved look on his oldest's face instantly. Before he could say anything, Daven came in the door with Shannon's leash in hand.

"Thanks for watching over her, Theo," he said warmly as he bustled in, failing as usual to stop the door from slamming behind him before Maurice could catch it. Theo let go of the collar and Shannon ran to Dav with all the exaggerated exuberance of a dog who hadn't seen her favorite human in 36 hours. He bent down to hug her, then looked around the room and seemed to realize he had interrupted something not so pleasant. He hastily latched the leash onto her harness and stood back up.

"Did you *just* get home, Hank?" he asked in surprise.

"Yeah. Don't ask. Thanks for going to get Floyd."

There were a hundred things Daven wanted to say about the fact that Hank hadn't slept for over a day, but he would never do so in front of an audience. Perhaps not even to Hank alone.

"No problem. See you tomorrow."

"I'll be in late. Around 10. I'm going to need to meet with you and Rupe right away."

"Of course. Talk to you then."

He left, and Floyd turned to look pleadingly at his dad, who simply turned and walked up the stairs without another word.

Floyd had no choice but to go to the study and wait in silence, writhing as he worried and fretted about what his dad was going to do and say about his failure to succeed at boarding school.

Soon enough the door opened, and Hank entered the room in jeans and a Henley. He stopped to hug Floyd briefly, then stood behind his desk, all business. "I hate to pee on your parade, but we have one piece of unfinished business to attend to. Let's get it over with so we can move on."

"You mean...my license?"

Hank extended the piece of pink paper to his son. "Yes. Shred it without argument."

Floyd reached across the desk and took the precious paper, swallowing his despair as he did so. Fighting with his dad within five minutes of being home would be incredibly reckless, and if this was the price he had to pay for being free of the boarding school, then so be it.

Hank had been steeling himself for a big fight, but he was pleasantly surprised with how quickly Floyd complied without any fuss. The boy simply turned and went to the shredder, flipped it on, then hesitated slightly before feeding it in with a visible sigh of resignation. Afterwards he just stood there, staring glumly at the still-grinding teeth.

"Turn it off," Hank said finally, once he couldn't stand the noise anymore.

Floyd switched it off and walked back to stand in front of his dad's desk, looking like his dog had just gotten run over by a car. "Dad, I'm sorry for all this. For fucking up. For being a failure. For everything."

Hank smiled a little. He never minded when his sons swore in private, and in fact was secretly amused by it. In public was another matter, of course...not that they had ever dared to do such a thing.

"Floyd, you're talking to a man who got kicked out of the Boy Scouts, two boarding schools, *and* college. Do you really think I'm judging you right now for merely *choosing* to leave a place that made you so unhappy?"

That brought a smirk out of the teen, and Hank knew then that everything was going to be okay.

"No, I guess not."

"What was it that made you so unhappy? I'm just curious. You don't have to answer, but I don't believe that you were really missing me and Theo that much."

Floyd nervously twisted his hands into the hem of his polo shirt. "I *did* miss you guys."

"Never mind, then. Tell me if and when you want to talk about it. Listen, I'm shot. I got to go to bed. You and Theo can order in whatever you want for dinner."

"Did you and Uncle Dav really meet with Harmon in San Diego?" Floyd asked tonelessly.

Hank felt his heart race for a moment. "Were you watching the news again?"

Floyd nodded. "This morning. It wasn't banned at school. Everyone watches it. I even know that Avery almost got a ticket but you talked the police officer out of it."

Hank sighed. "That's not what...okay, you're back to *not* watching it again. You know something is said about me almost every day that's going to upset you, and most of it is either bullshit or blown out of proportion."

"Not all of it." Floyd remained stone-faced as his dad crossed from behind the desk and stood less than a foot away from him.

"Son, I'm really glad you're back, and I'd like to keep it that way." Hank put his hands on his son's shoulders and squeezed reassuringly. "Whatever I tell you, or don't tell you, is for your own good. If you need to know, you'll know. We've talked about this a hundred times."

Floyd was too stricken to reply right away and Hank hardened his heart against the deep hurt he knew he had just inflicted. But he had to protect his son at any cost.

"Go figure out what you guys want to order for dinner. You know where the credit card is. Don't watch the news without my permission, ever. That's an order. I'm going to bed."

Floyd stood his ground. "Don't trust that asshole, dad."

Hank replied quietly, "I don't, and he knows it. Hell, everyone knows it, and the feeling is mutual. If it makes you feel better,

Uncle Dav was really happy with how the meeting went, and he told me I did great. If the most critical and pessimistic man in the world said that, then you *know* everything's good. Okay?"

That was supposed to make Floyd feel better, but Hank saw him tense up even more. Shit.

"I can't relax if I don't know what's going on."

"You don't need to know, Floyd. You're fifteen years old. Enjoy your childhood while you can and leave the rest of this shit to me. I need to go to bed, seriously. I'm dying here. Come on."

Floyd turned and opened the door and followed his dad glumly out to the kitchen. "I'm turning 16 on Monday."

"Yes, I know. That's two years from 18, when you can do whatever you want. Until then, you mind what I tell you."

"Yes, sir. Our phones are definitely being tapped, by the way. I keep hearing that click."

"Shit. Okay. I'll have the line disconnected." He turned around and embraced Floyd in another tight hug. "After dinner you go straight to bed and lights out. I'll wake you up at seven for breakfast and don't want any fussing. This weekend we're going to go look at the new house and then start moving in next weekend. You excited?"

Floyd grinned. "Yeah. I can't wait to see it!"

"Good. Do me a favor, after you order food go downstairs and find Avery. Let him know about the phone and what you heard. I'll talk to him tomorrow about it. Goodnight, Floyd."

"Goodnight, dad. It's really good to be home."

Floyd watched his dad disappear up the steps, and realized he wasn't really sure about that last part. Then he snuck into the library and parked himself in front of the little television that was haphazardly shoved into a corner, and turned the channel to the 5pm local news. It had already long started and they were past the headlines and into sports already. Damn. He changed it to CNN and sat down on the floor next to the couch to watch.

Half an hour later he nearly jumped out of his skin when the door to the library door opened with a creak, and he dropped the remote in his haste to change the channel. Thankfully it was just Avery.

"Hi," the man said quickly as he shut the door behind him. "Something you need to tell me?"

Floyd clicked off the TV and quickly scrambled up and went over to a bookshelf as if he had been browsing for something to read this entire time.

"I'm not sure what you mean," he replied nervously, then gave up the book charade and started to head for the door. "I need to go order dinner for me and Theo. Want anything?"

Avery stayed where he was, effectively blocking Floyd's exit. "You were supposed to tell me about the phones being tapped after you ordered dinner, both of which you didn't do. Then I find you in here watching TV against your dad's orders."

"Um. Are you…are you going to tell him?"

"*Out.*"

"Yes, sir," Floyd replied anxiously as he darted past his father's guard and hurried into the kitchen. Theo was in there, too, making a huge portion of macaroni and cheese, and he turned to glare at his brother.

"Where the hell have you been? I made us dinner since you never ordered it."

"What? Why didn't you ask Chef to make something?"

"Because it would take forever. Where have you been?"

Floyd shrugged. "Reading. Did you know dad met with Harmon?"

Theo stopped stirring the pot for a moment, then renewed the activity with vigor. "Yeah. I was kind of there. In San Diego, I mean. Not at the meeting."

"What…what the fuck, Theo? Why? You knew about this, too?" Floyd complained bitterly.

"Not like a had a choice. Dad told me not to talk about it. Hand me a plate."

"Fuck that. You tell me when these things happen, okay Theody?"

Now Avery's soft voice again, from almost over his shoulder. "Floyd, step outside with me for a moment."

Floyd didn't want to, but he knew better than to disobey any guard. If the statement had been phrased as a question he could stall, perhaps, but this wasn't a question. So he went, and Avery slid the door shut behind them. He looked livid, but his tone was perfectly calm and diplomatic.

"When Hank asks me tomorrow if you complied with his orders tonight, what do you want me to say?"

"I...I want you to say yes, of course."

"Good. Then go to bed, and leave Theo alone about Harmon. He wasn't lying, he can't talk about it. If you get on his case about it again, I'm going to have a word with your dad about what you were doing in his library tonight without permission. Understood?" Avery crossed his arms. "Your father expects so much better of you, Floyd. We all do."

"Yes, sir, I'm sorry," Floyd whispered shakily, thoroughly rattled. His breath hitched for a moment, and his eyes burned fiercely at the stinging rebuke. Avery had never spoken to him so harshly before. He sounded just like his dad. It hurt.

"Are you hungry?"

"Yes. I haven't eaten since breakfast."

"Then take a plate with you upstairs. Go. Lights out in thirty minutes. I'll be checking to make sure you obey."

Floyd nodded and swallowed hard. "Thank you. I'm sorry."

Avery patted him reassuring on the shoulder, then went back downstairs to his office, where he mentally prepared himself for losing his job if Hank found out he had interfered in a family matter. He knew Floyd would never throw him under the bus, but the fact that he had gone against Hank's wishes unsettled him thoroughly. So did the realization that he would willingly do it again if it meant saving the teenager from his dad's wrath, and vice versa.

That same evening

"Hey Dav. Listen, you're going to hear tomorrow that the audit didn't go well today. I just wanted to give you a heads up and ask you something."

Daven paused stirring his tea. "What do you mean, Rupe? What happened?"

"The strangest thing came up when they were reviewing our financials. Six different cash payouts were made for 'photographic services' last week. Do you know what that might be?"

"*Photographic services?* No idea. Did you ask Hank?"

"Yeah, I was talking to him when he got home. He thinks they might have been miscategorized, but it looks exactly like he paid off those damned photographers after all. The auditors red-flagged it to Stewart without giving us any time to investigate. We've got to figure it out before he gets summoned again."

"Well, I'm sure there's some back-up somewhere. The accounts payable rep who made the payments should be able to explain."

Rupert sighed. "That's just the thing that set off the alarm. We can't tell who did it. Our system allows anonymous transactions with Hank's written authorization, and he's used it a few times for highly confidential reasons. Like severance payouts and things, all above board. But not this time. It has to be a mistake because he says he didn't authorize a damned thing. Normally these transactions are hidden, but somehow they showed up anyway. If he can't convince Stewart this wasn't his doing, we're all in deep shit."

Daven abandoned his tea in the kitchen and went to sit down on the couch. "I don't think it was a mistake, but rest assured that Stewart knows Hank's smart enough not to lead a trail back to him by actually coding the transactions correctly and allowing them to be seen."

Rupe's heart nearly stopped at that. "What are you implying, exactly?"

"That someone is either embezzling from us and just happened to use a code that looks suspicious...or more likely, they're purposely trying to get Hank in trouble. I know you and Hank think everyone on the staff is perfectly loyal and upright, but I don't. Harmon wasn't telling the truth when he said he doesn't employ any double agents."

"You don't know that for sure."

"Neither do you."

Rupe mused over that for a few moments. "Jesus Christ. Let's hope you're wrong. But then again, if you are…never mind. Who is our most trustworthy person in accounts payable? I want only one single person to have access to making anonymous payments, so we can stop this in its tracks."

Daven thought about it for a moment; it was a toss-up between three men who had been on staff the longest.

"Probably Yannick. He's been with us for five years, never any complaints or trouble. He's a bit of an odd one, though, I think we should question the entire accounting staff to find out who did this. There's 24 of them, it will take time to do a polygraph on everyone."

"Time we don't *have* , Dav. Hank can only delay Stewart for so long."

"Well, we can't just choose a select few. It's either all of them, or none at all."

Shit. "Okay, let's do it this way. If we're going to choose one person to have access in the future, we should poly him alone to make sure he's above board. That way we don't have to explain or accuse anyone right off the bat. You want to pick Yannick, then?"

"Yes."

"Okay. If Hank approves we'll talk to Yannick tomorrow morning, poly him in the afternoon. If you're comfortable with him and can trust him with the access, I'm good with that. Then we'll poly the rest as fast as possible before Stewart can pull out his guillotine again. Hopefully, anyway."

Daven paused for a long, anxious moment before responding. "We have to eliminate the possibility that Hank did make the payments. It's our duty. He will understand."

Rupert groaned. "Right, thanks. Very comforting."

"Do you disagree?"

"Of course not. But I don't want to go there right now. Not after what happened to get us in deep shit last time."

Daven drummed his fingers on his lap. "No. But that's because we went behind his back with our suspicions. This time, we either ask him about it upfront, or we don't discuss it at all. Period. Which do you prefer?"

Rupert groaned again. "I'd prefer to walk a mile over hot coals than make that decision."

"Then I'll make the decision," Daven answered firmly. "You and I don't discuss it. He didn't do it, anyway, so there's no point."

"Are you absolutely positive about that?" Rupert asked after a long pause, almost timidly.

"No. But I'm willing to let it go and focus entirely on other possibilities. Are you?"

There was a long silence on the other end of the line.

"Rupert? Are you still there?"

"Ahem. Yeah. I'm sure he didn't do it. You're right, he's way too smart to let it be found. He would have used his own personal money, anyway. End of discussion."

Daven grunted. "Exactly. That settles that. See you tomorrow."

"Wait," Rupe interjected quickly. "No. We *have* to ask him, Dav. He knows that. If we don't, he'll think we are discussing it separately and we'll have Christmas Day all over again. I'll do it."

"No, it's my responsibility. I'll do it."

"Okay. I'll pray for you."

"No need. He's not going to hurt me."

"I was joking, Dav," Rupe sighed.

"Oh. Well, the meeting is at ten o'clock so try not to worry about it until then."

"Right. I'm sure I'll forget all about it."

"Good. See you tomorrow."

They ended the call, and Dav calmly went back to his tea, which to his dismay had become bitter and cold while waiting for his attention.

CHAPTER THREE

Saturday, January 29

Ten days after

Ventura Harbor, California

"Dav, don't unravel it. Just toss it way up. Got to go pretty hard, like-"

The coiled rope splashed into the water of the marina as Daven botched the throw to Hank, who had been reaching for it from the stern of his surprisingly modest 45-foot sailboat.

"You throw like a girl!" Hank complained with a grin as he wiped away the splashes of seawater from his face.

"Sorry. It was heavier than I expected."

"I got it, dad," Theo yelled as he dodged around his "uncle" and retrieved the line, throwing it smoothly into his dad's hands while clambering aboard at the same time. Floyd was busy at the helm, fighting against the tide to keep the boat in the slip so it didn't leave anyone behind.

"Uncle Dav," he called over the gratingly harsh noise of the new engine. "You coming?"

"Do I have a choice?" Dav grumbled as he waited for the bow to come closer before taking the huge step up from the dock. He made it without any further mishaps, to everyone's relief.

As Floyd navigated them into the open waters of the large marina, Hank walked along the decks and methodically pulled the fenders up over the sides.

"Boys, start untying the sails. Dav, come sit with me at the helm."

It wasn't often that Daven joined Hank and his sons on sailing adventures, and his clumsiness and general disinterest in the activity was primarily why. Not to mention his tendency to become seasick long before they could make it out of the smooth harbor.

"Sorry, Hank," he said sheepishly as he sat down next to his boss.

"No problem. Want something to drink?"

"Ginger ale, please."

Hank glanced aside at Maurice. "Ginger ale for Dav and the boys. Root beer for me. See if we have any Cheez-its." The man nodded and disappeared underneath the hatch to join the rest of the servants and the two guards, who always stayed below on these trips to allow the family some much-needed privacy. Once the drinks and food had arrived, Hank would close the hatch and it would almost feel like they were alone in the world again. Almost.

"I can't believe it's this warm and nearly February," he mused conversationally. "Got to love California. We'd be freezing our asses off in Kansas right about now."

"Mmmmm," Dav replied noncommittally, zipping up his windbreaker and looking slightly green. "Maybe I should get on a plane, then, since I prefer hypothermia over dry heaves."

Hank barked out a laugh, and his two boys turned around to look at him and grinned.

There was silence for about ten minutes, except for Hank's necessary commands to the boys in regards to the sails. He was never a tyrant at sea and was a surprisingly easygoing and humorous captain. Floyd and Theo loved these trips because they almost felt like a normal family again, and they didn't have to walk on eggshells around their dad for a few hours. Their mom had loved sailing, and the boat was named after her. Accordingly, Hank loved it, too, and he was at his most relaxed when behind the helm. For the Bancrofts, this was as normal as life would ever get.

As the boat nudged its bow into the deeper waters of the Pacific, Floyd pulled up the mainsail hand over hand while Theo worked on the mizzen. Once they were officially sailing, Hank cut the engine and adjusted his ears to the startling quiet while Maurice emerged with the drinks and snacks. While he wasn't really needed out here just to bring a few trays up and down, Hank always brought him along because he loved sailing.

"You take your seasickness stuff?" he asked with a straight face, as he always did.

Maurice grimaced. "No, sir. Going to be throwing up all over your beautiful boat today, I'm afraid."

"Try to keep it to a bare minimum this time."

"Yes, sir."

"Thank you."

Maurice disappeared below while Hank chuckled to himself. The man had an iron stomach and would possibly be the last person in the world to get seasick. But Hank always poked fun at him anyway, which was particularly fun to do in front of Daven, who was now a much darker shade of green.

"Hey, Dav. Take the wheel." That would give him something to do to keep his mind off his stomach. Hank picked up the two cans of ginger ale and went forward to hand them to the boys. They all sat down on the forward hatch and drank in silence.

"Dad," Floyd said eventually. "Can we just stay out here forever?"

"No. The dogs would miss you too much. How about all day, instead?"

"Sure. But don't you have work to do?"

"Nope. You guys want to take a turn at the wheel?"

"I do!" Theo interjected excitedly. With a strong breeze like this, Hank usually never let the boys take over the steering. But it was blowing straight, and the waves were minimal. Even Daven was having no trouble keeping her on course.

"Okay. Go take over from Uncle Dav."

Theo departed excitedly, and Hank was left sitting alongside his oldest son. They hadn't spoken much in the past week and a half, but when they had, Floyd had been pleasant and compliant, causing no trouble at all. It had been a remarkably peaceful ten days since he returned from boarding school.

"Hey. How are you doing?" Hank asked eventually.

"Good, thanks. You?"

"You seem a bit down. Just...you know, you can talk to me. I'm here. Anytime."

"Thank you."

Well, so much for that. Floyd was staring out at the horizon, and his mind was anywhere but on this boat. Hank patted him on the shoulder and stood up.

"Wait, dad..."

Hank staggered against a wave that pitched the boat as he turned back, and the momentum forced him neatly back down onto the spot where he had just been sitting.

"Oomph. Yeah?"

Floyd swallowed hard. "There is actually something that I need to tell you."

Oh god. Guilt detected. Hank knew his kids, and that's undoubtedly what Floyd's flat tone indicated. Well...so much for a relaxing day.

"What did you do?" he asked tersely.

Floyd shot him a hurt look. "Nothing!"

"Sorry. What's on your mind, I meant to ask?"

"Well, it's just that...that I'm sixteen years old now, and it doesn't make sense anymore for me not to know what's going on around me. I really don't like being in the dark. I was wondering if you would possibly reconsider your rule about not letting me watch the news."

Hank shuddered, then gulped down the last of his root beer. "Yes."

"Dad, please, I just want...wait. What?" Floyd stared at his father in wonder and surprise, eyebrows furrowed.

"I said yes, I'll reconsider, because you asked so nicely and told me what was bothering you without starting a fight. But I want to ask you something first, and I expect an honest answer. Have you been watching it without my permission?"

Floyd felt a lump in his throat. "Just once, the day I got home from Palm Springs. You went to bed so early and left the library unlocked...but I haven't done it again. Haven't even touched the TV at all, because I felt so bad about it, I swear. I'm sorry, dad."

Hank rested an arm lightly around his son's tense shoulders. "Yeah, I knew about that. Avery spilled the beans."

"He did?" Floyd responded in horror. "And you didn't even you didn't get mad?"

"Oh yeah, I was mad. Still am, but you haven't watched it since then, so I'll get over it. In the future we'll watch it together, and you're not to watch it without me, ever. Agreed?"

Floyd nodded, still in shock. "Why...why didn't you say anything about it?"

"Because Avery asked me not to. You feel like doing some fishing?"

Floyd stared askance at his dad for the third time in as many minutes. "Dad...I...are you feeling alright?"

Hank was desperate to tell him the truth. To lay down his burdens and tell *anyone* , really, that *no* ...he wasn't alright. Not by a longshot. That Stewart's total silence on the audit findings had instilled a sense of doom on him, keeping him awake for four nights straight. That he hated himself for allying with Harmon. That he disliked his own constituents and was secretly planning to destroy their ballot measures at all costs. That he knew Dav and Rupert quietly suspected that he paid the photographers off, despite his insistence that he didn't and their easy acceptance of his denial.

That doing the right thing had never felt so wrong, and that he knew his career would end sooner than planned, no matter what he did to prevent it.

Worst of all...that something dark within his soul *wanted* this. *Wanted* his name to live in infamy, along with his face from that famous photograph. *Wanted* to be a martyr for his party.

He didn't know why he couldn't fight off those thoughts anymore.

"Yeah, Floyd, I'm good. You know how much I love being out on the ocean. Makes me feel like myself again."

"But that's the thing. You're not *yourself* at all, dad. You're freaking me out."

"Hmmm. And here I was thinking you'd be relieved that I'm trying really hard to go easier on you and Theo. If you prefer, I can just take off my belt right here and-"

"No, no!" Floyd laughed nervously. "I *am* relieved. Please don't. Sorry I asked."

"I won't," Hank replied seriously. "The truth is that apparently I'm a big old softy when my boys are behaving. Who would have thought?"

The sarcasm wasn't quite lost on Floyd, but it didn't exactly hit its target, either.

"Oh. Okay. Dad?"

"What?"

"Do you think you'll be re-elected in November?"

Hank felt his blood pressure rise sharply at the query, but he kept his tone level. "I don't know."

"But we have enough money that it doesn't matter if you aren't, right?"

"Yes. We'll be fine, Floyd."

Hank withdrew his arm and shoved his hands into the pockets of his sweatshirt. He wanted to tell his son he wasn't going to run again and they'd all be free of this life, one way or another. And that was assuming he even made it to November without being thrown out of office.

"Look. A lot can happen between now and then. A lot *will* happen, and that's the only thing I can guarantee. Let's just focus on the present. Tonight we start packing for the new house, and in three weeks we move in. I want you to keep your attention on that, okay? And on school, obviously. Mrs. Aster is brutal with the homework, so you have a lot on your plate already without worrying about something that's ten months away."

Floyd nodded. "Okay, dad. I just worry, that's all."

"I know. Me too. Let's try to relax today. Want to fish for a little bit?"

"Sure."

Floyd got up and went aft while Hank stayed on the hatch, his thoughts shifting back to packing up the house, and once again wondering if he really should have hired movers instead of enlisting his servants for the task of filling up the pallet of boxes that had just arrived this morning. It wasn't exactly in their job description (not that they had one), but he hated beyond reason the thought of having strangers in the house. He knew he was being absurd by worrying about everyone thinking he was trying to be cheap by using "free" labor.

He went back to the cockpit to commend Theo's steering job, then said to Floyd as he was readying the poles, "Make sure they're secured this time."

Theo burst out laughing, then abruptly stopped himself as his dad threw a sharp look at him. Floyd had lost Hank's favorite pole overboard five trips ago, which the poor kid was apparently never going to hear the end of.

"I will, dad," Floyd replied with a sigh, his hopes of being forgiven dashed once again.

Hank suddenly remembered his vow not to be a asshole at sea, so he grinned, ruffled Theo's hair playfully, and went down into his cabin to lay down. He ended up dozing off for the better part of an hour. When he re-emerged into the sunlight, Floyd and Theo had given up fishing and were sitting way up on the bowsprit, waiting patiently for dolphins to appear alongside.

Daven moved aside to make room for Hank to take the helm and murmured very quietly, "I just had quite an enlightening conversation with Floyd. He's convinced Harmon is going to kill us both."

Hank groaned. "Oh geez. He's...I'm sorry, Dav."

"It's no problem. I tried to change the subject several times, but he's persistent. Have you changed your mind about meeting with him again?"

"No. Speaking of Harmon, though, I've got something bothering me and would really appreciate your perspective on it."

"Of course."

"I've been trying not to say anything for a while, because I'm not completely sure how I feel about the whole thing and didn't want to start any fights before I worked it out within my head. But I've got to be honest, Dav. We are completely wrong about supporting public flogging, and the tightening of restrictions on Bonded Retainers."

Dav nodded. "I know you think that, Hank. We all do. There's no other reason for you to delay approving the public statement for so long."

"What does Rupert say about it all?"

"He's frustrated, of course. Wants to get the thing out."

Hank took a deep breath and steeled himself. "No, I don't mean that. I mean...how does he feel about the measures? Does he support them?"

Daven took a long draw of his grape soda. "It's not for me to say, Hank. You should ask him."

"I'm asking you."

"Well, I'm not telling you, because I'm not inside his mind."

Hank noted a sudden shift in the wind, as did they boys. They jumped up to loosen the sails in order for a course change, and once it was done they started to come aft. Hank caught Floyd's eye and shook his head slightly, and noted with pride the way his son immediately understood the meaning. Floyd subtly redirected his brother around to sit on the bow again, and Hank picked up the conversation from where they had left off before he could lose his nerve.

"What would you say if I said we're going to oppose them both and ally with Harmon in our messaging?"

"We've run with Harmon's messaging before, Hank, and vice versa. So I would say, fine, let's do it. What is it about *this* particular subject that's upsetting you so much?"

"Oh, nothing. Just the little fact that our constituents are total assholes and will run me out of office for betraying them and their vengeful ideals. That's all, no big deal."

Daven nodded. "Probably."

"Probably? Thanks for making me feel better, Dav!" Hank replied in disgust.

"You didn't hire me to make you feel better. My job is to find out the truth to help guide your decisions. Opposing those measures is going to cost you. All of us, actually."

"Great. That's even more comforting. Thanks."

Maurice suddenly slid open the hatch to announce lunch was ready, and Hank snapped harshly at him, "Wait until I tell you *we're* ready!"

Daven stood up and set down his bottle. "I need to use the restroom, Hank."

"The head."

"What?"

Sigh . "The toilet on a boat is called...you know what, never mind."

"Okay. Be right back."

That was the end of the conversation for now; Hank knew. Daven had ways of defusing him that he couldn't fight back against, and suddenly having to make an exit for personal needs was one of them. He would most likely stay awhile for a while to let Hank's temper cool. Damn it.

Hank pulled out his phone, then remembered he had no signal out here. But he could still read emails that had already come in, and scrolled down to the latest from Harmon.

Hank, just learned of some new intel regarding measures that will be on the April ballot. I know it's far away, but we should talk. No doubt we'll disagree on all except one, which I think you should be made aware of sooner or later as it affects both of our sons directly. I think you catch my meaning. If you're up for dinner again, let me know. - Harmon

Once again, Hank felt a sweet taste of victory rush through his heart. That could only mean one thing; Harmon had introduced him to Colton Gamble, and now Hank's measure regarding prohibiting photographers from selling photos of minors had passed through the house. There was no reason for any of their constituents to downvote it. Soon Theo and Floyd would be free of the harassment that had made all of their lives so miserable.

February 9

FBI Headquarters - Philadelphia

Salome Danby was often unhappy, good fortune often missing out of her life, but this level of unhappiness was new and untested. She didn't know why she cared so much about Hank Bancroft, or why Stewart felt the same, or even why the president himself tried so hard to keep the man in line and in office. But they all did care about him, for whatever reason, which made the most recent report even more disappointing than the last.

"Salome, may I come in?"

Stewart was standing at the office door, realizing his boss hadn't even seen him approaching because she was so engrossed in the stack of papers in front of her.

"Sure. You may not want to, though, after what I'm about to show you."

"Oh god. What did Hank do now?" He sat down and took a mint from the candy bowl as Salome handed him a printed copy of an email that she had received the day before.

"Senator Gamble?" Stewart exclaimed immediately.

"Yes. Read it."

To: Office of Ethics and Integrity

Salome Danby, Director

Ms. Danby, it is my obligation to report to you that yesterday, Feb 8, Hank Bancroft called me from his cell phone to offer cash for pushing his recent measure through the House for the April 1 ballot. I declined, of course. Under the Whistleblower Act I exercise my right to decline to answer any further questions regarding this matter unless required by a lawful process.

Regards,

Colton Gamble

"There is no way Hank did that," Stewart scoffed immediately, handing the paper back to Salome in disgust. "Absolutely no way. He's smarter than that, not to mention more ethical. This is bullshit."

"Colton has no reason to lie. None," Salome refuted sternly.

"Except that he used to work for Harmon! That gives him all the reason in the world."

"Harmon fired him from his dream job, Stewart. They hate each other."

Stewart sat back in his chair. "Oh...that's right."

"Colton was really tight with Colbert, and I remember that the incident caused friction between him and Harmon. Add it to Hank's file. We can't ask him about it directly unless there is evidence, so we'll check his phone records next cycle. Have you questioned him about the photography payments yet?"

"No. We've contacted four of the six photographers involved in that incident, and none have had anything to say about it. They're either lying, or they weren't paid and it really was a glitch in the financials."

"Urbanes lying? To the FBI?" Salome asked in mock incredulity. "Who would imagine such a thing. Keep trying to contact the other two. There's no rush. We just have to do this right."

"I think it would be very strange of them to lie in order to protect an Seditionist."

"Not if they were promised future payments for complying. Or for their silence."

"Right. We've also discovered that Hank did disconnect his home phone. I'd say he knew we were tapping him, but the family is moving to a new house in two weeks and it could just be a utilities changeover."

Salome smiled a little. "No. He knew, and it's not a crime to unplug a phone. Leave it alone for now. It's not like we were getting anything out of it, anyway."

Stewart nodded. "Hank is much smarter than that. If he really *did* call Senator Gamble yesterday, I guarantee you it won't be in his phone records. He'll have used a secondary phone we aren't auditing so that we can't prove anything without issuing a subpoena for statements."

"Even then we can't prove anything. I couldn't ever have imagined Hank offering money like this before, but now that he's proved he's capable of it with that photographer business, I don't think we can put anything past him."

"No." Stewart was slightly depressed to discover he felt the same way. "I'm still upset we still haven't resolved the mystery behind his calls to a Colorado cell number at the time of Janet's murder, either. Until that's cleared, I guess we should keep all the possibilities on the table."

Salome opened her laptop back up, signaling the imminent end of the meeting. "I'm inclined to believe the senator, Stewart. Off the record, of course. You're free to believe whatever you'd like, but we can't let our opinions influence our investigation."

"No ma'am."

Stewart went back to his desk, and for an hour he grudgingly resisted the urge to pick up the phone and call Hank Bancroft to ask him about it directly.

He desperately wanted Salome to be wrong, but he strongly suspected she wasn't.

After another long struggle with his logic going around in circles, he gave in and picked up the phone.

Seditionist HQ - Los Angeles

Hank didn't want to get out of the car. He was tired and the day hadn't even begun yet. His calendar was already packed with meetings, and he wouldn't even have privacy at lunch thanks to the monthly birthdays party for the office. Normally he enjoyed those occasions immensely, as it took him out of his normal schedule and allowed him to socialize and relax for a little while before tackling the afternoon.

He dug his phone out of his pocket as the phone rang.

"Hey, Dav."

"Rupe and Taylor and I are in the conference room. Do you want us to wait, or shall we reschedule?"

Sigh. "I'm downstairs. Coming. Wait…I have an incoming call from Stewart. Shit. Don't leave, okay? Just wait for me."

He clicked over to the incoming call.

"Hank Bancroft."

"Morning, Hank. I just need a second. Are you alone?"

"Yes I am. How can I help you?"

"Quick question, off the record. Your measure is going to be on the April 1 ballot. Were you aware of that?"

"Not officially. Rumors only. Glad to hear it."

"And Colton Gamble helped you with that?"

Pause. "Yes. All above board and via official channels. Harmon introduced me to him directly. Why do you ask?"

"So...it was *Harmon* who introduced you to him?" That was odd.

"Yes. I thought it was strange, considering their history. But as I said, all above board. Is something wrong?"

Stewart cleared his throat. "No, sorry. The question I called to ask is whether or not there was any, uh, compensation that passed between the two of you for his assistance. Or any offer of compensation. This is not an accusation, Hank, let me be clear."

"Between me and Harmon? Of course not!"

"No, I meant...between you and Senator Gamble."

"I can't believe you're even asking me this," Hank replied, rightfully indignant. "Obviously you have some kind of suspicion, or you wouldn't have called. What's going on?"

Oh shit, Stewart thought frantically. *I never should have called. If Salome finds out about this, my ass is so grass....*

"Just look at it from my point of view. Passing a brand new measure in the House within a week is unheard of. And this Senator isn't known for his quick action on anything. Surely you can understand our concern?"

That relaxed Hank a little, and he backed off on the attitude, although his tone was still sharp. "I do. But if you remember that my measure helps Harmon's son as well, you'll realize who Colton was really in it for. He didn't care about what I want. He just wants to kiss Harmon's ass and try to get back on his good side. *That's* why he lit a fire under it. Any more questions, Stewart? I'm late for a meeting."

"No. Thank you for your time, Hank."

Hank hung up without saying goodbye, and stormed upstairs into the conference room where his team was waiting impatiently. He took a copy of Rupert's draft media statement out of his briefcase and slowly tore it to shreds as he talked.

"Alright, team. I've heard all of your arguments, opinions, and strategies. Thank you for your thoughtful input and valid concerns. I've made my decision. The Seditionists are officially opposing these March 1 measures. There will be no tolerance for public flogging, or indentured servitude for minors under our watch, and that's the end of it. Rupert, get out a pen and paper. We need a new media statement that allies us with the Urbanes."

Rupert reached into his briefcase to comply, then took a deep breath as he uncapped his pen.

"You might finally start a revolt with this one, Hank," he murmured quietly. "At the very least, our constituents will throw you out of office on March 2."

"*Another* revolt, you mean. Let them. You all agreed with me that these measures are wrong, never mind the ones that passed in October thanks to the damned elitists. It's about time we all got the balls to fight back against them." He looked at Taylor apologetically. "What's the female equivalent of that saying?"

"Something about ovaries, maybe? But we don't have a saying, because women are in a perpetual state of fighting back. Don't need balls, because we don't rest. Must be why they're retractable."

Hank closed his eyes briefly. "Yeah, never mind. Sorry I asked. Rupe, stop giggling and start writing."

CHAPTER FOUR

Urbane Headquarters - Denver

"It isn't just for show, Colbert," Harmon repeated for the third time. "Hank is putting his career at risk by aligning with us. He knows this is the right thing. You know what he told me? That he's totally prepared to lose his job over this March 1 vote. Come November, he probably will."

Colbert wasn't convinced by this line of thinking; he knew Hank far too well to resist cataloguing this sudden capitulation as anything but another devious scheme.

"Is that why you talked him into it? To turn his constituents against him?"

Harmon laughed. "Have you ever been able to talk Hank into anything? Because I haven't. He does what he wants, and *only* what he wants. This was *his* decision. Look, I know you hate the guy, but he's not up to anything this time."

"He's always up to something. Always. He was conspiring to get me thrown in jail while having dinner with my family on Thanksgiving Day."

"That was ten years ago. Are you ever going to stop bringing it up on a weekly basis?"

Harmon knew it was a rhetorical question, but he couldn't stop himself from asking anyway for the hundredth time. Colbert would forever be unable to forgive his former compatriot for publicly exposing their own party's private communications in the middle of the Second American Revolution. The immediate backlash over Colbert's unspeakably treacherous plans as leader of the Seditionists forced the rebels to all but disband and morph into multiple factions, and Colbert - along with his entire leadership team - was quickly jailed for the rest of the war by President Durdan for making terroristic plots against the government.

Hank's whistle blowing was the reason the more radical group of Urbanes came into existence in the first place, and it thrilled modern historians that one single clerk with a dislike of attracting attention to himself could cause such a rift in the historical timeline of the nation. And not just once - the infamous candid photo of him at a protest had started the war, after all. It thrilled the historians even more that the same man now led the party he had torn apart at the seams, and social studies textbooks went on for pages about the incidents. They claimed Hank ultimately saved the rebellion singlehandedly by insisting upon more peaceful conflict resolution, which was all part of the reason he was currently so popular amongst the more conservative citizens of the Reunited States. Which, in consequence, was also the reason why his followers had been steadily tightening the noose on criminal behavior since then.

Harmon had considered Hank a hero at the time, but that was before he discovered his own radical leanings. Once he did, he left the Seditionists and worked his way up over two years to take over as leader of the Urbanes. Then he hired Colbert the moment he was out of jail after the government fell, and the rest was history.

"I'm just reminding you, Harmon, in case you've forgotten," Colbert grumbled angrily. "Bancroft was my secretary, trusted by everyone with their lives, and he threw us under the bus faster than you can count to three. I never saw it coming, and you're not seeing it this time, either. He's up to something, and you're going to get-"

Harmon stood up abruptly. "Alright, that's enough. You can't keep letting the past dictate the future. We've cooperated with Hank before, and you barely said a word about it. Why complain now? Are you in support of those measures and haven't told me yet, or what? Explain to me what the problem is."

Colbert blinked a few times and uncrossed his arms. "The problem is that you're trusting Hank Bancroft after he has spent years trying to bring you down. I don't understand it."

"You're wrong. I don't trust him, and think he's a complete dick. You know that without even having to ask. These measures are for the good of the nation, and if he can help us get them passed, then more power to us. We need the support of his constituents."

"Not going to happen. He's going to oppose the measures. He's playing you. Daven and Rupert will never agree to go against the party line."

"They already have," Harmon interrupted quietly as he reached over to his printer and handed the new email from

Hank to his irate second-in-command. "I just got a preview of their media statement that's going out in ten minutes. Take a look."

Same time

Seditionists HQ - Los Angeles

"Well, Hank," Rupert said with a sigh as he placed the statement into the fax machine for distribution through the wire service. "It's been nice working with you. I suppose you've chosen new leadership for the party already? You're going to need them in about fifteen minutes."

Hank didn't look up, but smiled a little as he tapped his pen on his desk calendar. March 1 was 18 days away. Perhaps enough time to reason with his constituents, perhaps not...

"Relax, Rupe. We'll have until November to figure that out. Are you absolutely certain that holding off on a press conference is a good strategy? I feel like we should have one today."

"No," replied Daven from his post next to the window, where he was watching hungrily as a large group of people on the street crowded around a food truck. "I'd say no less than 24 hours, but I'm not the PR guy."

"Absolutely not today," Rupert agreed. "Even longer than that. I'd say 48 hours. Until then, say your prayers."

"I already have," Dav answered seriously.

"Stop it." Hank frowned as he set his pen back in the holder and stood up to stretch. "No more gloom and doom. We agreed on a strategy, so we have to willingly and calmly take the consequences. Neither one of you indicated you want to back down so far. Any change to that?"

Rupert and Daven looked at each other, then at Hank, then solemnly shook their heads.

"Right. So. There we have it." He looked at Rupert and nodded once. "Hit the transmit button."

Rupert appeared to count to ten before taking a deep breath and pushing the button, a move which he performed with his usual dramatic flair. Then the three men stood around like statues, rooted to the carpet as the fax machine began its ministrations. Lost in their own thoughts, no one looked at each other as the process was carried on. After several minutes when the transmittal receipt was spitting out and the tension was winding down, Hank finally spoke up.

"Gents. Look at me." When they had both complied, he took a deep breath. "I'm grateful to stand beside you in this moment. I'm proud of you both. Of all of us. We'll get through this, okay? We're doing the right thing. You *know* that."

"Yes, sir," they both said together in matching melancholy tones. *Sir.* Not what Hank wanted to hear at the moment from his two best friends. But he was quickly cheered when Daven's stomach rumbled loudly, breaking the seriousness of the moment.

"Sorry," Dav mumbled, his cheeks flushing red in embarrassment.

"I'm hungry, too," Hank replied as he turned to put his coat on. "Let's go down the block to Blue Daisy. My treat."

"Are you sure it's a good idea for us to appear in public right now?" Daven asked somberly.

"Yes," Hank and Rupe said together, then Hank added, "We have to appear as normal as possible. Business as usual. Disappearing from view after such a controversial statement would be the worst possible course right now. Come on."

The three friends left the room and went downstairs; Hank was too rattled to think of taking a moment for the others to grab their jackets from their offices down the hall. The little group crossed the street in silence, two of the trio clutching themselves against the wind, and all three shaking from the cold and frayed nerves.

Behind them their guards followed closely, peacefully unaware of the shitstorm that was about to slam them all.

The death threats started immediately. Hank's email address somehow became public by late afternoon, as did his cell phone number. The same fate befell Daven and Rupert. All three of them were inundated with messages from irate constituents, and Hank's assistant had quite a task on her hands trying to sort through the mess. She forwarded the few messages of support to his alternate, secret email address, which failed to cheer him even one bit.

But what did cheer him was the knowledge that people still had the lack of sense in this day and age to send their deeply disturbing threats in ways that made them easily identifiable. He had Ellen forward the worst email threats to his contact at the police department, and on the way home he would stop by to play the voicemails for them to hear. Those idiots would be quickly arrested, and hopefully unable to vote come March 1. The people Hank really worried about were the ones who might be serious about doing something, in which case they would keep their identities hidden.

But then again...all this had happened before, and all this would happen again. No one at Seditionists headquarters was fazed by the media and satellite tracks filling up the streets - it could hardly be worse than it was after Hank threatened Harmon last year on live television - but as Hank packed up to leave at 5pm he realized he had forgotten all about the impact this would have on Theo and Floyd. Last year, they had been at their grandfather's house in Wyoming when shit went down, and were blissfully unaware of all that followed.

This time, though...they would know. The house would be swarmed by media, the streets belatedly blocked at both ends by police. He looked at his phone for the first time in hours and saw seven missed calls from Floyd within the last half hour, then two from Theo.

Then one from Brittany only thirty seconds ago.

Shit.

He decided to call Brittany back first from the speakerphone on his desk while he packed his briefcase.

"You guys okay?" he asked quickly. "I'm leaving the office in five minutes."

"Theo's fine. Floyd's having a panic attack from all the mess out front. He thinks something happened to you. Maurice's helping him through it now."

"Let him know I'm okay and will be home soon. I have to go. Are the police there to keep the idiots off my lawn?"

"Yes. You need to talk to him," Brittany insisted, and Hank agreed.

"Hey kiddo."

"Dad! What the...what the..."

Hank tried to keep his voice cheerful. "Oh, the usual...your dad made the news again, but this time it's for a good reason. Everything's okay. I'll explain when I get home. You going to be okay?"

"They've been here for hours! Why didn't you call to let us know you're not dead?"

Hank couldn't very well say he forgot all about the very existence of his boys for five hours, so he dodged the question as best he could. "The guards could have let you know, they're all in contact with each other. Ask them next time. Can you-"

"Next time?!"

"Floyd. I'm coming home now. I have to go. Bye."

He hung up and then turned to find Daven standing in his doorway.

"Hey," Hank said casually as he closed the four latches on his briefcase. "Bit of a shitstorm out there."

"You think?"

Hank blinked in surprise; it wasn't like Dav to be sarcastic. When he did, it was always because he was extremely angry about something...and that was rare.

"Are you riding home with me?" he asked neutrally.

Daven shook his head. "No. Going to be here late."

"Nothing you can do in the next few hours will make this better. Don't argue with me, just get packed and let's go. What's wrong, anyway? You seem upset."

"I am. Floyd called me about a hundred times while I was in the strategy meeting. You really didn't think to let your kids know to expect all this mayhem on their front lawn?"

Hank sighed, wondering how to make this better and realizing he couldn't. "No, I didn't, Dav. I'm sorry. I just talked to Floyd and he's okay now."

"No, he's not. He's having a panic attack. I was standing right here and heard it all."

Hank froze. There was something really off about Daven's attitude that he didn't recognize, and he certainly didn't like the tone. But he wasn't going to start a fight with him about it when he was the one in the wrong.

"Alright. Floyd had a panic attack because his father is an idiot. Stay late if you want, then."

"I will. It's not like I have kids to go home to, after all. Kids that would love to know I'm still alive."

Hank walked over to his coat closet and took his time buttoning the woolen jacket all the way down. He felt his temper flare up a little over the man's untimely eavesdropping, but he fought it back down considering they butted in on each other's calls like that all the time.

"Dav, I said I'm sorry. No, I didn't inform the boys. It was thoughtless and stupid, okay? I'm the worst father of the year for like sixteen years in a row now, you shouldn't be surprised. Can you be done glaring at me now, please?"

Hank turned around to look at Daven to check on that last point, and instead found Avery there staring at him in confusion. Awkward.

Hank cleared his throat. "Uh. I wasn't talking to myself, I swear. Where did Dav go?"

"Went into his office about thirty seconds ago, boss. Are you ready for Vance to pull the car around?"

Sigh. "Yes. Let's go home, Avery."

CHAPTER FIVE

Same evening

Bancroft Household

Hank's anger at his guards arose suddenly on the way home, without him even realizing at first what he was mad about. There was just a sort of vague feeling of discontent swirling around in his brain, then it spread to his chest. By the time Vance had fought through the mess of cars to his driveway, he had figured it out and was thoroughly irate from head to toe. As they went through the front door he ordered Avery into his study even before saying hello to Maurice or going up to check on Floyd.

"Explain this to me, please," he began tersely as he shut the door behind him and circled around his favorite guard. "Floyd had a panic attack this afternoon because nobody bothered to tell him his father is still alive. Not only that, but I just learned both my sons were sent home early from school and nobody bothered to tell me. Are you all not communicating with each other? What's the issue here, exactly?"

"Sir, you won't let us tell the boys anything. Brittany knew Floyd was panicking, and she called me for permission to let them know what was happening."

"And you didn't think to ask me for it?"

"No. We already have explicit instructions that say otherwise, as you've reminded me time and again. And Brittany left you a voicemail about them going home early due to the press arriving at Rupert's house."

Neither explanation soothed Hank's temper. "Alright. My fault again for trusting that common sense will always prevail. Obviously, the boys can know I'm alive if they ask. Daven and Rupert are the only ones who have permission to inform them if I'm not. I also need to know when they go home early from school, and not by voicemail. Is that simple enough for everyone to understand, or do I need to dumb it down even further?"

Avery cocked his head a little and looked at his boss with an expression that subtly indicated he would love to throttle the mighty leader of the Seditionists to tiny little bits.

"Crystal clear, sir," he answered calmly.

"Is there something you want to say?" Hank challenged, not yet aware that he was wildly overreacting to what was really his own guilt over the matter.

"Not until you've calmed down."

"Take a number, it's going to be a long wait. Rewrite the policy and send it to me in one hour."

Hank strode past him and hurried upstairs to Floyd. He dreaded this conversation - confrontation, perhaps - and had a feeling he'd regret not waiting until he had collected his thoughts and was in a more polite mood.

Floyd was half-asleep in Theo's bed, while Theo was sitting next to him on the floor, playing video games on the television.

"No, don't get up," Hank said gently to both of them as he sat next to Floyd's limp body. There was a well-used paper bag on the nightstand.

"Hey, I'm here. You okay?"

"Feel sick," Floyd grumbled without moving. "Headache. What's going on? Are you in trouble again?"

"Not at all. I just released a statement today that didn't go over too well with my constituents."

"Your *whats*?" Theo asked.

"A constituent is a member of my party who is eligible to vote," Hank clarified. "Pause your video game for a second, please."

"How many do you have?" Theo asked curiously as he reached over to switch off the Nintendo.

Hank didn't want to say the real number - just over 120 million - because he thought that would be way too much for the boys to take in.

"About a third of the nation, give or take a little."

Theo's eyes went wide. "And they're all mad at you right now?"

"Not all of them." *Only the vast majority of them.*

Floyd flopped over onto his back and eyed his father suspiciously. His hands were trembling.

"So...you didn't do anything wrong this time?"

"Depends on who you ask. My opinion carries a lot of weight, so when I say or do something unexpected, everyone freaks the fuck out."

"Why was it unexpected?'

"It's just like I always say: we do what we think is right, even if everyone else thinks it's wrong, and then we accept the consequences. That's exactly what I did today, and I would do it again in a heartbeat."

Theo pitched in quietly, "If you did the right thing, what is everyone so mad about?"

Hank smiled a little. "Because they're confused about what the right thing actually is. They'll come around."

Floyd scoffed bitterly. "The other right thing to do would have been to let us know you were okay! You said Uncle Dav would always pick up my phone calls no matter what, remember? I called him like 50 times and he never answered, so I thought...I thought..."

Floyd's eyes were misty again, and Hank now had an enormous lump in his throat.

"Not his fault, don't be mad at him. None of our cell phones were working this afternoon. I was going to call you the minute you guys got out of school, but the day got away with me."

"It always does," Floyd muttered.

"I'm really sorry, kiddo," Hank said sincerely as he pulled the blanket up to Floyd's chin. "You're shaking pretty bad. Need some water?"

"Apple juice, please."

Hank looked at Theo, who immediately made his way to the kitchen.

Once he was gone, Hank leaned down to whisper in his other son's ear. "There's something I have to tell you. It's really important you keep it to yourself, because no one else knows yet, and they won't for a long time. It's absolutely critical that you never repeat it. I mean it. You promise?"

Floyd nodded.

"Not good enough. Say out loud that you promise. Swear it."

He did, somewhat nervously, and Hank took a deep breath.

"I'm not going to run again for office in November. This is my last term as leader of the-"

Floyd sat up and threw his arms around his dad, and thoroughly burst into tears. Hank couldn't help it; he cried a little too at the happiness the news gave his son.

"Dad! That's like...that's the *last* thing I expected you to tell me today."

"I mean it when I say you can't tell a soul. Not even Theo. If you do, I swear that I'll-"

"I won't," Floyd insisted urgently, between sniffles. "I *won't*, I promise. Did you get fired?"

"Ha. Who would fire me? I'm the one in charge. Lay back down and relax. You going to be alright?"

Floyd grinned and wiped his nose. "Yeah. Hell yeah, dad. I'm awesome. But why won't you tell Theo?"

"Because he has a big mouth. For now, nobody knows but you. Not even Uncle Dav."

"Wow."

"Yeah. I won't announce it until June or so. That's a long time to keep a secret, but I trust you. There's one more thing. I think it's a bad idea for you to watch the news right now, so I'm going to revoke my permission on that for a few more weeks. I'm not even going to allow myself to watch until this blows over. It's not healthy for either of us. Do you understand?"

Floyd looked deeply disappointed for a moment, but he didn't dwell on it. "Yeah, I guess."

Theo reappeared with the glass of juice and froze by the door, staring uncomprehendingly at the strange sight of his tearful but widely-grinning brother.

"Um. Sorry it took so long. I had to go to the fridge in the pool house." He walked into the room at a glacial pace, talking all the way. "But I told Maurice to put some more in the kitchen. Asked him, I mean. He said he would. Anyway, here you go."

"Thanks," Hank replied as he reached out for the glass. "He's okay, Theody, relax. We were just having a bit of a laugh after all this stress. Floyd, go back to your room and rest before dinner. Come on, up."

"I'm too dizzy," Floyd complained as he struggled against his dad's grip. "Can't I just stay here?"

"Nope. Up you go. Slowly. That's good. You're fine. Into your own bed. Thank you."

Floyd trudged out and Hank watched him disappear into his room, then he turned back to Theo.

"Thanks for your help with his panic attack. I know he appreciated it."

Theo turned his Nintendo back on and flopped onto the bed without making any response.

"You mad at me?" his dad asked after a moment.

"Yep," Theo mumbled.

Hank sighed internally. *What else is new?* he thought dismally. "Okay, well...dinner is in one hour and you know there's no attitude allowed at the table, so either get it out of your system now or forever hold your peace."

"Whatever, dad," Theo replied rudely.

"Wrong answer." Hank strode over and turned off the television with a quick jab to the power button. "Get your butt down to the spare room."

Theo didn't protest for once, and quietly turned off the game and got up. Hank almost felt sorry for him. No, strike that. He *definitely* felt sorry, and quite guilty for keeping such a huge secret from him.

"Wait. Just…never mind. Carry on with your video games. You know where to find me if you need to talk."

Theo didn't even do a double-take at the unprecedented turnaround. He was too tired from today's drama. "Most of the time I *don't* know where to find you, dad. That's why I'm mad."

Hank's heart fell a little. "I'll keep that in mind for the future. See you at dinner."

He fled down the stairs and decided to make an impromptu visit outside to check out the media circus. Avery scrambled up from his little desk in the hallway to accompany him out the front door, sighing inwardly along the way.

There were two state police officers standing on the screened-in porch, somberly guarding the front door like ancient sentinels at an Egyptian tomb. Hank's sudden appearance startled them both, but they quickly recovered.

"How's it going out here?" he asked mildly.

"Good evening, sir. All is well now that we've closed the street all the way to Olympic and Pico. Easy to keep the cars out, but the pedestrians are another matter."

"Hmmm. At least we won't have to worry about them when I move into my new house. The eight-foot walls should see to that."

"When do you move in?" one of the officers asked gingerly.

"Saturday." Hank rested his gaze on the long line of beat-up cars on the street. "Look at all those photographers. Don't know what they're waiting for. It's not like I'm going to stroll out and do a striptease for them."

"No, but maybe you should. It would make everyone forget about your statement pretty quick."

Hank laughed out loud, both at the wisecrack and the horrified expression on the man after he realized what he'd just said.

"Sir, I'm...I'm sorry, that was really-"

Hank waved the mortified apology away, still chuckling at the absurd imagery of the suggestion, then held out his hand. "Hank Bancroft, by the way, as you already know. Thank you for your assistance with this mess. May I ask why the state police are here alongside LAPD? I didn't realize pissing off half the nation would be such a big deal," he joked lightly as he shook their hands, suddenly feeling a lot better about everything.

The one who didn't make the joke said carefully, "There are all kinds of different agencies out here, even animal control." He pointed. "Those guys in green are border patrol from Texas. We're here in Los Angeles for a conference. It was just ending when the all-hands call for this, er, *incident* came through. Sir, it's my pleasure to meet you. I admire the stand you're taking against those horrible measures."

"Me too, sir," said the other officer quickly. As state employees they were not allowed to talk politics while on duty and must register as independents, but this was a human issue more than anything else. Hank felt another surge of joy and relief within his chest.

"Thank you. That's very kind. Where are you boys based?"

"Shasta County, sir."

Well, so much for the warm and fuzzy feeling. Hank's pleasant mood was suddenly overtaken by a dreadful sense of ice encasing his heart, and it didn't help that Avery visibly tensed up beside him.

"I see. Well, thank you for being here, and for your support on the measures."

"Best of luck, sir." *You're going to need it,* his tone said.

"Thank you. Goodnight."

Avery followed him in. "Shasta County, boss?" he hissed.

Hank grimaced as he dug out his phone. "I know. I'm going to take care of that right now."

"Captain Martinez," said the voice on the other side. "Oh, hello Hank. You okay?"

"Good evening. Mind telling me who parked two heavily armed dickheads from an Urbane shithole on my front porch?" he asked with a razor-sharp edge to his tone.

"What?"

"Shasta cops, of all places. Really? Why not Denver? Why not Harmon's own guards? Replace them with LAPD immediately, please."

Martinez sounded a little strangled, like he was trying not to laugh. "I put them there. The red-headed one is my son, and the other is his best friend. Really good eggs, both of them. They're stationed up north temporarily, and they hate it. You're safe."

Hank felt extremely foolish all of a sudden, but it was too late to take back his insults. "Jesus. I'm sorry. How was I supposed to know?"

"When you asked me for protection for your sons, did you really think I'd respond with *heavily armed dickheads from an Urbane shithole?*"

"No, I guess not. Sorry. But you could've given me a heads-up so I wouldn't have a heart attack when I opened the front door."

"Well, I *did* tell you to stay inside, so..."

"You know how well I listen," Hank admitted with an apologetic tenor to his tone.

"Indeed." Martinez grunted. "Can I stop by and talk about this mess in person? I'm actually out in front of Daven's house right now. He just got home, so we're all set here."

Aha...so Dav didn't stay late at the office after all. *He left not even ten minutes after me. Interesting.*

"Yeah, come on by. We're about to have dinner if you want to join. Just try not to say anything that will make my kids shit their pants."

"Fluffy clouds and ponies, got it. I'll be there in a few."

Captain Martinez whistled as Hank played the last of the voicemails for him in the study. There were only fifteen; the inbox had filled up after that. But Hank now had over 4,000 missed calls today. He was surprised the phone hadn't blown up yet.

"Phew. That's some heavy stuff. Don't delete those messages so we can record them at the station tomorrow. You're getting a new number, I take it?"

"Yeah, all of us have to." Just as he said that, the phone rang with another unknown number. He silenced it. "Even Floyd's number got out. You think I have any reason to be worried for my safety?"

"You've got half the nation pissed at you right now, so yes. You might want to consider having two guards with you all the time, instead of just the one. Maybe even a full-fledged police officer or two until this dies down."

"Don't say *dies* , please. And it's hardly half the nation. More like a quarter."

"A third," the captain mused. "At they're not all here in Los Angeles, though. Listen, I'd love to stay for dinner but I have to go check on Rupert and his family now. See you tomorrow?"

Hank's phone screen lit up again, and this time he was surprised to see that it was Harmon.

"Uh, yeah...I think we agreed on nine. I got to take this call, so Avery will walk you out. Thanks, chief."

The two men left, and Hank set down at his desk to answer the call.

"Hank's house of pain, how may I hurt you?"

"Ha, nice," chuckled Harmon.

"Wow, sorry...hope I wasn't on speakerphone," Hank realized belatedly.

"No. Glad to see your sense of humor is still intact after today. Do you have a minute?"

"Yes. What's going on?"

Harmon cleared his throat. "The reaction to your statement is overwhelmingly positive here in Denver. I'm sure it's quite the opposite in Los Angeles."

"You are correct. What do you need?"

"I'm afraid you're not going to like it. Colbert received a call from one of your employees about an hour ago. Said he's pissed about your stance against the party and wanted us to pay him for information on you. Remember the same thing happened to me last month? I don't have a phone number for you or anything, and no clue to his identity, but he said he's pretty high up in the organization."

Hank suddenly felt like vomiting. "Wait, why did Colbert get this call? Why not you?"

"I don't know. Anyway, Hank, we agreed to keep talking to him. To see if we can figure out who he is for you."

"Why would you do that?" Hank asked suspiciously, all alarm bells ringing at the highest volume. "Despite all the niceties lately, have you forgotten we're not exactly friends in this game? And how do I know Colbert isn't just making this up? He hates me."

"I can prove it to you."

"How? Did you record the call?"

"Yes, actually."

Fuck. Hank knew what was coming. A bargain, a blackmail...anything that could make this day worse was just about to happen in the next few seconds.

"Right. So, let me guess: I need to pay or do something in exchange for that recording, and for your assistance in finding out his identity."

"Well, to quote the smartest man I know: have you forgotten we're not exactly friends in this game? Of course there's a price: I want you to stop using double agents, just like I did. You can have the tape, and our cooperation, with a simple agreement on that matter. That's all I ask."

Hank's breathing hitched, and his eyes narrowed so much that he could barely see in front of him.

"No. Never. Are you recording this call, too? You know what, I don't care. We're done. Go fuck yourself. Why don't you go fuck Colbert, too? I know he's there, I can hear his mouth-breathing from here. Although I doubt he'd find any pleasure from your tiny little-"

Harmon's office - Denver

Harmon slammed down the phone and turned to Colbert with a tired shrug as he hit the "stop recording" button on the little black box next to his stapler.

"You happy now?"

"No, boss. That didn't quite go as planned," Colbert responded quietly, although he was silently rejoicing inside. It had gone *exactly* as planned. He wanted Bancroft pissed off at his boss as much as possible.

Harmon sighed heavily. "Right. So much for getting him to stop using double agents now. If that didn't work, nothing will. *Fuck*. Who do you think the caller actually was? Any ideas?"

"No idea," Colbert lied, already itching to call Yannick to congratulate him for being so convincing.

Harmon stood up and stared out his window, feeling depressed and guilty suddenly.

"Send him the tape anyway. Make a copy of it and overnight it."

Colbert's heart almost stopped; if not, then it certainly missed more than a few very important beats. "Wait. What? After what...you just...I don't understand."

"You don't have to understand; it's a direct order. Do it. I want it dropped at FedEx tomorrow by noon. And Colbert? No more of these games. I understand what happened tonight, but I need him on my good side. I know you hate him, and you have to put that aside or else we're going to have a serious problem. I'm going home."

Bancroft House

Hank was so angry about Harmon's call that he could barely stomach the idea of food as he sat down at the table with Avery and his sons - well, one of them, anyway. Theo hadn't shown up yet.

"Floyd, go get your brother," Hank ordered at 7:02pm. He didn't tolerate his kids being late for anything, and this would lead to a chat in the study if there wasn't a good excuse for Theo's tardiness.

Floyd flew up the stairs, and Hank turned to Avery. "Hey, what did you think about the chief's suggestion that we have a couple real police officers hanging around here for a while? I don't think it's a bad idea. I mean, we're down one guard anyway."

"Agreed. Why don't you ask him about those two on the front porch? Sounds like they want to get away from Shasta, and this could be a good excuse to get them out."

"Hmmm. Good idea. Did you send me the new policy?"

"Fifteen minutes after you asked me for it, yes. To your personal email. Once you approve it, I'll post it downstairs. You okay, boss? You seem...you look red."

"I wish I could explain, I really do. But it's a party matter. Internal thing. I need to talk to Daven."

"Not to pry, but...are you even on speaking terms right now?"

"Your guess is as good as mine."

They waited a few more minutes, and Hank got up to venture to Theo's room. He and Floyd were arguing, and Hank didn't need to hear what it was all about. He already knew Theo was still pouting and trying to make a statement, and Floyd was trying to convince him otherwise.

"...not that big of a deal, please. Don't get him mad. He's had a horrible day. Come on!"

They turned as Hank entered the room. "Floyd, downstairs."

"Dad, please don't, he's just upset about…a lot."

"I know. Move."

He crossed his arms and waited until Floyd was out of earshot. "Theo, you have to eat. If you think I'm going to just let you stay up here and-"

"I don't care what you do anymore," Theo replied angrily, flopping himself down on his bed.

"You have exactly one more chance to obey me. I'm going to count to five."

He got to four before Theo flung himself back on his feet and angrily stomped down the stairs. Once he got to the table, however, he was angelic and quiet. Floyd watched them both with wide eyes as they ate in silence. Normally, their dad would be chatting throughout the entire meal and asking everyone questions about their day, and pulling out answers from them that they were holding back. He was a veritable master at table conversation.

Tonight, however, he didn't say a word.

CHAPTER SIX

Bancroft House #2 - Los Angeles

Hank Bancroft was exhausted and terribly sick. The past 16 days had stretched his stamina and patience to the limits. Not only was he dealing with the backlash of his own party, but he had also moved into a new house, ignored Harmon and Stewart to the point of being summoned to Philadelphia, was nearly forced to fire Taylor for an inadvertent information leak (Hank sorely wished the "reply all" option could be removed from email altogether), and had been obliged to take the increasingly rebellious Theo into his new study almost every day. He was at wits' end with the boy.

There were a few bright spots. Floyd had been unusually angelic and encouraging, and Rupert not far behind...but it wasn't enough. The rest of shit he was putting up with was too much, and coupled with Daven's inexplicable coldness towards him lately, Hank was skirting the edge of multiple breakdowns.

The March 1 vote was occurring today, and by noon he found himself quarantined in his home with a sore throat so severe he could not speak at all. Even worse, he couldn't keep his eyes open long enough to read and reply to emails. The only person who would visit him now was Rupert, who had already gone through the same strain of flu and considered himself immune to getting it again. Hank prayed he was right, and he had rarely prayed for anything before.

"Hey, Hank, can I come in?" Rupert called from the bedroom door when he visited after work. Then, remembering Hank couldn't speak, he let himself in. "Shake your head if you want me to leave. No? Okay. I brought you some green tea."

Now Hank shook his head.

"Sorry, just a little joke. It's a London Fog with lavender, naturally. Your chef spent many dramatic minutes putting it together, so try to pretend you like it. What day are you due to go to Philadelphia?"

Hank held up three fingers.

"March 3? Yeah, no way. Look at you. Want me to call Stewart?"

Hank nodded after significant hesitation, and Rupert took a deep breath as he pulled out his phone.

"Stewart? I'm sorry to call so late. This is Rupert Aster, on behalf of Hank Bancroft. Yes, you too, thank you. I'm with Hank. He's too ill to come to Philadelphia on Friday. May we-"

There was a long pause, and Rupert looked puzzled through most of it. "But he, he can't...he can't speak or work right now, I assure you. His temperature is almost 103. You what?......no, that's not acceptable, I'm sorry."

Hank was so drained that he didn't care what proposal of Stewart's that Rupe considered acceptable or not, and he let his friend fight for him without trying to intervene. In fact, he could just drift off to sleep right now. *Yes, that would be really nice* . He started to slip out of consciousness a little, Rupert's angry but level words blurring together into a not unpleasant droning noise. In and out, in and out, until he could hear his blood rushing and feel his heart beating. Then the lights and sound inside his head went out altogether.

When Hank awoke again, it was pitch black outside and Rupert was asleep on the sofa on the other side of the room. He tried to call out for him, but no sound emerged, so Hank picked up the remote control for his television and aimed to throw it against the wall.

Unfortunately he had no strength, and the remote made it all of four feet away from the bed, with nary a thump on the thick carpet.

So Hank closed his eyes and went back to sleep again. This time, he woke to a doctor hovering over him, with Rupert pacing in the background.

"What the-" he tried, to no avail.

"You're alright, Mr. Bancroft. It's Doctor Milligan. I work at Palisades Hospital and you've seen me once before."

Hank looked at Rupert and held up three fingers again, with an accompanying quizzical expression.

"Yes, it took some wrangling but Stewart agreed to postpone until March 10. You're all set."

The three fingers changed to a thumbs-up, and then Hank tapped his wrist. Someone had taken his watch off.

"It's just after 5am," the doctor replied casually. "You're going to be alright in about a week. It's unusual to have such a severe strain of this flu in healthy, strong men like you, but you've been under a tremendous amount of stress. But I can-"

"The vote," Hank rasped desperately.

The doctor ignored that. "I can assure you that you won't see the end of the week if you don't get hydrated. Since you can't keep anything down, we need to move you to the hospital now."

"Obviously a good idea, but how are we going to manage it without an ambulance, and without the press getting into a feeding frenzy?" queried Rupert gloomily. They continued the discussion turned away from the bed in order to diplomatically ignore Hank's silent, writhing protest.

"The...vote..." he croaked in vain.

Rupert turned back around after a few minutes and swallowed hard. "Listen, you got to go to the hospital. I insist, no arguing."

"No, no, and no. Fuck you," Hank whispered slowly and painfully.

"Alrighty, then." Rupert let out a resigned sigh and looked at the doctor. "That's that. Hell will have to literally freeze over before this man agrees to go to the hospital. You've got to do your thing here."

"Alright. Then I have to call my tech in, and a nurse."

"Do it," Rupe said with finality. He didn't look at Hank as he left the room and went into the hallway. Floyd and Theo were both standing there, looking pale and scared.

"Hey guys. Good news, he's going to be fine. It's just the flu. I had it too, though not as bad. We're calling in a nurse to help him out for a few days and stay with him. Go back to bed, and after breakfast I want you each to pack a bag for Daven's house so you don't risk getting this thing, too. You're probably have to stay over for four or five days."

"Can't we stay with you?" Floyd asked quietly, and it was nothing against Daven. Just that it would be easier, since their school was in the same house.

"Unfortunately not. You know Dav is your legal guardian when Hank is unavailable."

"I know, but-"

" *No* , and don't ask me again. Back to bed, both of you."

For a moment Floyd was going to protest, but he took another look at Rupert's no-nonsense determination and wisely changed his mind. When the boys had gone, Rupe reluctantly went back into Hank's room.

"Okay, boss. While we wait for the nurse, I'm going to tell you about the vote." He looked meaningfully at Doctor Milligan, who picked up his chart and left the room.

"Well?" Hank queried in a rasp once the door had closed.

"Public flogging didn't pass. It was close, nearly a tie. All your long nights of writing and giving all those fiery speeches paid off, against all odds. Congratulations, Hank."

"Motherfucker," Hank muttered, unable to celebrate the win because he already realized that Rupert was cheerfully giving him the good news first in order to prepare him for the bad.

"What was that?" Rupe asked, genuinely not having understood the comment.

"Nothing. And?"

"I can't understand what you're saying, so I'll just continue. You already knew that the other one really had no hope of failing. Too many of the elite independents supported it, and in the end it wasn't even close. Even a large swath of Urbanes voted for it, which is a surprise."

Hank nodded, feeling sick to his stomach now on top of everything else. The measures to toughen up the parameters of indentured servitude and sentence the children of felons to such a life was about to become reality. And that, in part, was caused by the Seditionist's past stances on other related issues. Everything was cause and effect in politics, but had Hank foreseen this development, he never would have supporting cutting back on undocumented day laborers seven years ago.

Rupert pulled up a chair and sat next to his beloved boss, who was staring blankly at the ceiling. Gently he said, "I know what you're thinking, Hank. But please stop. We couldn't have predicted this back when we supported other measures that indirectly led up to it. This is never what we wanted. I'm going to take advantage of the fact that you can't speak right now, which means you can't argue with me, and I'm going to tell you something I've always wanted to say. You are a good man. Everything you've ever done - in your entire life - was for a good reason and for the greater good of all. The sacrifices you've made, the endless strategizing, the long hours, the writing, the speaking...none of it will be in vain because of one wrong measure."

"Four," Hank croaked. He was referring to this one, and the three that he had failed to stop last year.

"Leave it to you to argue even in this condition. Four, then. Out of how many? Listen, I'm not going to put up with you feeling sorry for yourself over this. Neither will Daven. Your conscience should be clear because you truly did the best you could to prevent this outcome. I mean...look at you right now, you've nearly killed yourself trying to do the right thing. But when you're better, we move on, and we do bigger and greater right things. Do I have your agreement?"

"No. I'm done," Hank declared with finality.

Rupert paused, his heart going into a freefall at the words. *I'm done...* and he obviously didn't mean he was dying. He meant he was done as leader of the party. Quitting.

He meant it, too.

"I'm sorry, Hank, still can't understand you. Rest your throat, and I'll...uh, the nurse should be here very soon. I'm going to check on the boys and call the doctor in for you. Be right back."

He fled the room and went outside, where the new red-headed guard and his friend were keeping station on the porch. The street was nearly empty except for one lone photographer's car, and the sun was just rising enough to show a streak of purple over the treetops.

"How's he doing, sir?" Martinez inquired.

"Don't call me sir, please. I'm Rupert, or Mr. Aster if you prefer. In about half an hour there will be a nurse and a medical technician arriving from Palisades hospital. Let them in once the doctor comes down and identifies them, not before."

"Yes, sir...Mr. Aster. How is he?"

Rupert wasn't trying to be evasive by not telling them how Hank was; he actually didn't hear the question at all amongst his racing thoughts. "Thank you. I'm going home, and I'll be back at 7 to have breakfast with the boys."

The guards nodded, and Rupe got into his car with a heavy heart.

Seditionists HQ - later that morning

"Dav, we got to talk," said Rupe gloomily as his colleague and friend entered the office an hour late, due to the unexpected arrival of Hank's boys at his front door first thing in the morning.

"About what?"

"In your office? Thanks."

Rupert made himself a cup of coffee before going into the office and closing the door firmly behind him. Daven was scowling and rifling through his briefcase, not looking up.

"Dav…I'm sorry for springing Hank's boys on you this morning. I really am, and I should have given you more notice. But I must say, I'm really disappointed at the way you handled it and how rude you were to all of us. Hank chose you as their guardian for a reason. What the hell is going on with you lately?"

"I don't want to talk about it," Dav said as he slammed his briefcase shut.

"I don't care. Talk about it anyway, or I'm going to make Hank wring it out of you when he gets back. Or I will, right now. You're being a total dick to everyone, and people are starting to talk."

Daven hung up his coat, then took a minute to dig out a file from somewhere deep within his closet.

"Fine. You asked for it. Here you go."

He all but threw the file to Rupe, who took it with dismayed astonishment and started flipping through it with increasing alarm.

"What the… *where* did you get this? Is this for real?"

"Appears to be. They came in the mail to my house just after the audit that uncovered them."

Rupe felt sicker and sicker as he studied the six receipts for a third, and then a fourth time.

"Holy shit, Dav. He *did* pay those fuckers off. Son of a bitch . Who sent these to you?"

"No idea. Came in regular mail, and the zip code it was sent from was our own. Somebody within our organization, probably."

"And you haven't done anything about it?"

Daven walked over and snatched the papers back. "Obviously not!"

Rupert wandered over to Daven's desk chair and collapsed into it. Hank was going to have a stroke over Dav hiding this development for so long, there was no doubt of it. "Fuck. What are you going to do?"

"Talk to him. I've been waiting until after the vote to do it, because we needed him focused on that. It gets worse. He allegedly offered Colton Gamble money for his help with passing his photography measure. Don't ask me how I found out, because I'm not proud of it. And don't even get me started on this infatuation with Harmon. I'm about ten seconds away from quitting every time I think about how he let the Janet investigation get buried just to win some bread points with the Urbanes."

"It's *brownie* points, Dav. Shit. Well, he's too sick to confront now. It would probably kill him to have an argument. You'll have to wait."

"I will. But if these are only little things I'm uncovering by chance, or by someone else exposing them, this could only be scratching the surface. Who knows what else he's up to?"

Rupert gaped at Daven as if he was on fire. "Do you remember what happened in December when we assumed the same thing over one single call? We were completely wrong about all of it, and we nearly lost our jobs to boot. This is Hank we're talking about. Hank *Bancroft* . We're godfathers to his children. Don't paint him in some ridiculous, nefarious light. There's going to be a good explanation, just like last time."

"Right. And the explanation will be: sorry guys, let me explain. I lied, and I really did pay them off ."

"Jesus, Dav. Don't get all high and mighty on me. If he did this - which we don't know for sure - he was desperately trying to protect his sons. Don't you understand? And in the end, it's truly just his problem, not ours. He's going to be the one who has to dig himself out of this."

"Except that he used Seditionists funds to do it, and the money was allocated from my department. So no, it's not *just* his problem. It's now mine, too. So don't tell me what to do, or how I should feel about being lied to!"

Daven was all but over the conversation, but as they were in his office, there was nowhere to go. They were both silent for a minute after that statement, fuming and nearly ready to physically fight each other for the first time since they'd known each other. It took all of Rupert's willpower not to stomp out of the office, but something was holding him back from doing that.

Then he realized what was really bothering him. He had been completely wrong to blindly defend Hank in the face of such evidence, and in the presence of a man who stood to lose so much from it. He should have had Daven's back on this one, and he failed him completely.

Rupe's voice was tight and full of emotion. "Dav...I'm sorry. You're right. I didn't mean to be flippant. I support you. Please forgive me. What's your next step? Is there anything I can do for you right now?"

Daven took a huge swig from one of the comically small water bottles he always kept in his coat pocket. "Thank you, and I accept your apology. Do you have a suggestion on how to proceed with some kind of investigation that we can keep hidden from Hank?"

"First we polygraph the entire accounting department and find out who made those payments. He was expecting that, anyway. And let's hope he doesn't come back too soon. We already poly'd Yannick, so I'll start with the other senior employees right away. This afternoon. With your permission, of course."

Daven looked at him sideways. "My what?"

"You're the big boss man while Hank's away. What say you?"

"Yes, proceed. You have my express authorization to do whatever you need to get it done quickly and efficiently."

Rupert rolled his eyes as he turned to leave the office. "Yes, sir, right away, sir."

"Thank you."

Daven didn't get home until almost 9pm, and he and Lucas found the boys sitting on the couch half-asleep, with Brittany sitting nearby reading the newspaper. It was the evening edition, in which Hank's illness was exaggerated and splashed all over the local section's headlines.

"Did you have dinner?" Daven asked all three of them at large, casting a wary eye on their guard, who got the message and subtly flipped the newspaper over on the table to hide its contents.

Theo nodded. "Yeah. How's dad?"

"The same. Your bedtime is 9:30pm, so why don't you get ready for that. Sorry I'm back so late. Without your dad at the office things can get a little hectic. Brittany, can I talk to you for a minute?"

The boys went back to their rooms, and Brittany and Daven went into the kitchen.

"I haven't even had time to ask about Hank today, or to even think about him," Daven admitted tiredly. "Have you heard anything?"

"Yes, I'm up to date as of about twenty minutes ago. High fever, very sleepy, can't talk. Nothing has changed. Everyone else seems fine in the house, and they've sterilized it top to bottom a few times today."

"Okay. Are Theo and Floyd behaving?"

"Theo's been a handful. I think his dad would have had a word with him about two hours ago for the way he was talking to me and his brother, but other than that everything's fine."

Daven nodded. "Thanks. Are you staying here?"

"That's up to you. I can if you want me to, and I wouldn't mind staying away from the plague house."

"That's fine, take the bedroom next to mine. It has its own bathroom. Thanks for your help."

Daven started with his nightly routine of doing random things around the house and was about to wish the boys goodnight when he heard them arguing loudly. With a deep sigh he made his way upstairs with Shannon close on his heels as the noise escalated while they argued about who could use the shower first. He was tired and didn't have time for this, but he couldn't exactly blow it off and hope for the best.

"Boys," he called calmly as he entered the bedroom they shared. "Come out here, please."

The noise abruptly stopped. Shannon jumped onto one of the beds and made herself comfortable while Floyd emerged first from the bathroom, with Theo close behind him. Dav was used to having Hank's sons argue around him (since they couldn't do it in front of their dad), and he had learned from years of experience how to intimidate them into silence without having to resort to making threats. All he had to do was cross his arms and look down at them disapprovingly.

"What's the solution to this problem?" he asked. Classic Daven - straight to the point.

"There's no problem, Uncle Dav," Floyd replied quickly. "We were just both trying to be first to use the bathroom." Theo stayed silent, thankfully.

"Do I need to decide anything for you in regards to that, or can you work it out on your own?"

"Theo can go first, it's no big deal. Everything's fine, Uncle Dav."

"Good. Proceed, then. My bedroom is right across the hall, as you know, and I prefer to sleep without being awakened by loud voices. Can I count on you to let me do that?"

They both nodded, eyes wide. Daven's tone was kind and friendly, and although the boys knew he would never lash out in anger or lay a hand on them, they wouldn't disobey him now if someone offered them a million bucks to do it. Their father often privately bemoaned his inability to have the same effect on them, much to Daven's embarrassment.

"Okay, then. I'm going to bed. As you know, you're not to leave this room for any reason until I open the door in the morning." That was only because they would likely wake Shannon up and incite a flurry of frantic barking. She was an excellent guard dog, if a bit overzealous. All of Daven's guards and regular visitors had gotten on his bad side at least once for making too much noise in the middle of the night and setting her off.

"Shannon, come along. Off the bed. Good girl. Goodnight, boys."

"Goodnight," they said together. The bedroom door closed, and Floyd turned and quietly but firmly shoved Theo to the floor.

"Bitch!" he hissed.

"Idiot!" Theo whispered back.

The door opened back up again and Daven peeked in.

"Oh, I forgot to tell you..." he watched in dismay as Theo scrambled off the floor and back onto his feet. Floyd cleared his throat, trying to get out some kind of reasonable explanation, but there was none. Anyone with eyes and a brain could gather what had just happened.

"Come here, Floyd," he said gravely, and Floyd obediently followed Daven into the hallway with a look of deep regret and shame on his face.

"You know what your father would do if he saw what I just saw, right?"

"Yes. I'm sorry."

"You're sixteen years old, beating up on a twelve year old, in my house. That's not acceptable, and your dad will be hearing about it when he's recovered. Go apologize to Theo, and then go to bed. Clear?"

Floyd nodded, eyes wide and wet. He hated disappointing people, especially Daven, and this was the first time he had ever had a reason to rebuke him in this manner. It hurt, and it was embarrassing.

"Do you have to tell him?" he tried, hoping desperately for a reprieve.

"I'm not going to tell him. You are, when he asks you if you behaved yourself. What I was going to say earlier is that I forgot to tell you both that school will start late tomorrow because Mrs. Aster has an appointment. We'll go out for breakfast at a restaurant, then take Shannon to the dog park. Brittany will wake you guys up at 8."

Floyd wiped his eyes with the sleeve of his sweatshirt and composed himself again. "Okay. That sounds nice."

Daven nodded, then reached out and patted a shoulder in what he hoped was a reassuring manner, but it felt more awkward than anything else. "See you in the morning. Goodnight."

By the end of day two, Rupe was starting to make himself crazy with the possibilities behind the receipts Daven had received. He even started talking to himself to keep track of his thoughts and bullet points.

Guilty of not covering his tracks properly....

That is so unlike you, Hank - the smartest man I've ever known. The most manipulative and careful man I've ever known. You've never missed a detail nor ever forgot them.

Which by itself alone argued for his innocence, because he wouldn't be that dumb. But then again, Hank had offered said bribes to Urbanes photographers on live television, with his son and a very angry Daven in tow.

Jesus, Hank. Maybe you really are that dumb. I mean, you did threaten Harmon on live television. Twice.

Putting everyone's careers on the line by using Seditionist Funds...

He would never put Daven's career on the line. Or mine. Never. But then again, he did nearly fire us for taking phone calls on Christmas eve, and then publicly shamed us for it...

The money was allocated from Daven's department....

That could have been a mistake. Errors in coding happen all the time amongst the more inexperienced bookkeepers...but, those with access to the anonymous account were highly experienced.

Back to square one again: Hank is paying off bribes with company funds and leaving a trail behind that leads straight to him.

...which would mean he's all but lost his mind, and I'm not willing to accept that.

If Hank intended to make an illegal bribe, why would he not use private funds instead?

...because personal banks do not allow anonymous ledger entries. It would have been too traceable.

And why the hell would he offer money to Colton Gamble to help pass that measure?

... desperation. Needed to save your boys from the press. Floyd's panic attacks becoming more frequent.

Colton Gamble had worked for Harmon once.

... Yes. Colton Gamble worked for Harmon once. Is that important? Is that a thing?

No, they had a falling out. Harmon hates Colton Gamble. They aren't even on speaking terms.

...but Colton Gamble is best friends with Colbert.

And Colbert hates Hank Bancroft.

Irrelevant. They've always hated each other, so why would Colbert start something now? And what would Colton Gamble have to gain?

Who sent the receipts?

An inside man. We'll never know, because we can't ask that question during the polygraph. It will expose Hank's crime. Or...not crime..or....fuck it all.

Rupe threw down his notebook and called Daven. "I've got nothing, Dav. I keep going in circles."

"I'm coming over."

Thirty seconds later they were face to face again.

"I have nothing, either," Dav admitted. "If anything, I'm more convinced he did it. At least Hank is still too sick to come in, or do much at all. Let's just hope he stays that way for another few days, or preferably until we can put him going off to Philadelphia next week."

The men looked at each other, horrified that they were on the same wavelength and harboring such dark thoughts.

"I didn't mean…"

"It's okay, Dav. I've been thinking the same: as long as he stays deathly ill, that gives us more time to save him. God help us…"

CHAPTER SEVEN

Saturday morning, March 4.

Daven's House

Daven was not used to having a full table at breakfast in his house - usually he dined alone at all meals - but he thought it was something he could probably get used to and enjoy. It wasn't planned, either, and just kind of happened as more people showed up at the house all at the same time. The boys were there, of course, and Brittany, Lucas, Rupert, and even Captain Martinez, who had stopped by to follow up on a report that someone was climbing over the back fence of the property. There were clear indications of someone trying to do that, but the officers had concluded the attempt was unsuccessful.

Daven had agreed to the boys' request to fix breakfast, much to his current regret. Theo was busy making a colossal mess with the waffle iron, and Daven had to almost physically hold himself back from trying to help him and prevent more mess. Theo had even spilled an entire carton of orange juice all over the floor in a moment of carelessness. As a neat freak, it had nearly pushed Daven over the edge, but he kept quiet.

Floyd, on the other hand, expertly cooked and served everyone oatmeal, sausage, and eggs, as well as pouring all the drinks and setting the table. He was obviously thoroughly enjoying himself and the company, and was happier than Dav had seen him all week.

As Theo slid a grossly deformed but perfectly cooked waffle in front of the very grateful police captain, Rupe finally put two and two together in regards to the man's last name.

"Are you related to Hank's new guard, by chance? He's a Deveraux, too if I'm not mistaken."

The captain reached for the syrup and smiled broadly. "My son. Thank god for Hank's intervention on that one."

Daven cocked his head curiously. "Oh? Was he previously unemployed for some time?"

"No, not at all. Worked as a state police officer and was transferred to Shasta six months ago, against his will. Toby went with him - that's his best friend since they were babies, practically - to make it more bearable. But it wasn't enough. I casually mentioned to Hank they hated it up there, then went on my way and forgot we ever had the conversation."

Rupe grunted. "Going from Los Angeles to Shasta County? What a grisly downgrade."

"That's why they can't keep any Southern California boys up there on a long-term basis and have to force them into it. Only thing it's got going for it is a big-ass lake that you can't even fish in anymore because of the tree-hugging plagues of Urbanes."

Daven asked, "So Hank had them transferred back to LAPD?"

"No. Not even two hours after hearing how unhappy they were - didn't even ask questions - he simply went out on the porch, sipping a beer, and asked them to join his own guards. Just like that. Offered a shit ton of money for 'em, too, didn't even try to bargain. The boys got back home a few days ago, pinching themselves daily and still not quite believing it all. Needless to say, their kids and wives are over the moon to have him home three days a week." He looked at Floyd and smiled. The teenager had sat down earlier to enjoy his own food but was now frozen still, fully enraptured by the tale he was hearing.

"He did that, sir?"

"He didn't tell you? Guess I'm not surprised. Your dad is a pain in the ass more often than not, but he's a good man. The best kind of man there is, and I'll fight anyone who says otherwise." He turned his attention back to Rupe and Dav. "It pisses me off, all the shit headlines he's been getting recently. Doesn't deserve any of 'em."

"Language, please," said Daven gently, cocking his head subtly towards the boys.

"Right. Sorry."

"We don't give a fuck about bad words," Theo piped up cheerfully from his station in the kitchen. Everyone at the table gasped, and then roared. Except Daven, of course. He smiled thinly, then stood up and went into the kitchen while everyone else continued to laugh and make conversation.

"How's it going over here, Theo? Making a mess, I see."

"I'm trying not to, Uncle Dav. Kept putting too much batter in, but I think I've got it now."

"Good. Remember that I told you there's no swearing in my house. Don't do it again, please."

"You swear all the time in your house," Theo replied cheekily, his grin indicating he meant no harm and had no intention of arguing any further. No, he was only basking in the attention from the crowd. The same type of positive and encouraging attention he didn't get very often from his father.

Daven gave in without a fight and reached way up into the cupboard to grab two more rolls of paper towels. "I guess you're right. Clean this shit up when you're done."

"I will. This waffle iron is going to be a bitch to clean."

"Let it cool down first, it's hot as fuck right now."

Theo giggled, and Daven opened the fridge, deeply depressed about the story Captain Martinez had just told. How he said he would fight anyone who didn't consider Hank a good man.

The words were strikingly familiar; Daven had once felt the same way. Just...not lately. And why not? He deeply admired Hank's huge balls in standing against his own party, was constantly moved by his rousing speeches given to hostile crowds that were quickly won over, and had been touched by the countless other good and positive things Hank had done for his constituents and even his opponents. For his friends. For complete strangers, like Martinez. Hell, the man had even ditched all his responsibilities in order to pursue Shannon around the city for hours, even though his friendship with Dav had already come to a certain end.

Somehow, Dav had forgotten Hank's true nature, and he suddenly hated himself for it. What's worse, it was his own fault. He was still bitterly hung up on the ugly consequences of the Christmas Day fiasco, even though he should be thankful Hank didn't fire him on the spot.

Even after Dav and Rupe had clearly proven they couldn't be trusted, Hank trusted them again anyway - after a few weeks of tension and petty bickering, to be sure - but he eventually forgave and let them back in, because that's the kind of man he was to his friends.

And what kind of friend am I being to him right now?

Dav continued to gather his thoughts while pretending to search for something in the fridge, then caught Rupert's eye as he grabbed the nearest bottle of what looked like root beer and sat back down. It was clear they were both thinking exactly the same thing.

We need to talk to him, Rupert's eyes said.

Daven nodded, then turned his attention to his cold, mangled waffle.

"Are you really going to put barbecue sauce on your waffle, Uncle Dav?" Theo asked in awe.

Bancroft House

Afternoon, same day

"Hey, boss," Rupert said quietly as he entered Hank's room with a bag of takeout from The Daily Grill. He hoped he could entice Hank to eat, but the odds seemed dismal; two other plates of uneaten food were already on the nightstand.

"Hey," Hank replied sleepily. "You're late. Can you close the curtains?"

"Sorry. Got caught in traffic." That was a feeble joke; Rupe only lived four blocks away. He walked around the room shutting the blackout curtains, which were so effective even in the middle of the day that he had to follow Hank's voice to make his way back to him.

"How are you doing?"

"Can't talk much. Hot. Nauseated. Annoyed."

"I'm sure. Stopped at your favorite place to grab you a chicken pot pie, despite my wife's insistence that it was too much for you to handle right now. It appears she's right. Again."

"Thank you, but you need to call me when you're going to be late, even if I am on my deathbed."

Oh...that's why he was annoyed.

"I apologize, Hank. Won't happen again. And you're hardly on your deathbed."

"Feels like it. Can you get Dav on speakerphone now, please? I want to get this over with."

Rupert flipped open his phone and realized with a start that he was almost 40 minutes late. Shit, he'd really lost track of time. Hank was still his boss no matter what, and this was a business meeting - one that Rupe himself had requested, and that Hank had agreed to despite his illness.

"Doing it now. I'm sorry," he repeated again, feeling like a complete dick as he dialed. The light from the phone enabled him to spot a chair in the corner, and he dragged it over next to the bed during the veritable eternity it took for Dav to pick up. Once he did, Rupert carefully laid the phone next to Hank so they could both hear and speak into it.

"Hello Rupert," Dav said robotically. "May I assume Hank is on the line as well?"

"Present, Mr. Johansson."

Oh boy…Hank was in a mood now. This couldn't be good. Rupert braced himself, already feeling overly emotional in advance from the epic argument he thought was inevitable.

"Alright, Dav. Since you volunteered to go first, please tell him from the beginning what we called this meeting for."

"Can't wait," Hank grumbled.

Daven took a deep breath. "Hank, I know this is going to be very upsetting. Please stay calm and let us talk this through from all points of view. I recently received a packet in the mail that implicates you in a bribery scheme. It was a packet of what appear to be original receipts for six payments made to Urbane photographers under your name.”

Hank started to sit up, which knocked the phone onto the floor and popped it shut. “What!”

Rupe put a firm hand on his shoulder as he reached down to fumble for his cell in the pitch dark. “Hank, please. Just listen. Lay down. We’ll explain everything. Try not to get agitated.”

“Easy for you to say!”

“None of this is easy for me!” Rupe snapped back harshly as he found the phone and re-dialed Dav as quickly as his trembling fingers could manage. It was the first time he could ever recall talking back to Hank in that manner, and it rattled him. He was relieved when Daven picked up on the first ring.

“Sorry about that, Dav. Technical difficulty. Go ahead.”

Dav continued as if he had never stopped. “We’ve been investigating them for several days to determine where they came from and who forged them. So far we haven’t found the hard evidence we need to prove they’re fakes. Whoever did this was on the inside, since everything lines up with our accounting and the timeline of the payments down to the minute. There’s no external party who has access to that information. But no one in accounting has yet failed a polygraph test designed to figure out who made the payments. Do you have any idea of who might be behind this?”

Hank was probably white as a sheet, but it was too dark for Rupert to see him. He made no response, but tensed up enough that the bed moved slightly.

"Hank?" Rupert gently prodded.

"How long...when did you get this package?"

"Three weeks ago. I only told Rupert on Wednesday, and we've been working frantically since then."

Why the fuck did you wait? Hank wanted to ask, but he refrained because he already knew the very uncomfortable answer.

"Okay. And what have you discovered so far?"

"The payments were made by cashier's check, likely bought in person. If we can determine where they were purchased, we might be able to obtain security footage and interview the person, or persons, who sold them. If we can confirm even one person who was paid with them, Stewart can issue a subpoena for a deposition."

"That's a lot of ifs. And a subpoena requires an indictment first, Dav," Hank said wearily. He was getting sleepy again, despite the shock of this news and the initial adrenaline rush.

"I believe Stewart can authorize a special investigation to prevent that. You'll have to ask him. Anyway, we have a handwriting professional coming in on Monday morning to analyze your signature versus those on the documents. We're already a quarter of the way through polygraphing our accountants. Lastly, we want to pull phone records to determine what calls were made between Colton Gamble and Harmon, and to see what evidence can be gathered from those.”

“Colton Gamble? Why?”

Rupe jumped in now, his heart pounding with a sick, deep thudding against his ribs. “He says you offered him money to help push your measure through the house.”

“For fuck’s sake. No, I did not.”

“Is there a recording of your call with him?” Rupe eventually asked, after a long silence from Dav.

“Calls, plural. We had about seven. No, because they were between our cell phones.”

Rupe felt like crying, he was that frustrated right now at Hank’s refusal to use his office phone for these calls so that could be recorded. They had had the argument countless times before.

Dav continued now. “Okay, well…then there’s no evidence, and Stewart will have to let that go. In regards to the receipts, there’s no way to complete the investigation before you go to Philadelphia. We can’t finish polygraphing the entire accounting department that quickly.”

“And the tape?” Hank was rapidly losing his voice again, and the question came out as a whisper.

“Yes, regarding the tape we got from Harmon. That’s next on my list to discuss. The voice analysis is due back Thursday, despite our rush job. They had quite a back-up at the lab we contract with, and no other lab is trustworthy enough to handle it because we didn't have time to vet them."

"Hmmm."

"Have you spoken to Harmon since we got it?"

"No. You know that."

Another long silence. Rupe and Dav were intensely curious why Hank was so pissed off at Harmon, especially considering the man had provided something to them for free that was incredibly valuable, but neither one of them had taken the precarious step towards asking Hank about it yet. He would tell them if and when he needed to.

"I'm really tired, guys. I need to go back to sleep. Proceed however you feel is best."

Daven paused. "Well, we would like to get your permission first to look into a few other possibilities. Today I was thinking of-"

"Not necessary. Do whatever you need to do."

Dav should have liked that answer, but he didn't. "Okay, are you just saying that because you're sick and don't have the energy to deal with this? Because that's not like you, and I'm not comfortable having free rein like this. I want to make sure you-"

"Sounds like you've managed fine on your own so far. Why stop now?"

There was an ugly but understandable bitterness to that remark. Hank had clearly reached his wits' end with today's news. Rupe hadn't forgotten his friend's vow that he was "done" with his job. Even though Rupe had pretended not to hear him at the time, and it hadn't come up again. But the memory of that remark upset him far more than he was comfortable admitting to himself.

"Thank you for your trust, Hank," Rupe said once he recovered his own wits. "You have our word that we're doing everything in our power to get to the bottom of this. We won't stop until you're completely cleared and all the questions are answered."

"I already know the answer," declared Hank tiredly. "Colbert is behind this."

"Most likely," murmured Rupert.

"We have him on our list of possibilities," Dav admitted. "But there's no evidence yet."

"There will be." Hank replied. "His best friend is Colton Gamble, and you know I don't believe in coincidences."

"We're exploring that angle. But it almost seems too obvious, don't you think? Everyone knows you hate each other, and that he's practically in Gamble's back pocket. He would have to know he'd be the very first suspect. And why would he want to start something with you now, after all these years? There are others with much more to gain from your downfall."

"Rupe and I know Colbert intimately. You don't. This is all him, and he's an impatient, arrogant bastard who will step on his own dick soon enough. That's when the red flags will start flying left and right. Keep your eyes open. I'm going back to bed, so let's end this for now."

"He's right about Colbert, Dav. I'll come by your house in a few minutes," said Rupe. He hung up the phone and turned to his best friend of ten years, feeling like the worst piece of shit on the planet.

"I'm sorry to have ambushed you with this while you're so sick, but I had no choice. You need to talk to the FBI on Monday. Or maybe Tuesday, depending on the results of the signature analysis."

"I forgive you for thinking I did it, Rupe," Hank said quietly. Peacefully, even.

"What? I never thought that."

"Don't lie," Hank murmured quietly. "I know you. I know the signs of guilt in your voice, in your eyes."

"My eyes, huh? It's pitch black in here, Hank." Rupert felt like crying, and his voice wavered with the guilt that Hank apparently knew so well. Damn it.

"Just admit it, it's alright," Hank added sleepily.

Rupert cleared his throat roughly. "I really need to get going so I can keep working on this with Dav, but I'd like to come by again after church tomorrow if that's okay. To see how you're doing and give you an update on the boys."

"Yes, please. I might ask you to heat up that pot pie for me, too." The bed rustled as Hank shifted slightly, and Rupert felt a burning hot palm rest on his forearm. "Whatever changed your mind, don't let anything change it back. I may be an ornery, impulsive fucker sometimes, and intolerable the rest of the time...but I don't lie to my friends."

That was all it took for Rupe's eyes to start leaking. "I know, Hank," he managed to get out. "I'm so sorry."

"It's okay. Go. See you tomorrow."

Hank patted Rupe's arm once, then slid his hand away and closed his eyes. Rupert wiped his sleeve across his wet face, and reluctantly left his friend.

"Goddamn, that was utterly agonizing," complained Rupert bitterly as he strolled through the front door of Daven's house and threw down his keys on the sideboard. "Would rather have had my-"

"Keep your voice down. Theo and Floyd are having lunch in the dining room. Come to my study."

They went in, and Daven poured Rupert a huge shot of bourbon without asking.

"He knows we thought he did it, Dav."

"Yes. He handled it all fairly well, considering."

Rupert held out his glass for a refill of bourbon, but Daven didn't oblige.

"No, I need you to be clear-headed right now. I have a friend in Castaic who is a handwriting expert on the side. Trustworthy and discreet. Do you feel up for a road trip today?"

"On the side? What does that mean? He's an amateur?"

Dav shook his head. "He was a professional, but retired to play in the ragtime band at Disneyland. The state still contracts with him on occasion for more difficult forgery cases."

"Wow. That's an odd mixture of skills. Hell of a commute, too."

"Do you want to come with me, or not? I need to leave in about ten minutes."

Rupe shook his head. "No. I want to stay near Hank in case he needs something. The boys can stay with me while you're gone."

"Thanks, but I'm taking them with me, and Lucas and Brittany. Rented a cabin at the lake for the afternoon so they can relax while I'm meeting with Asa nearby."

"Oh. Does Hank know you're taking them?"

"No. Probably wouldn't care, since he hasn't asked me about them even once in four days. It's really odd. Bothers me."

"He's horribly sick, Dav," Rupert answered hotly. "And he trusts you to take care of them without interfering. Don't worry about it."

The Long Way Around

Tooth and Nail

CHAPTER ONE

Friday, March 10 - Philadelphia

FBI Headquarters

"Okay, Hank. There's just something not quite lining up about this whole thing. Your explanation seems reasonable on the surface, but here's the thing: I received copies of the same receipts and a letter describing what they were, along with a photo of the packet that was sent to Daven. It exactly matches this one." He tapped the yellow envelope unnecessarily. "We launched an investigation immediately, and our conclusions are the exactly same as yours: the signatures cannot be confirmed either as genuine or fake, and the cashier checks are untraceable to a specific person without obtaining a warrant for the security footage from the location where they were purchased."

Hank swallowed his surprise in a too-large gulp of coffee, which burned his mouth painfully. His eyes watered, and he had to cough a few times before responding.

"You knew about this already? For how long?"

Stewart didn't answer that. "The Treasury Department traced all six purchases to a notorious bail bonds complex in San Bernardino. We've not had much luck with them before because their security cameras aren't the best quality, but we're working on it."

"Oh…"

"So my first question is, why didn't you inform us of this alleged plot the moment you discovered it?"

"I told you. I learned of it on March 4, when I was pretty much on my deathbed and out of the office. There was no point informing you when I didn't have enough information to hold a fruitful discussion. That was less than a week ago."

"You should have told me immediately, regardless. To do otherwise invited suspicion. I brought you here to see if you can help us launch a special investigation, which will allow us to obtain the warrant we need without pressing formal charges. But I can't do that at the moment."

"Why not?" Hank asked, feeling the world spin a little, in both directions somehow.

"Because there's a huge hole in your story that's yet to be explained. We know that Daven personally received the receipts at his house on February 13. So please don't tell me again that you weren't aware of them until March 4. On the surface, it looks like you held back investigating until after the March 1 vote in order to avoid negative publicity, which would have influenced your rallies."

"As I said, I only learned about them on March 4," Hank repeated hotly. "That is the truth. How do you know for sure that was the date he received them? Mail gets delayed all the time."

"I'm not at liberty to say how, but it's simply not up for debate," Stewart replied reluctantly. High-powered surveillance across the street had clearly captured Daven quizzically studying the bright yellow packet as he took his mail inside his house the evening of February 13, but the mere existence of that camera was strictly FBI knowledge.

"Not at liberty, huh? Well, I might not be 'at liberty' at all if this isn't figured out."

"That's what I'm here for. What happened to that packet between February 13 and March 4?"

Hank sat up straighter. "Was there anything illegal about us not informing you right away that we were investigating a possible forgery of an *internal* financial document? In fact, did we have any obligation at all to inform you of their existence until we had reached a conclusion of *our own* self-conducted investigation on *our own* employees, including myself?"

Stewart hesitated, then leaned back with a small sigh and shake of his head. "Technically, no."

Hank picked up his coffee again. "Exactly. Let's move on, then."

"I'm the one controlling this conversation, Hank, and we're staying on this topic for a minute. Since you claim you didn't know of their existence until March 4, I have to conclude that Daven himself - not you - held them back in order to wait for the March 1 vote to take place first. Possibly influenced and/or aided by Rupert. If that's the case, I need to know, because it will mitigate the circumstances and shift some of the blame away from you. Is that what happened?"

"Not even close."

"Then what? I need to give the president an explanation of some kind. Preferably one that's plausible, if you have one."

Hank leaned forward and set his cup down hard, causing a bit of coffee to splash onto the desk.

"I'd like to ask my question again, just for clarification. Was there anything illegal about our confidential investigation, or lack thereof? I seem to recall that you confirmed there wasn't, not even thirty seconds ago."

"Technically? No. But if it was delayed specifically to influence the vote? Absolutely. Looking at a felony on that one."

"Well, good luck trying to prove it."

Stewart stood up and shoved his chair back into the credenza in frustration. "I've had enough of this, Hank. I'm trying to help you, and you're stonewalling me at every opportunity. Go back to Los Angeles, and report here again on Monday afternoon if you've come to your senses by then. If not, I'll bring in Daven and Rupert instead to tell me *their* side of the story."

"They're busy on Monday. Monthly birthday luncheon at the office. How's Tuesday looking for you?"

Stewart raised an eyebrow at him. "You're being awfully cocky and defensive today. More so than usual. Are you sure that's in your best interests?"

"Are you sure that continuing this conversation is in my best interests?"

"Yes, because you're bluffing. I know you. You would never agree to let me summon Rupert and Daven here."

"Do it," muttered Hank as he reached over to pluck a Kleenex out of the holder and wiped up the spilled coffee to buy a few seconds to think. His bravado was failing as he realized the line was behind him now; he had crossed it with that simple *do it.*

Stewart sat back down and watched him for a few moments. Quietly he said, "Hank. I like you. I trust you. And you *know* that has always been true, despite our conflicts. Why don't you just tell me what's really going on in your head right now? If you don't, I'm going to have to transfer this case to someone else, because it appears my days of getting through to you are over. That's not a threat. If I fail to do my job and get enough information from you, an entire month of my time will have been wasted on trying to figure out how to exonerate you. I think I can guarantee that the next person who steps into this mess won't be nearly as enthusiastic."

Oh shit, thought Hank.

Stewart continued, "I'm not judging you for being defensive and angry. I'm not concluding you did anything wrong, or right, or whatever. But your behavior towards me - the *only* person in the position to help you right now - is indefensible, and I won't put up with it for one more minute. Tell me how you want to proceed. It's your choice."

Silence.

Stewart flopped his notebook shut after a minute of waiting in vain for Hank to speak again. "Alright. I'll summon Rupert and Daven, then. You can go."

"No. Leave them out of it," Hank said finally, giving up the bluff. "Daven held on to the receipts because he was afraid to confront me. Avoiding bad PR never even occurred to him, because his mind doesn't work that way. If they had gone to Rupert first, it's possible *he* would have held them back for that reason. Likely, even. But not Dav, and I would gladly bet my own life and career on that."

"What changed his mind about telling you?"

"Don't know. I never asked."

"It's good he revealed them when he did. We were waiting to see what you would do, and I was getting nervous. If he had destroyed them, or hid them from-"

"He would've *never* done that!" Hank retorted fiercely. "Even to imply it, or think that for one second, is, is-"

"I believe you. Calm down."

Stewart opened his notebook back up again and wrote for some time, then closed it one last time.

"Thank you for your honesty, however belated. Even if you aren't convicted of bribery, it's possible Daven could be publicly censured."

Hank's temper flared to new heights. "There is nothing illegal about what he did. You said so yourself!"

"A broken law isn't a requirement for censure. Poor judgment is usually enough, and I can hardly think of a more worthy example than that. At any rate, at least this makes me feel comfortable to launch a special investigation and get that warrant, which I'll proceed with on Monday."

"Okay. Well...thank you?"

"Don't thank me. I hate this as much as you do."

He looked over Hank's shoulder as his secretary caught his attention through the glass.

"Come in."

"Sorry to interrupt. The president is asking to see both of you in five minutes."

"Thank you."

The door closed, and Hank raised his eyebrows. "May I ask what *this* is going to be about?"

"Yes, we should have discussed it already but this thing with the receipts has taken all our time. Prepare yourself, Hank. It's highly likely that President Rickon is going to invalidate the passing of your upcoming measure."

"What! Why?"

"Walk with me, it's going to take a minute to get to the conference room." As they were hurrying down a long, empty hall, Stewart said in a low voice, "The rumor about you offering to bribe Gamble is running rampant, and he wants to talk about formally investigating in order to avoid accusations and bad PR. It's inevitable that the charges will be dropped due to lack of recordings, but the measure will get put back at the end of the line to go through the house again...probably to be put on the July or August voting docket."

Hank's anger resurfaced instantly, and he stopped in his tracks. "Are you serious? Not acceptable. There is zero evidence. I refuse to meet with him until these '*charges*' are dropped."

Stewart gaped at him. "But you haven't even been charged yet, and you might not be if the president approves to drop it. That's what this conversation is about, and you're lucky to get an audience with him at all."

"No. I won't be any part of it. Let me know when you're all done jerking me around."

"You can't just refuse to talk to the president. Come on."

"Oh, really? Let me show you how it's done."

Hank turned on his heel and made a beeline towards the back exit that led to his waiting car.

Stewart quickly caught up to him. "Stop being an idiot, Hank. Seriously, this is a huge mistake."

Hank kept walking, and Stewart followed in silence for the two minutes it took to traverse the hallway. When they reached the little lobby, Stewart snapped his fingers at the security desk, and the exit instantly locked itself with a resonating *clang*. Hank tried pushing it anyway, in vain, then stood there and just shook his head.

"You can't be serious," he grumbled under his breath as two guards came up to the men and kept a respectful but cautious distance.

Stewart was completely done with Hank's attitude, but he forced his tone to stay calm and gentle. "You can either come with me to talk to the president now, or we can formally indict you on bribery charges and have you held in Philadelphia until the investigation is completed. Your choice."

Hank laughed humorlessly. "Oh, I see. So I guess this means you're no longer on my side?" he challenged.

"Stop being so dramatic. If I *wasn't* on your side, I would just let you leave."

Hank looked out at his waiting car and did a double take. Avery had pulled up too hastily upon sight of him and accidentally jumped a good portion of the sidewalk with both right tires. Hank made a mental note to tease him for it later. Right now, there was nothing more he wanted than to dive in the backseat and speed off to the airport, back to the relative safety of his new house. But...*fuck it all.*

"Unlock the door," said Hank wearily.

Stewart turned to the security desk and nodded, and the door unhitched itself with a mechanical asshole. Hank strode up to the car and leaned into the open window.

"Don't quit your day job to become a valet."

"Sorry, boss. These streets are crazy narrow."

"Yeah. I just got called into another meeting. Need you to go back and wait a little longer, unfortunately."

"Will do."

"Thanks. See you in a bit. Stay off the sidewalk."

He went back in, turned to Stewart and began walking again, his former good humor partially restoring itself along the way.

"Nice trick," he remarked coolly. "I deserved that. Sorry for being a dick."

"Well, desperate times and all that. I'm sorry for threatening you. You know I don't want any of this to go south, so..."

Hank cleared his throat. "Yeah. Thanks. It's too bad you're my FBI handler. I think we could have been good friends in another life. You remind me so much of Daven sometimes."

Stewart laughed. "Having met Daven on one of his more awkward days, I'm not sure that's much of a compliment. But thank you."

"It's the highest compliment, I assure you. He does infuriate me to the core sometimes, but you can probably guess who's fault that is. Anyway, what would you suggest I say to president Rickon regarding this whole thing?”

“Nothing much. Just listen, agree to do what he says, and scoot the hell out while you have the chance. He’s been in a mood lately. At least take solace in the fact that you’re not the only person he’s pissed off at today.”

“Oh. Good. I think.”

CHAPTER TWO

FBI Headquarters, Philadelphia

Friday, March 10

Hank wasn't allowed into the conference room upon arrival; the president wanted to speak with Stewart first. Hank was obligated to wait a respectful distance away, and was not permitted to take out his phone. That gave him plenty of time to observe Rickon's dozen-strong security detail, which was remarkable for the fact that nearly all of them were female.

Hank suddenly regretted having all male servants and guards for so long, because Brittany had been an outstanding (and overdue) addition to the household, with unique strengths that the men never had developed. Like a maternal instinct, for example. That's why she was usually assigned to guard his sons. For the first time, he wondered what it must be like for her to live amongst 17 men and two boys...even the dogs were male. Most of the guards only lived at the house four days a week (the servants were 5 days), but Brittany was one of three who lived there full-time (along with Avery and Vance). He made a mental note to check and make sure all of her needs were being taken care of, as far as her accommodations and-

Hank dismissed this train of thought abruptly as Salome Danby suddenly strode into the anteroom carrying a binder that was much too small for the amount of contents it contained. Hank recognized it instantly as being Stewart's file on him; Salome must have stopped into his office to grab it in the way here. She darted into the conference room without a glance at anyone, and all was quiet again.

So quiet that Hank imagined he could hear his heart pounding and blood rushing. Or maybe he *wasn't* imagining it.

Seditionists Headquarters

Daven's Office

"What do you think is happening now?" Rupert asked for a second time as he sat across the table from Daven, who was busy being ridiculously picky about editing the long-delayed media statement to address the March 1 vote.

"I don't know. How could I *possibly* know?"

"I'm just trying to make conversation."

"And I'm just trying to work," Dav replied, a telling edge to his tone that indicated he was under more stress than usual. "Which is exactly what you should be doing, too. How's it coming with that list?"

"It's coming." Rupert sighed as he looked at his written notes. Hank requested a comprehensive list of all the headlines pertaining to him that he had missed during his illness, and Rupert had to write them out by hand because he had spilled orange juice all over his laptop yesterday and was still waiting for a replacement. He threw the pen down and massaged the painful muscle between his thumb and index finger. *Feels like I'm in school again* , he grumbled to himself.

"Sorry, what was that?" Daven asked without taking his eyes off his own task.

"Nothing."

"Let me see the list."

Rupert took a deep breath and gave him the notebook, swallowing his resentment for the hundredth time in ten days. He really didn't like Daven lording it over him like this. As usual, not having Hank around for so long drastically altered the dynamics between the longtime friends, to the point where Rupe always felt like nothing he did would be ever good enough for Daven. Like a little kid constantly trying to please his father. *Like Floyd* .

Daven put the list down, frowning. "This is taking too long. He wants it done before he leaves Philadelphia, so he can review it on the plane."

"I know, Dav. You do recall that he only asked me two days ago, right? I still have dozens of papers to go through, and then I have to type up this damned thing."

Daven grunted. "I'll start typing it up to save time. You keep reviewing the papers. Three hours. Not a minute longer."

"I *know,* for fuck's sake!"

That got Daven to finally look up, but he said nothing. He didn't have to; they both knew from past experience that Hank would nail Rupe to the wall if he disrespected Dav's authority in his absence. Like he was doing now.

"Right," Rupe said as cheerfully as he could manage. "Three hours. Got it."

Daven nodded as he moved over to his computer, taking Rupe's notebook with him.

"Dav?" said Rupe quietly a moment later as he hovered at the door. "I'm really worried about Hank. That's all. Sorry I've been a pain."

Daven picked up his fourth cup of espresso and peered over the monitor. "Hank can handle himself. Can you?"

FBI HQ - Philadelphia

Hank Bancroft was not handling himself well. The president was in a snippy, take-no-prisoners mood, and Hank was all but rising to every provocation that had come up since he walked in the door after waiting almost two hours like a schoolboy waiting to see the principal.

First to irritate him was the insistence from the president on addressing him as *Mr. Bancroft* . He was no longer simply Hank, because he was in trouble and it had to be keep being emphasized for some reason, in case he missed it. He did not; Rickon made his feelings on the matters quite clear.

Apparently Stewart and Salome had just laid everything out on the table that was going on with Hank and the Seditionists, and now it was time for the reckoning.

So that meant that secondly, Hank was entirely unappreciative of being ambushed by three people at once, and he made his feelings known. So did the president, who had similar feelings.

"You want to talk about being ambushed? How about me having to sit here today listening to 90 minutes' worth of bullshit going in your party. Rather, in one of this *nation's* political parties. You think it's all about you!"

"Which particular instance of bullshit are you referring to?" Hank fired back.

"You haven't talked to Harmon in several weeks, against our express instructions, is that correct?"

"Yes. He tried to-"

"Don't care," snapped the president. "Get it together, you're not children. And what's this about Daven holding back knowledge of a bribery scheme-"

Hank bristled. " *Forgery* scheme."

"Alleged forgery scheme, then, which conveniently he only informed you about after the March 1 vote? I have a mind to completely invalidate that day's measures, but I won't go that far since I think they're for the good of the nation."

"I see. Glad you agree that flaying the skin off human beings in front of children and women is probably a bad thing."

"Among other things, including your attitude. You're on dangerous ground, Mr. Bancroft. I expect you to address me respectfully from this point on."

Stewart and Salome were frozen in place, faces white. Apparently they did not see the president in this mood very often, and it was for damned certain they never saw anyone talk to him like that before. Hank picked up his water bottle and took an enormous gulp, then capped it again and set it down hard.

"With all due *respect* I find it interesting, sir, that you added the word *alleged* before the words *forgery scheme* , but you did not add it before *bribery scheme* . Do we not practice 'innocent until proven guilty' in this country anymore? You're the president, you know best, and I would be grateful if you could condescend to educate me on that point."

Hank got kicked out of the conference room for that comeback - discussion over - and was now sitting alone in Stewart's office again. He was running an hour late to catch his plane, and thought of poor Avery, who must be bored to tears waiting for him in the lobby with absolutely nothing to do.

When Stewart returned, Hank was shocked to see him in a state of open amusement.

"Holy shit, Hank. How the hell do you walk around with balls that big? I'm truly intrigued....please condescend to educate me on that point."

"Anti-chafing powder is a must. Buy it in bulk."

"Noted."

Despite his joking, Hank was more anxious than he had ever been in his life, save for Floyd and Theo going missing once for two hours. He knew he had gone too far with Rickon once again, and had been busy imagining all sorts of dire consequences in his head while waiting for Stewart to return.

"So? Am I fired, arrested, or what? Don't keep me in suspense."

Stewart smiled a little. "None of the above. You made your point, and the president has agreed to drop the matter regarding Colton Gamble."

"Oh." Shit, that was unexpected. "But not the receipts, I take it?"

Now Stewart was serious again. "No. In fact..." He opened his binder and pulled out six printed sheets. "Sorry to inform you that you're now under official investigation for that. We need your statement on all of these outstanding items in my file. A number of questionable items are being examined, some of which-"

"This is ridiculous," Hank said tightly.

"Let me finish. Your written explanation, in as many words as necessary, due in 14 days. In person. The president feels this is more... *suited to your temperament* , he said, to give you the opportunity to offer your thoughts in writing."

"What?" Hank numbly reached out for the papers, but Stewart didn't hand them over.

"No, I need to rephrase and clarify some of these items. Maybe add a few. They'll go out Fed-Ex tomorrow, to reach you Monday."

"What kind of questions?"

Stewart looked at the first paper. "One of them is in regards to Daven's motivations for holding back the receipts."

"I already told you."

"The second one…and these are not in chronological order, by the way…is in regards to calls you made to an unlisted Colorado mobile number on December. Things like that. Some of these are probably trivial."

Hank felt like he was going to have a heart attack. "Trivial? To whom?"

Stewart sat back in his chair, looking regretful. "Sorry. That was the wrong word. What I meant is that some of them are completely unrelated to the *alleged* forgery scheme . The president wants a full picture of all your activities since right before Janet's murder. You can't deny that a lot of shit has been going down since then. Mystery calls, blackmail attempts, etc. It's all very suspicious to him. Not to me, so much. Political shenanigans like this have been going on since the rise of mankind. But he's the boss, and we have to answer these questions for him."

Hank set his jaw and did not waver. "I told you. I'm being framed."

"And I heard you, but Hank...you have to prove it to me. Or at least give me something to go on. Someone to point the finger at. This is your chance. I'm working on it too, you know. Still trying to track down these cashier's checks to see who bought them. That could crack open everything. Trying to save you is becoming my full time job."

Hank's blood froze. *Trying to save you. Which means...I need saving. Which means...I'm in danger. From what?*

Stewart sighed and closed his binder and put the papers away. "There's one last thing. Your daily calls with Harmon must resume on Monday. Absolutely no excuses. If you fail to comply, you'll get your third warning. The final warning is after that, and you know what that means."

When Hank was able to speak again, it sounded to his own ears that his voice was 100 feet away from his mouth. "What you said earlier...that you're trying to 'save me.' Did you mean that literally?"

Stewart cleared his throat. "Literally? What do you mean?"

Hank knew then. Stewart was holding back. It was there in his eyes, clear as day. They had something else on him. Something darker than he could presently imagine. There was no doubt. That explained the wiretapping, among other things. *What the fuck...*

"Hank? You okay?"

"Quick question. Were you guys wiretapping my old house?"

Stewart looked startled for half a second, but then his guard instantly went up again. "You know I can't answer that."

"You were. I *know* you were. I heard it. That's why I disconnected the lines. Why did you do it?"

"Hank."

Hank felt horribly sick and dizzy all of a sudden, like the flu was starting all over again. But maybe this was the tail end of it; after all, he still had a slight fever only yesterday.

"I need to go home. Haven't seen my boys in ten days."

"Okay, we're done now. I'll see you on March...seriously, are you alright? You're white as a sheet." He reached into his refrigerator and grabbed another bottle of water. By the time he turned back around, Hank was passed out on the floor.

When Hank came to, he was surrounded by Avery and two female medics. Stewart was nowhere in sight.

"Sorry," Hank said thickly. His pulse was rushing in his ears, and his tongue felt three times as big in his mouth. It was a disgustingly sickening sensation. "Overtaxed...been sick. I'm alright."

"If you can sit up, sir, try it very slowly," said one of the medics.

"Yeah, I'm good. I got this."

Hank sat up and was treated to the sight of the office spinning in circles around him. The medics took his medical history and some vitals, and some kind of heart test, and determined he was going to be fine. Hank quickly recovered and Stewart reluctantly gave up his attempt to get an ambulance to transport him to the hospital. Hank was over two hours late for his flight home. The boys would be very annoyed by the delay, that was for sure. Probably Daven, too. He had to be sick of their bickering after ten days.

Seditionist HQ - Los Angeles - 2pm

Daven was grateful for the delay in Hank's return, because three hours had not been enough to complete the task. But five hours had. Rupert walked into his office to hand the rest of the list over, and then thanked his friend for typing everything out.

"No problem. Let me send this to Hank while you're here. Don't go. Close the door, please."

Within five minutes Dav had typed out the rest of the list (Rupert was always in awe of how fast his typing was; the fingers were nearly a blur) and emailed it to Hank. Then he closed his laptop with a decisive snap and looked over to where Rupert was sitting stiffly on the couch.

"I got a call from Hank," he said. "He's in the air by now. Will be home before 9.

"Did he say how the meeting went?"

"No, nothing. Which means-"

"-he got a serious beat down from Stewart," Rupert finished for him. "Or Salome."

"Or the president."

"Or all three of them."

Daven then did something incredibly out of character, and nearly unbelievable. Something that left Rupert's jaw metaphorically on the floor for a good amount of time.

Dav decided to leave the office early. It almost defied reality.

"Wait, what? Dav? Is that you? I'm hearing things. I'm in the Twilight Zone. Who *are* you?"

Daven went to his closet and took his coat off the hanger. "I'm someone badly in need of a break. And so are you. You're leaving, too."

Rupert stared at him. "I can't. I have a thousand things to do. At least."

"Not anymore. I'm the boss for three more hours, and I say we're done for the day. Let's go."

So they went. Daven chose Rupe's favorite bar at the end of Santa Monica pier, where they drank themselves silly and ate junk food until home school ended. Then they staggered back to their respective homes, accompanied by their bemused guards, to sort out the kids and return to real life.

Santa Monica Airport - 7:30pm

"Hey, Dav. I'm so sorry I'm late. Just touched down. I'll be there by eight."

"No problem. The boys are eagerly waiting for you."

"My house, or yours?"

"Yours."

"Okay, thanks. You okay?" Hank asked in concern. "You sound a little...were you asleep?"

"Yes, I am," Daven admitted. "I was, rather. Went to happy hour with Rupert. Knocked me out."

Hank felt himself grinning. He liked it when Daven loosened up, which was an increasingly rare occurrence. "That's great, Dav. Good. Glad you made time to go have some fun."

"I have a confession, Hank. Our particular happy hour commenced at 2:30pm."

"Oh, shit. Drinking on the job, huh? That's new."

"We went to the pier. I'm sorry. It was irresponsible and I take full blame for it."

Again, Hank grinned. "You don't always have to tell me *everything* , Dav. I wouldn't have asked. As long as you had a good time. I know it's been a difficult week. I'm only mad that I wasn't there to enjoy it with you. Anyway, thanks for the list of headlines. It wasn't as bad as I feared, especially the more recent ones. Looks like people are starting to calm the fuck down about the flogging initiative and focusing on other things. Like how much I'm leaving you in my will after I die of the plague."

Daven found himself shuddering at the thought. "Did you see the one that diagnosed you with bi-polar disorder? Or yellow fever?"

"Yeah. Surprised there aren't rumors out there that I'm pregnant. Goddamned paparazzi. Anyway, thanks again."

"Please thank Rupert, not me. He did all of the work on that, and my only contribution was to email it to you."

"I will. Thanks. See you in a bit."

"See you soon."

Daven set down the phone, and then turned around to find Floyd watching him with a wide smile. "Ha, I knew it! You were way too happy when you got home to be sober. Theo owes me ten bucks."

CHAPTER THREE

Bancroft House

Same evening

Hank exhausted himself into apathy on the flight home with all the thinking and worrying. By the time they were over Utah, he didn't care about his career, didn't care about the Seditionists, didn't care about the president. Nothing mattered for the time being, and it was refreshing to just focus on getting in bed and sleeping through the weekend. He was even seriously thinking of bailing on church for the second Sunday in a row, even though it would give the media (and his executives) a collective stroke.

The boys greeted him somberly at the front door, and Hank instantly picked up on their complete lack of enthusiasm at the sight of him. It hurt a little. A lot, if he was going to be totally honest with himself. He always suspected they liked their Uncle Dav better than him.

"Oh my god, dad," blurted Theo fearfully as he backed away. "You look so skinny."

Daven's eyes were almost as wide as Theo's. "Good to see you, Hank."

"Good to be back. Bit of a day."

"Did you bring us any pretzels, dad?" Floyd asked brightly - perhaps a little *too* brightly - after an awkward silence from the group.

"Of course. Have I ever come back empty-handed from Philly? In my grey bag. We kept them in the warmer on the plane this time, so they should still be fresh. I brought you some other goodies, too. Go look."

The boys lit up and finally stepped forward to greet him with silent hugs that lacked power - as if they were afraid to break him - but it was better than nothing. When they darted off to scramble through Hank's luggage he took the opportunity to go in the kitchen and grab a root beer for himself, and a ginger ale for Dav.

"Do you have a minute to talk?" Daven asked gingerly, quietly.

"About a minute is all I have left in me. My study."

--

Hank shut the door, then flopped down on his couch and stretched. "Do I really look *that* bad?"

"Yes, you do. What happened today?"

He wasn't about to tell Dav he had face-planted in Stewart's office, so he kept his tone light. "I got myself into a bit of trouble again, but I don't want to talk about it until Monday. It can keep. How were the boys? Did they act up? God, I was so sick. Thank you for taking such great care of them. I don't even think I even asked you once how they were doing."

"No, you didn't, because you know I would have told you if anything was wrong. We had some minor problems, but they were instructed to tell you personally. I'd rather not roll them under the bus."

"*Throw* , Dav. Not roll. It's better if you tell me, so I can hear it from multiple points of view."

Daven leaned against the desk. He couldn't take his eyes off Hank. He looked like a different person. Leaner, darker, wearier. Dangerous. It was frightening.

"How much weight did you lose?" he asked worriedly.

"Dav . Don't change the subject. I want to know if the boys behaved. If you don't prepare me, Floyd is going to take the blame for everything Theo did, and Theo will let him. If you want to be their guardian, this is the kind of shit you have to deal with. What if something happens to me tomorrow and they get turned over to you-"

"Nothing's going to happen to you," Daven interrupted hastily, a little too urgently. Hank was a little startled by the harshness and immediacy of his tone, and the two men stared at each other for a long moment.

If only you knew that for sure. Because I don't.

Daven cleared his throat. "Alright, fine. A few days ago they were arguing over the bathroom, and Floyd shoved Theo to the floor. There were three times Theo talked back to Brittany, and the third time I had to step in and send him to his room. He apologized to her and didn't do it again. That was all. They're good kids, Hank, and smart. Rupert says they've never once misbehaved in home school, and all their work is done in time and thoroughly. So...maybe go easy on them?"

Too late. Hank's anger had already flared at the imagery of Floyd manhandling his little brother, and he had no intention of going easy on him for it. But he stayed calm and collected so that Dav wouldn't feel guilty for spilling the beans.

"Thanks for the recap. Listen...I've been thinking. Are you prepared to take care of these kids if something does happen to me? And don't say it won't, because we don't know. You're their legal guardian upon my death, but I can transfer that power to Rupert, if you have any hesitation whatsoever after having just spent ten days with them. And I know there's more you aren't telling me, but that's fine. As long as it was nothing major."

Daven looked alarmed for a flash of a second, then breathed deep and cocked his head. "What happened in Philadelphia?" he asked gently.

Hank ignored the question. "So let me know how you feel. I want to be sure all my paperwork is in order before my next trip. Okay?"

"When's your next trip?"

"Two weeks."

Daven didn't blink. "I have to be honest, Hank. The fact that you're asking me this right now, just after your return from 'getting in trouble in Philadelphia' is really scaring the hell out of me."

"No need, it's unrelated. We just had a really rough flight home, and I was thinking about morbid things like planes crashing and having a stroke from the stress of dealing with all this bullshit. I mean, you read those headlines. It's a miracle I haven't jumped off a bridge already. Look, Dav, I promise to tell you about Philadelphia on Monday. Every bit of it, in excruciating detail, okay? I'm too tired right now. Thanks so much for everything."

"Alright. I should get going, then. Goodnight."

Daven encountered Avery in the driveway as he walked back to his waiting car. They solemnly shook hands, and Daven decided to test out a theory. Something his instinct had just triggered.

"How was your flight? Looked like it might be rough, with all the storms everywhere."

"Smooth sailing. Hardly a bump, fortunately. You know how much I hate flying."

Rough flight, eh? God damn it, Hank... "I'm glad to hear it. See you Sunday morning."

Dav could hardly sleep that night. It was the first time in memory that he had caught Hank in an outright lie, and the realization stunned and frightened him. He wasn't ready to be a father to Floyd and Theo, and he would never be ready to accept that Hank wasn't going to be around forever. But something about Hank's manner told him he might have to start preparing to face both possibilities.

Saturday morning

Bancroft House

Floyd had made the most luxurious breakfast Hank had ever seen outside a fancy hotel, and it almost seemed a waste that only the three of them would be able to enjoy it. But alas, Avery was asleep, Brittany was at the dentist, and Vance was just too weird for table conversation. The other guards were all either on duty or about to head to the gun range.

"Boys," he said between bites of omelet, "I understand from Dav that there were a few disciplinary problems this past week. I trust that you will learn from whatever happened and not repeat it again. Is there anything major I should know about?"

Theo and Floyd lowered their forks and stared at their dad. Floyd spoke up once he had swallowed his huge mouthful of eggs. "Uncle Dav didn't tell you what I did?"

"Why don't *you* tell me?"

Floyd swallowed hard. "Theo and I were fighting over the bathroom, and I shoved him to the ground to get in first."

"That's not what happened!" Theo put in. "Dav came to yell at us-"

"Yell?" interrupted Hank, shocked.

Floyd set his fork down and got all dramatic, as he was prone to do when retelling a story. "He didn't yell! He was literally like (Floyd pitched his voice down as low as it could go) *hey hey kiddos, what's the solution to this problem* and we agreed to stop arguing. Don't exaggerate, Theo."

"You're exaggerating, not me," refuted Theo. "There was no fighting, dad. Floyd just likes to get us in trouble."

"No, I don't," Floyd replied in confusion.

"If you didn't you wouldn't have told him-"

Hank knocked on the table. "*Boys*. Enough. I'm sorry I asked. Floyd, we'll chat later."

Floyd nodded and squirmed in his chair. "It wasn't-"

"I said later."

Floyd wrung his hands together a little in his anxiety. "Okay, sorry."

"Mr. Bancroft?" called Lucas quietly from the living room. "Mr. Johansson is here to see you."

"Tell him to come join us for breakfast. Got quite a setup here."

Daven came in and talked to Lucas for a minute before joining the family. "I didn't mean to barge in on breakfast. I actually came to see if I could go the shooting range with your guards."

The boys instantly perked up at that, and looked at each other with shining eyes. Daven's talent on the range was legendary, and the boys were eager to see him in action after so many years of hearing about it. It was part of the reason they were so intimidated by him, because his outward personality offered no hint as to the lethal shooting machine that lay inside. Even Hank's well-honed accuracy couldn't hold a candle to Daven's incredible eye.

"Of course you can go," Hank answered. "You know you're always welcome. Want to eat first?"

Daven hesitated, looking uncomfortable. "Can I talk to you for a moment, please? In private."

Hank hated leaving his omelet to get cold, but Dav would obviously not bother him unless absolutely necessary, which meant something was wrong. His skin prickled uncomfortably as he followed Dav to the study.

"What's up?"

Daven pulled the Saturday morning newspaper out of his pocket, and Hank took it wordlessly. The first page of the Politics section headline read:

Urbanes Hacked, Seditionists Blamed

"What the fuck is this?" Hank exclaimed, even as he started reading the story. Written by Hailey, of course. Who else?

Daven sounded exhausted. "Long story short, Hank...Harmon's executive team had all of their personal information released in some kind of information dump that was sent out on a listserv last night. Phone numbers, addresses, payroll, financials, bank account numbers. Everything. All twenty of them. It's been sent everywhere, no taking it back."

Hank kept reading, and his heart stopped on this part: *...an anonymous insider claims this is a retaliatory measure perpetrated by Hank Bancroft, controversial leader of the Seditionists, who is no longer on speaking terms with Harmon for unknown reasons. As Mr. Bancroft was in Philadelphia on Friday and departed hours later than scheduled, it is assumed he or someone in his party has been placed under investigation for this latest political calamity. He is well known to employ double agents within the organization, and this is not the first time confidential information has been released to unauthorized parties. In October-*

"Dav," Hank said shakily as he folded the paper back up. "This is exactly why I was asking you about guardianship of the boys."

Daven looked astonished. "You *knew* about this?"

"No, but I knew something big was coming. Something like this. Stewart...the way he was acting. *Fuck*. We need to talk. Now. Not here."

Hank quickly packed up his briefcase and went back out to the dining room.

"Lucas. Boys."

"Yaeghda?" Theo answered with a mouthful of chocolate milk.

"Go easy on that milk, Theo, it's a lot of sugar. Change of plans. I have to go to the office for a few hours, so the guards will take you to the range with them. Sit in the waiting room while they shoot, and do *not* bother them or ask to touch any guns. I swear to god if either of you misbehave, I'm taking my belt to you *both* when I get back, no questions asked. Understood?"

The boys nodded, faces white, and Hank left with Daven after throwing on a heavy coat.

Floyd watched the huge SUV pulling out of the driveway, which was immediately and closely tailed by all the press cars that had been rapidly accumulating within the past hour. Then he began having another panic attack.

CHAPTER FOUR

Seditionist HQ

Saturday, March 11

After two hours at the office talking in circles with Daven and Rupert and getting absolutely nowhere, Hank made an executive decision that the other two men strongly opposed: he called his rival.

"What the hell do you want?" Harmon answered irritably; he had not recognized the number and would never have picked up otherwise.

"Just wanted to tell you I have absolutely nothing to do with this so-called 'data dump.' Nothing. You *know* I would not lie to you."

"Don't ever call me again outside of the 10 minutes each weekday that I'm legally obligated to hear you breathe."

"I need your help trying to figure out-"

"Piss off." Hank stared at his phone as it disconnected, and then shrugged and dialed again. This time it went straight to voicemail.

"Don't leave a message, Hank," warned Daven. So Hank left a message, of course.

"Harmon, Hank here. This is my new cell number. Call me back today. We need to talk about this insider of yours who is accusing me of something he or she has absolutely no evidence for. I'll be pressing slander charges tomorrow, and need to know who to name in the lawsuit. If you don't tell me today who talked to Hailey, I'll name you, since what your employees say to reporters is ultimately your responsibility. Thank you."

"What the fuck, Hank?" Rupert asked in shock after Hank hung up. "Are you *insane?*"

Hank froze and stared at him with a ferocity that made Rupe want to be swallowed up by a hole in the floor.

"Excuse me?" Hank shot back icily. "So that's how you talk to your boss now?"

"Apparently I have to, because you're losing your goddamn mind!"

Hank bristled, so Daven stepped in between the two of them, his hands held up in a "calm down" gesture.

"Gentlemen, let's take a break."

"Go home, Rupert," said Hank irritably, peering over Daven's shoulder at him. "I don't need you right now if you're going to-"

"You don't need me at all anymore, looks like."

Daven rounded on Rupert. " *Stop it* . No one's going anywhere. Sit down, both of you, and start writing out the media statement before you have a stroke. I'll make us some more coffee."

Bancroft Home

"Just keep breathing slowly, Floyd. It's okay," coached Brittany, who had just returned from her dentist appointment in time to see the poor kid laid out on the couch for the third time this morning.

Avery had been awakened by the commotion and was now sitting anxiously nearby with Floyd's paper bag in one hand and a bottle of water in the other. "I'm going to call your dad."

"No," protested Floyd as he struggled to sit up. "I'm fine."

"Sorry, buddy, I have to. He's going to kill us already for waiting this long." He glared at Lucas, knowing he was in for a seriously bad time trying to explain this to Hank.

Floyd protested feebly, then threw up twice. Avery pulled out his phone while Brittany ran to get cleaning supplies.

Seditionist HQ

Hank Bancroft, leader of The Seditionists, has launched an internal investigation to determine whether anyone affiliated with his organization is responsible for the confidential data that was released-

"No," Hank said irritably, crossing out *anyone affiliated* and *responsible* on Rupert's third draft . "Try again."

Daven then out read his own edits to the draft: *Hank Bancroft, leader of The Seditionists, will immediately launch an internal investigation into the allegations.*

Hank looked up at his Chief of Staff. "Where's the rest? Or is that it?"

"That's it."

"Okay, um. No. Try again. Rupe?"

"Alright, how's this? *Hank Bancroft, leader of the The Seditionists, vehemently denies the allegations regarding his involvement and will immediately launch an internal investigation to determine whether any entity of his organization was involved in the incident.*"

"That's good. A bit cold, though. Warm it up a little, but keep the same words. My phone's ringing, hang on. Hey Avery."

"Sir, we need to take Floyd to the hospital. He just threw up some blood, not a lot."

"Shit. Like, out of the blue? Or has he been panicking?"

Avery took a deep breath, preparing himself for the rebuke of a lifetime. "He's been panicking. Hyperventilated three times since you left, I'm told."

"You were *told*?"

"Yes, sir, just woke up and came out to the living room to find him having his third attack. Still is."

"Alright. Whoever decided not to call me after the second one is fired. You can fill me in later. Take Floyd to Palisades, discreetly. I'll join you when I can."

"*When you can?*" Avery blurted, unable to stop himself from keeping the disgust out of his voice.

"You heard me correctly." Hank hung up, then turned back to the statement. "Dav, try changing it to *shocking and unacceptable incident.*"

Philadelphia

"Hi, it's Stewart. I just received the H.A. Times article. Guess we now know exactly what our mystery caller was predicting. I didn't think it would be something on this scale. Shocking."

Salome pulled her car off the road and idly watched two Amish buggies clopping through a field. "I'm on the way to Pittsburgh right now for a wedding. This was the absolute worst time for him to pull the trigger."

"I was just about run to FedEx to drop off the packet of questions to Hank. Should I hold off?"

"No, send it. We can always send another one. In the meantime, let's leave off investigating this new mess, because Harmon may want to handle it as a corporate espionage case rather than lay criminal charges. He would have a lot more leverage and control that way."

"What if either one of them asks for our help?" Stewart queried, which he knew wouldn't happen with Harmon, whose outright hatred for the FBI was well known.

Salome shrugged, even though Stewart couldn't see it. "Then we help, and make it our investigation. Until then, let's stay out of it. I do think that Hank's going to go after this anonymous person who accused him, and we can probably expect a media statement that will get him summoned again."

"Should I call him and warn him off?"

"Normally I would say no, but it might calm him to know that we're not adding it to our pile."

"Okay, thanks. Safe travels."

Stewart picked up the phone and dialed Hank's cell.

Seditionist HQ

"Fuck," mumbled Hank as his phone rang again. "Yes, Stewart? How are you on this beautiful, pleasant day, in which my world is absolutely *not* imploding around me?"

Stewart was not amused. "This is a courtesy call, Hank. I heard the news, but obviously the FBI has no jurisdiction over corporate espionage cases. We're going to stay out of it unless Harmon wants to press criminal charges, which he won't."

"Ah." That did calm Hank considerably, but... "What if he decides to?"

"He won't unless he has absolute irrefutable proof. Otherwise he will lose and have to pay the legal expenses for both of you, and his reputation would be damaged. There's nothing to gain by it. I would suggest not contacting him at this time and letting him sort it out on his end."

"Oh. Well...I, okay."

Stewart sighed. "You already talked to him, didn't you?"

"No. I just left him a message to call me. He hasn't yet."

"Okay. Like I said, no jurisdiction here, but you know I was a corporate lawyer in my past life. Don't talk to him, and don't threaten him. Everything you say or do at this point matters. Okay?"

Hank closed his eyes and took a deep breath. "Hasn't it always mattered? I can't take a shit without being criticized by the Urbanes."

Another sigh from Stewart. "You threatened him already, didn't you." It wasn't a question.

"Uh. Yeah, actually." Hank rubbed a knot on the back of his neck. "Basically said I was going to sue him for slander if he didn't name the person who talked to Hailey."

"Okay, Hank. That's...wow."

"I know. Listen, thanks for your advice. I've got to get back to writing this media statement and then get to the hospital to see my kid. Did you send the FedEx?"

"On my way now. It will arrive before 8:30am on Monday."

"Great. Can't wait. Have a good weekend."

Just as Hank said that, the call came in from Harmon. Hank picked it up immediately without a glance at Dav or Rupe.

"Harmon, I'm so sorry for that message. I'm a dick."

"Yes, you are."

"I shouldn't have threatened you."

"No, you shouldn't have. If anyone can tell you who this inside source was, it's Hailey. I have no idea, but I can assure you that I'll be sending a strongly worded memo to my entire organization letting them know that speaking to the press is always unauthorized."

Hank swallowed hard. "Thanks. I want to repeat, I have absolutely nothing to do with this."

"Someone in your organization does."

"And yours. Who do you think gathered this information in the first place?"

"One of your double agents, obviously," Harmon sputtered accusingly.

"Or an Urbane who has gone rogue and has nothing to do with me," Hank retorted.

There was a long silence on the other line. "I probably shouldn't tell you this now, because it might cause me to lose some early leverage. But we've just traced the listserv posting back to a computer in Santa Monica. So it was one of yours. I'll delete that voicemail, Hank, and we'll pretend it never happened. In the meantime, I want you to recall all of your double agents. If you don't, we're going to be having a very difficult conversation regarding what my next step is going to be. Let me know your answer by end of day tomorrow. Goodbye."

Hank looked at Dav, who was alarmed at the blood that suddenly drained from his boss's face.

"What did he say?" Dav asked urgently.

"Umm..." Hank was feeling dizzy again. "He...he said he'll start investigating, and we'll talk again at end of day tomorrow. Let's get that media statement done so I can get to Floyd."

CHAPTER FIVE

Harmon was smarter than most, but his biggest flaw as a strategist was that he lacked a vivid imagination. He certainly knew that there was far more to this story than just a rogue Urbane or Seditionist. Had he been able to think about it long enough, or creatively enough, his very first suspicion would have been that Yannick was somehow involved. And by extension, so was Colbert, the man who hated Hank Bancroft ten times more than anyone else.

But Harmon had no such imagination, so he asked Colbert to lead the investigation into how the information got into the wrong hands.

Seditionists HQ - Los Angeles

"Dav, I need to go to the hospital to see Floyd before he disowns me." Hank was looking at his phone; there were four missed calls from Avery and two from Floyd. "I need your suggestion on who we can trust in accounting to get involved in this mess with the receipts. I know you polygraphed everyone-"

"And everyone passed, which means we can't trust anyone," Rupert put in.

"Maybe we were asking the wrong questions," Daven answered plainly.

"Oh sure, let's just come right out with it. 'Hey, yes or no question, are you trying to get Hank Bancroft thrown in jail?' Jesus, Dav, really?"

Hank massaged his forehead with the palms of his hands. "Calm down. Before today, how many people had authorization to send anonymous payments? An exact number."

Daven looked depressed as he answered. "22."

"Alright. We can't undo that stellar decision to let everyone and their mothers have access, so let's move on. One of them has been on maternity leave, so that's 21. And now we only have one person who can do it, right?"

"Yes," Daven replied. "Yannick."

"Why him, exactly?"

"He's been around a long time. Impeccable record. Very private, and almost painfully respectful to everyone on the team."

Rupe put in unhelpfully, "Weird voice, too, but that's another story."

Hank stared at him. "Wait...what do you mean, *weird voice?*"

Rupert chuckled. "Kind of a pompous inflection, sounds likes he's talking through ten layers of cheesecloth. Annoying as fuck to listen to. Have you never met him?"

"Apparently not. I'd remember that. Okay, let's polygraph him again and offer him a 3% raise to confidentially help us with this investigation and keep an eye on things from here on out. Thanks, guys. I got to go see my kid."

Hank Bancroft had a vivid imagination, but even that wasn't enough to imagine that Yannick was a candidate for his mystery man. After all, he didn't know anything about him - about anyone in accounting, actually - and trusted Daven completely to put him in a position of such responsibility. As Vance was driving him to the hospital, he received a call from Harmon's cell phone.

"Long time, no talk. We're starting an investigation as of right now. I need more time."

Harmon sounded unconvinced. "Time for what? To come up with some kind of scheme to point the blame back at me?"

"No. Don't forget this is *your* problem, too. You need to move fast to find the person on your side who leaked this information in the first place."

"I'd love to, and you know how I can do that? By you telling me who you're paying in my office to get it! Or I could just have the FBI pull all of your financial records and comb through them over the next few months to find the mole. Everything can be traced, Hank. It's just a matter of time."

Hank was feeling incredibly smug at the moment, because he actually didn't pay his double agents at all until they decided "cash out" and quit their undercover jobs to rejoin Hank's organization. Only then would they get compensation in proportion to their accomplishments. Very few had actually taken that deal that so far, to Hank's surprise. Some agents had been with him for 7 or 8 years.

"Ignore your problem, then," Hank said flippantly. "Be prepared for more leaks, though. By the way, how do I know *you* aren't the one behind all of this?"

Harmon laughed. "Oh, I see. Trying to turn the tables on me, are you? You can't seriously think I released all my personal information. Social security number, bank accounts, everything, just to spite you."

That was exact the opening Hank was looking for, and if he didn't take it now, he might never have the chance again.

"Oh, come on. You have plenty of reasons to spite me, but you know has even more? Colbert."

"Colbert?"

"Correct. I know you chose him to lead this investigation, which is basically like sending in the wolf to count the sheep. I guarantee you he's behind this. Perhaps without your knowledge, even? You might want to check the bank account numbers that were allegedly leaked. Bet they aren't even his."

"Recall your agents, Hank," Harmon ordered tersely, now even more done with this conversation. "Then we'll talk again."

"Nope. This is where the tables are turning now: take Colbert off the investigation. Then, *after* you nail down the guilty parties and exonerate me, I'll remove agents from your organization and destroy all the information we've gathered that we could use against you if we were so inclined. You have my word. In the meantime, I'm going to continue my investigation with the assumption that I'll have as much time to conduct mine as you have to conduct yours. Are we agreed?"

"So you're basically threatening me into giving you more time?" Harmon asked in disgust.

"Threaten? No, no, don't be silly. Not at all. Technically, I think it's called blackmail," Hank said lightly, with a sarcastic laugh.

Harmon smiled - he had him now. "Right. Understood. Take all the time you need, Hank."

"Thanks! Chat with you soon, pal."

Hank disconnected the call and chuckled to himself in satisfaction.

Urbane HQ - Denver

Harmon slowly hung up the phone and turned to look at Colbert, who had blanched at least twice during the last part of call. He reached over and hit the STOP button on the tape recorder.

"You're sure that was being recorded, right?" asked Harmon skeptically.

"Yes, boss. Every word."

"And you heard him say *prepare for more leaks* and then outright blackmail me, right? I wasn't imagining it?"

"I did. Loud and clear. He was obviously joking, but..."

"Doesn't matter. We finally caught him in the act, the smug fucker. Let's make a few duplicates, then send the original to Stewart. I'm going to press criminal charges."

Colbert blanched again, panicking about having been called out and accused by Hank. "Wait. What if you...I have a better idea. What if you let Hank know we recorded that, and threaten to release it to Stewart if he doesn't cooperate?"

Harmon frowned. "Blackmail, with a blackmail attempt? That is some serpentine shit, right there. Damn."

"Or, we should wait until we have absolute proof that the listserv posting came from one of his guys. Why rush into this? It's got to be foolproof or we'll have to pay his legal bills. He hasn't yet admitted to this leak. Just threatening other leaks. I think we can nail him better than this."

Colbert was all but hyperventilating now. He could *not* let that recording get out, because Hank was right - the bank account numbers weren't his. He had transposed some numbers to protect his funds; a terrible decision, in hindsight. *Stepped on his own dick*, as Hank Bancroft would say.

Harmon was thinking as he tapped his pen against his temple. "This is all kinds of fucked up. I don't even know where to start. Do you think there's any possibility that Yannick is involved? I mean, we paid him through the nose for his past services. I can't imagine him turning against us. But he still works for them, right?"

"He had given his notice last time we spoke, a couple months ago."

"Shit. Well…maybe you're right. Let's take a few more days to get all our ducks in a row." Harmon popped the tape out of the recorder and put it carefully in his safe, while Colbert watched in silent horror.

"And of course we have to investigate our own team, too. I'm making a list of who to question first in regards to collecting all that data."

"I have an idea," Harmon said suddenly. "Let's give Yannick a call. Just ask him if he knows anyone in Hank's office who might have released our info either for him, or for his own reasons. Don't offer a penny for any kind of service. We'll start with him, and move on from there."

Colbert forced down the lump in his throat, but it took a few swallows. "Good idea. I'll call him."

Los Angeles

"Hey Dav, me again. I have to talk quick, just pulling up to the hospital. I've changed my mind. I want our entire senior accounting team placed on paid leave until further notice. All 21 of them, including Yannick. Confiscate their phones and badges, too. Laptops. Everything. We're not taking any more chances."

"I think that's-"

"Don't argue with me," Hank interrupted bitterly.

"-a wise move, I was about to say."

"Oh. Sorry. I want all of them intercepted as they arrive to work Monday morning and gathered into a conference room. Then we explain, and send them all home at once. Don't let anyone get wind of this before 8am Monday, or it could tip somebody off."

"Will do. I hope Floyd feels better soon. Say hello for me."

"I will. Thanks, Dav. By the way, I think we're going to be okay with Harmon. I sort of forced him into his own internal investigation, and now we'll have enough time to do our own."

"Forced? How?"

Hank still felt smug, and he replied lightly, "Oh, just doing what I do. Charm and wit gets you everywhere in this world."

"Okay. Well, good luck with that. Let me know when you are available to talk again."

"Will do."

CHAPTER SIX

Palisades Hospital

Los Angeles

Hank was feeling newly invigorated as Vance silently dropped him and Martinez off at the front entrance of the hospital. Press cars were already there, having tailed Avery and Brittany there hours earlier, and he could feel rather than hear the dozens of shutter clicks go off. It occurred to him too late that he should probably stop smiling, seeing as to what this errand entailed.

Floyd was asleep, so Brittany and Avery were standing at the doorway talking to each other in hushed tones as Hank walked up with Floyd's doctor on his tail.

"Room's not big enough for all of us," Hank murmured. "Why don't you guys go take a break? Is the cafeteria still open for lunch, Dr. Harborough?"

The blonde woman nodded cheerfully. "Yes indeed, 24 hours a day. But I'd stay away from the meatloaf if I were you."

The two guards left, and Hank went to sit down next to Floyd.

"Is this pretty much the same as last time?"

Dr. Harborough referred to the clipboard that was nestled in her left arm.

"Same cause, but not as drastic. I think he can go home in about 3 hours. We've given him a bag of fluid and medications for his stomach. Blood tests are all normal, at least the ones we don't have to wait a few days to hear back on. I would strongly suggest, though…"

Hank didn't want to hear about strengthening the anti-anxiety medication, and the doctor already knew he was deeply opposed to drugging his children into better moods.

"No," he said preemptively, loud enough that Floyd woke up with a start.

"Dad?"

"Sorry, kiddo. Didn't mean to wake you."

Floyd shifted around on his right side to look at his dad. "What time is it? What's going on? Why did you leave with Uncle Dav?"

Hank cleared his throat. "It's almost 2. Can't answer your other questions. I'm sorry."

"Are you in trouble again?"

"Floyd."

Hank looked up to find Theo glaring at him from his chair on the other side of Floyd's bed, but Hank ignored it. He was fully aware of what was on the boy's mind and had no interest in discussing it right now. Or ever.

"Want to go home," Floyd mumbled sleepily.

Hank looked at Dr. Harborough, who spoke up at last. "Floyd, you can go home at 5. I want you to eat something so we can make sure you're keeping food down. I'll be right back, Mr. Bancroft."

"Thanks." He waited until the door closed again before addressing his youngest. "Have you eaten?"

"Yeah. Hours ago."

"Good."

Theo's eyes narrowed. "*Hours*. Ago."

Oh boy. *That* tone. This was going to be bad.

"Right. I heard you."

"*Hours* ...in which you *weren't here* because your stupid fucking job is more important than your kids!"

Hank saw Martinez stiffen from across the room, so he stifled a rebuke and kept his tone pleasant. "Floyd, I'll be back in a minute. Theo, come with me, please."

"No."

Hank stood and latched a strong hand onto Theo's arm, effortlessly pulling him into the large bathroom that was attached to the hospital room. He didn't let go once they were in there alone.

"Theo. I hear you. I get it. But calm down or we'll be having a chat when we get home. Do you understand me?"

Theo angrily tried to wrench his arm away, in vain. "You're going to have to punish Avery then, too, because he said the same thing. You suck, dad."

Hank swallowed down the hard lump in his throat.

"Thought I told you not to be a tattletale."

"Whatever. Let me go!" This time Theo succeeded in flinging his arm loose, but there was nowhere to go; his dad was blocking the door.

"Okay. You've earned yourself a chat. But I'll make a deal with you. If you can behave yourself until we get home, I'll cancel it."

"And if I don't?" Theo challenged boldly.

"Going to be a hell of a discussion, then. Better clear your calendar for the evening." Hank stood up and calmly stepped aside to open the bathroom door for his son. "After you."

Theo hesitated, then darted through the door.

"Martinez," Hank said quietly. "You can station outside the door, if you prefer. Whatever you feel more comfortable with. I'll leave it up to you."

Just as he said that, a visibly stressed Vance showed up and quietly slipped into the room. "Boss, you got a sec?"

"What's up?"

Vance shook his head slightly and turned away, so Hank followed him into the hallway and shut the door.

"Yes?"

"There's a big crowd going nuts outside. All but calling for your blood. Took me forever to get the car parked because they were blocking the ramp to the garage."

"A big *crowd?* There were maybe a dozen people out there when we arrived."

"Not anymore, sir. Lots of people now."

"Fuck. Okay, come with me to the cafeteria to find Avery. Deveraux, stay here."

As Hank strolled through the double doors, he was struck dumb by the sight that greeted him. Every single person in the cafeteria had their back to them because they stood crowded around one single television on the wall, transfixed by live imagery of the angry scene outside. Everyone, including all the cafeteria staff and his own guards.

Hank slowly walked up behind Avery, who didn't see him, while reluctantly turning his own gaze to the screen. The sound was off, but the captions told the tale loud and clear.

-STUNNING LEAK WAS ATTRI-

-BUTED TO HANK BANCROFT-

-THE SAME MAN WHO-

-APPARENTLY HAS NO QUALMS-

-SENDING HIS YOUNG SON-

-TO THE HOSPITAL ALONE-

-LEAVING HIM TO FEND FOR-

-HIMSELF FOR OVER SIX-

-HOURS. HE ARRIVED ONLY-

Goddamn .

"Avery," Hank said sharply, startling his once-favorite guard. "What are you doing?"

Avery may have been startled, but there was no worry in his expression. He was not prohibited from watching the news like Floyd was, for one thing. And he was on break, for another.

"Monitoring the latest happenings, boss. For your security, of course."

"Of course. But I need to talk to you. In private."

Rupert's House

"Can't say I blame 'em, Dav. He should have been at the hospital." Rupert muted the television. "But at least we got the media statement done. Not that anyone's going to buy it. Jesus, what a cluster."

"Hmm. Do you think he's ever going to tell us who the four embedded agents are?"

"Not until he's on his deathbed."

Daven shifted uncomfortably. "You know...he won't let me tell him why I held back those receipts for so long. Didn't want to hear it."

Rupert shrugged. "Probably for the best, and you know why. He can't lie. You tell him, he tells the FBI, you get in trouble. He's protecting you."

"No, it's not that. It was something else. He *can* lie, by the way. Found that out myself last night."

"What do you mean?"

"Well..." Daven regretted having brought it up, but he did, so he had to finish the story. "He told me he had a rough flight home and it made him worry about what would happen to his kids if the plane crashed."

Rupert cocked his head. "You'd be their legal guardian. They'd go to you. He *knows* that."

"I know. That's what puzzled me, but it's not the only thing. The flight was perfectly smooth. Avery told me. Why would he lie about something like that?"

"I have no idea. That's odd. Maybe it's nothing. This whole thing is making him paranoid, and rightly so. You couldn't pay me enough to be in his shoes right now."

Daven opened his briefcase and rummaged through for a long moment before locating his target, a thickly bound version of the new indentured servant laws that had passed on March 1.

"I think the answer is in here. Between the three of us, he's the only one who's read the entire thing. Now, these statutes go into effect on April 1, right?"

"Yes. And?"

Daven sucked in a deep breath. "I was browsing this and happened to come across a clause that says *non-related legal guardians of minors are subject to the court's approval upon sentencing*." Pause. "You know what...never mind. I've said too much already."

Rupe stared at his friend. "And not enough. What's on your mind? Just spill it, for god's sake."

"I think..." Daven bit his lower lip as he debated whether or not to say the horrible words. "I think Hank isn't worried about dying at all. Maybe he believes he's going to jail, and that the court won't approve me to take care of Theo and Floyd."

"What? He's innocent."

"That's what we think. The FBI might come to a different conclusion."

"*Daven*." Rupert stood up as if to end the discussion. "We're not going there again. He didn't do it, end of story."

"You're not understanding what I'm saying," Daven sighed in frustration. "Our opinion doesn't matter in court. Facts do. If he's not brought down by those receipts, or those leaks, he's going to be brought down by something else. Whoever is doing this won't stop now. It's only a matter of time before the next thing happens, and we both know Hank's his own worst enemy when he's backed into a corner."

"Okay, Sherlock. I get it," Rupert snapped defensively. "So what do you propose we do, then?"

"Not us. It's really up to Hank. If he's convinced Colbert is behind this, he needs to let Harmon know and request his cooperation. In order to do that, he'll need to apologize and make peace with him first."

Rupe snorted. "Oh. Right. Good luck talking him into that one."

"If he disagrees and refuses, I'll let him know what the next step has to be if I'm right, and this keeps up. He'll want to protect the boys before anything else. If he refuses…"

"Which he *will* …then what's his plan B?"

Daven swallowed hard, then looked his friend in the eyes without flinching. "Quitting his job."

Palisades Hospital

Hank Bancroft was in a horrific mood after having it out with Avery about his remarks, and then learning he had to fire Lucas when he got home for making the unforgivable decision not to call him when Floyd was obviously in need of medical assistance. Theo picked up on the subtle danger instantly and dared say nothing as his dad returned and sat back down with a sigh.

"Hey, kiddo," he said to Floyd. "Dr. Harborough says you're good to go. Just waiting for the discharge paperwork."

"It's only 3."

Hank stroked Floyd's hair back into place. "Well, you're doing good enough to bail early. Listen, when we leave the hospital I want you to lay down on the back seat and relax. Close your eyes and just breathe. We'll take it really easy the rest of the weekend."

He felt Theo's eyes boring into him. The kid had seen the mob outside the window and wasn't fooled by his dad's attempt to keep Floyd from seeing them. But he also knew it was best for his brother, so he said nothing.

"How do you feel?" Hank asked.

"Headache. Tired."

"Me, too."

Theo snorted derisively at that, and his dad threw him a dirty look. "Just so you know? You got Avery in deep shit. I told you not to tattle."

The boy paled instantly. "What did you do?"

Hank ignored him. "Floyd, we have to make a decision regarding your anti-anxiety medication. I know it gives you some bad side effects, but if it's increased, these panic attacks won't be so bad. How do you feel about that?"

"Increase it," Floyd murmured. "I can't do this anymore."

"Okay." This was the first time Hank had let Floyd have any say in his medical treatment, and it was tough to let go of that control. He instantly regretted asking, because the answer was completely unexpected. Floyd hated his pills.

"Or," interjected Theo bitterly from the other side of the bed, "you can just have a boring job like normal people so that everyone's not stalking us all the time, and then Floyd wouldn't have to worry and be all drugged up just to function every day."

The truth was brutal, and it hit him like a cartoon anvil falling from the sky. That was the exact moment Hank Bancroft gave up the battle with his youngest and decided to wear his heart on his sleeve for the first time in his entire life. He looked around the room; they were alone. His throat was tight.

"Theo, you're right. We can't do this anymore. Wish granted. I've just decided I'm not going to run again in November."

Theo could only let out a tiny squeak in his surprise. His face lit up like a Christmas tree.

"You can't tell anyone," Hank continued. "I'll have to announce it in a few weeks. But tomorrow I'm going to call our builders up in Sacramento and start building the house near Yosemite. Do you understand what this means for all of us?"

"Yes. No. I don't...oh my god." He was grinning from ear to ear, and Hank said nothing more as he gave him a few minutes to process the news.

"Theo," he said eventually. Gently. "I want to talk to Floyd alone for a minute, okay? Can you do me a favor and go in the bathroom, and close the door? I'll come get you shortly."

Theo got up as if he was in a trance and did exactly as he was told. A very confused Floyd turned towards his dad.

"Dad? Why did you tell him like *that*?"

Hank shrugged and smiled a little. "Does it hurt to make him think I'm doing it for him?"

The teenager grinned sleepily. "Not if you keep letting me think you're doing it for me."

"I *am* doing it for you, Floyd."

Floyd sighed happily and closed his eyes. Hank should have been happy at this moment, too. Both his sons were on his side again, content and optimistic, and mostly behaving themselves lately. Life was good.

But all he could think about was that clause in the new laws. The one that had been running through his mind for two days like credits at the end of a movie. His heart skipped another beat as it started up all over again as he thought about how he had just stupidly and blatantly blackmailed Harmon: ... *non-related legal guardians of minors are subject to the court's approval upon sentencing of the felonious parent...*

CHAPTER SEVEN

Los Angeles - later Saturday afternoon

"Dad?" Floyd called as he made himself comfortable on his makeshift bed in the backseat. "Can we stop at Shake Shack?"

"No. Vance, straight home please. Floyd, lie down."

"I am. Can we go sailing tomorrow?"

"No. Hang on. Brittany, can you…"

"Got it," said Brittany as she got out of the car to clear the hospital's blocked driveway. Hank was impressed that she managed the task almost effortlessly and apparently with only a few words to the couple dozen angry people who stood with protest signs. It was too late to keep Theo from seeing them; he read the words and shifted his wide eyes to his dad, but said nothing.

"Dad?" came the voice from the backseat again.

"*What*, Floyd?"

"I'm hungry."

"I'll make you something when we get home."

The SUV pulled through the crowd slowly, and Hank looked back to make sure Floyd wasn't paying attention. He wasn't, and seemed content lying face down on top of all the blankets.

"Stay down. You don't look so good. Best to get you in bed when we-"

"No, I'm fine," Floyd protested. To Hank's horror he started to sit up at the worst possible moment, right when they were in the thick of the crowd. He quickly turned and administered an almighty smack to his son's rear end, much harder than he'd intended.

"I told you to lay down," he barked, feeling exactly like the total piece of shit father that he was lately.

"Ow!" Floyd yelped in surprise as he complied. "What the...sorry, I'm sorry."

"Oh my god, dad!" Theo objected loudly as he reached over the seat to try and comfort his brother. "You're so mean."

Hank fixed a glare at him. "Do you want to be next? Turn around and be quiet."

"But that's so fucked up, I can't believe you just did that!"

Hank abruptly hauled Theo facedown over his lap and held him down tightly.

"I told you to be quiet," he growled. "One more word and I'm spanking you all the way home, just like this. Got that?"

"Yes, sir," Theo answered tightly.

"Sit up. Put your seatbelt on."

Theo obeyed and kept his mouth tightly shut, although the ferocious glare he was giving his father nearly scorched Hank's eyebrows.

"Floyd, you okay?" Hank asked belatedly, but he didn't wait for an answer. Brittany rejoined the car as they passed through the kerfuffle, and Hank gave her a silent nod of grateful thanks.

As they got on the freeway, a van from channel 5 news abruptly pulled up alongside and stuck a camera out the window. Vance quickly changed lanes once, then twice more before losing them in the heavy traffic.

The entire car was dead silent except for Theo and Floyd's overlapping sniffles.

Rupert's House.

While conversing with Daven, Rupert saw a black SUV on the television screen out of the corner of his eye and grabbed the remote control to turn up the volume. An excitable young reporter was currently airing live in front of the hospital's driveway.

- has just left the hospital with his family, and it appears they're heading home. We've just learned from two Urbanes executives affected by the data breach that their bank accounts have already been siphoned of several thousand dollars, and that might be the least of their worries. Their social security numbers were released along with more than

enough info to allow false accounts opened in their names, identity theft, and other-

"Way to give people ideas, you dumbass."

Daven leaned back into his chair. "They'll do it anyway if they're so inclined."

-eager to hear what Mr. Bancroft has to say about this debacle. Of course, it hasn't been proven he was involved, but computer experts did trace the listserv posting back to a server in West Los Angeles. As we all know, that is where the Seditionist Headquarters is located.

"Yeah," grumbled Rupe, "because there aren't like five million other people in the same area who-"

"Shhhh!"

-and we're still not sure what to make of his lengthy meeting in Philadelphia yesterday, which happened to coincide with the president's trip to FBI headquarters. It's possible he was there to specifically meet with Mr. Bancroft, but that's just speculation and we don't know if they met or-

"*Everything* you say is speculation, dimwit!"

"Seriously, Rupe? I want to hear this, please."

- say for certain now is that the tide has turned against Mr. Bancroft as far as public opinion is concerned, his unexpected opposition to two crucial votes this month all but forgotten in light of this morning's news. Let's turn it over to Hailey

Hendricks, who is currently outside of the Bancroft home waiting for the family's return. Hailey?"

"Oh, fuck," Rupe exclaimed as he snatched up his phone.

"Rupe," Hank answered tersely. "Not a good time."

"You're telling me. Hailey Hendricks is broadcasting live from your driveway right now."

"What? Shit, we're like a block away. Thanks, I'll call you back." He hung up. "Vance."

"Boss?"

"Turn around and take the back entrance to the house. Brittany?"

"Radioing them now, sir."

There was a rear underground entrance to the house on the street that ran along the back side of the property, but it wasn't finished yet and had no gate or paving. The guards would have to hurry to run back and remove the temporary barriers, and then Vance would have to drive over construction materials to get there, but it was doable.

"Dad?"

"Not now, Floyd. Vance, take it easy. Slow and steady so we don't beat the guards there."

"We're being followed, sir. Four cars, maybe five."

Fuck. "Okay. Go through the Shake Shack."

"Dad?"

"Be *quiet* Floyd, for god's sake!"

"But I'm going to throw up. Carsick from laying down."

"Okay, sit up. Theo, get him a bottle of water from the cooler. One for me too, please."

Vance deftly turned the car around in a cul de sac and headed back to Pico Boulevard. The Shake Shack was an excellent spot to dodge press cars; they usually didn't follow their prey through the drive-thru because they would get stuck behind the gates that wouldn't rise until food was paid for and taken at the window. There was nowhere for them to wait, either, so most of the time Vance was able to break free of tails with this method. This time, however, three press cars followed him right in as if they were all attached to each other's bumpers with a chain. As they pulled up to the speaker, Hank moved to the left side of the car and rolled down the window. There was a tiny camera pointing straight at him.

Welcome to Shake Shack, this is Aston, may I take your order?

"Good afternoon, Aston. Do you know who I am?"

Yes, sir! We're studying you at school this month.

Hank blushed, as he often did at unexpected reminders of his fame. Or infamy, as some would say. "Ah. Well, I need a big favor. We're going to pull up to your window now without ordering, okay?"

Yes, sir.

Vance pulled up slowly. Hank was afraid to know what Floyd must be thinking, but there was no time to worry about it right now.

"Aston, we just need to sit here for about five minutes like we're waiting for an order. Then I need you to stall the cars behind me for a few minutes, please. We're trying to lose them so I can get my son home safely and privately. He's been sick."

"Vultures," Aston replied in disgust. "Yes, sir, don't you worry. Would you like some coffee while you wait?'

"That would be wonderful. Thank you."

She smiled brilliantly, obviously starstruck beyond repair. "And can I ask *you* a favor, sir? I kind of secretly read my textbooks at work when business gets slow. You know? Between orders, nothing else to do. Happens a lot."

"That sounds very...dedicated." Hank wasn't sure where this was going.

Aston gleefully turned around and pulled out a Sharpie from somewhere, along with her history book. "Would you autograph this for me, Mr. Bancroft? Right here in chapter 22. There's where you first come in, way back when you were born."

Way back when? Ouch. "And how did I die?" he teased, flipping to the later chapters as if searching for an answer to his destiny.

Aston shrugged. "I don't know, we haven't gotten that far yet. Do you mind signing it?"

Hank froze. "Uh. Doesn't this book belong to your high school?"

"Not anymore. Going to steal it now." Aston grinned.

"I'll just pretend I didn't hear that." Hank dutifully signed the book, adding a "stay in school" note with a smiley face.

"Thank you! I'll get your coffee now."

Hank turned to Brittany after Aston walked away from the window, not knowing whether to laugh or cry. "*Way back when.* For fuck's sake. Like I was roaming around with the dinosaurs or something."

Brittany cleared her throat - which sounded suspiciously like a camouflaged laugh - and spoke quietly into her lapel mic to get an update from the house.

"Do you get asked for your autograph a lot, dad?" Theo asked in awe. He had never seen this happen before, because their guards always prevented strangers from getting that close to their dad everywhere they went.

"Not so much anymore. Mostly during the war, and right after."

"Did women ever ask you to sign their boobs?"

Hank almost choked on his water, and Vance let out a strangled bark.

"Seriously, Theo? Where on earth did you get that idea?"

"Saw it after a wrestling match. And a concert. I don't remember the other thing."

Hank was going to deny it, but there was nothing to be lost by lightening the mood in the car a little. "Okay, well...yeah, they did. Your dad was a stud once, you know." He winked at his son.

Theo was full of mischief suddenly. "I bet you did it. Didn't you?"

"Never, actually. I was married to your mom, and that's not acceptable behavior for a husband. For a good husband, anyway. Brittany, what did Avery say?"

"He said they need about three minutes. Working hard to clear a path."

"Thanks. Floyd, are you alright?"

"Yeah, I guess," came the grumbled, unhappy reply. He couldn't possibly be amused by anything at the moment.

Aston came back to the window with the coffee and waited until Brittany finally gave the go-ahead to leave. Hank handed the young woman $50 first. "This is for the replacement book.

Just say you lost it and don't steal anything else, ever. Okay, we're ready to go. Thanks, Aston."

The gate instantly lifted up, and Vance pulled out as quickly as he could manage without actually leaving smoking tire tracks. Two seconds later the long flimsy arm fell back down again so fast that it crashed down on the roof with a bone-crunching THWACK! that made everyone jump.

"Son of a bitch!" Vance exclaimed under his breath as he floored it and turned right onto Olympic.

Hank held back laughter as he turned to look out the back window; Vance was as lovingly protective of the SUV as Hank was of his Thunderbird. "Yeah. She may have timed that poorly, but it did the trick. They're trapped. Okay, get us home."

"Goddamn, going to have a hell of a time buffing out that motherfu-"

"Vance!"

"Sorry, boss."

Sunday

The church that the leaders of The Seditionists attended had informally been considered off-limits for protests and media attention, and Hank was glad to see that today was not a break in tradition. There were, as usual, photographer's cars parked across the street and in the square, but that was all. It was almost too quiet.

Rupert and Daven were already there, and Hank took his usual place in between them.

"Hey guys," he whispered. "Surprised I didn't get any other calls last night from you two. Hailey must've shit a brick once she realized I slipped past her."

"Hank!" Daven admonished with a fierce and increasingly common *we're in church, you idiot* type of hand gesture.

Hank looked up in the balcony, where his grumpy sons were just sitting down. "You know, I have an idea. If you're not busy, why don't guys come to the servant's luncheon with us after this? It's rather fun. Not sure why I haven't invited you before."

Daven looked askance at him, but Rupert butted in first. "Would love to, thanks Hank. You would too, right Dav?"

"I would?"

"Great, it's settled then. I've always wanted to see what the famous Bancroft Sunday Bruncheon is all about."

"Why do you want us to come?" Daven asked suspiciously, ignoring the looks from Rupert that were clearly designed to shut him up.

Hank looked hurt. "Do I have to have a reason? Maybe I just want you there because you're my closest friends, and my kids idolize you. You should be there."

Daven was supremely discomfited by this gesture, since it fit neatly into his theory that that Hank was preparing to possibly lose his kids and wanted their godfathers to get more comfortable around the household. Just in case?

"I'm sorry Hank, I'm just confused. You're so secretive about your family one day, and the next you're inviting us to this. It just makes me wonder what's really-"

"Dav," Rupert said warningly. "This is not the time or place for that particular discussion."

Hank looked back and forth between the two of them. "What *particular discussion?* "

"Nothing, Hank," Daven whispered quickly, and quieter than before. "We're just not used to this. I mean, even after ten years I don't know how many servants you *have,* and now I'm about to have lunch with all of them. You're quite the secret keeper, you know, so this is...new. That's all."

Hank's nerves prickled. "We have 11, so now you know. *Secret keeper*? What does that mean, exactly? And why are you so offended about me asking you to a brunch with my household?"

"I'm not offended. I'm alarmed."

Hank raised his voice just over a whisper, although he felt like shouting. "Oh, really? Well forget it then, sorry I asked. You're uninvited."

"Thank you."

Rupert reached over and put a hand on Daven's knee, keeping his face carefully neutral. "*Stop it*, both of you. We are *in church*, in case you haven't noticed. You're acting like children."

Children. Hank looked up again at his boys, who were watching him curiously.

What's wrong? Theo mouthed.

Uncle Dav is being an asshole, Hank mouthed back.

"I understood that, Hank," Daven hissed.

"Good," Hank replied shortly, as he angrily flipped open his bible.

"Oh my god," muttered Rupert. "If you were my kids you'd both be over my knee by now. Shut up, the sermon's starting."

Hank ignored him, his mind already elsewhere, as usual. Theo had giggled at the *asshole* remark, but Floyd had no reaction at all except for a deeper scowl. He was still upset about getting smacked in the car yesterday, and Hank didn't blame him, and he flushed hotly again at the reminded. *What kind of father does that to a kid that just got out of the hospital? Oh that's right, my kind.*

Hank was stone-faced as he sat with Daven and Rupert in the limo a few hours later from the hotel back to the house. The bruncheon had gone well, but Hank refused to talk business until it was over. Now the boys were in the other car so that the three men could talk, and Hank was thoroughly ready to set fire to the Sunday newspaper he was currently holding.

"Okay, this is...they're talking about our double agents. How do they even know we have them? Has Harmon been talking to the press himself on this side? That's completely illegal."

It was true; in this era of government Hank, Daven, Rupert, Harmon, Colbert, and Umber were expressly prohibited by law from speaking to any political reporter off the record or even casually. Even to be seen greeting Hailey at a party could get any of them censured on the spot, for example. Not that Hank would ever give her the time of day, of course, except at press conferences. If Harmon had talked to the press, well...that was something.

Rupert looked deeply bored by the whole thing already. "Oh come on, we've been through this before. All Harmon had to do was tell someone like Zane, and *he* could run off and tell Hailey. You know that law is really just for show."

Hank looked sharply at his friend. "I wrote that law, Rupe, and it's not just for show."

"I'm sorry," Rupert said sincerely, feeling utterly foolish that he had forgotten that detail.

"Furthermore," Hank added, "this article claims the Urbanes don't employ double agents. That's another thing that should only be at Harmon's level of knowledge, and Colbert's. And Umber's, but certainly no lower."

"It does make us look really bad in comparison," Rupert conceded.

"And this bullshit right here." Hank jabbed angrily at a paragraph in the second article on the front page.

Sources say the FBI is currently investigating Hank Bancroft for bribery. Two men who spoke under strict conditions of anonymity reached out to a reporter at this paper to claim they were personally given $3,000 by an inside agent of Hank Bancroft in exchange for unspecified services, and that they have the receipts to prove it. Furthermore, one of these men claims he has information on the December murder of Colbert's driver that could lead to a revelation of Mr. Bancroft's involvement in the assassination, including several calls he allegedly made to the killer just five days before the incident. As if that's not enough, at least one man who claims to work for the Seditionists in Los Angeles has let us know he offered his services to the FBI as an informant. We will be updating this column daily as this extraordinary story evolves.

There was an ugly silence in the car for a long time, which Hank eventually broke.

"Guys. What the fuck is going on?"

"We don't know," Rupert said. "We're doing everything we can, you know that. But I have a plan."

"What?" Hank rasped. "Speaking of plans, theirs is already working. I truly feel like I'm the one going crazy, not everyone else."

"Well you're not, so let's talk about it. You're convinced Colbert is behind all of this, right?"

Hank nodded. He felt like he was having an out of body experience all of a sudden.

Rupert pressed on calmly. "Right. So...you should tell Harmon that and ask for his help."

"I already did."

Daven was startled. "Oh...you did? When?"

"Friday night. He just laughed. Colbert's leading the investigation for him. I also told Stewart. Without evidence, he's completely unwilling to pursue it. So, forget that. I'm sorry I didn't tell you sooner, but it just was something I don't really want to talk about."

"That was an important thing to leave out, Hank. You have to keep us informed of these things."

Rupert nodded. "Agreed. So much for plan A."

"Yep. What's our plan B?"

Daven and Rupert looked at each other, each unwilling to tell Hank to quit his job yet. It was too soon, and there was still a lot of work to do.

"We're working on it," they said together.

CHAPTER EIGHT

Late Sunday night, Bancroft House

Four hours into his research Hank had made no discoveries, and no decisions. He hadn't picked up his phone, either, despite both Daven and Rupert trying to reach him in the past half hour. To say his despair was at its lowest ebb wouldn't have been much of an exaggeration; the worst was when Mary died. This was only a very distant second.

He threw aside the newspaper as the expected knock broke into his thoughts. "Come in."

Floyd came in reluctantly, looking for all the world like he would rather be walking over lava than get any closer to his dad.

"Sit down."

Floyd obeyed, then looked at his hands and said nothing, so Hank began without any preamble.

"You're still mad at me for what happened in the car yesterday."

Nod.

"Floyd, you *know* that when I tell you to do something, you do it, even if you don't know why. I want you to take a look at this and tell me if you can figure my reasoning for making you lie down." He picked the newspaper back up and handed it to his son. "Look at the picture. What do you see?"

"Protesters." He peered closer. "Wait, that's Brittany, and...that's our car."

"Yes, this is us as we left the hospital yesterday. Those protesters were angry with me."

Floyd picked up on his meaning immediately. "Oh. You didn't want me to see them so that I wouldn't panic again."

"Correct. Now do you see why I did what I did?"

"Yeah."

"Sorry, what was that?"

"Yes, sir," Floyd amended. His eyes darted back to a pair of familiar, unpleasant objects on the credenza. Hank followed his gaze and then felt his heart fall a little.

"I'm not going to paddle you, Floyd. You just got out of the hospital, for god's sake."

"That didn't stop you from..."

Floyd quickly trailed off and fell silent.

"Good choice not to finish that sentence, kiddo," Hank replied stiffly.

Floyd took a deep breath. "Sorry. Did you really fire Lucas, dad?"

The unexpected change of subject left Hank felt slightly disoriented for a moment. "Uh. Yes, I did. A few hours ago."

"Because of me?" Floyd wiped a stray tear from his eye. "I talked him into not calling you. Begged him. This is my fault."

"Not completely, but you did play a big part in it. Floyd, you're 16 now. Old enough to where your decisions don't affect just you alone anymore. Almost everything you do and say impacts someone else, too."

Floyd swallowed hard. This discussion was far worse than any corporal punishment.

"I'm sorry," he whispered miserably. "Please hire him back."

Hank's eyebrows raised way up. "What? You don't even like him."

"That doesn't mean I wanted this, dad."

"I'm sure he didn't, either. I just hope you'll both learn something from this and not repeat your mistakes. And I also expect you to stop sulking around, pronto. Go to bed."

"Dad."

"What?"

Floyd took a deep breath and braced himself for backlash. "You're right, I'm 16 now. Old enough to hear the truth. You could have just told me in the car you didn't want me to look out the windows because you thought it would panic me. Maybe next time you can just tell me what's going on so that you don't even *have to* tell me what to do, and I'll just figure it out for myself."

Hank swallowed hard. Floyd was growing up so fast; it was both fascinating and difficult to witness.

"I hear you, Floyd. I do. But sometimes I don't have time to explain myself, nor should I have to even if I do. You know better. Next time, the belt comes out."

Floyd looked about to cry at that.

Hank felt hellishly sleepy all of a sudden, and his son turned to a blur for a few moments. "Okay, discussion over and you're forgiven. Just remember I'm going to protect you as long as I can now, because I'm not going to be around forever."

"Dad! Don't say that."

Hank sat back in his chair. "Sorry, I'm confused. I thought you said you were old enough to hear the truth."

"But not *that!* "

Hank didn't really have time for this, he realized. Daven and Rupert had called again, there was still the email to Stewart to finish, and he had to plan out his meetings for Monday. Nothing had been finished, only partially started and abandoned. It was already nine o'clock.

"You can't have it both ways, Floyd. Either you get treated like an adult, or like a child. Which is it? Let me know so that we can stop arguing already."

Floyd was breathing hard again. Too hard. *Fuck*. Hank stood up.

"Never mind. We're both tired, and I can see you're starting to get too stressed. Go to bed."

The intercom button light up, and Hank kept an eye on Floyd as he triggered the microphone.

"Yes?"

"Mr. Johanson's driver is at the front gate, sir. Asking if he can come in."

"Is Daven with him?"

"Yes, sir," replied Martinez.

"Tell me that, then. Let them in." He fought back his irritation (which was over nothing, admittedly) and turned to his son again. "Come on, upstairs we go."

"I know the way, dad," Floyd protested as Hank followed him out and up the stairs.

"Just checking to make sure you're going to be okay. You're red."

"I'm *fine*."

"Okay. Goodnight." Hank turned and went back down the stairs to the front door, where Daven had just exited his car.

"I need some air. Let's walk."

Daven stared at him. "What's wrong?"

"Nothing. Haven't really taken advantage of all these grounds. With these walls, we could plan World War 3 and no one would ever know. Why are you here, Dav? It's kind of late. Not that I mind, but you've got me worried."

"Right. Well, first of all, because you didn't pick up your phone. Secondly, because Rupert and I feel like it would be best if you took a couple of days off and just let us work on this thing while you stay out of the spotlight."

"Yeah. Sounds good."

Daven stared again. "Really? We were sure you'd fight me about this."

"I'm guessing you drew the short straw when you guys were deciding who had to come over and give me this suggestion."

"No. Rock, paper, scissors. Something I learned from Floyd and Theo."

"Always go rock."

"I went paper."

"That's what you get. Anyway, I'm not mad. I can work from home and do a few things without causing chaos at the office."

Hank cleared his throat and tried to ignore his racing heart. "I, uh...you know what, Dav. There's something I need to ask you. You're not going to like it."

"Yes?"

Hank hesitated and didn't say anything for a while. Daven didn't prompt him.

"Okay," he said eventually. "I've asked you before, but you didn't seem sure about your answer. Do you *really* want to be the legal guardian to my sons? And don't get mad, but it's just...at the banquet, you seemed so uncomfortable and unhappy. Awkward as hell. I felt like you didn't want to get to know the household at all, or maybe you and the boys just aren't as close as I thought you were. And it's okay if so, it really is. They're a huge, life-changing responsibility."

Daven looked crushed. "I'm sorry, Hank. I just...I don't think I'm ready to be a father to them. And it's not because of them. It's because of you."

"What?" Hank askance, looking confused. "What does that even mean?"

"You're acting like they're going to be handed over to me tomorrow. I can't accept that you won't be around for longer than that. Why don't you just tell me what's going on and stop dropping hints all over the place?"

"I'm not dropping hints! I'm being realistic. Dav, I could be killed in a car accident in the morning. Or a week from now. I guess I just started worrying once I realized how short life is in the past few months."

Daven said plainly. "You're lying. You also lied about having a rough flight home on Friday, you lied about why you wanted me and Rupe at the banquet, and you've been lying by omission for weeks in regards to what's going on between you and Harmon. Tell me the truth now, or I'm going to walk away and not come back for any reason. I'm dead serious, Hank."

Hank had stopped in his tracks some time ago, and he found himself unable to move or speak for several long moments.

"This is the only chance I'm giving you," Daven continued. "Because we both know tomorrow is going to be too late."

Hank stuffed his hands inside his coat; he was freezing now, but it wasn't the temperature. "Fine. Ten years ago I visited Colbert in prison to apologize to him for what I'd done to bring him down, because for some absurd reason I felt guilty about it. You know what he said to me?"

"What?"

"He thanked me for visiting him, and then said he would return the favor someday."

Daven was unimpressed. "Okay. That's nothing. People make threats all the time, Hank."

"It was more than a threat. It was a promise. I can still see his face, and hear his tone, and feel my body go numb every time I think of it. He's been obsessed with me ever since. Even Harmon mentions it on occasion. This whole thing has been years in the making, Dav."

"Then we have years of trails to follow."

"No. He learned his lesson the first time about not leaving trails. How do you think I got him?"

They walked in silence for a few more minutes until Hank had the courage to speak again.

"It's not that I'm giving up or anything. I want to fight this." He thought about how he had blackmailed Harmon, but decided not to mention it at the moment. "But the truth is, Dav…I always knew this was coming. That it was only a matter of time."

"That has to be difficult to live with."

"Yeah. Going back to Harmon. I've been going after him so hard over the years for several reasons, all of which you know…but also because I knew that if he goes down, so does Colbert."

Daven paled a little. "Oh. That explains a lot."

"Then I started to become friendly with him, of all things…and *that's* when Colbert swooped in and got me. I let my guard down, Dav. Turns out I actually like Harmon, who'd have thought? What a cluster fuck."

"Likeable or not, he got Janet killed. You know that. God knows what else he's done."

Hank went so quiet for a minute that Daven thought he'd gotten separated from him in the dark.

"Hank?"

"Right here. We don't need God to tell us what Harmon's done, Dav. We've got double agents for that. And if I'm going down, so is he."

The Keeper of the Lost

King of the Castle

CHAPTER ONE

Daven's house, same evening

"Rupert, we have a problem. Hank agreed to stay away from the office for a few days."

"But...wait, that's what we asked him to do!"

Daven grunted. "Now we can't keep an eye on what he's doing. He's given up already, thinks he's lost this battle. He's going to focus on bringing Harmon down instead of absolving himself."

"Wait. I'm confused. Back up, Dav, you're freaking me out."

"Sorry. We talked for about two hours just now. He's going to recall his double agents, get all the dirt he can on Harmon, and take him down with him. Those were his words, not mine. He seems to be uninterested in trying to find a trail back to Colbert anymore. Told us to keep trying, but there was no point. He's convinced Colbert can't get caught."

Rupert's hair stood up on the back of his neck. "Oh, fuck. This is not good."

"It gets worse. He wants to do a press conference tomorrow at four o'clock. Not a media statement, mind you, but a full-on press conference. I think he's finally lost his mind, Rupe."

"Shit, well...he's the boss. I'll start preparing. In the meantime, it's your job to talk him out of it. I'm not going to get caught in a lurch if you can't succeed."

"Agreed. That would only make things worse. Wish me luck."

Seditionist HQ, 4pm

Daven was not successful in talking Hank down, and now he and Rupert silently leaned up against the back wall of the press room and watched their boss with a level of fear and awe they had never quite felt before. First off was Hank's media statement.

"Thank you all for coming," he stated calmly, and cheerfully. "As usual, I will start this off by reading our official media statement regarding the recent allegations against me and our organization in general:

The Seditionists are aware of the numerous allegations made Friday and Saturday against Hank Bancroft, leader of the party. Only one of the allegations are true: we do in fact utilize a small number of informants within the Urbanes organization. This practice is not, and has never been, illegal. Their work is limited to passive monitoring for illegal activity and reporting on the general morale of the party's employees and its constituents. Their purpose has never been to sabotage operations or release unauthorized information, and they are not paid for their services. However, in an abundance of caution, we have made the decision to recall all such persons back to Los Angeles effective immediately, and will not engage in this practice in the future."

There was a collective, excitable gasp from all around the newsroom. Daven let out the long breath he'd been holding, and Rupert fidgeted with his tie for the hundredth time.

All other allegations are categorically false and will be proven as such in very short order. Mr. Bancroft has personally made the decision to step down as leader of the Seditionists while these investigations are ongoing, in order to prevent situations at the office that may create tension or result in conflicts of interest. Daven Johansson, Chief Strategist, will lead the party until further notice. The investigation itself will be conducted primarily by Rupert Aster and Taylor Bowen, with the gracious assistance of an FBI auditor.

Hank set the statement down and hit the green button on his podium. "I have ten minutes for questions."

Urbanes HQ - Denver

"My god. Balls of steel, that man. No matter how much I hate him, got to say it." Harmon whistled low and took another handful of chocolate covered almonds from the jar on Colbert's desk.

Umber shook his head, but didn't avert his eyes from the television. "For a smart man, he's not very smart sometimes. Putting his entire accounting staff on leave? Jesus Christ."

Colbert leaned forward. "Shhh, I think this is the last question. Bet you anything Hailey's going to get it."

Seditionist HQ

"Yes, number 27."

Hailey stood up, looking as smug as usual. "Mr. Bancroft, do you think these charges are just a string of easily explainable coincidences, or do you believe you're being framed?"

Daven and Rupe simultaneously tensed up. Again. They absolutely hated when Hank went for a free-for-all on questions like this, especially against Hailey.

Hank smiled. "Ms. Hendricks, I don't believe in coincidences. Next question, please?"

Daven glanced at his friend, who was sweating bullets. "He's doing pretty good, actually. Holding his own."

"Wish I could say the same for me," Rupert grumbled. "I'm one more question away from wetting my pants."

Hank punched the green button again. "Yes? Mr. Lowly."

Urbanes HQ - Denver

Colbert held his breath and tried not to draw attention to his sudden angst. Mark Lowly was one of the photographers Yannick paid off.

"Mr. Bancroft, it's well known that you offered to bribe photographers not to take pictures of your sons. You admitted

204

as much, and were publicly censured for it. How is it that you now claim you made no such payments? Is such a statement supportable?"

"As I already said, Mr. Lowly, these payments were unauthorized. We're investigating them."

At this, Hank looked right into the Denver station's camera and smirked. It seemed to Colbert that the man was looking straight at him. Mocking him. Daring him.

"Wait, I don't get it," said Harmon slowly. "Who would be doing this to him? *We're* not. I mean...doesn't this seem incredibly strange? I know he has a lot of enemies, but if he's right, this is a pretty sophisticated operation."

Umber, who was secretly a huge fan of Hank's chutzpah but would never admit it to these particular men, laughed a little nervously. "Well, as long as he doesn't pin it on us, I don't care. Maybe one of his agents went rogue. More likely, he's guilty as hell. He's bribed people before, for god's sake. Almost got jailed for it a few times."

"Years ago," Harmon scoffed.

"Nobody's doing anything. He's guilty as hell, boss," said Colbert, as calmly as he could manage. Bancroft had no chance.

Until he did something totally unexpected, that is.

Hank cleared his throat. "I'm sorry, we've run out of time for questions. I want to strongly encourage the six photographers who allegedly received these payments from me to please call the FBI with information as to how, when, and where they received the money. Whether their answer implicates me or someone else, it's incredibly important that this information be made known as soon as possible in order to allow us to complete the investigation. If you do not call on your own accord, it is highly likely you will be subpoenaed to travel to Philadelphia to give testimony once my trial begins. Here is the number FBI's tip hotline. Oh, and forgive me for neglecting to mention that we even know where the cashier's checks were purchased, and we're very close to obtaining video of the person who bought them. We are hoping to link that person to the person who made the false payments. Possibly it is the same man or woman. Thank you for your time, and have a nice evening."

Oh, holy fuck... Colbert said to himself as he saw his entire future crashing down around him. If Yannick was identified, Harmon would see through the entire charade in a heartbeat. It was time to think fast.

"Boss, I think you ought to pull the trigger with that tape, now. Shoot this thing down before it grows wings and the public starts supporting him and saying we're framing him."

Harmon nodded. "I was thinking the same. He was pretty convincing, huh?"

Umber looked at the floor. "He's got *me* convinced we're framing him, for god's sake. I hate to admit it, but Colbert's right. We need to get the jump on him now."

"Agreed. Alright. We have to protect ourselves..and our party, more importantly. Let's do it. I'm going back to my office."

Seditionist HQ

Hank's office

Daven immediately busied himself making an espresso while Hank began packing up his things and prepared to go home for a while. *Hopefully not forever*, he mused.

Rupe was the first to speak. "Hank...I have to say, I'm incredibly impressed with how well you handled yourself. I'm sorry I ever fought with you about this press conference in the first place."

"It's alright, Rupe. You weren't wrong."

"What you said about the FBI subpoenaing the photographers, though. Was that true? I mean, we don't even know who they are, unless you know something we don't."

Hank grimaced. "Yeah, about that. I sort of made it up on the spot. I'm going to have hell to pay for that when Stewart hears about it, if he hasn't already-"

Hank's phone rang, and it was Stewart. "Speak of the devil. I'm going to put him on speaker so don't say anything, okay?"

The men nodded, and Hank answered the phone.

"Hank Bancroft."

"Hi, Hank. Stewart. Just watched your press conference."

Hank closed his eyes and took a deep breath. "I'm completely prepared for you to rip me a new one. Go ahead, I deserve it."

There was a brief pause. "You mean over the subpoena thing? No. I thought it was quite clever. Hell, if it leads to tips I can use, all the better for it. I was calling for something else. Did you receive the questionnaire packet yet? FedEx said it was delivered at 10:30am."

"Yes, I did."

"Good. The other thing is that I have some potentially upsetting news, Hank. Harmon has indicated he wishes to meet with me tomorrow. He's flying out tonight on a red-eye. I didn't want you to hear it on the news first."

Oh, shit. "Okay. Thanks for letting me know. What does that mean for me, exactly?"

Stewart replied, "He hasn't actually told me, but I think you know what it could mean."

"Yeah." There was only one reason Harmon would ever willingly meet with Stewart.

"You should prepare to meet with me to discuss this. If he...god, I hate to tell you this over the phone in this manner. But if he does have enough evidence for us to press criminal charges-"

"You'll have to arrest me." Hank swallowed hard. "When?"

"Assuming that's the reason he's coming, Thursday. Possibly Friday. You really should make finishing that questionnaire a priority."

Hank's throat was dry, and he had to swallow a few times to reply. "Make it Monday. I need one more weekend with my kids."

"Just a second."

Stewart put him on hold; he didn't dare look at Daven or Rupert in the meantime.

"Hank," said Rupe softly.

"Shhh."

It seemed like an eternity passed before Stewart came back on the line. "Just spoke to Salome. She guaranteed no earlier than Monday."

"Thank you."

"Hank, don't despair too much yet. It's possible he's only going to-"

"No, it's not. But thanks for trying to make me feel better. I better get back to work. Or home, rather, since I have no work at the moment."

"Sure. I thought you did an outstanding job on the press conference, and it was a good idea to step aside for a little while. We'll keep you updated from my end."

Hank hung up the phone and turned back to his closet. He was strangely calm and focused.

"Can I talk now, Hank?" asked Rupert softly.

"Be my guest."

"We're going to find a way to get you out of this. I promise."

Hank laughed a little. "You shouldn't make promises you can't keep. I'm going home, gents. Dav, I'll call you in a little while. I have some ideas to pursue for the investigation."

Daven still said nothing. He hadn't said a word since the press conference, not even the slightest glint of approval, and it hurt Hank's feelings.

"Goodnight, guys. You okay, Dav?"

"No."

"Me either. Keep in touch, okay?"

CHAPTER TWO

Bancroft House

Tuesday morning, March 14

It was rare for Hank Bancroft to feel sorry for himself, but here he was doing exactly that. The questionnaire Stewart had sent him was intense, but by lunchtime he got halfway through it before getting completely stuck on one odd question:

On December 19 and 20, three calls were made from your cell phone to the number (303) 975-4153. Please explain the nature of these calls, including the recipient's name.

He had looked at his phone records just to be sure, and found that he had indeed made those calls. Most likely while he was at home, judging by the time they were made. But for the life of him, he couldn't remember why on earth he would have called any Denver numbers back then. He searched his email for a reference to it and found nothing. Rather than skipping this question and moving on to the next, he just sat there and stared at it for a good hour or so before picking up the phone and calling Daven.

"Hey Dav, do me a favor? Have Taylor search for some info on this number. I'll explain why later, but it should be a priority." He gave the number.

"Will do. Are you okay, Hank? Haven't heard from you all day. Sent you a couple emails."

"I know, sorry. I'll get to them right now. How are you doing?"

Daven sighed. "Remember how I said I never wanted your job? I still don't."

"I know. With any luck I'll steal it right back from you soon. I need you to stop by tonight and sign some paperwork related to your guardianship of the boys."

"Hank-"

"Don't start with me, Dav. It's just precautionary, something I should have done it a long time ago."

Long silence. "Fine. What time?"

"Whenever. Thank you."

FBI HQ - Philadelphia

"Harmon is here, sir," sang out the receptionist on Stewart's intercom.

"Send him in." Stewart slammed shut the binder on Hank Bancroft, and braced himself for an incredibly rough meeting. He couldn't stand Harmon in any shape or form, not even to watch him on TV, and he especially hated the fact that his dislike for the man caused a bias towards Hank that he couldn't control despite being completely aware of it. He knew he would have to set that aside and be completely objective, but it wasn't going to be easy.

"Welcome to Philadelphia," he said, handing Harmon a bottle of water as he walked in. "Long time no see. Please have a seat."

"Thank you." Harmon declined the bottle of water. "Brought my own, thanks."

"Alright. Let's get down to business, then. What brings you here?"

Harmon looked nervous, which was unusual. "I'm convinced that one of Hank's informants stole personal information from our databases and provided it to Hank for distribution."

"Okay. What's convincing you?"

"Our IT experts traced the listserv posting to a 10-block radius in Santa Monica. Within that radius is the Seditionists headquarters." He pulled out a notebook full of papers and handed one over to Stewart. "I'd like to ask that the FBI verify this information."

Stewart studied the map, then looked up. "You said your IT experts already traced it."

"Well, I'm hoping you have the technology to narrow it down further. Those ten blocks happen to contain hundreds of offices and homes."

"Right." Stewart took the cap off the bottle of water he had offered, and drank some himself. "You already know we have that technology."

Harmon nodded, but he didn't seem smug or victorious about any of this. Reluctant, almost. Stewart was intrigued by this remarkable change in his behavior since their last meeting, but he forced himself to stay business-like.

"May I ask why you're in such a hurry to turn it over to us? You haven't even finished your own investigation yet."

"The Urbanes are not framing Hank. I know he's accusing us, but under oath I will tell you that's not the case. I have nothing to do with this. The public, however, might not feel the same."

"Ah. I see. You're worried that public opinion is going to turn against you, and you're trying to prove your innocence before they have the chance."

"Yes."

"Which, in turn, means proving Hank's guilt before he has the chance to pin it on you."

"Yes." Harmon thought of the tape in his briefcase but left it alone for now; he needed more leverage first.

"Okay. So...you came here to ask for my help in what, exactly? Besides trying to find the exact location of the listserv posting."

Harmon shifted in his chair. "I have no doubt his agents have done harm within my organization, and that he's entirely responsible for this data leak. That's what I want to focus on. But I want to make it a civil matter, not criminal."

"You can't once the FBI is involved. You know that."

"I'm asking you to make an exception."

"Why? If you're so convinced he's guilty, then-"

"Because I don't want his kids to become Bonded Retainers, that's why," Harmon interrupted irritably. "That law is bullshit and should have never passed. We both fought it, and somehow we lost. I'm not going to let him just...just tell me, can you make an exception, or not?"

Oh, this is different . A tender side of Harmon that Stewart never knew existed.

"We might not have to make an exception. The boys have another legal guardian. If Hank is convicted by March 31, Daven likely gets custody of them. The old law allows for that if the guardian has been in place for over five years, which he has. After April 1, the courts have to approve him, and I doubt they will. Especially if he's tied up in this whole mess, or implicated in any way. I can't predict what will happen."

"So we need to do this today."

"Yes. I can order his arrest as early as tomorrow if you have definite proof of any felony that he committed. That should leave enough time to get it wrapped up by March 31."

Harmon was floored. "You're trying to rush a trial for him? One that might not leave enough time to look at all the possibilities."

Stewart nodded. "Therein lies the problem. I've been busting my ass trying to find something to help, but right now it's all just a waiting game."

Harmon stood up and started to leave. "We'll go to civil court, even if I can't prove a damned thing. Forget it. Thanks for your time."

"Harmon."

"What?" he snapped.

"Just because you're taking it to civil court doesn't mean we're going to drop our criminal investigation of all the other charges. If you prove your case there, it's going to be proved here. Possibly too late."

That gave Harmon pause. "So...what are you telling me to do?"

"I want you to tell me the truth. Do you have hard evidence that Hank committed a felony?"

Destroy the tape. This is not worth it. Hank was just joking.

Stewart saw the flash in Harmon's dark eyes, the affirmation couched in denial. "No."

"I don't believe you," he replied calmly. Quietly.

Harmon scoffed. "Well I guess we're at an impasse, aren't we?"

Stewart let a warning tone slip into his next words. "I'm sorry, I was under the impression you were trying to help Hank. My mistake."

"I am! And rushing into a trial is not the way to do it."

"I'll keep that in mind. And you should keep in mind that, as the aggrieved party, you would have the right to benefit from a plea bargain that might include being able to obtain the deed to his children."

"Oh, right. Hank Bancroft is going to waive his right to a trial, say he's guilty, and turn his children over to me while he traipses off to prison. What kind of drugs are you on? What the hell would I even do with his kids, for god's sake?"

Then...the bombshell. Stewart looked him straight in the eyes and didn't waiver. "Deeds are transferable to any free adult, Harmon. It wouldn't require the approval of a court."

That startled the man, and the sudden realization of what Stewart was secretly telling him to do seemed to hit him like a ton of bricks.

"You want me to...you...holy shit. He's going to get convicted anyway, isn't he? You already have him, but you can't move fast enough."

Stewart fought to hide the relief he felt that Harmon was figuring it out on his own, and he completely ignored the question since he had no authorization to confirm such a thing.

"You really should educate yourself better in these matters if you're thinking of pressing ahead. I would recommend pages 561 through 567 of the Courts & Law review. Might help you see things more clearly and aid in your decision. I'll have some copies made for you." He reached over to his intercom button and instructed his secretary to pull out the book and copy the pages for his "guest."

Harmon left with no further comments, and Stewart suddenly felt like crying. He desperately needed anything he could get to convict Hank as quickly as possible, and he had done the best he could to force Harmon into seeing it, too. But he was afraid that Harmon wasn't imaginative enough to read between the lines and see the full potential of their options. That he could transfer the deeds to Daven. Had he understood?

Salome came out from behind the door of the listening room. "Jesus. That was an unexpected turn of events. I got what you were implying right away, but did he?"

"I'm not sure. I could see the gears turning, but the light bulb dimmed there at the end. At any rate, I failed. He didn't leave his proof. I'm guessing I'm out of a job now, too."

"Don't be ridiculous."

The intercom lit back up again, and Stewart punched it irritably. "Yes?"

"Sir, Harmon is asking to come back in for a moment. Said he left his phone on your desk?"

There was nothing there. "Yes, he did. Tell him to come in and get it."

Harmon walked back in a minute later, and his eyes got wider upon spotting Salome. "Sorry, didn't mean to interrupt."

"That's okay. What's up?"

"I assume you were listening," he said to Salome, who nodded.

Harmon put his briefcase on the desk and unlatched the sides. "I just have one more question for you both."

"Yes?"

"Would I be able to negotiate the boys out of indentured servitude altogether?"

Salome answered. "No. The current law is that if Hank gets convicted in a state court, the minimum indenture for them is 20 years."

"Until March 31, you mean."

"Correct. After that...it's for life."

"With castration at 16, and all that fun, wholesome stuff."

Salome crossed her arms. "We didn't write the laws, Harmon, and I can certainly assure you Stewart and I don't agree with them. But yes, that is true."

"Can you guarantee we can get this done by March 31?"

"If Hank agrees to the plea bargain, yes."

Harmon opened his briefcase and handed Stewart the tape.

"Then I would like to press criminal charges against Hank Bancroft in the state of Colorado."

CHAPTER THREE

FBI HQ - Philadelphia

Same day

"I don't know, Salome, this whole thing still rings false to me. I can't accept it."

Stewart was miserably reviewing the latest transcript of the call from their mystery informant, the same one who claimed Hank Bancroft paid him to murder Janet. He hated being back to this same dreary subject. The tape Harmon had given him today wasn't the solid proof he had hoped for; no, that was a differently felony altogether and made exactly zero difference to this particular investigation. The meeting with him had led to nothing more than the same number of unanswered questions they had started with, to everyone's deep frustration.

Salome cleared her throat and rearranged her desk needlessly for the fifth time this afternoon. "Me either, but you know we have to stay objective. If we don't track down this caller, we're never getting anywhere. No clues yet at all?"

"No. I don't understand it. Why is he playing us? What does he have to gain by staying anonymous? I mean, hell, he could easily hide behind the Whistleblower Act and gain our protection rather than incriminating the hell out of himself. This is like putting together a puzzle that's missing all the edges. I mean...look at this part."

Bancroft called me several times in the days before Christmas on a temporary phone I purchased just for this job.

Stewart sat up a little straighter, his heart pounding again. He didn't want to believe it, but he could hardly dismiss the connection without comment. "Those might be the three calls on the phone records we audited. You know, the ones we asked him about?"

"Yes. The number with a Denver area code that was deactivated the day *after* Christmas?" She reached into her desk drawer and pulled out the binder. "If this caller can verify the number, we can verify him and this whole shady story."

"He'll never give it to us. He'll think we can track down where he bought it, and therefore identify him. Not a chance."

"But we can't. We've tried already, you know that."

"But *he* doesn't know that. Salome, I think we should let him know we have the number, and tell him we can find him."

Salome stared at Stewart uncomprehendingly. "Why? Wouldn't that scare him off?"

"We should also tell him we now have surveillance video of the person who purchased the cashier's checks."

"Why?" Salome repeated.

"To force him into shitting or getting off the pot. Excuse the expression. All he's done is just throw tidbits at us and disappear. Maybe we can scare him into giving us everything all at once, so we can get this thing damned thing settled before the 31st."

Salome shook her head. "I'm sorry, but no. We're not going to resort to scare tactics. That's an old United States tactic, and we're not that anymore. We're better than them."

Stewart scoffed. " *Better*. Right. This waiting game is bullshit, Salome. You know it is. We have to move *now* . Christ, with the surveillance video coming back on Thursday we almost have everything we need except for this asshole's identity! All we need to do is confirm he really does work for the Seditionists, and this conviction is certain. That's it. And we have less than two weeks to do it before..."

He didn't have to say anything else; they both knew what was at stake.

"We wouldn't be in this position if that March 1 vote hadn't passed. But that doesn't mean we're going to resort to lower ourselves to scare tactics. Let's try something else," Salome suggested, ignoring Stewart's insolence. "Hank's convinced that Colbert is behind this, right? And he doesn't think this person actually works for him, but is just a go-between?"

Stewart nodded. "He has zero evidence, though. And so do we."

Salome smiled a little. "I'm willing to look further into the possibility anyway. Let's stop by Denver on the way to Los Angeles. If Colbert shits a brick upon hearing that we have *two* videos of our suspect as well as tracking down his phone number, we'll know he's involved."

Stewart grinned, approving of the plan, but…"That's pushing it awfully close to Monday. We're going to run out of time."

"Alright. Then we'll go tonight and meet Harmon in the morning, and Hank in the afternoon. Get packed."

Bancroft House

Tuesday night 6pm

If any moments in Hank's life had ever seemed impossible to overcome, they were now deemed inexpressibly easy compared to answering the phone when Stewart finally called with the news about what Harmon wanted. He felt as if his arms were suddenly made of lead, and the ringing was as loud as cannon fire in the confines of his study. After several long moments of pondering whether he and the boys could get away with sailing off into the wild blue yonder and disappearing, he ruefully dismissed the idea and turned bodily around in his chair to yank the phone out of its holder.

"Hello Stewart."

"Hello Hank. Got a minute?"

"Just one minute? Seems like I have the rest of my life in your hands."

Stewart hesitated, then declined to acknowledge the bitter sarcasm. "I'm really sorry to tell you that both Harmon and the FBI are moving forward with criminal charges. I'll have to arrest you on Monday. I'm sorry."

Hank counted to ten before he responded. He had never expected to be having a conversation like this, not in a million years, but here he was. Here *they* were.

"I see. Why didn't he just pursue a civil lawsuit?"

Because I made him do this, and I hate myself for it. "We'll talk more later. I'm quite limited in what I can say right now."

"Alright. Guess I'm flying to Philadelphia on Sunday night, then."

"No, anytime Monday is fine. Just arrive before midnight. Listen, I've been speaking to Salome about this whole thing for a couple hours after Harmon left, and she's insisted on interviewing Daven and Rupert first. We're actually on the way to Denver in about two hours, and tomorrow afternoon I'll need to meet with you all in Los Angeles. Separately, of course."

Alarm prickled along the hairs of Hank's neck. "What are you going to ask them?"

"Anything within our due diligence, Hank. We have to. You know that."

"They didn't do anything wrong."

"Never said they did."

Hank gulped down the last of his whiskey, but didn't even realize he was doing it. "What time?"

"I don't know yet. Maybe 2pm."

"What are the charges, exactly?"

Stewart took a deep breath. "They'll be detailed in the official subpoena I'm bringing tomorrow."

"Super. Can't wait."

Stewart paused, hating everything about every word on this conversation. He would give anything to be calling just to bitch Hank out about something stupid, like he had so many times before. A dumb, childish infraction that wouldn't lead to such a drastic end.

"There's one last thing for now. As of this moment you're officially prohibited from contacting any member of Harmon's team for any reason, by any method. If you even try it, you'll get nailed for contempt. So just don't."

"Hmmm. Would that be a felony in this context?"

"No, but it won't help your case in any way whatsoever."

Hank shrugged, the gesture unseen by his conversation partner. "Fair enough. I have no idea what I'd say, anyway. Can Daven or Rupert talk to them?"

"Not at the moment. After Monday, yes."

Another pour and drag of whiskey, and suddenly his mood turned from somber to downright foul. "Peachy. This night just keeps getting better. Are we done?"

"Yes. There's no need to be rude to-"

Hank hung up the phone and immediately hit his intercom button to staff quarters. He had one more weekend with the boys was suddenly determined to make the most of it.

"Maurice, report to my study on the double. Bring a notepad."

"Yes, sir?"

"Arrange for the boat to be transferred to Dana Point on Thursday or Friday, and then have it ready by 10am Saturday for a day sail. I'll send you a shopping list to you soon for food and drinks. You can come with us or not, your choice, but either way I need you down there getting everything set up before we go. Sorry to butt in on your weekend."

"That's alright, sir."

"Secondly, reserve 3 hotel rooms Saturday night at the Ritz-Carlton in Laguna Niguel, tickets for Disneyland on Sunday, as well as lunch and dinner reservations at Club 33. We'll also need the usual cast member escorts."

"Yes, sir."

"Cancel the banquet for Sunday. Let the hotel know we'll pay them anyway since it's late notice."

"Yes, sir. You're skipping-" Maurice stopped himself; it wasn't his place to ask, even though every fiber of his being wanted to protest. The media would tear Hank apart as a heathen come Monday if he didn't go to church. The only time they didn't was when he was down with the flu recently, in which not a single whiny protest was lodged in the papers thanks to Rupert's strongly worded request to the press.

"No, we're not skipping church," Hank replied to the unasked question, apparently unperturbed for once by Maurice's nosiness. "We'll go to Crystal Cathedral since Theo's always wanted to see it, and head to Disneyland afterwards. Lastly, the servants don't have to return home until Monday at three, including you, so reschedule the bus."

"Yes, sir."

"Thanks Maurice, that will be all for now."

The man left, and Hank wearily hit the intercom button again. "Avery. My study, please."

While he waited for his guard, Hank had about two minutes to wonder what in the hell he was going to tell Theo and Floyd. No matter how he did it, the boys would be inconsolable. What fresh hell for poor Floyd, who couldn't even see his own house on television without having a fit. The poor kid would probably end up hospitalized again, and there wasn't a damned thing Hank could do about it.

Knock, knock.

"Come in."

Avery carefully entered, still wary and wounded from having been thoroughly dressed down for saying in front of Theo that Hank should have been at the hospital with Floyd instead of at the office. He knew he deserved it and fully understood the reason for it, but that made it no easier to swallow. Hank had a ferocious way with words when he was angry, and some of his more choice phrases were still ricocheting painfully around Avery's consciousness.

Hank was calm and almost friendly, however. That was unusual, considering his incredible penchant for holding grudges longer than was reasonably acceptable. "I realize you have planned time off next week, so I would like to take Martinez with me to Philadelphia on Monday. We might have to stay for a while." *Maybe years, in my case* .

"I can go, boss," Avery said quickly, not wanting to cause any drama. "My days off start on Thursday. If we're back by then, it's fine."

"We might not be," Hank quietly responded after an awkward silence. "I can't really say why."

Oh, shit...he's done it now . "Then I should go with you. I'll change my plans. Don't worry, sir."

Hank looked immensely relieved, which perked up his guard somewhat. "Thank you. We'll also be going on a weekend trip. More details later. I have a lot to do tonight, so forgive me for being vague. You can go."

Avery ignored the dismissal and stepped forward, taking a deep breath. "Speaking of forgiveness...I sincerely hope you've forgiven me for what I said in front of Theo."

Hank looked away and rifled through a binder that was laying out on the credenza. "I'd be lying to you if I said I did," he responded, not unkindly. "But I am trying."

Avery took another deep breath, steeling himself for what he was about to say next. "Hank, when you summoned me to your office I was busy shuffling through the live camera feeds."

That got Hank's full attention again; he turned around in his chair. "And?"

"You know that I don't like to get the boys in trouble, right?"

"Yes, I know. Worst part of your job, you've said a thousand times. What's happened?"

It was true. Avery hated this part of his job. Hated it more than anything else in the world, but he had no choice. This is what he was paid for and had agreed to do. "Floyd snuck out of his room and he's in the pool house."

Hank didn't have to ask what his son was doing. He knew without question.

The intercom lit up, interrupting the conversation. Hank punched the button irritably.

"Mr. Johansson is here, sir," said Martinez, who was stationed in the guardhouse.

"I assume you let him in?"

"No, sir. Waiting for your permission."

Avery nodded approvingly; Martinez was learning fast after several early faux pas that had drawn his new boss's ire.

"Good," Hank said, approving of the caution as well. "Send him up. Thank you."

Hank turned back to Avery. "Thank you. We'll talk some more tomorrow."

"Shall I tell Floyd to-"

"No," said Hank decisively as he stood up to go deal with this latest mess. "I've got it, and I won't mention who was watching the cameras. Thanks."

"I'm sorry, Dav," Hank said grumpily as he returned to his study to his waiting friend and slammed the door behind him. "Had a slight issue with my oldest."

"Is he alright?" Dav asked with true concern, and not just out of courtesy.

Hank stopped himself from rolling his eyes in frustration. "Floyd is not allowed to watch the news without me. One guess as to what he was just doing?"

"I have no idea," Dav replied seriously, and Hank gaped at him.

"Watching the news. Really, Dav?"

"Oh. What did you do?"

Hank sat down hard. "What I had to do. The kid disobeyed a direct order; he knew what to expect. Have you made up your mind about the guardianship issue?" he barked without intending to. Daven looked aghast at him, and Hank flushed.

"Sorry. Way to launch right into business, right? Forgive me. It's been a hell of a day. Let me rephrase. Have you made a decision regarding my request to take guardianship of the boys if something happens to me?"

Dav nodded. "Of course my answer is yes. It was never going to be anything else."

"Really? Could have fooled me," Hank muttered bitterly.

Daven sat down in Hank's guest chair. "Is something wrong, Hank? Besides Floyd, of course. You seem unusually-"

"Is anything right?" Hank interrupted. "I'm going to Philadelphia on Monday. In the afternoon, specifically."

"Why? Were you summoned?"

Hank tensed, not wanting to tell Dav the truth yet, but not wanting to lie to him, either.

"Not yet. Dav...we need to have a serious talk. I don't know if right now is the time to do it, but I don't see how waiting is going to make this easier. Just be honest with me. What was the real reason you held back those receipts for so long?"

Daven took the bottle of water Hank offered. "You told me to never tell you."

"I'm asking you now. It's important."

"I'm not going to answer," Daven replied calmly as he took a drink. "Per your orders, if you don't recall. You were adamant."

"And why do you think that was, exactly?"

"Because then you would have to tell the FBI, and I'd get in trouble."

Hank felt like his world was spinning suddenly. "Fine. Then just answer yes or no: did you hold back because you didn't want it to cause bad PR and influence the vote?"

Daven stared at him coolly, expression unreadable. The guess wasn't exactly correct; he had only done it to keep Hank focused, not to distract the voters. But either way, the desired end result was essentially the same. Dav had seriously messed up, but he sincerely had not realized it until this moment. How much he had put Hank's career in jeopardy with his good intentions.

"No comment."

"Okay, let me put it this way. If that's what you did, for god's sake, *don't* tell anyone that. Attempting to influence the vote with something like that could be considered a felony. Do you understand me?"

"Loud and clear."

Hank paused breathlessly, seeing a rare burst of fear that crossed Daven's eyes for a fraction of a second like a shooting star. "*Fuck.* You did. I knew it. You've been around Rupert too long. Jesus, Dav."

Daven took another long draw of water. "Is Stewart going to interview me?"

"Yes he is. Tomorrow."

"Hank, you of all people should know I'm not going to let you take the fall for something I did."

Hank stood up and walked to his window, frustrated beyond description. "No. I am literally ordering you to keep your trap shut about the vote, understand me?"

Daven cocked his head like a quizzical beagle. "You can't order me around, Hank. I'm the one in charge now."

Hank froze, his heart in his throat. Coming from anyone else, that remark would have been an egotistical, hurtful, even threatening statement. Coming from Daven, however, it was simply the truth watered down to its barest element. He regularly made stark observations like this without any ulterior motives or malice, a fact which usually comforted Hank. This time, it didn't. He felt like breaking anything within reach suddenly, but managed to keep himself still.

"Right. Dav, you should leave before I lose my temper and say things I'm going to deeply regret."

"I'm not afraid of your temper. Besides, isn't there something I have to sign in regards to Floyd and Theo?"

Hank had forgotten all about it; now he seethed impotently as he returned to his desk and pushed the thick packet over.

"This is to accept the responsibility for handling my estate and take over complete guardianship of my sons. I'm leaving everything to you. All my property and finances, too."

Now it was Daven's turn to freeze in horror. "Hank. No. I can't."

"You can, and you will." He tapped the cover of the bound pages. "*This* is why you can't be guilty of a felony. Because then you'll have *nothing,* and neither will the boys. This is for them, not you. Now do you understand me?"

Daven looked down. Horrified, but calm. "What am I supposed to tell Stewart, then?"

"That you held back because you were afraid of confronting me after what happened at Christmas. I'm a tyrant, everyone knows that. Play that up and he'll be fine. It's what I already told him."

Daven could not meet Hank's eyes suddenly. "You're not a tyrant, and I'm not agreeing to that or signing this until you answer one simple question."

"What?"

"Are you going to Philadelphia on Monday to be arrested?"

Hank picked up his whiskey bottle again. "I thought you said it was a simple question."

"Are you?"

"Look, anything could happen between now and then. I'm just being practical and cautious."

Daven didn't back down. "Answer the question, Hank. Without drinking that entire bottle first, if you don't mind."

Hank hesitated, then swallowed another mouthful and nodded as he locked eyes with Dav. There was a very long silence between the two friends.

"When were you planning to tell me this?" Daven finally asked, astonished.

"Give me a break, Dav. I just learned about it less than hour ago and I'm still in disbelief."

"I'm sorry. What evidence do they have?"

"I don't know yet. Enough, apparently. I really don't want to talk about it right now," Hank added sullenly, hating himself for being so outwardly cold toward the man who was trying to save him and his sons. Although it made sense since part of him, Hank realized reluctantly, resented Daven for getting him into this mess in the first place by holding back the damned receipts.

Another long silence.

"Well, we need to talk at some point. Like tomorrow morning. Now everything you've been saying lately makes sense. Give me the pen, please."

Hank didn't comply yet. "Wait. What are you going to tell Stewart about the receipts?"

"Whatever you want, as long as it keeps you from taking the blame. Pen?"

Now Hank handed it over. "Thank you. Just know that there's no one else I would trust more to do this for me."

Daven nodded. "There's one more thing. I don't think you should send the boys to Maui."

"Why not?"

"I want them with me," Daven insisted.

"You'll be at work. That makes no sense."

"It makes a hell of a lot more sense than sending them away and disappearing, and leaving Millie to deal with the aftermath. She doesn't know them as well as I do."

Hank almost immediately launched into to a protest, but then he remembered something crucial: Daven's own father had left the family without a trace years ago. Hank backed off immediately, knowing what a sensitive and painful subject that was for his dear friend. He suddenly had no desire to inflict the same agony upon his own sons.

"You're right. She won't know how to handle Floyd. Can they stay with you next week? I'll have Maurice connect with you guys and do all the shopping, and Chef can come by and do the cooking."

"Or I can just stay in your house. It will be less disruption for the boys, and more private."

"Yeah. Good idea. If you don't mind, let's just do that for as long as necessary."

"Any idea how long that might be?" Daven prodded anxiously.

"Anywhere between one day and forever, I guess," Hank said offhandedly as he tore open a huge bag of peanut M&Ms.

Daven stared aghast at him, the serious of the situation suddenly cloaking his heart in a frozen, tangible heaviness.

"For god's sake, Hank. It seems an odd choice to be so flippant about this."

"I can either be flippant, or I can be hysterical. Let's just try to stay positive, okay?" Hank replied quietly, mouth and hands full of chocolate. "Want some?"

"No, thank you."

Daven turned back to the packet with a deep sigh and quietly signed the papers. Much to Hank's relief, he didn't notice the clause that automatically turned custody of the boys and all his property and finances over to him at 11:59pm on March 31 if Hank wasn't free by then.

A few minutes later the enormous deed was done, and both men didn't know what to say to each to other.

"Thanks, Dav," Hank managed, heart lodged firmly in his throat. "Want to stay for dinner?"

 "I would like to, but my appetite is completely gone and I'm fairly certain you wouldn't enjoy my company right now. Thank you, though. Can we please talk in the morning?"

"I'm busy until noon or so. I'm sorry that I've been keeping you out of the loop. My four informants are meeting me here in the morning. It's crucial that their identities are protected, so I have to keep you out of it."

Daven shrugged. "You don't think Harmon will suddenly notice four of his people have disappeared from the office in the same week you recalled your agents? They won't stay secret for long."

"You're right. But I'd like to just talk to them alone, okay? I'll fill you in later and give you names so we can relocate them to our office. Call me at noon."

"Alright. Goodnight, Hank. I implore you not to give up yet. We've still got a long way to go with our investigation."

Hank nodded. "I know. Thank you. Um, on another subject altogether, do you remember that code to dial when you want your caller ID to be blocked?"

"I think it's star six seven. Why?"

"I just want to make a quick call to a restaurant but don't want my number to get out again. Thanks."

Daven left, and the moment the door shut, Hank snatched up his phone and dialed Harmon, taking care to block his number first.

Denver, Colorado

Harmon usually never answered unknown callers, but cell service at the Denver airport was infamously spotty, and with his lack of technical savvy he thought perhaps some kind of signal weakness was preventing the number from coming through. He did make sure not to say his real name, however...just in case.

"Hello?"

"Hi, handsome. How's your day been?"

"Who is this?"

"Who do you think?" answered the gruff voice on the other line.

Harmon found himself breathless all of a sudden as he got into his car on the tarmac. "Ah. If you're calling to threaten me again-"

"Not at all," Hank replied easily. "On the contrary, I'm calling you with a friendly reminder."

"You're not in the position to be reminding me of anything right now, *friend.*"

"Oh, I think I am. Code 314.3 of the political integrity code prohibits our parties from releasing names of our own employees, as well as those of each other's parties. Speaking of

239

which, you're going to be missing four people at roll call tomorrow. Just wanted to give you a head's up."

Harmon felt his throat go dry. "Your informants, I gather."

"Right on. As a *friend*, I just wanted to make sure you didn't get your little hands slapped for doing something so silly and preventable like publicizing who they were to anyone outside the need-to-know group."

"Duly noted."

"Good, good," Hank answered, his tone obnoxiously chipper. "Well, you're welcome. I'm looking forward to reconnecting with them tomorrow. No doubt they'll have a lot to tell me about their time spent in your wonderful organization, so thank you for confirming you'll help keep them safe. Have a nice evening."

"Hank, wait-"

The line went dead.

CHAPTER FOUR

Tuesday night, Bancroft House

"Well, that was a really stupid thing to do, asshole," Theo said matter-of-factly after Floyd finished explaining where he'd been and why his eyes were red, even though he did feel sorry for his brother in spite of it all.

Floyd threw his hands up in frustration and flopped around on Theo's bed to face the wall. "I knew you wouldn't have any sympathy, bitch. I'm freakin' sixteen years old, but he keeps treating me like I'm twelve!"

"More like five, but act like a dumbass and you're going to get your dumb ass whooped. It's not rocket science."

"Okay, Theo. You can stop now." Floyd didn't say it, but he wasn't mad about the consequences he'd just received; he was only indignant about being kept so isolated from the outside world. Furious about what he had just learned from the mouth of someone who didn't even know him.

"Here he comes," Theo said quietly, reaching over to mute his video game as the sound of a heavy footfall on the stairs made its way into the bedroom. Floyd didn't move, he only stiffened as Hank entered the room like a shark searching for his next prey.

"Dinner's ready, boys. Sorry it's late, I had to meet with Uncle Dav. Go downstairs," Hank said tiredly, keeping his eyes on his oldest. Theo went, but Floyd didn't move, as Hank expected. He waited a long moment, then sat down next to him and rested his arm on Floyd's side, patting him reassuringly.

"Okay. You can stop pouting now, kiddo. It's over and done with."

"It's not over," Floyd muttered.

"Excuse me? Did you not hear me say you're forgiven?"

"But I haven't forgiven *you* yet. You said I could watch, then I couldn't. You're an Indian giver."

Hank's heart fell a little, and his resolve hardened even further as he took a tight grip on Floyd's forearm. "Don't use that phrase ever again. It's racist. And I thought you understood where I was coming from in regards to the news. Do I need to repeat myself?"

"Please don't," Floyd grumbled as he shifted his weight around into a somewhat more comfortable position. "Or else I'll be forced to poke out my own eardrums, I swear."

Hank held back a snigger. Floyd had a tendency to be unintentionally amusing when he was this pissed, which was doubly unfortunate because also he hated being laughed at. Especially when he was angry. It was a fine line to tread, so Hank tried to inject some lightness into his tone without going overboard.

"Well, we don't want that, it's messy. I won't say a word. What did you learn from your little expedition today, then? Any juicy news about myself that I should know? I mean, sometimes Hailey knows what's up before I do, so maybe you can give me a briefing of what's going on in the life of Hank Bancroft."

"Don't know. I only got to watch like five minutes before Avery narced on me."

"What did you learn in those 5 minutes?"

Floyd hesitated, not knowing whether his dad was baiting him or genuinely trying to find out what the headlines were. His tone was bitter when he finally answered. "The Santa Anas are blowing."

Hank glanced out the window automatically; it was pitch dark but he could easily imagine his palm trees tipping over quite a bit from the infamous windstorms that periodically sapped the sanity out of Los Angeles residents for days at a time

"Air moves sometimes. Huh. Who would've thought?" Hank was secretly relieved; that meant he wasn't at the top of the ticker for once. *But not for long.*

"That really hurt, dad," Floyd complained in a mumble as he rubbed his backside; his efforts to dull the sting becoming more fruitless with each passing minute.

Hank was not sorry, not one bit. "It was supposed to. Kiddo, you knew exactly what was going to happen the moment you turned on that television. Did you really expect me to go easy on you when we've been through this twice before? Stop pouting and come down to dinner."

"I'm not eating again until you let me watch the news on my own."

"Since when did you start giving me ultimatums? I don't think so." He gripped Floyd's shoulder as he stood. "Attitude ends now. Up. I won't tell you again. Food's getting cold."

Philadelphia Airport - Tuesday evening

"You know, I've been thinking," began Salome as she stuffed her carry-on suitcase into the overhead bin. "You're exactly right. We need to ask our caller what that mobile phone number is. Or was, rather. I mean we already have it, right? So whether or not he gives it to us, he's in the same boat as far as possibly being tracked goes."

"I'm not following, sorry."

Stewart sat down in his window seat, glad for once that he didn't have a stranger seated next to him all the way to Denver. He wanted to talk to Salome. Needed to talk to her and find any way out for Hank.

Salome dropped down into her seat and deftly snapped the seatbelt shut. "I mean we tell him we have the number, but unless he can confirm it's the same one, we are no longer taking his calls seriously. When you think about it, that makes the tracking issue irrelevant."

"Shit or get off the pot, like I said," Stewart answered wryly.

"Precisely. When he calls back, you have to ask him. Give him part of the number outright so he knows we're not bluffing, and ask him to finish it. If he can't, we simply won't take his calls any longer. End of story, investigation over and whatever he's trying to gain now is all lost."

"Right. The problem is, I almost don't want him to be able to verify it. That would mean he's not lying."

"I know," Salome agreed glumly. "Just keep in mind that Janet deserves justice, and it's our duty to get it for her. Let's just hope he calls back sooner than March 31."

Bancroft House - same evening

"Boys," Hank said heavily, with a rapidly pounding heart as they finished off the last of their burgers. It had taken him almost half an hour to get up the courage to even address the matter at all. "I have to go to Philadelphia on Monday, and I'll likely be there all week. Uncle Dav is going to come and stay with you guys here. I fully expect a glowing report of your perfect behavior when I get back."

Floyd's eyes were wide, and he was frozen in a state of lifting a chip to his mouth. "You've never been gone that long. What's going on?"

Tell him the truth. "There are some meetings I have to go to," he said with a dry throat, absurdly self-conscious of how stilted he sounded. "There's also an investigation ongoing that

I'm a part of, which requires me to answer and ask lot of questions. It will take time due to all the people involved."

"An investigation about what?"

"My, my. Aren't we demanding today? An investigation, period. That's all you need to know for now."

"I want to know everything," Floyd insisted stubbornly.

"Too bad," Hank replied simply, cocking his eyebrows with a *don't push me* expression.

Floyd put down his chip and stood up quickly; it reminded Hank of all the times Maurice had suddenly stopped in his tracks to wonder if he had unplugged something or another.

"What are you doing?" Theo asked, puzzled.

"I don't feel good." He all but ran off, and Hank followed him to his room while Theody remained seated in confusion, staring after them with a pickle hanging out of his mouth.

"Floyd? What's wrong with you?" Hank asked irritably as the boy dodged him several times on the stairs. He obviously wasn't upset about his stomach. "Stop."

Floyd ran into his room and slammed the door, and locked it behind him. In the past, that would have caused Hank to all but blow a gasket. But he had his keys in his pocket, so he calmly took them out and opened the door. Floyd was in the bathroom, sitting on the edge of the tub with his face in his hands, and Hank shut the door and sat down placidly on the toilet next to him.

"Did the food make you lose your mind on top of making you sick? Don't you ever slam the door on me again, much less lock it."

"Mmmm," Floyd replied noncommittally, shoving his chin deeper down into his jacket.

After about thirty seconds of nothing but silence and heavy breathing, Hank had a feeling he knew what the real problem was and braced himself as he asked quietly, "The news. Was it really five minutes of talking about the Santa Anas?"

Floyd didn't answer at first, but he shook his head after some hesitation. *Fuck.*

"Okay. Tell me exactly what you heard. It may not be accurate and you could be getting yourself all upset over nothing."

"Yoone gaijins cical prisad cax aded."

Hank reached up and pulled Floyd's hands away from his face. "I didn't catch that. What?"

"Nothing," the stricken teenager amended.

"Floyd," Hank admonished, fighting back his own panic and dread. "It's important to me that you get the truth directly from the source, rather than some half-assed reporters. What did you hear?

Floyd ignored the question again. "If you really go to jail, does Uncle Dav become our new dad?"

Hank's pulse started thudding painfully at his temples. "Don't jump to conclusions, and please tell me you didn't breathe a word of this to Theo."

"Of course not. But does he?"

"Just try to relax. You don't even have the facts yet. Tell me what-"

Hank watched aghast as his son turned and threw up in the tub several times. He patted him on the back reassuringly until he was done, then handed him a towel from the etagere. Floyd snatched it out of his hands.

"I told you so," Floyd said frankly as he wiped his mouth. He was calm. Too calm.

"That you didn't feel good? I'm sorry. I'll go get you something for your stomach."

"No. I meant...that you should have quit your job a long time ago. You wouldn't listen." Floyd shook his head again. "You never listen."

Ouch. Hank stared at his oldest in consternation. "Floyd, this is really not helpful. Are you alright? In any pain? Do you need to go to the doctor?"

The boy tipped his head against the wall, his eyes glassy and moist, staring at nothing. "No. I told you so," he repeated softly. "I *knew* it was too late."

Hank rubbed his temples vigorously. This was all going to hell in a hand basket, and there was nothing he could do about it.

No way to placate his son or make this any better. All he could do was acknowledge his increasing irritation at Floyd for disobeying his orders not to watch the news. At least the boy's color was coming back into his cheeks.

"Alright, you seem fine. You're sixteen now, as you keep reminding me, so if you want to discuss this as adults then we should do it. I'll tell you as much as I can. Let me know when you're ready,"

Floyd stood up a little shakily, but self-assured and confident, having collected himself admirably in record time. "I'm fine, sir. I don't need to talk, but thank you for the offer."

"Right. Well, it's only seven-thirty. Maybe you'll change your mind. Do you have homework?"

"I already did it, sir."

Hank fought the urge to roll his eyes. "Stop with the *sir* thing, Floyd. I hate when you resort to theatrics. I don't want to fight with you, especially over something as important as this. Go do something constructive, or educational, or-"

"Something educational? Like watching the news?" Floyd retorted mockingly.

Hank eyed him dangerously. "You're one more smart remark away from me taking off my belt again, kiddo," he warned quietly.

That was all it took to set Floyd straight; he swallowed hard and forced himself back in check again. Hank saw the fight drain out of him instantly, his eyes soft again. *There, that's better.*

"Thank you. If you really feeling alright, go drink a glass of water. Then it's bedtime and lights out. You need rest. We'll talk some more tomorrow."

"I'm fine." Floyd sighed as he went...but at least he went at all, Hank told himself.

This day was a fucking nightmare.

Bancroft House - Wednesday - 8:30am

Floyd was still nauseated and pale the next morning, so Hank let him stay home from school with the caveat that he was restricted to his room until 11:30am. That was because the informants arrived precisely as scheduled at 8:30, and Hank sat them all down nervously in the library and locked the door. Before saying a word, he walked around handed them all water bottles. They looked exactly as anxious as he felt.

"Welcome back to Los Angeles, team," he said carefully as he sat down and pulled the cap off his favorite pen and flipped open his notebook. "You've obviously already realized your presence will be missed in Denver, but Harmon's been warned not to name names. At any rate, since you went under pseudonyms, nothing should happen even if he does. Thank you again for your services. No matter what happens in the next three hours, you are all guaranteed a full relocation package, a job in the organization, and compensation for your little side job. So let's get to it and not waste any time. Mick, I'll start with you since we've spoken most recently. What's been happening in the legal department these days?"

The man cleared his throat twice before he could speak. "It's been quiet, Mr. Bancroft. Ever since Harmon got his last warning and censure, he's been stopping most litigation and offering settlements to almost everyone just to clear the slate. I don't believe anything's going to be pending that's going to be of help to you right now. But I did happen to be one of three people who had access to the papers filed against you, and learned something interesting right off the bat."

Hank sat up straight, forgetting all about writing anything down. "What's that?"

"He's got a...maybe we should speak in private?"

"No. I trust you all implicitly. Go ahead."

"Yes, sir." Mick opened his briefcase and pulled out what looked like maybe a couple dozen pages stapled together and looked around the room. "I...let's just say I trust you all implicitly, as well. We've been through a lot in the past seven or eight years. Anyway, I had a feeling we'd be recalled, so I took a copy of the attorney-client privileged draft complaint. It will help you mount your defense far ahead of the trial."

Hank didn't move, not that he could even if he wanted to. He cocked his head towards the back of the room. "There's a shredder in the corner. Feed it in there, and leave this room. You should have never-"

"Sir, I haven't read it myself, I just took-"

Hank's voice was like ice and fire all at once. "Stop talking. You should've *never* brought that here. I ought to turn you in myself. Come with me, please. Leave that face down on the chair for a moment. Nobody touch it."

Mick did, and stood up somewhat unsteadily as Hank led him directly across the hall and into his study.

"I'm so sorry, Mr. Bancroft. I meant well. Please don't-"

"Did you make a second copy?" Hank interrupted quietly after he'd shut the door behind him.

Mick looked like he didn't want to answer, but Hank asked again, and he nodded grimly. "Yes. It's in a secret pocket in my briefcase."

"Good. Shred the one on the chair in front of the others. I don't care how much we trust them, we're keeping this to ourselves. As you leave the house, place the other copy in the drawer of the side table by the front door. And even though I'm going to give you a big fat bonus for it, don't ever do this again. Got it?"

Mick nodded, so they went back into the room, and he dutifully picked the papers back up and fed them into the shredder.

"Thank you, Mick," said Hank coldly, resuming his authoritative demeanor and throwing eye daggers at the man. "We'll pretend this never happened. Please confirm there are no other existing copies."

"No, sir," the man replied shakily. "You can look through my briefcase, if you'd like. In fact, please do so that there's no suspicion later. It would make me feel a lot better."

"I won't, since it's my ass on the line. Pamela, would you do the honors?"

Pamela obviously didn't want to, but she complied and searched it thoroughly in full view of the others. Much to Hank and Mick's relief, she did not find the hidden pocket.

"It's clear, sir," Pamela finally declared.

"Good. Then this incident is forgotten and forgiven. You may leave now, Mick."

The man silently packed up his things while the others watched breathlessly. On the way out he muttered, "I'm sorry," once more. Just loud enough for everyone to hear. Hank nodded approvingly, then looked around the room and took a deep breath.

"Alright. Don't repeat his mistake, ladies. No more felonies in this room. If you have any, keep them to yourself. Who'd like to go next?"

Seditionists Headquarters, Los Angeles - 9am

"Tell me you found something, Taylor. Anything."

Taylor handed the report to Rupert. "The number comes back as disconnected on December 26. It's not traceable, unfortunately. I've been working on it for 16 hours straight and…nothing."

Daven took the report away from Rupe. "There's *nothing* we can do? At all?"

Taylor shook her head. "Maybe one day the technology will give us the ability, but right now it's a dead end. The only option would be to check the surveillance footage of every single cell phone store in the 303 area code. There are 435 of them, and we don't even have the time frame in which the phone was first activated. Needle in a haystack, gents."

Rupe shrugged. "Well, maybe the FBI can figure it out. Let's get back to work, then. Thanks, Taylor."

Urbane Headquarters, Denver - 9:30am

Salome carefully studied Colbert's face and body language while Stewart falsely claimed to have two surveillance videos on the subject, as well as a confirmed phone number and voice recording.

The big man didn't show any signs of distress at the news. Not a single tell, nothing to indicate he was in the least bit alarmed at the suspect being unveiled. If anything, Colbert looked completely bored by the proceedings altogether.

He's not involved, Salome silently concluded with sudden clarity and reluctance. Harmon wasn't responsible, either, that much was already certain. She knew with just one glance that

Stewart was thinking exactly the same thing based on Colbert's lack of reaction:

Fuck...what now?

Bancroft House, 10am

"Hey buddy," Avery said as he rose from his desk when Floyd came down the stairs. "You feeling any better yet?"

Floyd was putting on his jacket and backpack. "I'm fine. Take me to Rupert's house."

Avery looked at him askance. "No. You're supposed to be in your room until 11:30. Back upstairs, and get a move on."

"Or what? You'll narc on me again?" Floyd challenged rudely. "You used to like me."

Avery tipped his head to the side slightly, willingly allowing the deep hurt and frustration he felt to show on his face and in his voice. He was simply done with this kid lately.

"You're right, I used to like you. Back when you listened to me and let me help you out. I don't feel bad about narcing on spoiled brats who disrespect me, though. Are you going back upstairs, or not?"

The deeply ashamed look on Floyd's face at this unprecedented outburst satisfied him immensely.

"I'm sorry," Floyd said hoarsely. "I don't....I didn't mean it."

"Then go upstairs," Avery responded sternly, worried that Hank would suddenly exit his library and come upon this little scene.

"Okay. Sorry." Floyd turned and ran back up the stairs. It wasn't until he let out his breath that Avery realized he'd been holding it. Two hours later when he returned to his desk in the hallway, he was pleasantly surprised to find a brief thank you note from Floyd on his keyboard. He read it, then glanced aside into the dining room, where the teenager was just sitting down to lunch with his dad. Floyd was watching him, so Avery smiled a little and gave a thumbs up.

Floyd nodded and turned his attention back to his father. He was a good kid, Avery knew. Always had been

CHAPTER FIVE

Wednesday afternoon

Urbane Headquarters - Denver - 1pm CST

Harmon was eager to get this meeting over with, and not just because he hated the FBI. Stewart, in particular, who always seemed over-eager to push his buttons. But this time it was Salome who was testing his patience with her long checklist of open-ended questions. They seemed to be almost near the end of list, much as Harmon was near the end of his patience. He was also starving.

Salome didn't seem aware of her interviewee's desires whatsoever, and she persisted without pausing. "Next. You're aware you have Seditionist informants in this specific office, I understand."

"Had. Yes."

"And if they become known, it's against the law for you to release their names outside of a need-to-know...wait a minute. What do you mean, *had?* Past tense?"

Harmon frowned. "Hank assured me there were only four, and they would be gone today and not replaced. We have exactly four employees missing today. He keeps his word, if nothing else."

Salome could feel Stewart's eyes on her. "I see. When did you have this discussion, exactly? It's strange you never mentioned it before."

"Because I was waiting for you to ask. We talked last night, very briefly."

"You called him?"

"No. He called my cell. Around seven-thirty, I think. Something like that."

"You're just as forbidden as he is to communicate. Why did you pick up the phone?"

"Didn't know it was him. He blocked his number."

Salome tapped her pen on her teeth.

"Show me."

Harmon pulled out his mobile phone, scrolled down to the "calls received" list, and handed it to her wordlessly. She looked at it, wrote something down, then handed the phone back.

"Thank you. So, you've figured out who the four employees are, correct?"

The man scowled and nodded. "Their identities will remain confidential, I assure you."

"Excellent. Will you please excuse me for a moment? I need to confer with my colleague to see if there's anything else we need to ask. Then we'll be out of your hair."

"Certainly. Please use my conference room." He stood up and opened a door for them, which led to a small conference room with no other doors. Very private, but they still walked over to the far side of the wall in an abundance of caution.

Salome whispered, "I thought you told Hank not to contact him?"

Stewart flailed his hands in frustration. "I did, about an hour prior to him doing it. I even sent him an email shortly afterwards saying the same. He knew better."

"Christ," Salome muttered. "And Harmon's just sitting there, smug as a Cheshire cat with that same knowledge. I'm going to strangle Hank."

"Not if I get to him first. At least there's no *actual* proof he called."

"Right. So do you believe Colbert is involved with this whole payments business?"

Stewart shifted uncomfortably from one foot to the other. "Based on his body language alone? No, I saw nothing to indicate he has anything at stake here, other than obvious satisfaction at watching Hank go down. Makes my stomach turn."

"Mine too. This is such a cluster fuck."

Stewart sighed heavily. "Salome, I think we should ask about those four employees. What departments they were in, at least. If even one of them had access to all that leaked information, it could be damning. I'm hoping none of them did, but I'd rather know sooner than later."

"You're right. Anything else?"

"Not that I can think of."

They went back in the room and sat down. Salome purposely didn't touch her pen or notebook to ask the next question. "Harmon...about these four employees. Were any of them high-level enough to have access to the information that got leaked about your 20 executives?"

Harmon scoffed. "High level? Hardly. All four of them are administrative assistants. Unfortunately, one was assigned to the legal department and had access to some of the documents we filed yesterday in regards to the case."

Despite his horror, Stewart had to take a private moment to appreciate and admire the fact that Hank had managed to install not one, but *four* assistants within the company. Not executives, as he had suspected. It was a brilliant stroke. After all, Hank himself was the one who single handedly brought the country to its knees while working as a lowly, underpaid office clerk for Colbert. He knew firsthand what kind of access to information these positions really had. And how no one would ever suspect their lowest-level employees could even wield such power.

Salome seemed to be thinking the same, but she kept the conversation on track. "Right. So to repeat the question, did any of them have access to the information that got leaked?"

Colbert answered for his boss. "Collectively, yes. Each of them had access to some part of it."

"I see." Salome redirected her attention back to Harmon. "So you seem to think the four were working together. Were they close friends, by chance?"

"How would I know?"

"Right. There's very little we can do without proof of an actual crime. If you find any, let us know. Do you have any further question before we take our leave?"

Harmon looked at Colbert. "Will you give us a moment, please?"

Colbert scowled, but complied. Stewart and Salome held their breaths as Harmon leaned back in his chair and studied them aggressively for a few moments.

"I want to be clear on something, just in case it's been lost in translation. I don't give a fuck about Hank Bancroft after all the grief he's given me in ten years. I've almost lost my job because of him how many times? But that doesn't mean I'm taking any pleasure in watching this all go down. Even if he's guilty as hell, this is not something that satisfies me on any level."

Stewart nodded. "We know. No one's accusing you of enjoying this."

"What I *do* care about are his sons. I have children of my own, as you know. Are we going to be able to wrap this up by March 31, or not? Because you said we could, but this...this is taking us nowhere fast. I'm getting concerned that you might have misled me."

Salome took a deep breath. "You were not misled, but that brings me to the next question. You have some work to do in regards to constructing your plea bargain. Why haven't you started it yet?"

Harmon scoffed. "There's one small detail that you might have overlooked. How am I supposed to get Hank to agree to it if you won't let me talk to him and explain my reasoning?"

"You won't. You *cannot* contact each other again, period. That's the law."

"What am I supposed to do, then? By the time I can talk to Daven and Rupert, *they* won't be able to speak to Hank, either. He'll never agree to it, and I can't exactly write in there what I'm planning to do with the deeds or else everyone will see right through this whole charade."

Salome shrugged. "Then I suggest you choose your 3rd-party negotiator wisely. Someone Hank trusts would be a good start. That's how you can get through to him after Monday."

Harmon all but threw up his hands. "Are you nuts? Hank would never trust anyone I'd be willing to name as my negotiator."

"Figure it out. I can't get involved in your strategy. We're supposed to remain neutral, and that's what I intend to do."

"You..." Harmon looked irate, but his voice was even. "You all but *forced* me to do this. I didn't want to take it this far. And now you're just going to just leave and tell me to *figure it out*?"

Salome looked unmoved. "You made your bed, and now you have to lie in it. Nobody asked you to come to Philadelphia in the first place. Any further questions?"

"No." Harmon stood up, conversation over. "With all due respect, feel free to get the fuck out of my office now."

"That went well," Stewart muttered as they got in their car to go to the airport. "Can I ask you something? With all due respect, of course," he added facetiously, in mock salute to Harmon.

"Of course."

"Why did you...why did you taunt him at the end? Maybe taunt isn't the right word. I was just surprised that the conversation took such an ugly turn."

"Unpleasantly surprised, I gather," Salome remarked with a smirk. "You seemed to be upset with me."

"Yes, actually. I feel like that did more harm than good. Do you mind letting me in on your reasoning, so that we're on the same page?"

"Sure. It's simple. I'd much rather have him pissed off at us than have him pissed off at Hank. Whose side do you think he's on now?"

“Oh.” Stewart smiled widely. “ *Oh* . Nice.”

“Right. What’s that saying you like so much?”

“Shit or get off the pot?”

“Yes. He hasn’t done a damn thing since we last talked on Monday. Bet you anything he’s already making a list of possible negotiators to help Hank, even as he’s cursing at our backs. I may have given him a stroke, but it was exactly what he needed to hear.”

“I’m impressed.”

“Thank you. Call Hank, if you don’t mind. Let him know we’ll be at the office by 2:30. I want to meet with Rupert first, then Daven. That will leave Hank for last and give us all the time we need.”

Stewart pulled out his phone. “I’ll bet you a million bucks he coached Daven on what to say to us about those receipts. Or rather, what not to say.”

“I don’t bet on bargains, sorry.”

Urbane HQ - Denver - one hour later.

“Lester Boyd. Harmon here. Long time no talk. How have you been?”

Startled silence. “Holy...I mean, hello, sir. Fine, thanks. You?”

"Good, good. Listen, I need you to come to Denver to meet with me. I can't explain over the phone. Are you available Friday? I'll send my plane for you."

"Yeah, uh…got some meetings to cancel, nothing major. Is everything alright?"

"Can you get to Richmond airport at…let's say 6:30am? It's a three-hour flight. That will put you in our offices by 8am my time, and we'll make sure to get you back in time for dinner."

"That works. Is there anything I need to prepare or read up on, or anything?"

"No. Just be at the Signature terminal as agreed. We'll talk when you get here, but not until then. Understood? And obviously, this is extremely confidential. I'll call your boss now to make an explanation for your absence."

"Great, thanks. See you Friday."

"Good. Thank you."

CHAPTER SIX

Wednesday afternoon

Bancroft House

As much as Hank wanted to eat lunch, his anxiety entirely prevented him from achieving that goal. He kept busy pushing his food all around his plate and not accomplishing much otherwise, except adding to his worries. Floyd was in the same boat but Hank had never been the type of parent to insist that his children eat everything, or not waste food they were given; in fact he was quite the opposite and had a standing agreement that Chef could indulge them with whatever they wanted. Except for Theo's sugar addiction, of course, which Hank kept under tight control. It was a wonder neither of the boys weighed 300 pounds at this point, but both of them were lean and generally made good choices.

"How are you feeling?" Hank asked suddenly, breaking the silence.

"Fine, dad, thank you."

"Not hungry?"

"Not really."

"Me either." Hank poked at his chicken again and let his thoughts wander to the lawsuit papers in the side table. He couldn't decide whether he should read the illicit document before or after he met with the FBI. If he waited, he couldn't give away anything to indicate that he had them...which is what he was afraid of if he did read them in advance. But then again, knowing in advance what he was up against could help-

"Can I go to Rupert's house after this?" Floyd queried.

"No."

That was the end of that. Floyd started to roll his eyes but stopped at his dad's warning glance, and got up to take his dishes into the kitchen instead.

"Sit down, Floyd." His tone was telling, and the teenager took a deep breath as he complied.

"Dad, I really don't want to talk right now. I'm sorry."

Hank took a huge gulp of root beer. "Wasn't asking you to talk. I have a meeting this afternoon that's going to determine what happens come Monday. Honestly, at this point, I have no idea what the hell to expect. But I promise I'll keep you in the loop, okay? I don't want you watching the news because it's going to scare the shit out of you. They love to exaggerate everything, and even lie outright, and you know that."

"So I've heard." Floyd's reply was obviously meant to be humorous based on his expression, which was not challenging, so Hank let it go without comment.

"I'm going to leave the house at two for the office, and I'm taking Avery with me. I trust you not to disobey me again."

Floyd looked down at his hands. "I won't. What time will you guys be back?"

"Around six. Come to think of it…do you want to go see a movie while I'm gone?"

"Wow, dad. You're letting me skip school to go to the movies? Are you feeling okay?"

"Just marvelous." Hank stood up and folded up his napkin, and Floyd followed suit. "I'll tell Brittany to take you to the Cineramadome." That was where the Bancrofts were allowed to use the back entrance and go in and out of movies unseen. "Then I need to go to my study and prepare for this meeting."

"Who are you meeting with?"

Raised eyebrow. "Floyd."

"You said you'd keep me in the loop," Floyd reminded him politely.

Hank sighed. "Right. I did. The FBI, and Rupe and Dav."

He worried Floyd would throw up again, but the boy merely nodded. "Okay. Good luck, dad."

"Thanks, kiddo. Go change."

Hank ventured downstairs to talk to Brittany, and stopped in his tracks when he saw she was watching the national news. Naturally, his own face was plastered onto the screen.

"Oh god," he moaned as he walked in. She jumped up and grabbed the remote to mute it, as if she were just as forbidden to watch as Floyd. But on the contrary, all the guards were expected to be on top of the latest whispers about their boss and they often had the news running all day down in the basement. Usually with the captions on so it didn't drive them crazy.

"Sorry, sir," she said, swallowing hard.

"That bad, huh? Put it back on. And I've told you a hundred times not to apologize for doing your job."

He sat partially on her desk and braced himself for what he was about to hear.

- expected to defend himself against what appears to be multiple charges laid by the Urbanes, the details of which we do not yet have. Sources from inside the party state that at least one indisputable felony charge is pending, and a statement from the FBI is still yet to be released. Calls made to Rupert Aster, PR leader for The Seditionists, were not immediately returned. We'll come back to this story as it develops.

The shot changed to the front of the house - or walls and roof, rather - where a news media truck was parked at the bottom of the driveway. Hank had seen the top of its satellite dish on his way down the stairs. He crossed his arms.

"That wasn't too awful. What else were they saying?"

Brittany looked rather wild-eyed at the question. Hank never spoke about such things with his guards. Idle discussion amongst them about Hank's work life was strictly off-limits if it didn't relate to security issues, with special consequences for those who engaged in outright gossip - as Avery had recently found out when Hank docked him an entire paycheck for his comments at the hospital.

"Well…" she hesitated, then shut her mouth tightly as Avery rounded the corner and came into the office, stopping in his tracks at the sight of Hank.

"Sorry, boss. Didn't see you."

"Stay. Welcome to the party," Hank said wryly. "It's okay, Brittany. Just tell me."

"Boswin News is saying you'll be put in jail next week, but seem to have no idea why," Brittany replied shakily. "It's been breaking news all day, with no substance. Our local news hasn't said anything. The Denver news is going a bit nuts with speculation, but again, nothing confirmed."

Avery and Brittany both couldn't meet his eyes, Hank noticed. He didn't blame them. "They mention anything about me going to Philadelphia on Monday to be arrested?"

Both of them nodded hesitantly, but made no verbal reply.

Hank replied matter-of-factly, "What a historic occasion…first damned time they've ever told the truth. Whatever happens, your jobs are safe, so don't worry. Daven is going to stay with the boys while I'm gone, however long I'm gone. They'll need you. End of story. Brittany, can you take Floyd to the movies, please? Avery, I have to go to the office at two."

"Of course," they said together, and Hank made his exit abruptly, knowing he was being an ass by casually throwing out a shocking statement like that, but at least the incident made up his mind for him. He grabbed the papers out of the side table and made his way up to his bedroom with a newly hardened resolve.

Colbert's Car - Denver

"Hey, Colbert. Sorry I took so long to call you back."

"You shouldn't be calling me at all now that you're not working. How long did Bancroft suspend you guys?"

Yannick coughed in surprise, then amusement. "Suspend? That implies some kind of wrongdoing. We were placed on administrative leave. Paid, may I add? So I'm doing a lot better than you right now."

"Well it's a damned good thing you didn't go pick up those cashier's checks yourself. FBI has the surveillance video."

"Ha. Told you so. They can track anything. So what do you want me to do next?"

Colbert waited until someone passed behind his car and out of sight again before responding. "Not much you can do at the moment. How long are you kicked out of the office for?"

"No idea. And they're probably going to poly us all before they bring us back. Hope I can pass it twice. It was hard enough not breaking a sweat the first time around. Hey...how did you know they have the video?"

"Just got out of a meeting with the FBI. They also have the number you paged Hank with. They're all over him like white on rice, and he did exactly what I expected him to. Going to have me a visit to see the man in jail, finally."

There was a pause on the other line. "*Finally?* How long have you been planning this?"

Colbert smiled to himself. "Twelve years? Ever since he first stabbed me in the back. I have stories, my man. Stories for days. Hard to believe it's almost over."

Yannick bit the inside of his cheek. Something about this wasn't right, suddenly. Everything was...perhaps very wrong, perhaps not. Maybe he was just being paranoid.

"I see. So this isn't exactly all a business venture, then?" he asked lightly.

"All you need to know is that I've got more than enough cash to keep you going until it's done. And I'll be in touch again when I need something else."

"Don't you mean *we?*" Yannick asked quickly. "You and Harmon?"

"Of course." Colbert started a little when he looked into his rearview mirror and saw Umber come into the garage. "Got to go."

There was no getting out of the man seeing him, so Colbert quickly pretended like he was looking for something in his glove compartment. Umber, of course, would never miss an opportunity to be nosy, and he walked right up to his colleague with a smug look on his face.

"Hoy there. Sorry to interrupt. You've got a private office for doing that kind of thing, you know. Unless you're into the whole exhibitionism scene." He waved his hands around in a suggestive fashion on that last part.

Colbert got out of his car. "Not my thing. Just looking for my phone charger."

"Right. Well, if I didn't know better, I'd say you were up to no good out here."

"But you know better, right?"

Umber smiled. He was no fan of Colbert, but he had to tread lightly due to his BFF status with Harmon. "Of course. I'm off to lunch. Ta ta for now."

Seditionists HQ - Los Angeles

"Mr. Johansson?"

Dav hit his intercom irritably as he walked back into his office. "Yes?"

"Mr. Bancroft on the phone for you. Says he's been trying to call your cell."

"Put him through." He looked up at Rupert, who had followed him in after they had just eaten lunch together. "Want to stay, or…"

Rupe wanted to do anything but stay, but his curiosity got the best of him. "Yeah."

"Hey Dav. Did you get my email about the FBI coming to see you and Rupe at 2:30?"

"No, sorry. I've been at lunch."

Hank huffed in annoyance. "If you're going to ignore your cell, at least keep an eye on your damned emails. I've been trying to get a hold of you for an hour."

Daven crooked an eyebrow at Rupert. "I'm sorry, Hank. Rupert is here with me. They're coming at 2:30, you say?"

"Yes. Am I on speaker?"

"Yes."

"Okay. They're going to meet with you first, Rupe. Don't even ask me what the questions are going to be like because I have no idea. It's absolutely imperative that you don't try to act like you're hiding anything."

Rupert glanced at Dav, then back to the phone. "I have nothing to hide, Hank."

"Yeah, I know. But you guys haven't met Salome. If you hesitate on anything, or act like you're trying to spin your answer, she'll pick up on it and start to probe, and it's going to hurt like a son of a bitch. Be honest and candid. Don't fuck around with these guys even in the slightest. Dav, you remember what I told you the other day?"

The receipts. Hank had told him to lie, which was the opposite of what he was saying now. "Yes."

"Good. I'm going to be at the office by 2:30 and we'll talk some more then."

"Hank, why aren't we having our lawyers attend as well?"

Hank cleared his throat. "Yeah, that's the other reason I was calling. I just got off the phone with Brody, and I want him present in everything we do from here on out."

Daven scrunched up his nose. "Brody Camber? He's too young. He's...Hank, he's brand new."

"I agree, Hank," Rupert replied. "He's still got that deer in the headlights look every time someone asks him even the simplest of questions."

"Yeah. He also idolizes us all, and he's hellishly smarter than he looks. Ever had a conversation with him? You'd be surprised how tough it is to keep up."

"Hank-"

"Dav, I've decided on this, and you're not going to change my mind. Everything we say from here on out, he hears. Got it? And don't you dare tell me you're *the one in charge* again."

Rupert looked at Dav in surprise and mouthed, you said *that?* Daven shrugged a little, then turned his attention back to Hank.

"Yes, I hear you. We've got it. See you at 2:30, then?"

"See you then. I'm leaving in just a few." Hank hung up.

"Wow, Dav," Rupert said with a grin. "Way to take the ball and run with it. Was the water in his espresso machine even starting to cool off before you started pulling rank on him?"

Daven ignored him and frowned. "Brody Camber? *Seriously?*"

Hank was of course fully prepared for everyone to be staring at him when he arrived back at the office, but it still threw him off a bit and he felt little more than an exotic animal on display at the zoo as he followed Daven into a conference room.

"I won't lie," Dav said quickly as he shut the door. "Sorry, Hank."

Hank sat down and leaned way back in his chair, crossing his hands over his belly. "Well. You have to, Dav. It's official. I'm fucked."

"What do you mean? What's happened?"

Hank felt strangely calm under the circumstances. "Harmon recorded me in a conversation that can only be construed as blackmail. The FBI has the tape. No jury in their right minds, Urbane or Seditionists, would ever deem it otherwise. I'm looking at five years, minimum, no matter what happens with all the other charges."

Daven was nearly beside himself. "How could you...why would you...Hank, after all the..."

"I know. But what's done is done. So you're going to lie, and you're going to get out of the implication that you fucked around with the news of those receipts in order to avoid alarming our constituents and influencing the vote."

"That was never my intention!"

Hank huffed. "Fuck your *intention*. It doesn't matter. Perception is reality, and that's what you have to accept. Just like I have. Blackmailing Harmon was never my intention, either. It came out as a sarcastic comment in a moment of anger, yet here I am. Nobody is going to believe that you-"

Daven stood up to cut him off. "No, Hank," he said firmly. "There's got to be another way."

Hank closed his eyes for a long moment. When they reopened, Daven was deeply unsettled by the feeling that a stranger was staring back at him.

"If you don't lie, I'm going to lose the boys for a minimum of 20 years, because you will *never* be granted custody of them if you throw yourself onto your sword. You take yourself down, you take *them* down, too. Do you understand me, or not? I'm not sure how much clearer I can possibly be."

Daven shook his head and stared at the floor, unable to accept what he was hearing.

"Dav?" Hank prompted. "You're *going* to lie, I don't care how much it pains you. Consider it a punishment for fucking up with those receipts. *Then* you're going to take care of my boys and run this organization. That's what you signed up for the other day, and I expect you to honor that agreement. Are you hearing me at all? Feels like I'm talking to a brick wall."

Daven walked around the conference table in silence, sliding his finger thoughtfully along the back of every chair.

"Need an answer, Dav," Hank said a minute later. "By the way, Stewart and Salome have no idea I'm aware of the tape, so don't mention it."

"What? Then how do you know of it?"

Hank hesitated. "I can't tell you."

Daven threw up his hands in frustration. "For god's sake, Hank. I can't handle all of this right now. You know what? You ask too much of people sometimes. And this is...this is too much."

"I know. I'm sorry for that. But right now, I just need a yes or no answer at the very minimum. Are you going to lie to them, or not?"

The conflicted man in his trademark coat looked away for a minute - which felt like hours to Hank - then finally caught Hank's eye and nodded.

"Thank you," Hank breathed out in relief.

Daven turned and abruptly left the conference room without another word. Hank jumped when the door slammed, but he didn't move to follow his friend. He just sat there, mindlessly twirling his wedding ring around his finger in silence for a full hour, until the expected knock on the door announced the arrival of Stewart and Salome.

CHAPTER SEVEN

Seditionists Headquarters

Wednesday afternoon

"Hey guys," said Hank casually as a file of downturned faces piled into the conference room. "Bringing the whole gang, huh?" He moved aside to make room for Rupert, Daven, Brody, Salome, and Stewart around the table.

Stewart shut the door behind him, but didn't sit down.

"Hello, Hank. Sorry to visit you under these circumstances. Since you're all here and in one room, I wanted to quickly go over what's going to happen on Monday."

"The apocalypse?" Hank joked, not caring about the astonished side glances he received from Rupe and Dav.

Stewart didn't react; he knew Hank well enough to understand that he turned to black humor when he was nervous. "At exactly noon we'll send in an FBI tech to put a special tape across your office door that's illegal to breach. You'll have three hours *after* that to send out a press release, or have a press conference if you prefer, before you need to go to the airport. I would suggest that Daven release an additional statement immediately after your departure."

No one on the room seemed to be breathing all of a sudden, except for Hank.

"Understood. That sounds...very humiliating."

Stewart swallowed hard. "It's not meant to be. You're not going to be dragged out in handcuffs. It's literally just a guy in a suit who will be in and out in five minutes. You'll go to the airport on your own, and travel with whoever you want. We have no intention of turning this into a spectacle."

Hank smiled a little. "Wonderful. I'm looking forward to seeing what the inside of a Philadelphia jail cell looks like. If they're anything like the ones in Los Angeles, I'm in for a fun time. And probably dysentery."

Confusion clouded Stewart's expression at that statement. "Wait, Hank. Back up. We're not locking you up on Monday, for god's sake."

Hank heard Daven and Rupert finally breathe out together. "Oh. I thought...I mean, under arrest usually means 'in jail' to me."

Salome spoke up at this point. "It doesn't for you. You're literally the most famous person in the nation, hardly a flight risk. We'll let you stay in a hotel while the investigation is ongoing."

"I don't want special treatment," Hank lied.

"Trust me, you do. Besides, it's not your decision. I do want to add that before noon Monday, your organization is to maintain your silence and not speak to the media or make any statements." She looked around the room. "Mr. Johansson, Mr. Aster, any questions?"

Daven looked at Hank, but there was hardly any recognition in the glance. Dav was like a man defeated, and Hank knew it was because the lie had been told. He was profoundly relieved, no matter how much his friend hated him for it.

Rupert asked carefully, "When will the FBI be releasing details of the charges to the public?"

Salome replied, "That's something I need to discuss with Hank. He will have a lot of control over what gets said on Monday, depending on how he wishes to proceed. However, the FBI will craft the statement, not the Seditionists or the Urbanes. We have no intention of enabling any more public slap fights between your parties."

"Right," Rupert replied in obvious disappointment. "So you're saying that absolutely nothing is up to us from this point on, as far as PR goes."

"Untrue. Stewart just told you you'll have time to make a statement or a press conference between noon and three on Monday."

"Yeah, but that's after the fact. What about before? Excuse me for not appreciating the fact that we basically have to sit on our hands and let the rumors get out of hand while you two get to sit back and enjoy the show."

Hank snapped out of his reverie at the remark as Salome bristled.

"Rupe," he chided warningly. "Let it go. We'll talk later."

"Seriously, Hank? No. It's bullshit. You should see what the news is already saying. Which, by the way, I blame the FBI for." He turned to Stewart. "Why did you let this get leaked?"

"Rupe, if you don't shut up-" Hank began, but Salome held a hand up and everyone instantly settled down and fell quiet again.

"It's alright, Hank. I'll answer that. The Urbanes leaked it, not us. They have been reprimanded for it already."

Daven looked at Hank and scoffed. "Harmon wouldn't have done that," he muttered. "Not while he's barely holding on to his job."

"Colbert all the way," Hank agreed bitterly.

"Umber," put in Rupert sullenly. "Wolf in sheep's clothing, that one."

"But smarter than Harmon and Colbert put together, and that's not saying much," Hank refuted hotly.

"Let's settle down, please," Salome said firmly. The room went silent again. "If there are no further questions or arguments, we should move forward."

"No," replied Dav.

"This is bullshit," muttered Rupe under his breath.

"*Rupert*," Hank growled.

"No questions, Ms. Danby," Rupert amended politely, finally accepting that he was pushing Hank too far.

She nodded. "That will be all then. We'll be in touch again soon."

The door shut behind the two men as they left, and Hank looked at Brody for the first time. "You doing okay?"

"Yes, sir," the young man answered confidently.

"Do you wish to speak with me alone before we get started?"

"No, sir. But you need to tell me if you're uncomfortable answering a question *before* you answer it, not afterwards. I will ask for clarification, or have it rephrased or removed from the record. Don't say anything ambiguous, try to stick to yes and no and short explanations. Understood?"

"Yes, sir." He smiled wryly, idly wondering at the same time if Brody had also spoken to Dav and Rupe in such an authoritative manner. He could imagine both men being deeply offended by such unexpected sassiness from the new guy, and the thought amused him for a few precious moments.

Stewart opened his binder and picked up a pen. "Let's start with the subpoena. I had to rewrite it on the way to Los Angeles to include some revisions from Harmon. The very first thing I want to ask you is extraordinarily delicate, to say the least, and your answer could determine if there will be additional charges."

"Way to jump right in," Hank mused bitterly. "Not even a softball question first, huh? By the way, please accept my apologies for Rupert's behavior. I'll be having a word with him later."

"It's alright, Hank. He was fine in the interview, and he's not exactly wrong about his concerns. I'll revisit that issue with the president and see what he says."

"Thank you."

Stewart looked down at his notes, obviously feeling uncomfortable about the incident nonetheless. "Moving on. Harmon wants to lay additional charges of unlawful corporate espionage because he has evidence that one of your informants took copies of proprietary documents at your direction. If you're aware of any such actions, you need to tell me now. If we find out later, things are going to get ugly very quickly."

Fuck. Hank cleared his throat. "I know of one such action. One of my informants tried to bring me a copy of an Urbane's legal document on his own accord. I was incensed, to say the least, and made him shred it on the spot. I never laid a single finger on it, nor did I ask for anything like that to be taken."

Salome was stone-faced. "What kind of document?"

Fuck, again. "A draft of the original lawsuit complaint."

Stewart's jaw dropped. "That's...okay, that's a felony offense on its own."

"I'm not telling you who it was, so don't ask," Hank bristled.

Brody leaned over to his new boss and said quietly, "You don't have to tell them. Stay calm."

Hank took a deep breath and tried again to answer Stewart more diplomatically. "Yes. I'm aware it was against the law.

That's why I ordered it shredded immediately, in front of the group, so that four people could witness it. I never touched it."

Salome set down her pen and picked up a bottle of water. "Was this person searched for additional copies of the document, including his belongings?"

"Yes. None were found." That was the truth, technically. The secret copy had not been found when Pamela searched the briefcase.

Salome and Stewart exchanged glances, and Hank suddenly became deeply uncomfortable. He hadn't yet shredded the second copy; it was in a locked drawer in his desk at home. He vowed to immediately shred it after reading it once more, the moment he got home.

"Right, so…" Salome took a deep breath and drank some more water. "This is a problem, Hank. If I had your offices searched right now, would we find any other illicit documents?"

"I believe a warrant is required to search my offices. Is that correct, Brody?"

"Yes, sir."

"We're not searching anything," Salome clarified irritably. "I'm asking you a question, and I expect you to answer it."

Stewart caught the momentary flash in Hank's eye that indicated he was about to lie. Something he had never seen before in him, but had seen a thousand times before in other people. It was unmistakable.

"No. You won't find anything," Hank said steadily.

"Thank you. Moving on-" she stopped herself as her phone rang. "I'm very sorry, gentlemen, this is the president. I have to take it. Please excuse me."

She got up and disappeared into the private washroom that was connected to the conference room.

Stewart cleared his throat roughly and looked at the lawyer. "Mr. Camber, with Hank's permission will you please leave us alone for a moment? Thanks."

Hank nodded, and the young man left. Stewart looked Hank right in the eyes and didn't waver. "You're lying, Hank. Stop it, or I will seal up both your offices within the hour and you'll never get the chance to go back in. Do you understand me?"

Hank shifted uncomfortably in his chair. "Do it, then, if you're so convinced."

"You also told Daven to lie. Tell the truth from this point on, or I'll do it for you. We clear?"

Hank picked at a piece of loose laquer on the table and smirked. "Just from this point on, huh?"

Stewart sighed and shook his head. "Jesus Christ, Hank. You've really...I don't even know what to say. Get your lawyer back in here, please, before I say something I'll regret."

"Like what? What else could you possibly do to dig my grave any deeper?"

"You're trying to blame this on me? Unbelievable! I'm trying to help you, you stubborn fucker," Stewart hissed.

"I appreciate the support," Hank replied insincerely.

"Support that's *always* been there, by the way, if you'd ever take a moment to realize it. Haven't you ever noticed that everyone is on your side, except you? Even Harmon, for god's sake."

Hank sat up straighter. "Even Harmon? What the hell does *that* mean?"

"Forget it. I need to stop talking." Stewart got up and pulled open the door to let Brody back in before either of them could say anything else.

Hank just sat there in silence, feeling like he had received several gut punches in a row.

Your transparency will be the death of you.

I'm trying to help you, you stubborn fucker.

Everyone is on your side, except you.

Even Harmon.

"Well, that was fun," Hank said blandly as he strolled into Daven's office two hours after he had last seen him. Rupert was there, too, looking just as depressed as Hank felt.

Dav stood up. "What happened? Everything okay?"

"Ha. When was the last time anything was okay around here?"

"What's going to happen now?" asked Rupert with deep concern. "And please, no more joking."

"Well...I have four days to mount my defense for the charges that are coming on Monday. Blackmail, espionage, bribery, et cetera." He held up the subpoena. "It's all in here. The worst part is something I need to discuss with Daven alone, since it concerns the boys. Not that I don't want you in on the discussion, Rupe, but it truly doesn't make sense to-"

"It's alright," Rupert replied quickly. "I understand. You two definitely need to talk."

"Wait, let's not jump ahead," Daven insisted. "Besides the tape, Hank, what else do they have on you?"

"What tape?" Rupe asked, puzzled.

Hank rubbed his temples. "Guys, I...there's so much I need to tell you. Let's meet in the morning, okay? Clear your calendars. I've got to go home."

Hank didn't show up for the meeting on Thursday morning, so around 10am Daven took a car to the house to check on him. He already knew he was okay - as in alive and acting normally - because he had spoken to Avery already once he had gotten too concerned to wait any longer.

He was shocked to the core when the guard at the gate turned him away.

"Mr. Bancroft doesn't wish to have any visitors right now. Sorry, sir," said a clearly embarrassed Martinez.

"I...but...does he know it's me?"

"Yes, sir. Just spoke to him. He said to deny you entry."

You've got to be kidding me, Dav thought, stunned beyond description.

"Very well, I...thank you?"

He went back to the office and continued reading through all of Hank's old emails to find any way out of this mess. Again. Around 4pm, Rupert all but burst through the door.

"Dav! Turn on the news!" He ran to the television and quickly found the right channel, and Daven watched in stony, shocked silence as Hank appeared, walking confidently down the stairs of a private plane.

- arrived approximately half an hour ago at the private airstrip in New Castle, about 35 miles outside of Philadelphia. He was taken into custody by Salome Danby on the tarmac and is presumably being driven to FBI headquarters. A spokesperson for the FBI has stated that a statement will be released in two hours. As the story develops we will continue to update you.

The shot changed to a blurry aerial view of the town car, not moving in the standstill traffic on 95.

Daven couldn't breathe, or speak. He was vaguely aware of his cell phone ringing in his pocket, and strictly by force of habit he pulled it out mechanically and flipped it open.

It was pretty much the last person he could imagine having anything coherent to say to at the moment.

"Hello, Floyd."

"Uncle Dav? I'm sorry to bother you. When are you going to be home? I'm kind of freaking out."

Daven's chest tightened. "Right now, Floyd. I'm coming. Hold on."

CHAPTER EIGHT

Daven realized on the way to the Bancroft house that Floyd would probably be on the floor in a fit of hyperventilation when he arrived, but he didn't have the name or number to the boy's doctor, nor any idea of if or when she needed to be called. It didn't occur to him, though, that there were 17 other people in the household - plus Theo - who already had this information. He was used to living completely alone, so the thought of 20 people living under one roof, and who all looked out for each other, was completely foreign to him.

Therefore, when the gates to the estate opened up immediately upon the arrival of his town car (the guard didn't even bother to come out of the booth) he raced up to the front door with an oppressive feeling of barely controlled panic. Just like Floyd was feeling right now, he figured.

Brittany opened the door for him with a small smile, and Daven was surprised to find Floyd and Theo merely sitting on the couch, chatting and eating Cheez-Its like nothing was wrong. He hesitated, then went and sat down beside them, dreading what he was about to hear next.

"Hello, boys. How are you doing?"

"Not so good. Dad's not coming back," Theo blurted casually. "Want some Cheez-Its?"

Daven paused, shook his head, and studied Floyd's calm expression in deep confusion. "Floyd, I thought...you said you were freaking out, so I raced here as fast as I could. What's going on?"

"He wasn't freaking out," Theo answered with a mouthful of crackers. "He's fine!"

Floyd flipped to the next page of his comic book. "Yeah, I'm fine, Uncle Dav. We just got home from school. But dad's in Philadelphia for a little while, so he wants you to stay with us."

"Forever," interjected Theo with all the sullen attitude that only 12-year old boys were capable of.

"Maybe. Is that why you're home early?" Floyd asked offhandedly.

"I...sure. Yes." Daven turned to look helplessly at Brittany, whose expression offered no further clues. He turned back to the boys again. "When I find out what your dad is up to, I'll let you know. In the meantime-"

Floyd answered, "It's okay, we already know. He left you a note in the study with the rules we have to follow and stuff until he gets back." Floyd stood up and set down the box of Cheez-Its. "I'll show you where it is. Want something to drink first?"

"No, thanks."

Daven followed the teenager in wonder, feeling like he was in the Twilight Zone.

Until they arrived in the study, that is. It turned out Floyd had just been staying strong and unconcerned for Theo's sake;

once the door shut and he was alone with his "uncle," he completely lost it. Daven grabbed the box of Kleenex and caught Floyd just as the boy collapsed onto the couch and all but melted into him in tearful anguish.

After half an hour of calming Floyd, who thankfully didn't have a full-fledged panic attack, Daven slowly peeled himself off the couch and moved towards the manila envelope on the desk. It contained just a few sheets of paper topped by a handwritten letter on Hank's personal letterhead.

Floyd looked up at him questioningly from where he was lying listlessly, so Daven felt compelled to explain. "I don't think your dad meant for you to see this, based on the way it's sealed. I'm going to read it to myself first, okay? And I'll share with you what I can."

He only got a bare nod of a response, but that was enough, and he tore open the flap in fretful anticipation.

Dav - I left early for Philadelphia to make sure there was enough time to wrap this thing up before March 31. Enclosed is a list of all the standing rules I have for my sons. Floyd will follow them except for the one about not watching the news, so I've had all the televisions removed and locked in basement storage, except for the one in my bedroom sitting room, which is off-limits to the boys at all times. The door's passcode is 1182. Theo is pretty good on the whole, but watch his sugar intake carefully or he'll be bouncing off the walls 24 hours a day.

Also enclosed is a list of usernames and password for all of my online accounts, as well as the combination code to my safe. In there, you'll find more information which you can access on April 1 if I haven't returned by then. As for the investigation, you and Rupert are to stay out of it completely from now on unless you are asked specifically for information by the FBI. There's nothing else you can do at this point. Go back to work as usual and be the amazing leader that I know you are (need to work on your people skills, though...they're a little rusty.) I'll be in touch as soon as I can. Stay true. -Hank

Daven read it four times, his heart falling further and further into the abyss each time - then looked across at Floyd, who had sat up and was fully alert again.

"What did your dad tell you?" he croaked. "Try to remember exactly."

"Yes, sir."

"Don't call me sir."

"Sorry. Dad said he...he..."

Daven set the letter down and crossed back to Floyd, taking the chair directly across from him. "I know this is hard, but you have to tell me. I didn't have time to talk to him before he left, and his trip was a complete surprise to me."

Floyd nodded again, then wiped his eyes for the hundredth time. "Last night when he got home from work, he said he was going to be gone for a while. Like, maybe years. We..."

"Be strong, Floyd. Continue."

"Sorry, I'm trying. He said a lot, I don't remember it all. But I understand what's going on. He's going to Philadelphia to try to get exhilarated."

"Exonerated," Dav correctly, much less gently than he intended.

"Exonerated. But he doesn't know if he can. He doesn't think he can. He said...he'll probably be back before I graduate college."

Daven stood up, unable to bear another moment of sitting still. This was a bloody disaster.

"I don't really know what else to say, Uncle Dav," Floyd continued, fearing that the man was annoyed at him, rather than at his father. "We spent all our time since then just being together, and saying goodbye, but he still made us go to school this morning after he left for the airport."

That sounded just like Hank; as hardass as ever even under the most dire circumstances. "How is Theo doing?"

Floyd shrugged. "Fine. I don't think it's hit him yet. Anyway, then dad told me to call you at four o'clock because you'd know by then that he was in Philadelphia."

Daven nodded. "Anything else you need to tell me?"

"Not really. Not work related, anyway. He told us we had to listen to you and not give you a hard time. Which we won't, Uncle Dav, I swear."

"I know. Floyd, you look pale. Why don't you go lay down for a little bit in your room? I'll meet you there in a few minutes. Can you grab me something to drink? I don't care what. I need to call Rupert to let him know you're okay, and then I'll be right there."

"Okay. Can I take the dogs up with me?"

Daven hesitated. "What would your dad say to that?"

"He'd...." Floyd hesitated. "He'd say no. They aren't allowed on the second floor."

"Then no. Go on, I'll see you in a minute."

Floyd pulled himself up with a grumble and left, and Daven dialed his friend as fast as he could manage. Rupe picked up halfway through the first ring, his tone angry and hurried.

"What the fuck is going on, Dav? You disappeared on me and I've been dealing with a fucking five-alarm fire here without any kind of guidance or information. Thanks a lot for just bailing out and leaving me a hell of a mess to clean up."

"Calm down. I had to tend to Floyd. Turns out Hank left me a letter." Daven read the most relevant parts to him and was met with a deafening silence on the other end of the line.

"Rupe..?"

"Yeah. I'm here. What the fuck are we supposed to tell our constituents? Never mind them, what about our own employees? Not to mention the media. God damn it, Hank."

Daven put the letter into a drawer that had the key in the lock, then removed the key and put it into his pocket. "First of all, stop cussing at me. It's not helping. Secondly, don't worry about the media. We're under a gag order so they don't matter at the moment. Send out a company-wide email to let our employees know we'll have an all-hands meeting tomorrow at 10am."

"What are you going to say?"

"I have no idea yet. I'll call you back in an hour."

He almost put the phone back in his pocket, but changed his mind and left it on the desk. There were well over 50 missed calls already, and the buzzing reminders were annoying him. Theo wasn't in the living room when he passed through, so he went straight to Floyd's room and shut the door behind him. Then he pulled up a desk chair next to the bed. Floyd was facing the wall and under all his sheets and blankets.

"There's a root beer for you on my nightstand," he mumbled, and Dav reached over and took it gratefully.

"Thanks. Are you alright?"

"Yeah. Sleepy. I was up all night."

"Okay. Do you need anything?"

Floyd didn't say anything at first, but then he flipped onto his back and stared at the ceiling. "I got in trouble with Mrs. Aster today."

"For what?" Daven asked with a slight choking reaction; he was so *not* ready to be a father and this kind of talk made him extremely nervous.

"I wasn't very nice to her."

"Okay. You want me to talk to her and explain?"

"Yeah. Please."

Daven nodded. "Consider it done. Don't worry about it. You were under a lot of stress today."

"Uncle Dav?" Floyd said after a long moment of silence.

"Yes?"

"I think I'm going to throw up."

Me too, thought Daven as he reached behind him for the trash can.

The Nevermore

First and Last

CHAPTER ONE

FBI Headquarters - Philadelphia

Friday morning, March 19

"Okay, wait. I'm confused. You want to do *what*, Hank?"

"You heard me," Hank answered gruffly, and he felt rather than saw Brody stiffen next to him.

"Yeah, but...no." Stewart irritably threw down his pen, which he knew had not yet run out of ink but was still refusing to cooperate. "When I said you had a lot of input into our press release, that didn't include throwing *yourself* under the bus."

Hank shrugged. "I'm only concerned about the well-being of my party at this point. They must go on without me, and if the public thinks Dav and Rupe were involved in any of this bullshit, they'll defect in droves."

"I get it. But-"

Hank leaned forward in an almost threatening manner. "Apparently you don't, or you wouldn't be arguing with me about it."

Stewart didn't flinch and hardened his own tone in response. "In the ten years I've known you, I've *never* had to tell you not to lie. But here I am, saying exactly that twice in less than a week. There won't be a third time. The answer is no, and that's the end of it."

"For all you know, it's not a lie. I haven't even told you anything yet."

"If you truly expect me to believe that Daven forced you to turn yourself in, you're batshit crazy, Hank. I know you. And I understand why you'd want to deflect the blame from him, I really do. But you're jumping way ahead. We haven't even discussed the charges yet."

Hank stood up and began pacing around the room angrily. "The only charge that you'll ever be able to prove is blackmail. The rest is bullshit. You know that."

"No, I don't," Stewart said simply. Quietly. Almost hesitantly.

Hank turned to him with a shocked expression. "*What*?"

Stewart took a breath so deep that it hurt his lungs. "I *believe* it, but I don't *know* it. Not yet."

"Colbert does, but you don't fucking care about that," Hank retorted with a scoff.

"Mr. Bancroft," Brody said suddenly. "Please retain your calm demeanor."

Stewart nodded, keeping his eyes on Hank. "Agreed, thank you. You need to sit down and answer these items you ignored on the questionnaire, or else we can't proceed."

Hank sat back down and snatched the papers off the desk. "This phone number that I allegedly called three times around Christmas. What's it in regards to? I don't even know how to answer."

Stewart hesitated again, not wanting to fight or cause any reason for Hank to dislike him. "Look, just answer the question. Who was the number to, and why-"

"I don't *know*! Is it illegal to call phone numbers in Denver now? Why are you even suspicious about it at all? I think I deserve an explanation. No, scratch that. I absolutely, 100% deserve a goddamned explanation about why you want to know. And where is Salome, by the way?"

"Not here."

Hank bit back his retort that would have included a snotty reference to 'Captain Obvious.' "Yeah, I can see that. Is she listening to us?"

"No. As I mentioned, this conversation is being recorded, but she's not listening live. She'll hear it later. No one else is listening, either. This is you and me. Answer the question about the phone number, please."

Hank smiled sardonically and gestured with his palm up. "You first, please. I insist."

"A moment." Stewart lifted his phone receiver and dialed a number, which was obviously Salome's.

"Mr. Bancroft would like an explanation of why we're asking about the 303 number. Yeah, that one. May I tell him?" He paused, looked at Hank and shook his head slightly, then looked away again. "Thank you."

As he hung up the phone, he mouthed "sorry" so that it couldn't be heard on the recording.

"I can't tell you until after you answer the question to the best of your ability."

"No. Brody, what are my rights in regards to this matter?" He turned to look at the young man, who was bleary-eyed from being unprepared for the red-eye flight that Daven had hastily sent him on to intercept Hank.

"None that I'm aware of, sir. The question isn't out of line so far."

Hank sighed, giving up the fight at last. "The only thing I can think of was that it was Janet's cell phone number. She was delivering a document for me when she was killed. I called her once to my memory, though. Not three times, but that was three months ago. Maybe I only spoke to her once, but had to call three times to reach her? I don't know."

Stewart's heart skipped a beat as he looked down at the phone records. That would still not explain this. Then he pulled up Janet's profile again and matched it to one single call on Hank's records. He *had* called her once, he wasn't lying, but Stewart already knew that.

"You did call her once. It's right here, and it's not the same number. Any other reason you might have called it?"

"I want to know why you're asking me, or I'm not saying another word," Hank said steadily. "Brody, don't interrupt me, please. Stewart, you either tell me what this is all about, or you put me in jail now and I'll fight until the bitter end alone because I'm not putting up with this. End of story."

"Alright, alright," Stewart said wearily, rubbing his forehead and hoping the nausea would go away sooner rather than later. "We got a call from someone claiming to be her killer. About six weeks ago. He called me again last night and gave me that number, and said you called it three times, and on the right dates. He also had detailed knowledge of the crime scene that was never released. The phone was deactivated on December 26 and is untraceable, even by us."

"What the fuck," Hank muttered to himself in disbelief.

"So now," Stewart continued miserably, "you see why I'm asking. This looks bad, Hank. That's why I'm pushing you for a reasonable explanation. Anything you can tell me will be helpful."

"What kind of *detailed knowledge* did he have, exactly?"

Stewart looked like he wasn't going to answer, but he did. "That she was carrying a list of confidential information about Urbane executives. The same list that got leaked a few weeks ago. He has the copy she was carrying, he says. So...I don't really need to add anything to that, I think."

"Did you record this 'mystery' call?"

"Yes. And you will be able to listen to it after we're done with this initial deposition. Monday, most likely."

Hank shook his head for a few minutes, it was all he could do.

"Okay. So let's say she was carrying such a list, just for the fun of it. You're implying that I had her killed *before* she could drop it off to me? How does that make any sense, logistically? Why not do her in afterwards?"

"Well, our mystery caller said he thought she'd made the drop. When he realized he messed up, he ran, deactivated the number, and hasn't been in touch with you since. Went rogue on you is what he claims."

"His *claims* are utter bullshit," Hank said angrily.

"Alright," Stewart said, still trying to write something down with his misbehaving pen. Hank wordlessly handed him one of his own, then waited silently as the man took down his notes.

"Anything else to add on this issue at the moment?"

"No. I need to talk to Daven," Hank said quietly. "Will you allow me a few minutes alone?"

"You can have ten minutes. I'm going to make some more coffee." He reached over and stopped the recording device.

"Thank you." Hank turned to Brody after Stewart was gone. "You can listen if you want, but it's going to be pretty uncomfortable, not going to lie."

Brody nodded decisively. "I'll stay."

"Hank?" answered the sleepy, astonished man on the other line. "Are you alright?"

"Yeah. Dav, I'm sorry I left without telling you. Things got crazy real quick. Are you alone?"

"Yes, I'm in your guest room. The boys are still asleep. What's going on?"

Hank glanced at the clock; it was 5:15am in Los Angeles. "Jesus, sorry to wake you. I didn't even think about the time change. Hey, listen, I got your voicemail regarding your meeting this morning with your staff."

"*Our* staff, Hank."

Pause. "Right. Look, I've been thinking about it and decided I want you guys to stay completely neutral. Don't go into anything specific, or say something like you're certain I'll be found innocent, blah blah blah. It's really important that you don't take my side. Just say this is what's happened, this is what we know, now we have to wait to see what comes next. You have to be as non-committal as possible. End of story."

There was a long pause on the other line. "What *exactly* is going on, Hank?" Daven asked suspiciously.

"Nothing, yet. Haven't even met with anyone today. But whatever I do next is in your own best interests, whether you like it or not. Okay? Promise me you won't fight, and that you'll stay out-"

"Hank-"

"Don't interrupt me, please. You and Rupe *cannot* take my side. Especially you. Remember what I said about the boys."

"So this request is personal, rather than business."

"No," Hank answered hastily. "It's both. Maybe not equally, but both all the same."

Daven didn't say anything for a while, then he demanded, "I think I'm owed a better explanation than that. What are you up to?"

"Nothing!" Hank fired back. "Are you going to do as I say, or not? I need to know before I proceed here."

"Fine, so you just want me to tell everyone 'okay, nothing to see here, back to work' and think this is just going to blow over?"

"I don't want to fight with you, Dav," Hank said tiredly, returning to his normal tone. "I'm trying to protect you first, and the party second. It's extremely important that you are personally distanced from me as much as possible right now."

Daven scoffed. "I don't feel the same, Hank. It's my duty to stand up for you. As a friend, not even as an employee. It astonishes me that you're caving in and giving up just like that, and I won't accept it. I'm going to defend you, like it or not."

Hank closed his eyes and rubbed his temples. "Dav. We've known each other for too long, that's the problem right now. You're not seeing the big picture because your heart is getting in the way. Normally I would appreciate that, but not today. Use your brain, please. If you're dragged into this...if you defend me, and I go down anyway, you'll be associated with that forever. And so will the party."

"I don't care," Daven replied simply. "You're innocent. My loyalty to you is more important than this job. The party can burn down to ashes for all I care."

"You don't mean that."

"Yes, I absolutely do."

Hank knew he wasn't going to win the argument at this point unless he changed tactics drastically, and that was going to be extraordinarily painful. He dodged a wary glance at the recording device to make certain it was actually off, then inhaled deeply.

"Okay. Dav, I...maybe you shouldn't be as loyal to me as you think. I haven't been perfectly honest with you lately, and there are things that you don't know..." His voice broke a little, but he got it back together quickly. "Look, I'm not giving up. I'm fighting this. But I'll say it one last time: distance yourself from me before it's too late. For you, and the party. But mostly for you. You need to get back to work and move on. Don't fall on your sword for me. And if I'm cleared, we'll all get back to work as usual, and no one will be worse for wear. Are we perfectly clear now?"

There was no answer from Daven, as Hank expected, and he was surprised to feel a strong burn in his eyes and tightening in his chest.

"Dav?" he prompted after a minute.

"Yes. I'll do as you say," he replied calmly. Icily.

Hank wiped his eyes. "Thanks. I'll be in touch again soon, okay? Just...stay true. Keep our good work going until I get back. Say hi to the dogs for me."

"I will."

"Alright. Goodbye for now." He hung up before Daven could say anything that would make him burst into tears, then turned to Brody.

"Maybe you shouldn't have been listening," Hank said with a humorless laugh. "You don't know me well enough to know that sometimes I have to trick Daven into doing what's best for him."

Brody was just staring at him wordlessly.

"Are you alright?" Hank asked after a moment, concerned that his young lawyer was about to bail on him. "You can go home, if you want. I don't-"

"No, sir," Brody said firmly. "I'm staying. You're right that I don't know you well, but even a stranger could tell you weren't being truthful with Daven. You haven't done anything, have you?"

"No. Well, not what they're accusing me of, anyway," admitted Hank.

Brody hesitated a little. "You still don't think Harmon is behind all this?"

"Oh he has something to do with it, but he's not the mastermind. He's not smart or devious enough. Colbert is the puppet master here; of that I have absolutely zero doubt."

Brody nodded. "They cannot legally ignore you if you accuse him outright. Formally, I mean. But without evidence it could be construed as slander, so you have to be careful."

"I'm pretty sure slander charges are the least of my worries right now."

Hank leaned back in his chair again and stared at his phone, which was still flipped open and glowing. The urge to call Dav back and smooth things out again was overwhelming. But he hit the power button and flipped it shut, then picked up the questionnaire as Stewart re-entered the room.

CHAPTER TWO

Bancroft House - early morning - Friday

"Of course he was lying, Rupert! How could you possibly think otherwise?"

"Sorry," Rupe said contritely. "I didn't mean to imply...look, I'm just having a hard time absorbing this whole thing. Not to mention I'm still half-asleep. We've been through this before, you know. It's like freakin' Groundhog Day."

"What? I don't understand that reference."

Rupe was a little shocked at that. "You haven't seen the movie? Never mind. I mean this whole doubting him back-and-forth between you and me. Doesn't this happen every few months? Usually I'm the one being the devil's advocate because we have to look at this fairly, but that doesn't mean I'm accusing him of anything. We *know* he's done stupid, shady things in the past, Dav. This isn't-"

"No. If you're not going to get on the same page with me, just forget ever discussing this again."

Rupert sighed. "Fine. This linear thinking isn't constructive, just so you know. But if Hank wants us to distance ourselves, we have to do it. He's still the boss as far as I'm concerned. No offense, of course."

Daven stared at the ceiling fan as it slowly made its way around in endless, meaningless circles. *Kind of like this investigation, and my relationship with Rupert, and politics in general...*

"I can't do it, Rupe. I just can't sit by and say nothing in his defense. I'm going to quit."

"Right, because that solves everything, huh? Coward's way out, if you ask me."

Sigh. "I know. You're right. But it's tempting, all the same."

There was a knock on Daven's door, and he sat up so fast it made him dizzy. Shannon leaped off the bed like a flying squirrel and immediately launched into a frenzied barking fit at the door.

"Shannon, shush. Hang on, Rupe. Going to put you on mute for a moment. *Shannon* !" He climbed out of bed and went to open the door, where Theo was standing there expectantly.

"Everything okay, Theo?"

"Chef wants to know what you want for breakfast."

"Already?" Dav exclaimed as he looked at his watch.

"We eat at 7, Uncle Dav. Are you hungry yet?"

"Yes, just tell him to make whatever he's making you two. Thanks. Listen, I'm on a call and I have to finish it up. I'll be out soon."

Theo's eyes widened. "With dad?"

Daven's heart dropped a little. "Uh, no. But it's about your dad, and it's really important. I'll see you at 7, okay? Please take Shannon out and let her into the yard."

Theo frowned and took her collar wordlessly, leaving Daven feeling sorry for speaking more harshly than he intended. Hank's remarks about his rusty people skills came flooding back to him. He would have to work on that, for sure. But not right now.

"Rupe, I don't even know what to say at the staff meeting. This has really thrown me for a loop."

"Okay, let me think about it and get back to you. Try to stay focused and don't let the boys see you rattled. By the way...you know I don't like to disagree with you, but Hank's right. We have to stay neutral, and that would apply for anyone in the same situation. To do otherwise could backfire on us to the point where we can't recover."

"Honestly, I wouldn't even care."

"*Daven*," Rupert admonished. "You're not acting anything like the leader Hank wants you to be. We have 509 people directly counting on us. Do you think he'd be proud of you if he heard this conversation? Proud that you gave up within five minutes and were willing to throw everything away to do the opposite of what he's asking you to do?"

"No," Daven admitted grudgingly. "He'd tear me a new one."

"Correct, and you'd deserve it. So get yourself together, and let's meet at the office at 8:30."

"Alright. Thanks. See you then."

Daven hung up and then made his way upstairs to Floyd's room in order to keep himself occupied enough to not have to think about this whole sorry situation. He was surprised to see all three dogs in bed with the teenager, wrapped around his body protectively.

"Hey, Floyd," he said softly as he approached the bed. "Time to get ready for breakfast. Are you awake?"

"I don't want to, Uncle Dav."

"Okay. You don't have to eat, but you need to go to school."

"I know," came the muffled reply. "I will."

Dav weighed the option of admonishing him about the dogs, but didn't see any benefit to being a hardass about it. Floyd was clearly comforted by their presence, and the three pairs of dark canine eyes were watching Dav so smugly that it seemed fruitless to challenge their cozy stronghold. Instead, he left and stood in the doorway of Theo's room.

"Floyd doesn't want to eat. Can you tell Chef when you go down?"

Theo was sorting through several shirts in an effort to decide what to wear. "But he always says that, and then he changes his mind at the last second. All it takes is some bacon."

"Good to know. Why didn't you take Shannon outside like I asked you?"

"She didn't want to go. It's like she suddenly weighs 500 pounds when you try to get her to do something she doesn't want to."

"Fair enough." That was indeed quintessentially Shannon, the most determined and stubborn dog he'd ever known. "But how did she and the other dogs get upstairs, then?"

Theo shrugged. "I opened the gate to let them all come up. Dad's not here."

This was an argument for another time, Daven knew instinctively, but he couldn't just let it go. "Your dad's rules still apply, Theo. Next time don't do that, or at least ask me."

"Or what? You'll take a belt to me?" Theo responded bitterly, still not making eye contact. "It's a stupid rule."

Oh boy, thought Daven. *Danger zone.* He walked fully into the room and shut the door behind him, then sat down on Theo's bed next to the pile of shirts.

"I don't believe in corporal punishment, as you know. Stop what you're doing for a second and look at me," he commanded gently, but firmly. "Thank you. I'm really disappointed in you, Theo. I've been here all of one day - less than one day, actually - and already you're testing me. We will follow *all* of your dad's rules...yes, I include myself in that, because there are plenty of things I can't do, either. It's what he wants and expects us from us. Let's not let him down. Are we agreed?"

"But it's not like he'll ever find out, since he's not coming back."

Daven closed his eyes briefly, silently vowing that he wouldn't let his sudden surge of strong emotion take over. "Go put the dogs in the yard, and don't argue with me."

Theo's posture relaxed, the fight in him disappearing instantly. "But I'm not trying to argue," he said quietly, his voice trembling a little. "Dad always lets Floyd sleep on the couch with them on bad days and it helps a lot. I was just trying to make him feel better. Sorry, Uncle Dav."

Daven froze, then before he could stop himself, he capitulated. "Okay. They can come upstairs from now on."

Theo stared agape a time him. "Really?"

"Yes. I don't want Floyd sleeping downstairs at night. So you boys will have to make sure the doors are always closed to the other rooms so they don't destroy anything."

That cheered Theo up beyond compare, but the now severely depressed Daven went back to the guest room in defeat. When he emerged forty-five minutes later the dogs were outside and Floyd was hovering over the bacon, just as Theo had predicted. *Thank god.* Floyd *was* visibly better, if not downright cheerful, but Dav knew Hank would ream him anyway when he found out.

But...maybe he didn't have to tell him. Just this once.

Denver, same time

Lester Boyd hadn't seen Harmon in many years, not since he'd left Colorado and headed for warmer climate. They had been good friends, and Harmon gave him a job for life at a party-affiliated training school, but his involvement with the party itself was long over. That's why he was still in a bit of a daze as he waited in the conference room for his old friend, but he was smart enough to realize that this undoubtedly had something to do with Hank Bancroft. But what, he didn't know and couldn't fathom.

Colbert, though...he was another story altogether. Lester and Colbert hadn't been on speaking terms since pretty much their first meeting. He couldn't understand what Harmon saw in the quietly dangerous man who locked eyes with people during conversation like his life depended on it. It was unnerving and intimidating, exactly what was intended. That was why Lester stiffened when he heard the distinctive voice just outside the door. The knob turned along with his stomach.

"Lester Boyd," Colbert sing-songed as he entered the room with Harmon. "Long time, no talk. You look old, my friend."

"Thank you?"

Harmon silently shook hands with him, but Colbert just sat down and spread papers in front of himself as cheerfully as if they were all about to play dominoes.

"Thanks for coming," Harmon said guardedly. "You must be incredibly curious why I asked you here, and I'll explain. I'll also compensate you for the time you had to take off from work. But first I want to ask you something. Are you following the news in regards to Hank Bancroft?"

Lester cleared his throat and sat up straighter. "Only out of morbid curiosity, really. Those media idiots don't really know what's going on and their theories change every five minutes."

"Right. Well, as you know, I'm not a fan of Hank's personality and tactics. We've fought a lot over the years, and only recently started getting along and working together on some measures."

"So I've heard," Lester said with a grin. "Nobody thought you and Hank could agree on the color of an orange."

Harmon didn't smile back. "You're not wrong. But one thing we have always agreed on is how we would do anything to protect our children. Hank is facing prison time, and the reason behind it is highly confidential. I've been tasked with finding a mutually agreeable negotiator, which is why I asked you here."

"You mean...to negotiate what's going to happen to Floyd and Theo?"

"Yes. I know you two aren't exactly friends, but you spent six years with the boys and ten years with Hank. Do you think he'd be willing to speak to you on my behalf regarding the plea bargain? If you agree, I can tell you everything. Then you'll have to meet with him and discuss terms. He's a good father, he'll do what's best for his boys."

A good father. He wondered how Harmon knew that, and felt a cold surge of nostalgia at the sudden recollection of what Hank's parenting was like back in the days just after the revolution. To a casual observer, he'd actually been a terrible father to the boys, especially to Floyd - controlling, harsh, and downright unreasonable the majority of the time. Lester had often stepped in to comfort young Floyd after a punishment. But Hank wasn't what he seemed; he spent half the time struggling to protect them, and half the time spoiling them senseless, which was what he vastly preferred.

Good father or not, he deeply loved his sons. If they were threatened in any way, no force in the universe could survive the wrath he would unleash on the culprits. Lester had seen it with his own eyes. They were threatened now, and Hank must be out of his mind with worry.

Lester cleared his throat again, and then took the bottle of water that Harmon hastily pushed over to him. "Thanks," he said after he drank half of it. "I said I'd kill Hank the next time he saw me. So I would say my chances of getting any conversation out of him would be 50-50. Useful conversation, on the other hand...maybe a 10% chance. There's just one problem beyond my ability to solve, though."

"What's that?"

"He'll never bargain. Not with you, with me, with anyone. Never has, never will. He'll go down swinging first, and damn the consequences."

Harmon knew this, of course. "Let's just get to the end result that I'm hoping for: as the aggrieved party Hank's sons can be deeded to me via the plea bargain. I'll transfer them to Daven myself after the trial, if he makes it through."

"*Makes it through?*"

"Yes. I learned yesterday that Daven is also implicated in at least one of the charges the FBI is bringing against Hank. A minor one, but enough to potentially earn him a class 2 felony and put him out of the running as their guardian."

Oh...fuck. Lester almost choked, but he managed to keep a straight face. "Okay. But deeds can only be transferred once a year. Hank will never agree to you having them for a year, or a day, and that's if he even believes you'd actually do it. Not in a million years, with a million words and a million promises."

"I know, but we have to try. Didn't say this job was going to be easy. And I can't compensate you for it, either. We have to move fast if you're going to agree, though. I'll need you in Philadelphia on Tuesday at the latest."

"Move fast?" Lester asked. "Why rush it? Something like this...you'll need all the resources and time you can get."

Harmon glanced aside at Colbert; Lester really *was* out of the loop now on the world around him now that he'd all but left the party.

"I think we're going to need more time than I allotted for this discussion." He stood up. "Let me go clear my calendar."

Seditionist HQ, 10am staff meeting

Daven felt all but paralyzed as he stood in the wings at the little basement theater that was housed in the office park. Rupert had hastily rented the venue from the owner of the building for an exorbitant fee, and all 488 employees present were jammed in shoulder to shoulder, waiting eagerly for news from their executives. He prayed no one would think to call the fire department and report a violation; the last thing the Seditionists needed right now was more bad PR over jamming their entire staff into a fire trap.

"Dav," Rupert said gently, moving closer towards his new boss. "It's 10. You got to go out and talk to them. Come on."

"I...Rupe, I've never been so nervous in my life."

"I don't envy you, but you have to do it. Go get it over with."

Daven took a deep breath. "Alright. Where's the mic, Taylor?"

Taylor glided over and handed it to him, then put a finger over her lips and turned on the switch. The light on the bottom of the mic glowed green and squealed briefly; Rupert imagined feeling his own heart squeal back in response as he handed over the little speech they'd written together. He felt damnably sorry for Dav, but this was his job now and he had to do it. Hank had been through much worse a dozen times over.

Daven closed his eyes, prayed silently for what seemed like an interminably long time, and walked out onto the little stage without any further adieu.

"Good morning," he said first, and everyone murmured the same back in response. Dav froze; not because of stage fright but because he was afraid that his tone of voice would lack the conviction and strength he needed to get through this. It was hard enough to convince people of something you believed in, and much harder to convince them of something you didn't. He looked down at the paper and realized his hands were shaking; which oddly helped steady his nerves. *Let my hands shake, then...as long as my voice doesn't.*

"We're under a media gag order right now, so this message is for your ears only. We will make a public statement on Monday." Deep breath. "Hank Bancroft has been taken into custody pending charges that could lead to a criminal conviction. While the investigation is ongoing, I will be the interim leader of the Seditionists."

He stopped, folded up the paper and put it in his pocket, imagining Rupert all but screaming from him from the wings for going off-script after just two sentences. *How often have we both done the same to Hank?* he wondered briefly, sadly.

"Hank wishes for me to not defend him, to not say he's innocent, to not...put myself in a position where it could backfire and give me a bad name if the worst happens. I fought him hard on that, but ultimately agreed that it was in the best interests of our party - of all of *you* - that we allow him to independently proceed through this investigation, no matter what any of us personally believes. But I've worked for Hank for 10 years and been friends with him for 12, so you can probably imagine exactly how I feel about this entire situation. Which is that the accusations are complete bullshit, by the way, in case you have any doubts. But again, Hank told me not to say that, so I won't."

"Jesus Christ," whispered Rupe to Taylor in shock. "Dav has gone rogue. Never thought I'd see the day."

"I knew he had it in him," Taylor responded with a smirk.

Daven stopped to take a deep breath and then walked up to the very edge of the stage, taking a moment to try to look at every face in the room. "Just because I'm up here on stage five feet above you does not mean I consider any of you below me. *All* of us have *equal* responsibility to honor Hank's legacy by respecting his wishes to continue our good work in his absence, and to not waste time and words speculating about what could be. Therefore, at this time I will make no further remarks on the situation, because I don't have time for it. It's back to business for all of us. We have an April 1 vote coming up, and several of the measures still need a lot of work as far as rallying our constituents to oppose them. I would encourage you to avoid the news for now since we don't need the distraction of mindless media speculation. As I mentioned, our media statement will be released on Monday. Thank you for your cooperation."

He walked offstage and handed the mic back to Taylor, then looked at Rupe as he loosened his tie, expression as guilty as a dog who had been caught raiding the trash.

"Go ahead," he said with a resigned sigh. "Chew me out for not following the script."

"You think I should?" Rupert answered seriously.

"If I was Hank, you would."

"You're not Hank. He usually went off-script to spite me. You did it to honor him. I'm actually *really* proud of you, Dav." Rupe's voice cracked a little, and even he seemed surprised at himself for saying it.

Daven froze with his tie half off. "Wait. What?"

Rupert clapped him on the shoulder, feeling a warm glow course through both of them. "You did good. Really good. Hank would hate it, but I loved it. It was what our team needed to hear. Just don't give that same speech to the cameras on Monday, please, or I might have something vastly different to say about it."

"I won't. Is it too early to go get lunch?"

"Not really. Blue Daisy opens at 10:30. Want to walk over?"

"Yes, please. I need a drink."

CHAPTER THREE

FBI HQ - Philadelphia

Four hours into the interview, when it was time to break for the afternoon, Stewart was all but at the end of his rope with Hank's answers. Not that there was anything wrong with them, but...ironically enough, come to think of it, the problem was *exactly* that there was nothing wrong with them. No conclusions could be drawn, no coincidences struck away, no questions answered...nothing. They ended the morning where they had started it, and the only thing gained was a new level of frustration and distrust from both sides.

The next hour or so was going to be much harder. Exponentially harder. Stewart had to introduce the idea of a negotiator, which he knew Hank would absolutely throw a shit fit about. Then, as the day ended, he would have to call Harmon and inform him that Janet might have been carrying the list of confidential information for Hank. He wasn't looking forward to either task, to say the least, so he just sat there alone, forcing down the tasteless whatever-was-on-his-plate, wondering what the hell Hank was thinking right now.

He sure knew what his own thoughts were like, and they're weren't pretty.

Hank roamed around the room restlessly while Brody hungrily ate another snack, and wondered what the hell Stewart was thinking about. It took a tremendous amount of willpower to fight the temptation to call his sons. They were in school, he knew, and what exactly was he going to tell them anyway? What was he going to tell Daven, for that matter? Or anyone? He knew he was screwed on just the blackmail charge alone; the rest of it almost didn't matter at this point.

Then there was Harmon. How tempting it was to call him, too. Stewart never explained what he meant when he'd said Harmon was on Hank's side, and the real translation of what that meant was an agonizing itch that Hank couldn't scratch. He resolved to ask the question directly, and then automatically pulled his phone out of his pocket to call Daven.

Los Angeles

"Hello Hank," Dav answered gruffly. "I have Rupert with me. Is it ok if I put you on speaker?"

"Sure."

Rupert took a deep breath and sat down in Daven's desk chair, ignoring the astonished side-eye he was getting from his new boss.

"It's weird not having you here, Hank," Rupe said matter-of-factly. "Can't wait for you to get back and start bitching about Daven's caffeine intake again."

"You mean the fact that he goes through an entire package of my espresso pods every day? I don't miss that. Damned things are expensive. Hey…did a guy come in to seal up my office door?"

"Yes," Daven answered quickly, then he covered the phone's microphone with his hand. "Out of my chair," he hissed in irritation at his colleague.

"I can imagine what everyone must be saying," continued Hank glumly, his voice tinny and far away over the flip phone. "Don't tell me, it will just make me more depressed."

Rupert answered in a positive tone, although his body language was saying something else to Daven entirely. "I would love to tell you what they're saying, actually. It would raise your spirits quite a bit."

"Hmmm. Speaking of which, Dav, how did the meeting go this morning?"

"It wasn't a meeting," Daven said as he sat down in his reclaimed chair, while Rupert took the couch off to the side. "I…I just had some things to say."

"Did you distance yourself from me like you promised?"

Dav shot a warning look at Rupert before responding. "Hank, I made it clear that we as an organization were to let you proceed through the investigation independently and without offering any opinions to the contr-"

"Just answer the question, Dav," Hank interrupted tiredly. "I wanted you to not back me up and stay entirely neutral. Did you, or did you not do specifically that?"

The long silence that ensued answered the question for them all.

"Right," Hank sighed, sounding rightfully disappointed. "Maybe you should take me off speaker for a moment. I want to say something to you privately."

Daven picked up the phone and took a deep breath as he hit the button. "Yes? It's just me now."

"Look, Dav. I know I'm not in charge of you right now, but-"

"You are, Hank. Until this ends, one way or another."

Pause. "If you really believe that, you wouldn't have disobeyed me. *Again.* Tell me exactly what you said."

Daven hesitated. "I'd rather not, because you might have a stroke."

"That might be a blessing in disguise. Tell me."

Dav did, almost word for word.

"Okay," Hank eventually responded. "Obviously it's no surprise that I'm really pissed off with you right now, and it frustrates me to the extreme that you can't understand why. If my boys really don't matter to you that much, then I might as well just turn them over to the state right now and save us all the trouble. Because I'm going down, Dav, whether you want to believe it or not. It's time to get some fucking common sense, accept the reality of this situation, and start thinking about someone other than yourself. Are you hearing me?" His tone and volume had escalated dramatically, shocking Daven to the core. It took him a few moments to find his voice.

"I'm not going to apologize for supporting you, Hank. I never will, no matter how angry you get."

Hank scoffed angrily. "Fine. Tell that to the boys when you're not approved to be their guardian after this shitshow goes through the courts. I'm sure they'll understand that you couldn't set your pride aside for five minutes to save them 20 years of slavery."

"It's not pride. It's loyalty."

"I don't give a shit what it is, you're endangering my sons and I don't appreciate it one bit. Put Rupert back on the phone."

Dav shakily hit the speaker button once again. "Okay. He's back on."

"Rupe?"

"Yes, Hank?" he answered in a timid voice while watching Daven worriedly; the man had suddenly gone ashen and looked about to vomit.

"I'm going to give it to you straight. If Dav doesn't toe the line, he's going to get dragged into this mess even further, which means Floyd and Theo are in serious trouble. The Seditionists are to stay neutral and not defend me, period. I said it before and I'll say it until my dying breath. Do you understand why?"

"Yes, sir, completely understood." Rupert never called Hank *sir* unless he was dead serious and totally sincere...which wasn't very often at all. Therefore, Hank knew for certain that his friend needed no further explanation and would do as asked without question.

"Thank you," he breathed in relief. "Daven? What about you? Are you going to comply with my wishes now?"

"Yes, sir." It was even more rare for Daven to use the honorific, and Hank was satisfied at last.

"Good," he responded happily, tone back to normal again. "Then get back to work. The April 1 vote is coming up, and Harmon wants to work with you on it. I expect you to cooperate fully with him despite this entire sorry situation, because our constituents are more important than personal grudges. I'll be in touch soon."

Daven said nothing more as Rupert bid their boss farewell and ended the call almost as pleasantly as it had begun.

"Jesus, Dav," Rupe breathed shakily as he closed the phone and handed it back to his friend. "I never realized how scary he can be over the phone. In person, yes, but this is new. We'd better do what he says. Are you...are you alright? You're white as a sheet."

"I'm fine," Daven snapped as he got up to get some coffee. Then, remembering what Hank had said about the espresso pods, he stopped and resolved to curb his caffeine habit. Maybe that would ease his temper somewhat.

"Sorry, Rupert," he finally said. "I'm not myself today, obviously. I'm going to call Hank back and apologize. Do you mind…"

"Not at all, leaving now. Lock your door so you don't get interrupted."

"Thanks. I haven't forgotten about our lunch. Just give me a few minutes."

"Sure."

Daven got up and made the espresso anyway, swiftly abandoning his plan to cut back in favor of a quick fix of energy. Then he sat down in front of his desk phone and stared at it gloomily, unmoving.

After twenty minutes he still hadn't dialed the phone. He didn't want to. He knew he unfairly pointed the finger at Hank for this entire situation, for thrusting him prematurely into this job as CEO and father figure. Positions he *didn't want*, he realized with a jolt for the very first time.

Even as the ugly truth set in, he hoped and prayed he would come around and actually want these things. Sooner, rather than later.

If he'd had the *choice* to take them, would he want them then? Was his reticence only because the boys and this job were forced on him? Was he being completely unreasonable and childish?

He didn't know. It was possible. All that was for certain right now was the fact that forgiveness and understanding weren't his number one priorities at this time. Saving his friend *was*, but he wasn't being allowed to even attempt it; his way blocked by the very man who needed saving.

It was such a fucked up situation, and to put it plainly...Daven blamed Hank entirely and resented him bitterly for it. Even as he fought not to, and knew it was wrong.

But he also knew sitting around and moping was accomplishing nothing, so he shoved the phone angrily away and got up to collect Rupert for lunch at Hank's favorite restaurant.

Had Daven known that he would never have the opportunity to speak to Hank again, the morning would have ended quite differently.

CHAPTER FOUR

Friday night - Los Angeles

It was suppertime at the Bancroft house, and Floyd and Theo waited politely and silently at the table while Chef kept the food heated for them. Normally, Chef would be home in Eagle Rock with his family on a Friday night but Daven didn't know that, and had earlier in the day asked him to prepare a nice meal for dinner. Vance had taken pity on the man and promised to drive him personally home afterwards, an offer which Chef had gratefully accepted.

The servants all instinctively knew tough times were ahead, even though - like Floyd and Theo - they were not allowed to watch live television in the house. They could watch movies and TV series on tapes that Maurice would rent from Blockbuster on a weekly basis, but that was it. It was a rule universally resented by all of the indentured staff, but considering the lengths to which the man ensured their comfort and happiness in other ways - some quite extraordinary, such as the weekly banquets with their families - no one ever dared to complain, nor to even think of complaining. It almost seemed treasonous to even grumble about such a minor thing.

Maurice was also here, but that was normal since he lived in the house full time. At the moment he was busily canceling all the arrangements for the planned weekend sailing trip and Disneyland, taking some comfort in the fact that neither of the boys had known about the outings before Hank had left for Philadelphia. He couldn't imagine either one of them even wanting to go anyway, considering the circumstances...well, maybe Theo would. He was too young to be perturbed by much, thankfully.

At a quarter after seven, Floyd got up from the table and told Theo he was cold and going to get a sweater. Instead, he snuck downstairs to Brittany's office. She was there, watching the news and drinking tea with an absent-minded expression.

"Hey Floyd," she said warmly. The next words out of her mouth should have been, "you aren't allowed down here," but the truth was, she didn't care. The poor kid had been through enough lately and didn't need his guards hounding him.

"Hi." Floyd looked up at the television, then back to Brittany. "Do you think dad's coming back?" he asked quietly.

Brittany frowned, then set her cup down carefully. "He hasn't told me what's going on. But I've heard from Avery that it's...that it's possible Hank, I mean, your dad, might have to stay away for awhile." She glanced at the news footage. "The news is even less helpful than Avery was, no big shocker there," she said skeptically.

Floyd sat down on the corner of her desk and began to watch the news, pointedly crossing his arms to show that he didn't care about the rule saying he couldn't. But the screen went black suddenly, and he turned to look at Brittany. His words of protest died on his lips; she was holding the remote with a resolute and business-like expression, finger still on the power button.

"We can talk all you want, but I'm not turning it back on."

"Just for a minute?" Floyd pleaded.

"Nope. I'd like to keep my job, Floyd. I really like being here with you and your brother."

"Okay. Sorry." Floyd shrugged and went back upstairs. He bypassed the first floor and went straight to Hank's sitting room, punching in 1182 in the entry panel, marveling at how easy it was to figure out the code. His dad used Theo's birthday for pretty much everything.

He parked himself on the couch and turned on the TV, feeling his stomach turn at the sight of Hailey Hendricks reporting from a driveway. *His* driveway, actually. Of course.

Before I send it back to you guys in the studio, I wanted to stress that the media statement distributed only an hour ago made it clear that the party is taking a huge step back from Mr. Bancroft, by outright refusing to defend him or even take his side. It almost seems like - and you might have to kind of read between the lines for this one - that Mr. Johansson is perhaps even responsible for the quick exit to Philadelphia. One can imagine that he is deeply concerned about his own role in all of this, probably even afraid of how it will impact his career, and is taking steps to mitigate the damage as much as possible.

What do you mean by responsible, Hailey? asked a weasley-looking studio anchor as the camera flashed to him. *Surely you don't mean Daven Johansson is responsible for Hank's arrest?*

Hailey smiled in a sinister fashion that made Floyd's skin crawl. *It's possible when you think about why he would suddenly step back from his closest friend of twelve years and act like he doesn't even know him. We've even been advised there was a call between Harmon and Mr. Johansson today to discuss the April 1 vote. Perhaps those two have allied, I don't know, but it all seems rather fast and suspicious. Like Mr. Johansson has already moved on and left Mr. Bancroft to his fate. To me, that makes it seem like he knows he's guilty. Perhaps he's even cooperating with the FBI, since we know Johansson and the FBI met on Friday in his office, right here in Los Angeles. If I didn't know better, I'd say he's seized the opportunity to be the next leader of the Seditionists. Who wouldn't, under the same circumstances?*

Very intriguing possibility, Hailey. You've got the studio folks all riled up for more, as I'm sure our viewers are, too. We'll get back to you soon. Let's jump to the studio for weather now. The Santa Anas are apparently responsible for knocking down a power line in the Camarillo area and sparking a wildfire that is currently gathering-

Floyd leaped to his feet and slammed his hand down hard on the power button of the television, almost knocking the screen over in the process. He couldn't breathe, and his hands were numb, not feeling the stairwell railing at all as he raced back down the stairs. The wall rumbled next to him on the landing, indicating the massive garage door opening or closing. Either way, that meant Uncle Dav had arrived at last.

Floyd veered into his room, locked the door behind him, and dived under the covers, laying perfectly still as Hailey's shrill accusations repeated in his brain over and over again. Less than two minutes later his heart stopped when he heard Daven Johansson - the *next leader of the Seditionists* - knock on the door to his room. Floyd pulled out his cell phone and called his dad as fast as his shaking fingers could manage.

Two times. Three times.

There was no answer.

The door to the room jiggled a little, then opened wide. Floyd pulled the blanket tighter over his head and held his breath.

Friday night, Philadelphia

Hank laid back down in his hotel's bed and seethed freely for the third hour in a row. He was still beyond appalled at Harmon's offer of a negotiator, and had nearly physically assaulted Stewart just for mentioning it. Fortunately he kept his wits about him, and carried on the conversation to the bitter end...during which he had somehow agreed to the negotiator - on his own accord, not coerced - and he was pissed as hell about it. But he knew Stewart was trying to help, and that was the only saving grace in this situation.

What was worst of all was that his phone had been taken away from him after Harmon quickly reported to Stewart that Hank had called him. It was true; Hank had given in to his curiosity immediately after the tough conversation with Daven. Rather than submit to charges of contempt and go straight to jail, he agreed to give up the phone in exchange for maintaining his freedom...well, what limited amount of freedom he had, anyway. His hotel room's phone was taken out, and a guard stationed outside to prevent him from leaving. But as pissed off as he was about the situation, he knew it was better than jail and therefore resolved to make the best of it. Stewart had promised to give him back the phone the next morning at 10am, and warned that any further attempts would result in a felony contempt charge.

So now there was nothing to do but seethe, order room service, and sleep. Hank did plenty of the first one, and even more of the second just out of spite (until he got cut off by the irritated guard), and exactly none of the third. It was a very long night for the soon-to-be former leader of the Seditionists.

Los Angeles

"Floyd?" asked Daven gently, not stepping into the bedroom just yet.

"Mmmph?"

"Uh...dinner is ready. What are you doing?"

Floyd mumbled that he was cold, and Daven waited a few long moments and then walked up to the bed, keeping a respectful distance.

"Come down and eat. The food will warm you up."

"I want to talk to dad."

"I do too, Floydie. We can't until tomorrow. Come down and eat."

"My name is Floyd," he replied sharply.

"Okay, *Floyd* . In a bit of a temper, I see. Shall I have chef bring up a plate for you?"

Floyd turned around and peered at the man he suddenly could feel no warmth for. "Chef is supposed to be in Eagle Rock."

Daven cocked his head. "What do you mean?"

Floyd turned back around and faced the wall, saying nothing. Let him flounder and figure it out for himself.

Daven didn't take the bait; he knew exactly what Floyd was doing. "Alright, I'll ask Theo. I know why you're upset, and you're right. I should have called. The day got away with me. I didn't mean to get home so late. Will you come down to dinner?"

"This isn't your *home* ," Floyd blurted hotly. "It's mine and Theo's, and it belongs to our *dad* . Remember him?"

Floyd didn't even care that Daven's expression was at once crestfallen and stunned and hurt. He set his jaw even tighter, resolving to say nothing further.

Dav responded in a strangled tone. "Alright, Floyd, we're going to nip this in the bud right now. Let's have a talk."

Floyd threw his covers off and sat up abruptly. He absolutely hated the *let's have a talk* spiel; it didn't matter who said it, or for what reason - good or bad. "Theo's waiting for us," he grumbled irritably.

"He can wait a minute or two longer." Daven sat down on Floyd's desk chair. "Truthfully, Floyd, I trip over saying the word *home* every time I say it when it's not referring to my house down the street. It's really awkward, but I mean well. What would you prefer me to say instead?"

That threw Floyd off completely; he had been spooling up for a fight and was now being asked for advice instead?

"Say *the house* ," he finally mumbled.

"Deal. Now, if there's something bothering you besides that, and besides the obvious fact that you're missing your dad, please tell me. I believe open communication is the key to preventing and solving all problems."

Floyd took the ball and ran with it. "Fine. I heard the party was going to release a media statement today in regards to my dad. What did it say?"

Daven didn't hesitate; he reached into his pocket and pulled out a paper that had a few typed sentences on it and all kinds of handwritten notes.

"This is what you're getting all bent out of shape for? Why didn't you just ask me to begin with?"

"Can I read it?"

"Sure."

Floyd took it as if it were on fire and read it carefully.

Daven Johansson, interim leader of The Seditionists, is obliged to issue a blanket "no-comment" statement for the duration of the trial of Hank Bancroft. Party business will continue as normal, effective immediately. A press conference to discuss the April 1 voting docket will be held on March 25 at 10am PST. This will be followed by twenty minutes of Q&A, led by Daven Johansson and Rupert Aster. Questions will be screened to ensure they are topical.

Floyd read it three times, then looked up with a carefully blank expression. "What does the *topical* thing mean?"

"It means that questions not relating directly to the April 1 vote will be ignored because they're not the point of the press conference."

Meaning questions about his dad. Floyd was feeling hot again. "You didn't defend dad at all. Why?"

Daven took the paper back and folded it up, slipping it back into his pocket for safekeeping. He was only slightly mollified to realize Floyd hated it as much as he did. That it hurt his own heart as much as it hurt Floyd's, even if it was just a statement aimed directly at the media and not at his own constituents. That would come later and it would be much harder to craft, even with Hank's guidance.

"It's complicated, Floyd," he finally said, reluctantly. "I wouldn't even know how to explain."

Floyd's heart suddenly flushed ice cold at that. So it was exactly as Hailey had said, after all. Daven was distancing himself from his dad in order to protect himself. Abandoning him. Possibly he had even been the one to… *no* .

"I'm not hungry, Uncle Dav." *Uncle Dav.* The words sounded traitorous on his dry tongue. "You should get down to Theo or he's going to start pouting. I'm going to bed."

"Alright. You know where the refrigerator is if you change your mind." Daven stood up and went to the door. "Goodnight, Floydie."

"Floyd."

"That's right, sorry. Goodnight, Floyd."

Daven waited for a response and got nothing.

Floyd waited for the door to shut, then got out his phone again and dialed his dad in vain for almost two hours.

CHAPTER FIVE

Saturday morning - Philadelphia

Hank Bancroft finally did fall asleep, but it wasn't until 9am. He was awakened at 10 by Stewart, who wished to return his cell phone as promised.

"Morning, sorry to wake you." Stewart set the phone down on the credenza - after thoughtfully plugging it into the charger he had also taken away - and started to back out of the hotel room again. "It goes without saying that we'll be monitoring your calls, so..."

"Yeah, I know. Hey, what's on the agenda for today? For me, I mean."

"Nothing, actually. You're confined to the hotel grounds, of course, which shouldn't be too much of a hardship."

Hank smiled a little. "Yeah. I'm sure the public would love to hear how their tax dollars are going towards putting a disgraced criminal up in a five-star hotel for a week."

"That's *not* what you are, and besides, they're not paying for it. It'll be billed to the Seditionists, of course."

Hank recalled all the ridiculously expensive room service he had ordered last night and grimaced hard. So much for sticking it to the man. "Oh. Well, then...you couldn't have put me up at the Hilton again or something?"

Now it was Stewart's turn to grin. "You'll have to take that one up with your chief of staff. I was going to put you there, but Daven threw a fit and insisted on this."

Of course , Hank groaned internally. "Right. I'll be sure to knock another star off his chart, then."

Stewart nodded, then got serious again as he pointed back at the phone. "I know it's totally none of my business, but you have quite a few missed calls from your son. About 40 or so. I had to turn the vibration alerts off, it was driving me nuts."

"I'm sure. Thanks. So when do I have the pleasure of the FBI's company again?"

"Tomorrow morning. Do you want to go to church?"

"No."

"Okay. I'll be here to pick you up at nine. We'll spend most of the day going over your deposition and making any corrections or clarifications. Monday will be your day to decide where you want to go next, and the negotiator will arrive on Tuesday."

Hank swallowed hard. "Do you know who it is?"

"Yes, but I can't tell you. I'm sorry." Stewart blushed as he vaguely waved around the room. "You should, uh...try to get as much rest as possible today. I apologize for interrupting your sleep."

"Mmhmm. Thanks." Hank was secretly amused by the fact that Stewart was apparently just *now* finding it awkward to be holding such a serious conversation with one of them half-naked in bed.

"Okay. See you tomorrow."

"Wait," Hank said quickly, "Is my guard at this hotel, also?"

"Yes, Avery is next door, room 1147. I know you prefer connecting rooms, but under the circumstances-"

"I know. Don't worry about it. Thanks."

Stewart left, and Hank laid back and stared at the ceiling for a long time until he remembered the remark about all of Floyd's missed calls. He waited a few more minutes, then dragged himself into the shower to clear his mind and think about what he was going to say to his kids.

Los Angeles - Saturday morning

Daven hadn't slept all night, either. He was too busy actively hating everything and everybody, and turning over a thousand different scenarios in his mind - almost all of them dire and bleak. It was almost 8am, and he was no longer able to resist the urge to call Hank. 11am in Philadelphia; surely the man was awake by now even though he was well-known for his ability to sleep far past the noon hour.

So he picked up his phone and dialed, still somehow not surprised to find himself listening a few rings later to Hank's voicemail message. Still asleep, then. He dialed Maurice instead, who picked up instantly.

"Yes, sir?"

"Don't call me sir, please. Did the boys eat?"

"Yes, sir."

"I said..." *Sigh.* Some things just weren't worth the fight. "Great, thank you. What's on their schedules today?"

A slight pause and ruffle of papers. "Floyd has therapy at nine for two hours, and Theo has hockey practice at the same time. After that, they're free. Most Saturdays Hank would take them sailing after that."

Daven groaned. He was *not* going sailing, end of story. "I didn't know Theo plays hockey. With who?"

"Well, he has private lessons at the country club. Hank won't let him play on a team yet, although he's quite good. It's a bit of a security issue."

The thought of Theo playing a team sport completely by himself depressed Daven inexpressibly, and he resolved to fix that right away. The boy needed companionship and friends.

"Right. Can you give me a list of all the youth teams in the area and contact numbers for them?"

"I already have such a list, sir. I'll print it for you immediately."

"Just email it to me." Daven gave his email address. "Listen, I want to ask you something. Last night Floyd mentioned that Chef should have been in Eagle Rock. Was that true?"

"Uh, yes, sir. The servants go home on Friday afternoons."

Daven bristled a little, but then backed off just as quickly. He didn't want to start off on the wrong foot with this man, who was obviously just trying to do his best under very trying circumstances.

"Okay. You need to tell me these things in the future," he said, trying his best to keep the statement from sounding like a reprimand. "I'm kind of running blind, here. I have no idea how Hank runs his household."

"Sorry, sir. I just assumed…I mean, you've known him for so long, and the boys…I thought you would fit right in without any guidance."

Fit right in. Hardly. "I'm afraid that's not the case." Daven felt himself soften up suddenly. "Listen, let's have lunch together today and talk about this. I need all the help I can get, and your input will be invaluable."

"Certainly, sir. What would you like to eat so I can obtain the ingredients this morning?"

"No, I mean at a restaurant. I have a list of ones with private rooms that I'll email you."

There was a shocked silence. "Sir, I can't…I'm indentured, I can't be seen…it's not proper."

Daven sighed. "I don't care. Pick a restaurant and let me know so I can call and make a reservation."

Another shocker. "But I…I'll make the reservation, of course. Sir, are you sure about this?"

Maurice sounded rather shaky, and even though Daven detested the indentured system and the societal imbalances it created, he knew he was making the poor man highly uncomfortable and that it would help to take a more authoritative stance.

"Yes," he amended, "you should make the reservation, of course, and arrange for transportation. Who is the weekend driver?"

"Vance is always here on the weekends for the family. I mean...for you and the boys, sir."

The family.

Daven swallowed hard again. "Great. We'll eat at noon at King's Head, if they have a room available. Let me know. Gather whatever lists and information you think is of the highest priority for me to know first."

"Yes, sir. And what will the boys do while we're gone?"

Oh, right, the boys...it's not just me anymore. Get your shit together, Daven.

"Have they been to the Getty?"

"No, sir."

"Okay. They'll go there. I'll arrange it with Brittany."

"An *art museum* ? Is he serious?" Floyd whined as wrangled the polo shirt off over his head and looked for something else to wear, per Daven's instructions. "And I have to freakin' dress up?"

"Not dress up," Maurice corrected. "But something nicer than a polo shirt. Slacks and a dress shirt will be fine."

He went into Theo's room and found the boy already dressed exactly correct, of course.

"I've been wanting to go to this place for months!" Theo exclaimed happily. "How did he know?"

"He probably heard it from your dad. Are you ready to go?"

"Yeah."

"Okay, the car is outside. Have fun."

Maurice went back into Floyd's room and found him in the same state as before - but now holding clothes in each hand - shirtless, pouting, and in no mood to go anywhere.

"Floyd, the car is outside waiting."

"I don't care. I'm not going." He jumped a little as the sound of Daven coming up the stairs reached his ears. "Maurice? Tell him I'm not going."

"Yes, you are," said Daven gravely as he stood in the doorway. "The shirt you're holding in your right hand is fine. Put it on, and let's go."

Maurice was astonished to see Floyd drop them both on the floor and turn defiantly away from Daven to sit on the bed. "No."

"Floyd," pleaded Maurice quietly, almost a whisper. "Don't. Your dad wouldn't want this."

"He's not here," Floyd shot back, glaring at Daven at the same time.

Daven, of course, had no idea why Floyd had suddenly taken such a disliking to him. It hurt, but he kept a straight face.

"Would you like to come to lunch with me and Maurice instead? We're going to be discussing how your dad runs the household, and how we should proceed from here on out if he doesn't return. Your opinion matters, and I'd like to hear it."

Once again, Floyd was completely thrown off by Daven asking him for his opinion outright, rather than launching straight into a fight. It was so completely different from his dad. But then again, maybe his dad would still be here if it wasn't for Daven.

"He's going to return, so you're wasting your time," Floyd blurted out, even knowing it wasn't true. He had somehow already accepted he wouldn't see his dad again for a while, but it felt good anyway to say he'd be back.

Daven entered the room and looked at Maurice. "I think we need a moment, if you please." Then, to Floyd after they were alone: "Floyd, you know your dad's in trouble. We talked about this already, and he even told you that himself. I can't just take over this household without any kind of guidance, whether it's for five days or five years. You and Theo need stability, and so do I. Now, do you want to go to lunch with us, or do you want to go to the art museum? There is no third choice."

"I'm not going anywhere," Floyd insisted quietly. Just as he said that, his phone rang with his dad's ringtone. He bolted away from Daven and snatched it off the bathroom counter.

"Dad!"

"Hey, kiddo. How are you doing?"

"Not good. Daven is trying to make me go to an art museum!" Floyd whined again.

"Really? The Getty? You should go, it's really cool. We had a company holiday party there last year. Theo's been wanting to go forever."

Floyd glanced back at Dav. "Dad, I really want to talk to you... *alone*," he added significantly.

"Alright, call me when you get home."

"But I don't want to go."

Hank chuckled a little. "That's what I said, too. Like father, like son. Look, I can't talk right now anyway. I just called to say hi. When you get home around six I'll have all the time in the world, okay? Call me then. Don't miss the room with all the Rawson tapestries. Some of them are over a thousand years old."

"*Rawson tapestries.* Oh my god, dad. You're such a nerd." Floyd smiled, then gave in at last. A thousand years old sounded pretty cool, actually. "Alright, I'll go. I'll call you at six, okay? Isn't that late over there?"

"Nope. I'll be just starting my day at this rate. Talk to you then, son. Love you."

"Love you too, dad."

Floyd waited until his dad hung up, then he slowly picked his shirt up off the floor and put it on. Daven was no longer in the room, and Floyd hadn't noticed when he left. So he walked down to the car alone and shoved Theo over as he got in.

"Hey! Sit in the back, asshole," Theo protested.

"We can both fit here, bitch," Floyd replied grumpily, with another shove.

"Not if you keep eating as much bacon as you did this morning," Theo shot back with a firm shove of his own.

"Boys," warned Brittany calmly, although she wanted to laugh instead.

"Sorry," the brothers mumbled together.

The car pulled away from the driveway and into the street. From the passenger seat mirror Brittany pretended not to see Floyd suddenly put an arm protectively around his brother and pull him close. Theo squirmed away in silent protest at first, but then changed his mind and went back in for a re-do. Floyd draped an arm around him again, and covered them both up to their shoulders with the car's resident cashmere blanket.

The boys were quiet and still all the way to the museum.

CHAPTER SIX

Tuesday, March 28

Mayfair Federal Prison - Negotiating Room

"Fine. I'm not walking away. I have the official offer here." Lester laid out four pages on the table and shoved it through the tiny little crack on the table to the other side of the wire partition. "As the interested party, the Urbanes decide the penalty. If you confess to all charges and agree to be executed, then Harmon will deed-"

"*Executed?* What the holy fuck?" Hank nearly screeched. He swiped all the papers off the table with both hands and jumped up. Lester calmly continued

"-as I was saying, Harmon will deed your sons to my training school for nine months. I don't have to tell you that I'll take excellent care of them, but saying it anyway just in case you've forgotten how much they mean to me."

"What about me? Do I mean nothing to you?" Hank demanded. "I can't believe you bought into this Urbanes brainwashing shit."

Lester stared at him. "I'm not an Urbane anymore. I'm an Independent who works for an Urbanes-funded organization, like thousands of others. And I'm not here for you."

Hank answered quickly, and firmly, gesturing wildly around the room as he did so. "So this isn't about me, Lester? Are you serious? This is all about me and the knowledge I have of Harmon's crimes. He's asking me to trade my life for…for…you haven't seen my sons in ten years. You don't know them. They won't even *know* you . Floyd might, but Theo definitely won't. He was only two. And even if Floyd does remember, the last time we were together, you had a shotgun pointed at my chest. You think he's just going to let that go?"

Lester shrugged. "You do have that effect on people."

"So I just have to confess to everything, huh? That's your idea of justice?"

"You're guilty as sin, Hank, and everyone knows it. Time to think of the boys now."

"They're *all* I'm thinking about, Lester! Floyd is already 16. I can't believe you, of all people….no. I'm not signing anything." Hank was almost in tears, which is extremely rare for him. "Leave me the fuck alone. Maybe I should have been the one threatening to kill *you* ten years ago. And maybe I should have done it."

"Hank," warned Lester in a low tone. "Calm down."

Hank fixed him with an astonished expression. "Easy for you to say."

"This isn't my doing. This is Harmon, and you need to agree to it," Lester said placidly. "For the boys. You have no other option. You're already nailed with blackmail and that's a five year sent-"

“I know that. Goddamn, stop repeating yourself.” Hank turned his back to Lester and drummed his fingers on his hips impatiently. “Harmon isn’t the only one who can propose terms for this plea bargain. I want to talk to him.”

“You can’t.”

“Fuck you. I can, and I will. Arrange it for the sake of Floyd and Theo. Or else what happens next is your fault.”

Lester scoffed. “Nothing you could say would make me think that.”

Hank turned around, eyed him dangerously, then smirked. “Oh Lester, you know I love a challenge. So here’s the deal: arrange for me to speak to Harmon today, or be prepared to live with yourself when my boys are separated forever. Because that’ll all be on you, I guarantee it. I’ll do it. I’ll let this fall apart, just to make a point. I *know* you. It will *break* you to have that on your conscience.”

Lester breathed hard for a few long moments. “You’re a...you haven’t changed a bit, let’s just put it that way.”

“But you have, Lester. And I hate what I’m seeing. Do the right thing and give me at least a glimpse of the man who I fought with side by side through the years of the revolution. He’s got to still be in there somewhere. I have faith.”

Lester’s eyes narrowed dangerously. “You’ve never had faith in anything, asshole.”

The smile was gone now. "Well, maybe I *have* changed, then. But at least it's for the better, which is more than I can say for you."

Hank sat back down and crossed his arms, glaring at Lester with conviction and daring.

Lester sighed. "Fine. I'll see what I can do. For Floyd and Theo, not for you."

Hank wasn't granted the call with Harmon. He fully expected that and didn't blame Lester, however. Instead, he asked to call Daven and was granted the request. He was taken to a private room in the jail's offices for the task.

"I want my guard to be on the call as well," he told Stewart firmly. It wasn't a question. "He's going to start looking after Daven now, and I want to tell them both what my next steps are."

Stewart looked at Avery, then nodded. "I don't see why not. Come with me. You have 15 minutes."

"Thank you ever so much for your kindness," Hank replied facetiously, with a mock bow. "Avery, come on."

"Boss? What do you mean I'm going to-"

"Shhh." He shut the door of the little room behind him and watched Stewart settle in the room next door, purposefully keeping his back to the glass.

"Give me your phone," Hank whispered.

"What? Sir-"

"Your phone. Take mine and call Daven, but tell him to hold in silence until I'm done with this call. Mute us. Don't disconnect the line."

"Hank, no. You can't," Avery protested, having realized in dismay what his rebellious boss was up to.

"Do it, or fly back to Los Angeles today and leave me to fend for myself. Your choice."

Avery grumbled and rolled his eyes a little, but he finally took the proffered phone and handed Hank his own.

"Good afternoon," Hank began formally a few moments later, not sure whether to be relieved or not that his rival actually picked up the phone. It might have been better if he didn't. "I hope your day is going a lot better than mine."

"Holy shit," Harmon replied in shock. "You just don't know how to give up, do you? Goodbye."

"Okay. Guess you'll never know what I'm about to tell you, then. Too bad." Hank sighed dramatically, then paused as he heard Avery quietly explain to Daven why he was calling, and he almost missed Harmon's reply.

"-balls to call me again?" asked Harmon in wonder, and not a little admiration. "Only you would think you can get away with this."

"That's the goal. My charm and wit goes a long way, you know. I'll bet you $100 you don't report me."

"You know I won't," the other man responded, his tone more puzzled than usual. "You're in enough trouble already."

"That didn't stop you from reporting me the first time," Hank nearly spat back.

"Well, I was pissed off because I'd just found out Janet was the one who leaked our info."

Hank paused, wanting to scoff at that nonsense, but realizing it would get him absolutely nowhere at the moment. The last thing he needed was to lose the chance to have one final word with Harmon.

"Are you alone?" Hank asked carefully.

"Yes. Are you?"

"Obviously. Stewart thinks I'm calling Daven." Hank said a quick prayer under his breath. "Look, I know you're trying to help. The FBI has made it clear to me that without agreeing to a plea with you, this trial will never be wrapped up in time. I understand it was your idea to push it along faster to help out the boys."

There was the sound of a cleared throat from the other line, twice. "Not exactly my idea, no."

"Right. Anyway, I just want to know why you're pushing for execution. Do I really scare you that much?"

Harmon was obviously incredibly uncomfortable; Hank could hear him shifting in his chair. "I was advised that you confessing to all charges was the fastest way to wrap up the trial. Some of those charges require capital punishment. It's an ugly situation Hank, but you have to admit that you pretty much brought it on yourself."

Hank's heart raced at that. "Ah. So you think I'm guilty, then. Corporate espionage, Janet's murder, that big whole list."

"I'm not sure about Janet's murder. I've asked for it to be removed from consideration. But everything else? Absolutely. I have no doubt. If I did-"

"Of course you're not sure about Janet," Hank laughed harshly. "Because *you* did it. You, and Colbert, and some unknown motherfucker in my organization-"

"Hank-"

"-and I think you're afraid I'll find proof of it. That's why you want me gone. I see right you through you, my friend. You're more transparent than Saran Wrap."

Harmon ignored this line of questioning and went a different direction entirely. "Let's forget about Janet for a moment. I'm doing what I'm doing to help your sons, not you. I don't care what happens to you."

"You don't say."

"But I'm willing to sweeten the pot a bit if it helps."

"How on earth do you sweeten a pot of shit?" Hank asked with another dark chuckle. "The answer is no, I'm not agreeing to a fucking thing. You're scared because you *know* my informants gave me a lot of ammunition. I may be making you a plea bargain of my own if they can get their dossier together fast enough. But if not. Daven will take you down for me, and he'll have all the time in the world to do it. You are just as fucked as I am, my friend."

That seemed to set Harmon back on his heels, and Hank heard his quick intake of breath. "Okay, Hank. You like to say you're a realist. So let's get real. Even if I dropped my case and went down on charges myself, the FBI isn't going to stop their pursuit of you. Five years in jail, *minimum* , Hank, for what they've proven already."

"I'll take it. Maybe you and I will be cellmates. Wouldn't that be fun?"

Harmon's tone went dark; he was no longer in the mood for Hank's bullying. "Fine. Let me put it another way. Let's see what happens if you don't agree to a plea. Take me out of the picture entirely, Hank, and your boys go away for life because the FBI cannot wrap this up by March 31. But I can get it done with this plea bargain. Floyd and Theo? I'm their savior. You should be *grateful* that I'm offering to trade your life for theirs. Not threatening me."

"You're right. I'll send you a thank you card from death row."

Harmon ignored that, his blood now boiling. "And to get more *real* - you know who forced me to pursue the blackmail charge on you and offer a plea bargain? Stewart. I wanted to do this in civil court. He is literally the reason we're talking right now. When this all came up, I was only looking forward to suing you and making a nice chunk of change from that tape."

Hank's throat went dry, and his lungs started to hurt. "That's bullshit," he croaked without conviction.

"No, it's not. But everything you've said is. I'm done with this conversation. Goodbye."

"*Wait* . Just...wait." He was relieved to still hear breathing on the other line. "What is this... *sweetening the pot* you were talking about?" he asked quietly, carefully.

A long pause in which Hank was afraid Harmon had cut the connection, then a heavy sigh. "This has to remain between you and me. I can't put it in writing...but I guarantee you I will transfer Floyd and Theo's deed to Daven after the one-year waiting period."

No answer.

"Hank?" Harmon pressed after a minute.

"I'm here. If you're feeling so charitable, why don't you just transfer them to him right away?" he asked skeptically.

"You know why. Daven is under investigation, too. If he gets hit with a felony...and even if he doesn't, the courts can pull it back. It honestly makes no sense for me to do that, regardless. The public will see it as a bribe to get you to plead guilty, and the last thing I need right now is another PR nightmare at the hands of the Seditionists."

Hank closed his eyes and suddenly felt like a runaway train was barreling straight at him. "Fuck me, this is out of control. You know what, though? If you hadn't given them that tape recording, I'd still be free!"

Harmon refused to feel guilty about that. "For now. You're lucky I did. As I said, Stewart knew it was the only way to-"

"What else do they have on me?" Hank asked offhandedly. "I mean...this is..."

"Have you not seen the list of charges yet?"

"Of course I have." Hank rubbed his temples. "So I'm fucked, is what you're saying. You think Daven won't be approved."

"Correct. The courts can't risk it. I have nothing to do with the Daven issue, so you can take that up with him."

Harmon was right. Hank felt like he was going to throw up. He had to agree to the plea.

It was over.

It was well and truly over.

He was going to die within the week.

"Okay, so..." Hank took a deep, steady breath despite the jangling of his nerves. "You do realize you're going to turn out to be the villain in this scenario, right? The public is going to hate you. And the Urbanes."

"No. The terms of the plea bargain will remain confidential for ten years. That's one of the caveats. Your kids are stuck with me for a year, whether you like it or not.

Stuck with Harmon. Well, considering Daven's cavalier behavior lately, this might be the better option, Hank thought darkly.

"So what happens to them during the twelve months?"

"Already worked it out," Harmon continued brightly, heartened by the fact that Hank was finally seeing the light. "They can go to Lester Boyd's school for 9 months, then work for three months in a home of my choosing. After that...well, they become Daven's servants for the next 19 years. And we both know he won't treat them like actual servants."

Hank rubbed his temples yet again. "I can't believe this shit."

"Hank, even as much as you hate me, you know I would *never* do anything to harm your children. They'll be in good hands."

Hank knew it was true, as much as he hated this man. "What kind of school is it?"

"House servant training. Top tier, safest bet there is. And it will keep them together for the entire term of their indenture...even if something happens to Daven."

"That works," Hank said quickly, not really believing this was even happening and that he was even speaking such words. His eyes were still closed, his head throbbing in pain. "But I want their deed to go to Lester. Not you. And I want this entire agreement in writing. Verbal is not enough."

Harmon was puzzled. "Lester *Boyd* ? That's, uh...under what rationale?"

"Under the rationale that I don't trust your sorry ass."

"And you trust *him* that much?"

"With them, I do." It wasn't quite the truth; Hank didn't really trust Lester either, but he was enormously worried Harmon would lose the deeds if he was taken down by Daven and Rupert. Not if... *when* . Because after his best friends found out about his death and figured out what had gone down in Philadelphia, it was over for Harmon, too. Lester was the safest bet.

"That makes no sense. I'm the one who's trying to help them," Harmon added, still puzzled.

"They go to Lester, or you can hit me with another blackmail charge in about five seconds," Hank threatened icily, although it was all for nothing, really. His informants had almost nothing at all to go with, to his great disappointment. But Harmon didn't know that, so he wasted no time grabbing at the opportunity to get them out of the picture.

"Agreed, then. Looks like I picked the right negotiator after all."

Hank was silent for a long time, and Harmon didn't prompt him.

Eventually Harmon said, "Well...I'm going to revise the draft of the plea bargain and send it back to Stewart for your review.

I hope you take it, Hank. There's not much time to keep fighting about it."

"You're telling me. Before I go," Hank continued, "I'm going to give you some priceless advice for free: get rid of Colbert. He's been playing you like a fiddle all along. Dump his ass now, or you're going to be next to fall."

"Really. And what evidence do you have, exactly?"

Hank cut him off firmly. "Let's just say I'm so certain he's behind this, that I don't blame you for this situation. I'm not even mad. Ten years ago when I visited Colbert in prison, he vowed to do the same for me. Now he's come to collect on that promise. My time is up."

"He...*what* are you talking about?" Harmon queried, genuinely bewildered.

Hank ignored the question. "Good luck if you decide to ignore my warning. You're going to need it."

Harmon closed his eyes and took a deep breath. "Hank, just so you know. I never wanted-"

The line disconnected, and Harmon slowly opened his eyes to the sight of the phone trembling slightly in his hand. In the background, through the glass, Colbert slowly came into focus. He was standing by the coffee maker with Zane, bantering and grinning like he didn't have a care in the world.

Harmon watched him for a long moment, then pushed the dark thoughts aside and pulled up the plea bargain document on his laptop.

"Hank?" prompted Avery quietly. Hank took his phone back with a gulp and hung up on Daven without a word.

"Avery...I..."

"This is bullshit," Avery said plainly, and he yanked his phone out of Hank's hands and left the room angrily. Hank followed him silently, feeling like a child trailing an angry parent. Stewart was waiting at the table, watching them curiously.

"May we continue?" he asked calmly. "Or do you two need a minute?"

"We're good," said Avery tightly, ignoring the piercing glare Hank shot him. "I'll go back out the lobby if there's nothing else."

He didn't wait for either man to answer and simply walked right out the door, slamming it hard behind him.

"Okay then," Stewart said after an awkward pause. "You want to go after him, or-"

"No. Thanks." Hank sat down hard and dutifully handed his phone to Stewart, who scrolled through the call log. He spotted the 7-minute call to Daven, and handed the phone back.

"Thanks. On second thought, bring Avery back in here please."

"Why?"

"Just do it. Now, if you please."

Hank got up, his heart pounding. What the hell was Stewart going to… *oh, shit*. He stuck his head out the door and Avery came in immediately, still ablaze with fury.

Stewart stood up and put a hand out.

"Your phone, please."

Avery threw him a blank look. "My phone? Why?"

"I want to see the call log, if you please. Although it's not actually a request."

Hank sucked in his breath and struggled to keep a neutral expression.

"Yes, sir." Avery reluctantly dug his phone out of his inner pocket and handed it over.

"Thank you," Stewart said, somewhat sheepishly. He scrolled through the list very briefly, and then handed it back. "Sorry, I'm just doing my job. Thank you."

Avery nodded and left after cocking an eyebrow at his boss. Hank was astonished that Stewart continued the conversation as if nothing untoward had occurred…it just wasn't possible that he hadn't seen the call to Harmon. It was even more impossible for him to ignore it, if he had seen it.

Hank could hardly concentrate on Stewart's words as he was escorted back to the portico into a waiting car, and during the long ride to the hotel, he kept his face carefully expressionless in order to not give away that he was royally pissed off with the man for forcing Harmon into this situation...even though he was doing it to help Hank.

Hank was immensely relieved to finally be dropped off at the hotel and glanced at Avery with a look that clearly said "follow me, " but he was ignored. So instead of going to his own room, he boldly followed Avery into his and slammed the door behind them.

"If you have something to say, just say it," he challenged irritably.

Avery threw his boss a glare that all but set the room on fire. "Actually, no. I have zero desire to talk to you right now."

"What the hell?" Hank exclaimed in surprise as he followed his guard to the far side of the room, running both hands through his hair in frustration all the while. "Then just answer one question and I'll go. How did Stewart not see that call?"

Avery was breathing heavily as he continued to throw eye daggers at his boss. "Did you really not know that I carry two phones? One for work, one for personal?"

"No. I didn't know that." The realization then hit him like a brick in the face, and his heart raced a little as he stared at Avery's back. "Oh, shit. So you handed him the wrong phone."

"The *right* phone, you mean. You're welcome."

Hank's head was swimming a little. Actually, quite a lot. His tongue felt three times thicker than usual, too. It was a close call... *way* too close.

"Jesus Christ on a pogo stick. Avery, I can't tell you how grateful I am for your-"

"Don't bother, Hank. I quit," Avery said simply, without any heat.

"Avery!" Hank gasped.

Avery crossed his arms and kept his tone steady. "You acted unethically and put me in danger - and not the physical kind, which is the *only* kind I agreed to when I signed up for this job. So I consider this a breach of contract and expect an appropriate severance package."

Hank had never known Avery to be even half as angry at him before, and he was shocked into speechlessness at this declaration. He held up his hands in a *seriously* ? gesture and stared open-mouthed, feeling indignant and crushed all at once.

Avery was suddenly outwardly serene again, but an emotional explosion was simmering just below the surface as he crossed the room to the other side and yanked his suitcase out of the closet. "I'll stay here long enough for my replacement to arrive. Who do you want me to send over, sir?"

"Deveraux," Hank croaked after a moment. "I'll arrange it. You need to relax."

"I'm fine, and I'll take care of it. He should be able to make the 9pm flight and be here by dawn."

Hank felt his heart rise into his throat and stick there nauseatingly.

"Thanks." Hank noticed his hands were shaking, which irritated him even more. "You're right, I acted in an unforgivable manner. But may I ask why you're so furious that you want to just walk away? It seems out of proportion, no offense."

Avery did not waver. "Because I couldn't remember which pocket held which phone, and nearly had a heart attack on the spot trying to remember. It was sheer luck I grabbed the right one, but if Stewart finds out what I did...like I said, I didn't sign up for this."

He turned and jerked opened the suitcase and laid it open on the bed. Hank kept quiet for a minute while the man angrily threw all his belongings in, then spoke again quietly during a break in the furor.

"I'm sorry, Avery. I accept your resignation, since you insisted. But please reconsider. We've been friends for six years; don't let it end like this."

"No, I'm your employee and nothing more. *Former* employee, as of tomorrow."

Ouch , Hank thought with a sharp pang to his heart. It was a well-deserved jibe, but still. He softened his tone down to one he almost never used, except with Floyd when he needed soothing.

"Hey," he began impulsively, hesitantly. "Stop what you're doing for a second and talk to me. *Please* . It's important. Just...one more minute of your time is the last thing I'll ever ask of you."

Avery did stop, obviously deeply concerned about Hank's unusual pleading tone.

"Yes?" he asked with a visible degree of trepidation.

Hank wandered over the bed and sat down, defeated and tired. He reached back to grab one of the pillows and put it over his lap as if it could offer some kind of comfort and protection.

"Listen, Avery...I, uh..." His voice cracked briefly and he had to take a moment to regroup. "I'm not going home. This is it."

"Yeah, I gathered that."

Hank gripped the pillow tighter. "I need...I'm *asking* you to stay and take really good care of Dav. Please."

Avery wasn't moved. "He has his own guard already. As for that conversation with Harmon. I only heard part of it, not enough to piece together all that's going on. But it sounded to me like you were negotiating a prison sentence with him."

"Yeah, I was," Hank lied.

"Prison," Avery repeated flatly. "You said you were innocent."

"Look, it's complicated. I can't get into it. But this trip to Philadelphia has turned a one-way ticket, and that's the ugly truth. Will you stay with Daven? He will need you. I'll have your contract turned over to him tomorrow if you agree."

Avery just stared, his body at a complete standstill and his face frozen into an expression of disbelief.

Hank stood up and gently put the pillow back in place. "I'm sorry, this is a lot to take in without warning. I'm truly sorry about the phone thing. Honestly I had no choice, though, and I'd do it again if I had to. Hate me if you want, but it's the truth. Let me know in the morning what you decide."

Avery cleared his throat twice before responding. "I don't need time. The answer is no. But with your permission I'd like to stop by and say goodbye to the boys tomorrow."

The boys. Oh god . Hank had no intention of telling Avery what was going to happen to them; obviously the poor man hadn't heard enough of the conversation to realize the deeds he kept referring to were Floyd and Theo's. He must have thought Hank was referring to transferring the house servants, since everyone on the planet knew that Daven was the Bancroft boys' next guardian.

"Of course you can see them. And visit them whenever." Hank was suddenly exhausted. "But don't bother calling Martinez. You and Brody can fly home together tomorrow at noon. I won't be needing a guard or a lawyer any longer than that."

CHAPTER SEVEN

FBI Headquarters - FBI

Tuesday evening

It wasn't often that Stewart was left dumbfounded by new developments (after all, six years on the front lines in the Army tended to leave one nearly immune to surprises in later life), but he was entirely numb after he read Harmon's plea bargain. Salome was in a meeting, so he picked up the phone and called the leader of the Urbanes after he was finished digesting the new terms. Well, perhaps *digesting* was the wrong word.

"Harmon. Stewart. Listen, uh…what on earth went down between Mr. Boyd and Hank? I've just read his alleged agreement to these terms."

"Not alleged," Harmon corrected. "He did agree to them, and those were the amendments he wanted."

"How do you know that? I just left him an hour ago and he hadn't made any decision yet. He made it clear he had no interest in continuing any further negotiations with you."

Harmon cleared his throat roughly; being just as forbidden to talking to Hank as the reverse, he wasn't willing to admit his part in the affair.

"Well, maybe he just needed time to think."

Stewart set his coffee down hard, the realization behind's Harmon's caginess slamming him in the chest like a kick. "You two did talk. I *knew* it. And you told him."

"Told him what?"

"That I'm behind this. You did. Or Lester Boyd did. Don't lie. That's the only reason why he would have clammed up on me so quickly, and with such hostility. Because he never needs *time to think* , as you put it. The man makes massive decisions at the blink of an eye, always has. You know that."

Harmon swallowed hard. "I told him nothing. Lester might have."

"Bullshit. I can see right through you, even over the phone."

"No, you can't, because you're wrong. Can we please go over the document now?"

Stewart threw the papers down. "Oh sure, no problem. You just want Hank to die, is all. No big deal, let's just get it over with, huh?"

"Did you just call me to bitch me out, or are we going to get some actual work done here?"

"We're not doing a damned thing until you tell me if you spoke to him today. Yes, or no?"

Harmon gritted his teeth. "No. Why don't you ask him, if you're so sure? You know he can't lie."

"You're correct. Hold on."

Stewart pressed down the hold button with an angry jab, then set the phone on the desk and got up to pace his office. The truth was, he didn't want to confirm that Hank and Harmon spoke. If he didn't hear it directly, he didn't have to report it. He waited a few minutes to give himself time to breathe and calm down, then picked the receiver back up again.

"Alright, you two didn't speak. My apologies. Let's go over these terms, one by one. Starting with the corporate espionage confession…"

Hilton Philadelphia

Late evening

Lester Boyd couldn't sleep. Hank hadn't changed a bit, no. But his comments about the way *Lester* had changed was really driving him to distraction. The two men had lived one of those dangerously special kinds of friendships, where they each knew too much about the other. That was never a good position for two men of strong opinion and fiery temperament. As such, they had parted ways ten years ago knowing they were equally doomed if one turned on the other. So they hadn't done that.

Until now…Lester had been the one to turn on Hank this time. He had reason; the man broke every law in the spectrum and had somehow become a bigger asshole than he was before. Hell, he'd even threatened to separate his own children just to make life all that much harder for Lester. Hank deserved to go down.

So why couldn't Lester Boyd sleep? He didn't want Hank to die, for the boys' sake. Their grief would ultimately lie at the feet of the man who convinced Hank that death was the right decision. And that man was Lester. So he knew, even now, that his own life would forever be plagued with the guilt he had been so desperately trying to avoid earlier today.

Hank Bancroft had won. Again.

He didn't know at this time, of course, that it was all Harmon's doing. Or more accurately, Colbert. He wouldn't find out for a while; it would be months before his world turned upside down for a third time. In the meantime, he emptied the contents of his hotel room's minibar and finally passed out asleep at 4am Wednesday morning.

Ritz-Carlton Philadelphia

4am Wednesday morning

I don't wish for you to blame yourself in any way. I'm not convinced that the Seditionists are on the right path, and it would-

Hank scratched out these sentences for the fourth time and began again.

The Seditionists, under my direction, has lost our way over the past year. I'm counting on you to bring us back to a place where we can think again of the best interests of all citizens, not just our own constituents. While I wish for Harmon to be removed at your hands, you cannot let the effort obsess you and-

Obsess you. No...preoccupy?

-overtake your efforts to re-establish a firm hold on proper morals and ethics. Therefore, it is under my express command that you hold off from-

Hank tore up the entire paper and sighed in frustration and anger. This flowery language was not his specialty, and he needed to be more direct with this particular recipient, who wouldn't be impressed by being forced to read between the lines. He grabbed a fresh sheet of paper, and as an afterthought exchanged his black pen for a blue one in the hopes that would somehow help sweep away his writer's block.

Dav,

I'm sorry we didn't get to speak again before my death. Honestly, I wouldn't have known what to say. That I fucked up? That you and the boys have to pay the price for that? That I probably destroyed everything we've accomplished? How do I even possibly start to make amends? The answer is retribution, with my own life. Forgive me for taking the coward's way out.

I know the Seditionists are in good hands with you and Rupert, but you have to keep in mind that bringing down Harmon isn't your first priority. Getting us back to a position of trust and esteem must take precedence over everything else. Your constituents are counting on you to put them first.

Hell, the entire nation expects that. And you must put them first. Always.

When you get custody of the boys on April 1 next year, be prepared for them to be very different than they were before. Floyd's going to be angry. Theo's going to be even angrier. They may hate you. They will probably hate me. All I can say is, they love their Uncle Dav and will come around eventually. Have patience and treat them with more understanding and gentleness than I ever did. Floyd will test you until you're ready to have a nervous breakdown, and Theo? Well, he's young. He has no filter and no stop button. But you do. Use them generously.

In my plea bargain agreement, which is sealed for ten years, I took all responsibility for the recent errors in judgment you committed under my watch. That's why you were pardoned unconditionally. Just don't make any further mistakes, because I can't protect you a second time.

That being said, always remember that none of what happened to me was ultimately your fault. I chose to live my life on the razor's edge, and always knew the consequences could be dire. I'm at peace with the knowledge that my legacy will live on through the great things you and I accomplished together over the past decade.

Farewell, my loyal friend. See you on the other side...

Hank

PS

Really got to work on your people skills. Still rusty.

Hank didn't read the letter a second time for errors or clarity. He couldn't. His eyes were tired, and rapidly filling up with moisture. He folded up the paper and carefully slid it into the envelope, but didn't seal it yet. Stewart said he would have to read it first to make sure nothing in it would cause further legal problems with Daven.

Setting that letter aside, he swung his chair around to the other side of the desk and picked up the plea bargain that had been delivered by courier almost 6 hours ago. He'd hadn't signed it yet, because he was planning to demand to meet with Lester one more time in the morning. He'd say it was for a clarification, but in truth, he just wanted to be able to confront the man about his part in this and rub salt in the wound one last time.

Eventually Hank realized he didn't want to read that either and folded it up, too, forcing himself to stop thinking about all of this for at least a minute. So he took a shower and started to go to sleep as the sun was just starting to tug at the very edges of the horizon.

Then he realized he might not ever have another chance to see that sight, so he dragged himself to the reading chair by the window and watched Philadelphia transition from black and white into full color.

Anyone else would have winced at the thought of Independence Hall being the last thing he saw before he closed his eyes to rest, but Hank always did appreciate the black humor in such irony. There was a smile on his lips as he drifted off to sleep in the big fluffy chair that reminded him fondly of the one at the office Daven had hated so much and threatened to torch in Rupert's front yard.

CHAPTER EIGHT

Seditionists Headquarters

Friday, March 31

"Daven... *Daven* ." Billie waited a moment more, then cleared her throat loudly. "Mr. Johansson."

"*What* ?" Dav looked up from his notebook at last. He was in a rare temper, and everyone at the office had been afraid to set foot within 20 feet of him all day. Even Rupert.

"A gentleman is here to see you. Won't tell me his name, but he says-"

Daven stood up upon spying a familiar face peeking around the corner at him. "Thank you, Billie. Come in, Stewart. Shut the door. Why didn't you tell me you were coming?"

"I couldn't. I'm sorry."

Stewart sat down, looking for all the world like he would rather be anywhere else. Inside of an active volcano, perhaps. Daven's heart dropped a little.

"What news of Hank?" he demanded roughly; Hank's comments on his rusty people skills were the last thing on his priority list right now.

"Nice to see you, too. Alright, let's get down to it. I can't tell you anything unless you sign a confidentiality agreement that binds you and the Seditionists organization to permanent media silence on the topic of Hank's trial and outcome."

"Permanent!" exclaimed Daven furiously. "That's bullshit. What kind of idiot yahoo thought I would agree to that?"

Stewart's eyes narrowed. "I did, or I wouldn't have flown all the way out here. Calm down, Mr. Johansson. You need to come with me. My car is waiting-"

"No. I would show you out, but I'm very busy. Goodbye."

Stewart fully expected this; his tone remained steady and placating. "Fine. I can see you're under a tremendous amount of stress and not open to suggestion. So let me switch to facts. If you *don't* come with me, you're going to be very unpleasantly surprised and confused when you get home. Show me out, please."

Daven fixed him with an icy glare. "You know the way."

"Do it anyway. I won't ask again. You might want to pack up for the day."

Daven froze, hearing the warning in his tone. "Will I...will I be able to come back tomorrow?"

" *Yes* . You aren't being arrested. My sincerest apologies if I gave that impression."

"But the boys are expecting me home in an hour-"

"*Daven* ," Stewart snapped as he stood up, not willing to argue any further. "Let's go."

There was something in his tone now that made Daven comply, despite every desire to the contrary. He remembered Hank's words from a recent conversation: *Stewart has always been a friend to me...do as he says* . So Daven got up reluctantly, gathered his things, put on his coat, and quietly walked the man out the door and down the hallway to the elevator.

Stewart whispered. "We're going to Hank's house. Just get in the car and don't make a fuss. Don't even talk. Understood?"

Daven stared at him, bitterly swallowing the automatic protest. "Yes, understood."

"Thank you."

Daven was not just unpleasantly surprised when they arrived at the Bancroft house; he was astonished. Every single member of the household staff and guards were waiting at the door in terrified silence. He spun around to Stewart in bewilderment as they walked down the long hallway to the study.

"What the hell is going on?" Daven demanded in front of the entire FBI entourage that had followed them into the house from three different cars.

"We'll talk in a moment," Stewart replied coldly as he reached into his jacket pocket. "This conversation will be recorded for the protection of both of us. Will you come with-"

" No ."

"Come with me, Mr. Johansson. My group will stay out here." Stewart all but shoved Daven into the study and then slammed the door behind him, after which he hissed forcefully, *"I'm on your side, for fuck's sake! Cooperate, damn it."*

He then set the recorder on the table with a flourish and jammed down the red button while glaring dangerously at Daven.

He raised his voice so it could be heard through the door. "Daven Johansson, I hereby inform you our conversation is now being recorded until I return to my car. You almost must sign this agreement before I can say anything more. Do you understand?"

"Yes, we're being recorded. Got it. I'm not signing a damned thing. What's going on?"

Stewart closed his eyes to the pain that was throbbing behind his eyeballs, and lowered his voice to a normal level. "If you don't *sign. the. agreement. I'll have to leave* ."

"Goodbye, then. Thanks for the ride home."

Stewart inched the paper closer to Daven and raised an eyebrow. "At least read it first. If you still don't agree, I'll go without another word."

Daven read the two paragraphs and was surprised to realize he didn't disagree with the reasoning behind the demand. The FBI simply wanted to control the messaging themselves to prevent both parties from savaging each other in the press. It wasn't a bad idea at all.

"Will Harmon have to sign this, too?"

"He already has, and he wasn't happy about it either. But do you understand why we're asking for this?"

Daven grabbed a pen and scrawled his name much larger and messier than normal.

"I have to admit it does make sense. Alright, I signed. Now talk."

"Thank you. Three days ago, Hank pled guilty to all charges. His sons are being indentured for twenty years as of tomorrow at noon. Do you understand?"

Daven's jaw fell open. "I......no. What? Are you serious?"

"Floyd and Theo were taken into the FBI's custody about an hour ago. That's why we're here."

Daven was thoroughly appalled. "You just...you just came in and *took them* ? Without notifying me first?"

"We had to. Hank wouldn't agree to it any other way."

Daven sat down hard. "He *agreed* to this? You've got to be fucking kidding me," he said, realizing at the same time how much he sounded like Hank in that moment. "This is...I can't...did he leave me any kind of explanation for all this?"

"Yes, actually. You'll be summoned to Philadelphia on June 15 to personally retrieve a letter he wrote you. I will also have more information to release to you at that time."

"Why would Hank make me wait so long?" Daven asked mildly. The fight in him was suddenly gone; he just wanted to talk now and was desperate to wake up from this nightmare.

"I can't say. I have on me the original paperwork Hank signed to transfer the boys' deeds to an anonymous party operative, as well as a copy of the charge sheet where he signed his name next to the guilty plea. You may view the documents now if you're in the right frame of mind."

Daven shook his head; not to say no, but in sheer disbelief. "He didn't do a damned thing. This was coerced out of him. Wasn't it?"

"A plea bargain is mutual coercement, technically. I think what you're asking is how do you know this signature is legit? That he wasn't under duress, or under threat if he didn't sign?"

"Yes," Dav answered shortly. Bitterly. "Exactly that. Show me, please."

Stewart did. "You will see they are all co-signed by myself and the president, as well as Salome Danby. The very reason I brought them with me was to assure you he wasn't forced into signing."

Daven parroted flatly as he handed the papers back, "So you're telling me the boys are...for twenty years..."

"Correct. Now, as you know, deeds can be transferred after one year, but until then they will be taken to a completely confidential location. Only five people will know where they are, and you cannot change that."

"Oh, really?" Daven replied sarcastically.

"Yes, really. I realize you could probably figure it out with all the people you know. But the terms of that confidentiality agreement you just signed strictly prohibits you from trying. Indirectly, that is."

Daven looked down to the paper, feeling silently enraged again.

"Now on to my final topic," Stewart continued quickly, "The FBI has dropped our investigation on your part in all this, and it won't be reopened."

Daven was eerily calm. "I had no part in this. Did you assholes even investigate Colbert at all, or was that too much to ask?"

Stewart stiffened. "Furthermore, you are expressly forbidden from retaliating against the Urbanes or the FBI in any manner whatsoever. Retaliation means a lot of things, including the refusal to be civil in official communications." He shifted his glance to the paper Daven was still holding. "You may keep a copy of the confidentiality agreement for your records, and show it to Rupert and Taylor if needed. No one else is permitted to see it."

Daven turned around to the copier and made 2 copies, then handed the original back while the fury in his heart converted rapidly to black despair.

Stewart looked down again at the recorder. "I know that your next question will be regarding Hank's sentence. I can't tell you that either, but it's in his letter. You'll know on June 15."

Daven leaned over to the device and spoke directly into it. "This is bullshit. You should all be ashamed of yourselves for letting an innocent man and his sons get separated for twenty years."

"Noted, thank you," Stewart replied dryly, a bit shocked at the outburst. "Make sure to memorize the terms of that agreement, because even one slip-up will send you to jail."

"So the boys are no longer in Los Angeles?"

"Well, yes. They're on the plane, waiting for me. We're taking them to their father first, of course, so he can say goodbye. His sentence begins tomorrow at noon."

"I refuse to believe Hank actually agreed to any of this," Daven muttered stubbornly.

Stewart shrugged. "I don't blame you for that, to be perfectly honest. But his letter should help ease your concerns."

Daven scoffed. "Well, then. I would suggest you hurry up and join the boys on that plane. The faster, the better."

Stewart cocked an eyebrow at him, but didn't react otherwise to the rude dismissal. "Goodbye, Mr. Johansson. We will be in touch."

He reached over to shake Daven's hand silently. Daven took it for some reason, he didn't know why. He secretly preferred to strangle Stewart. But the man quickly transferred a small, folded square of paper to his hand during the gesture, then left. Daven stood there dumbfounded, watching the security cameras until the three black cars disappeared out the front gate. Then he sat down hard and yanked open the piece of paper, accidentally tearing it in half from haste.

I believe Hank's claim that he was framed. We will talk more on June 15 when you come to get the letter. In the meantime, if you quit, or piss off PH and get yourself fired (or worse), I won't get approval to investigate Colbert's possible hand in all this. Be patient. I need time to think and plan how to proceed. Your silence and perfect obedience to me from now on is critical.

Daven numbly read it a few times, then went upstairs and sat down on Floyd's bed, absently scratching the bellies of the boy's two dogs as he pondered the note. "PH" meant President Hendrickson, and it would take very little to piss the man off. He and Daven actively disliked each other from their first meeting, and had never bothered to make any effort to get along. Hank was always hopeful the two men would finally click whenever an occasion put them in the same room; even trying to seat them next to each other every year at the White House's Reunited Day Dinner. He had finally talked the butler into it last year, but then Daven had deftly swapped his nameplace card with someone else's mere seconds before everyone sat down. Daven smiled at the memory of his little trick. Hank hadn't even been mad; he was too busy being impressed by his friend's ninja-like stealth and determination.

Starsky and Hutch soon fell sound asleep upside-down, and Daven reached down between his legs to massage Shannon's neck for a while. He didn't know what to do next, and was still feeling nothing over the loss of Hank's freedom. Or that of

Floyd and Theo's. But he knew himself well; his tendency towards delayed reactions never meant lesser reaction. This apathy was merely the calm before the storm. The guilt, regret, and million questions would rush into his psyche all at once, and he was on the verge of being extremely miserable for at least a week.

When the intercom rang to announce dinner, it broke him out of his reverie at last. He peeled the dogs off his lap, hungrily ate the meal Chef had prepared for him, and asked Vance to drive him to church afterwards. He wanted to pray for Hank, and the boys, and even for Stewart. Especially for Stewart, maybe, he mused as he sat down in a pew and closed his eyes.

That was the plan, anyway. But the dam broke early and hard, and he ended up praying mostly for himself.

CHAPTER NINE

Friday night, March 31

Philadelphia

In a way, the last ten days had been the happiest of the Bancroft boys' lives. Their father may be all the way across the country, but he was acting how the boys thought all dads acted - meaning, not like a dictator. That's how he was on the boat every time they went sailing, and the boys loved it.

They'd all talked on the phone for hours. The man had a terrific sense of humor, who knew?

But now they were all in Philadelphia again, and Floyd in particular was dreading the possibility that the new warmth and love they'd heard over the phone would evaporate in person.

"Hey kiddo."

"Hey dad!" Theo called happily as he rushed out of the town car and into his father's arms.

"I've missed you. So glad you're here. Get any sleep on the plane?"

"No. Floyd slept the entire way, though."

"That figures. Come on, let's go to the room. What's taking him so long to get out of the car?"

Theo shrugged. "He's probably asleep again."

Hank released his youngest, then went to the car and stuck his head in.

"Hey Floyd. Put the Game Boy down and come out."

"I don't want to."

Hank clambered into the car and motioned Theo to wait with the driver.

"I know you're mad at me, but don't be a brat. There's only-"

"I'm not a brat," Floyd protested sullenly.

Hank reached over and took the gaming device gently out of the boy's hands. "I'm really glad to see you. You know we only have 14 hours. I explained this on the phone. Let's not spoil it."

"I don't want to."

"I know, because you don't want to say goodbye. Neither do I. But that's not until tomorrow. So let's go get some room service and watch TV for a bit."

"Why did Avery quit?" Floyd blurted abruptly, and Hank's heart stopped beating for a moment.

"Because he thought he wouldn't be needed anymore and got his feelings hurt when I asked him to join Daven's team."

"You didn't fight, did you?"

"Of course we did. I was really mad he wanted to leave, and I got my feelings hurt, too. There was some yelling. But leaving is what he wanted, so I wished him the best and said goodbye. Don't let that change your opinion of him. He's a really good man and deserves to be happy."

To Hank's great relief, Floyd accepted that explanation readily. "Oh. Okay."

"Let's go upstairs. I'm cold. And there's Boston cream pie on the room service menu."

That was enough to convince Floyd, and Hank climbed out after him with a grin.

At 3am, Floyd woke up with a gasping, violent start. His dad quickly came over to the bed and sat down next to him, speaking in a soothing tone and putting a warm hand on his shoulder.

"Floyd, you're with me in the hotel in Philadelphia. You okay? Sit up for a minute."

"You're awake, dad?"

"Yeah. Sit up. What were you dreaming about?"

Floyd searched his mind. "I was dreaming...something about Daven, I don't remember."

"Hmm. Anything to do with why you're being so mean to him?"

"Mean? You'd be proud, dad. I've never been more polite to anyone in my life."

"That's not what Theo says. Go back to sleep and we'll talk again in the morning."

Floyd laid back down. *Shit. So much for the new warm and fuzzy Hank Bancroft.*

\---------

It was 7am and Floyd was slowly shoveling sausages into his mouth while Theo slept on the other bed, drooling all over the bedspread. Their dad was sitting on the desk chair, absently rubbing Floyd's neck and back as he talked.

"You can't misdirect your anger like this. He didn't do anything, and doesn't deserve the way you're treating him."

Floyd bit his lip. He hadn't yet admitted what he heard on the news, about Daven being responsible for all this. His dad would certainly be furious, there was no doubt; maybe he'd even ask Daven to punish him. So Floyd had said nothing over the past week. He spent his time carefully avoiding Daven altogether, only responding to him with exceedingly polite *yes, sirs* and *no, sirs,* and not letting the man get within three feet of him or offer any comfort whatsoever.

"Floyd?" prompted Hank. "What's gotten into you? Did he do something to upset you?"

"Yeah. He doesn't have any feelings, dad. He's a robot. Maybe that's why Avery left."

Hank actually laughed out loud, and Floyd looked at him sideways. "Why is that funny?"

"Oh, if you only knew, Floyd. He's quite the character, isn't he? Look, I...there's something I really need to tell you before Theo wakes up. Are you done eating?"

"Yeah."

"Okay, put the plate down and let's go into the living room."

Floyd got up and stretched, feeling like he had just swallowed a brick. There were only five hours left until his dad was going to leave them for a year, and his stomach churned again as if he had eaten live snakes.

"Sit down, kiddo. This is, uh..." He put a hand on Floyd's knee and stayed silent for a few long moments. Floyd felt his adrenalin suddenly course through his body like a racecar on the track.

"What, dad? You're scaring me."

Hank looked up, and his eyes were a little wet. "I don't want you to live with Daven just yet. He's going to be way too busy as the new leader of the Seditionists, and won't have enough time to raise you the way I want. I've decided to send you to a boarding school in Virginia."

Floyd's expression was blank. "Just...just me?"

"You and Theo," Hank amended. "You'll stay there for a full year and no one will know where you are. You'll never have to worry about the Seditionists, or photographers, or news people trying to invade our lawn, or anything like that. It's a very safe environment."

"Okay," Floyd answered, not really upset about the news yet.

"The thing is, Floyd...you're going today."

"Today?" Floyd exclaimed.

"Today," Hank repeated. "I'm going to jail at noon, as you know, and at that time you'll be driven down to Richmond. It's about four hours. It's a training school, actually."

"For what?"

This was the hardest part of all, and Hank wasn't even sure he could ever get the words out.

"It's...just remember you're there for your own safety and security, and you'll be with Theo."

Now Floyd was really alarmed. "A training school for what?" he repeated loudly.

"For house servants. You and Theo both have-"

"We've been *indentured* ?" Floyd shouted.

Hank stood up now, too. "Yes, but only temp-Floyd, calm down and let me talk."

"Dad!"

"Floyd, *quiet*. Stop shouting. There's no reason to panic. I need to tell you all the details of what my-"

Floyd ran back into the bedroom, grabbed his coat, and slipped out the door. He took the emergency exit stairs and bolted into the lobby and out into the street. Hank and his guard didn't catch him in time.

Five hours later, the FBI came to collect their prisoner. Floyd hadn't been found yet.

They took Hank anyway.

THREE DAYS LATER

Seditionists HQ, Los Angeles

Monday morning, April 3

"Dav?" called Rupert nervously as he knocked on his boss's door. "Got a minute?"

Daven shut his laptop and pulled himself back to the present. "Yes. Come in."

Rupert visibly nervous and subdued. "You skipped church yesterday. The media is having a field day with it. Hailey, in particular. She's practically glowing."

"I don't care."

"You should, because Hank's going to kill you when he finds out."

"He won't find out," Daven answered coldly, and Rupert looked like a deer caught in the headlights as he sat down and crossed his legs one way, then the other, then back again.

"Alright. Well, Millie just called me. The boys haven't shown up for home school yet, and none of the guards are answering the phone at the house."

Daven said nothing and reached aside to grab his "World's Okayest Co-Worker" mug. The tea scorched the roof of his mouth painfully, but he didn't flinch. *Let it burn,* he thought miserably. I deserve it.

Rupert watched him closely, knowing he had to tread very lightly if he was going to get out of this conversation unscathed. "Wow. Finally using the mug I got you like six years ago, huh? I don't know if I'm more surprised by that, or by the fact that you're drinking tea."

Daven turned the cup around so the design was facing away again. "More like world's worst," he grumbled. *Uh-oh* , thought Rupert. Daven beating up on himself was rare, but always a very bad sign.

"Oh...so....Hank went down, didn't he?" Rupert asked quietly. Daven got up to lock the door, then stared out the window, not wanting to look at his friend's face for fear of starting a new grief cycle all over again. He steeled himself and spoke normally.

"Hank pled guilty and was taken to prison. The boys are now indentured and were removed from the house on Friday."

Rupert was stunned. "Excuse me? The boys were supposed to go to you. That's why they rushed this trial in the first place. What the fuck happened?"

"I don't know anything except that it was his choice. He wrote me a letter which I'll receive on June 15. I'm hoping he can explain himself then. Maybe we'll speak on the phone, eventually. For now, I…"

…I don't want to talk to him ever again. Daven mentally pushed back the nearly overwhelming fury he felt towards Hank for the incomprehensible decision. He wished he could see him one more time, just to throttle him into confetti.

Rupert said nothing for a long time. Daven heard some sniffles, so he turned to hand over some Kleenex and waited some more.

"Alright," Rupe finally said. "So what now?"

"Stewart had me sign a confidentiality agreement. I want you to sign it, too." He went to sit down, took the paper out of his pocket, and read it out loud.

"Permanent silence?" Rupe shot back angrily. "I'd have thought you would rather quit than agree to those terms."

"I may dislike the president, but he's smart enough to realize that without this agreement, our parties will spend months tearing each other apart instead of doing our jobs. I only wish he would have some the same for Hank so that he could never have instigated the problems we still have with Harmon. It's a smart move."

Rupert was shaking his head. "Dav…I don't feel the same. I can't agree to this. Ask me for my resignation if you have to."

Daven handed his colleague a pen. "You're not quitting. You're going to stay and help me get this organization back on its-"

"Dav, why would you-"

"- *back on its* feet again. That's going to take both of us. We'll still have say in what the FBI releases. We just can't release it ourselves. Tell me how that's unreasonable. Don't you dare threaten to quit on me again. You hear me?"

Rupert looked up, startled into awed silence.

"Sign it," Daven repeated firmly, before there was time for another protest. Daven's expression was unreadable, but his voice was like a thundercloud of hell about to break loose. Rupe had never heard that tone of voice before, and it shook him. So he took the pen and signed, vowing to bring the subject up again later when he might not lose his closest friend over it.

"Now," continued Daven in his normal tone, "first things first. We need to get our accounting staff back into the office. The books are going to be a mess if we don't. Can you facilitate that for me?"

"That's...it's more of a Human Resources thing, but yes. I'll get it started."

"Good. Thank you. And then I need you to gather up the latest-"

" *Wait* , Dav. Please. For god's sake, at least give me five minutes to process this clusterfuck before you throw me back into the fray."

Dav set down his mug and frowned. "Sorry. I've had three days to think about it and all I want to do now is talk about something else."

"Understood. Just bear with me a little longer. You *know* Hank was framed, right? Can't we do something?"

Daven thought again about the papers he'd been shocked to find in Hank's safe on Saturday. That was something he could tell his friend about, and it might help him move on.

"Stewart said we can't. It's done. There's something else I have to tell you. You're not going to like it."

Rupe looked crushed. "Oh, god...what? I'm afraid to know."

"Well, you need to hear it. I found out on my own that Hank's informants were making photocopies of proprietary Urbane documents for him. At least one, anyway, but it was a big one. I found it in his safe. That would explain why he always refused to tell us who his contacts were."

"Holy shit. What was it?"

"A first draft of the lawsuit Harmon filed against him. In Harmon's own handwriting, along with all his side notes and remarks."

The hair on the back of Rupert's neck rose and practically crackled from tension and fear. "Oh, fuck...Dav...that's political espionage, plain and simple."

"Yes. There's zero chance it was planted, because Hank put his own notes all over it, too."

Rupe breathed in deeply and felt like crying again. "Jesus, I've never felt so torn in my life. Who knows what else they took. Do you still have it?"

"Yes. I want to hold on for it a little bit, in case Hank appeals."

"Appeals his own guilty plea? For god's sake, Dav, you're not thinking. Get rid of it now before the FBI finds it. Nothing it says is going to help him now, if it didn't already."

"But if Stewart knew about it, he would have told me to open the safe while he was standing five feet away from it. He didn't, so he doesn't know."

Rupert went pale and clammy. "What if they show up with a search warrant? Jesus Christ on a pogo stick. How can you be so calm? You know what, it's not even safe to be telling me this. You...you *really* shouldn't have told me that."

Daven shrugged. "Like I said, I thought the knowledge that he was guilty of at least some of the charges would help you move on. It has for me. And I think it's important for you to know how much I trust you. Want to grab some breakfast with me?"

"No. I mean...thanks, but I need some time alone because I'm disturbed by how cavalier you're being about this. Seems like you don't even care what happened to Floyd and Theo," Rupert accused, even knowing he wasn't being fair. Daven wasn't exactly prone to emotion even under the roughest circumstances.

"Rupert...you of all people should know what the last three days without them has been like for me. But right now I have a lot of work to do. I'm going to the cafeteria. I hope you can pull it together by the time I get back."

"Depends how long you're gone," Rupert replied with a shrug as he got up and left. He was very upset, and Daven knew he had to change tactics quickly or his friend would walk out the door and not come back.

Got to work on your people skills, Dav. Still rusty.

————-

Philadelphia, Monday afternoon

FBI Headquarters

Stewart rubbed his eyes as he fought with a terrible case of writer's block. Not that he didn't remember everything that happened, of course, but he had difficulty articulating it properly without breaking out into a fit of righteous indignation and accusations. This was an official report for the president, and he had to stay professional.

The prisoner was taken to Mayfair Facility and the execution postponed indefinitely, approved by Salome Danby. Approximately 90 minutes later Floyd was located by municipal police in the parking lot of Oregon Diner in South Philadelphia.

The part after that was where he had re-written his account at least four times already.

Floyd was taken by police car to Mayfair Facility and met by me, whereupon he refused to get out of the car. Mr. Bancroft was informed of this predicament, and did not grant me permission to force Floyd to exit the vehicle. A phone call was proposed as an alternative, but Floyd again refused and became emotional. Salome Danby instructed me to ensure Floyd was not having a panic attack, which he said he was not.

Stewart had to get up and walk around his office for a few minutes. He hated everything and everybody for what happened next.

After approximately 30 minutes, at 2:07pm, Floyd exited the car on his own accord and requested to be taken into the facility to say goodbye to his father.

Stewart wiped his eyes.

They embraced for approximately two minutes, during which less than twenty words were exchanged. No time limit had been given; they broke apart on their own accord. Floyd left willingly and was taken back to the hotel by police to rejoin his brother.

"Fuck you Harmon, Colbert, FBI, and everyone else involved in this bullshit," Stewart said out loud. Then he put his pen to paper again, reinvigorated by a bitter energy he had never felt before.

Hank Bancroft was executed by lethal injection at 4:00pm after reciting his final words to myself, Salome Danby, and Lester Boyd (3rd party negotiator). Please find attached the transcription of this statement.

Five long pages, single-spaced. It had been a hell-raiser of an impressive speech, too, and one which could easily start a third revolution if it got into the wrong hands. The man knew how to get a message across, to say the least.

I returned back to FBI Headquarters rather than the hotel as planned, as the emotional toll of this day exhausted my ability to continue. Salome Danby proceeded to the Ritz-Carlton on my behalf. The Bancroft boys were transported to ISTMS at 6:00pm and arrived at 10:02pm.

The report wasn't perfect, and would have to be expanded a little for more clarity, but Stewart stopped there and thought about Hank's speech again. He had taken a copy for himself, and already knew that when the investigation of Colbert was over, he was going to be calling Daven and asking for a job with the Seditionists.

MONDAY EVENING

Seditionists HQ - Los Angeles

Daven walked into Rupe's office and shut the door behind him.

"Rupert...we need to talk about what happened between us this morning. I don't want to leave it until tomorrow."

"Me either. Please sit down."

"Thanks. I should have just told you it wasn't a good time to talk in the first place. I have so much going on. I still need to explain to the household, or rather, *not* explain where the boys are. It's not going to go over well, so I've been putting it off. Hank's guards are totally in the dark too and getting on my case every five minutes for updates. Avery quit last week, by the way."

"Avery *quit* ? *Avery,* of all people? Why?"

"No idea. He left Hank alone in Philadelphia and came to say goodbye to the boys while I was at work. Theo told me."

"What a dick!"

"I'm not sleeping well," Dav continued tiredly. "The dogs are anxious about the boys missing and won't eat. I'll have 11 servants to get rid of, and almost all the guards. Not to mention two huge houses to be emptied and sold, and a boat, and cars. All the while settling Hank's personal financials and running this organization in a new role I don't feel qualified for, under the threat of jail time for making one mistake by saying something I shouldn't. My nerves are totally shot. I'm almost past caring about anything but me right now."

Now Rupert was softened up, too. "Can't blame you for that. Good god. I'm sorry. By the way, you *are* qualified. There is no one else who can do this."

"Thank you for saying that. Maybe I'll believe you one day." Daven ran a hand through his hair. "I'd like you to sign a one-year contract. I'll double your pay if you do."

"Jesus, Dav!" Rupert breathed shakily. "No. Absolutely not. I don't do things just for money."

"Then what's it going to take for you to stay?"

"Who said I was leaving?" Rupe exclaimed.

Daven spread his arms out and made a vague, all-encompassing gesture to include the entire building. "Why on earth would you *want* to stay? Do you have any idea what we're in for when the press figures this out? It's just a matter of days before everyone starts bailing on me, employees and constituents alike."

Rupe was shaking his head slowly. "I don't get it. Remember what you told me this morning? You literally said *I think it's important you know how much I trust you* . And now you're all but bribing me for a contract? What happened between then and now?"

"I realized leaving is the smartest thing to do. The safest. I would if I could."

"Then why don't you?"

Dav pursed his lips. He couldn't say that Stewart told him he can't quit, but he wanted to so desperately that it physically pained him. "I want to stay and continue Hank's work."

"I don't believe you. You want to stay behind to take down Harmon and Colbert."

"That would be a nice bonus, but no. I can't touch them, at my peril."

Rupe got it now, and his heart started to hurt, too. "I see. The FBI is forcing you to stay. For how long?"

"I don't know. For longer than I want, certainly." Daven looked broken for a moment, and Rupert suddenly felt the need to do absolutely anything to help his friend feel better. They had come so far together, why not keep going a little longer?

"Alright," he agreed, forcing out a cheerful, casual tone. "If you're that determined to be stuck with me, I'll sign a contract. Draft one up, but don't change my pay. It wouldn't look right. Just buy me dinner at Yamashiro and we'll call it even."

"Yamashiro? It might cost me less to double your pay," Dav remarked humorlessly.

"Most likely, yes. I do want a certain clause included. One that says we work together as true partners. I want to know everything that's going on with this organization. Also, you have to take my advice if I think you need rest. You drive yourself too damned hard. It's not sustainable, and god knows no one else is remotely qualified to run this ten-ring circus if you work yourself to death."

Daven nodded. "Alright. Fine. Whatever." He looked irritated, like he was going to argue, but he didn't say whatever was on his mind. Instead, he reached out to shake hands. When Rupert took it, Dav then stepped forward and pulled Rupert into a tight embrace. It was brief, but significant and unprecedented.

"Hugs now too, huh?" Rupert joked as he wiped away new moisture from his eyes and stepped back. "I might have to upgrade that mug of yours. Hey, Millie is making dinner now. Want to join us?"

"No, but thank you. I'm not in the right frame of mind. We'll talk tomorrow. Go be with your family."

"Dav…I know it always makes you uncomfortable when I say it, but you *are* part of my family, and there's always a place at our table for you. When you're ready, of course."

Daven blushed a little, as usual.

"I can't. I really need to meet with the household tonight. They're a mess. It's not fair to leave them hanging any longer."

"Oh. What are you going to tell them?"

"Well, I'm letting go of all the guards except Martinez and Toby. Then I'll tell the servants that they're going to be freed. All of them are more than halfway through their terms, so now I can legally cancel the rest of their sentences."

Rupert was stunned. "Dav, there's a massive penalty for owners to do that. Eleven of them at probably a hundred thousand a piece…that's more than your house cost."

"It's not a money issue. I intend to abolish this whole system, and who better to set an example than the new leader of the Seditionists?"

"Wait, wait. With all due respect you're being completely unrealistic. Our party is *responsible* for this system. You were one of its biggest proponents! A quarter of our constituents have servants of their own."

"But only about 5% of Harmon's. Rupe, I'm not talking about abolishing it overnight. We still have three years before we can even publicly *suggest* revoking the law. I'm talking about you and I being the drivers of a steady, gradual shift towards abolition. The program started as an alternative to prison overcrowding. It's quickly on its way to becoming full-on slavery again with every new vote."

"It's what our constituents want. You are paid to represent *their* interests, not yours. And they're going to be very confused with why you're suddenly changing trains now...or worse, just claim you're doing it only for Floyd and Theo."

Daven didn't budge. "They can claim whatever they want. Deed holders are in the minority. So we'll focus on the majority."

"In theory, yes, but...I don't know if it's possible, Dav."

"Exactly. You don't know. So why not try?"

Dav sounded so much like Hank with that statement.

"But considering our biggest supporters are the wealthy with huge households, this might be the end of both our careers if we succeed."

"God, I hope so. I hate this job."

Rupert sighed and gave up. Daven's logic and persuasive skills were not quite as irresistible as Hank's, but he had learned a lot from the man over the years. "Okay, fine. Why not. Does this mean I have to get rid of my servants, too?"

Daven fixed him with *that* look. "What do you think?"

"Right. How about I allow you to tell that one to Millie yourself?"

"I will if you insist, but as her husband it seems you-"

"Dav, I was joking. Just...let me know what you decide, so I can look into the costs."

"I've already decided."

Rupert smiled a little, feeling both dread and warmth at the same time. "Why do I have the feeling you're going to be more of a hardass than Hank Bancroft ever was?"

"That would be a difficult feat, and one that I'm not interested in accomplishing."

"Can I bring back my favorite chair, then?" Rupe joked hopefully.

Daven looked at him askance. "That hideous fluffy thing? Absolutely not."

The
Strongman

Rescue at Sea

CHAPTER ONE

Wednesday afternoon, April 4

FBI Headquarters - Philadelphia

"I'm just saying, it's complete bullshit," Stewart muttered to as he walked to the President's office with his boss.

"You'd better use different words to Rickon," Salome said quietly. "That's not saying I'm disagreeing with you, but-"

"I know," snapped Stewart, then he backed off just as quickly. "Sorry. It's...it's not your fault."

They walked into the antechamber and found the president already standing there, looking grim. He beckoned them both wordlessly into his office, and Stewart handed over the sealed report.

"Sir, it's all in there as requested."

"Thank you," Rickon responded with a sigh. "An ugly business, for sure. I don't want either one of you thinking for a minute it was your fault. We all tried to talk Hank out of this, so if you're a failure, then I'm a failure, too."

Stewart glanced aside at Salome and took a deep breath. "I just...sir, it seems..."

"What? Speak freely."

"Yes, sir. In my humble opinion, it's unconscionable that we aren't telling Daven he's getting Theo and Floyd in one year. Not to mention keeping that from the boys themselves. And who's going to break the news of Hank's death to them? I just feel so wrong about this whole thing."

"Sit down and let's address all that," the president replied mildly as his hand hovered over his intercom. "Is this a tea or coffee kind of day for you?"

More like whiskey, actually. "Neither, sir, thank you. I think we should tell Daven. It will help keep him in line and out of trouble, and screw what Harmon wants. It's cruel."

The president shook his head. "It was written in the plea agreement that he wouldn't be informed, period. Hank agreed to it."

"Because he had to," Stewart replied, keeping his tone level. "His kids were being used as weapons against him. He would have signed anything!"

The president looked at Salome, then back to Stewart. "Harmon was rightly trying to protect himself. If the public knew, they would lynch him. Hell, Daven himself would probably lead the mob."

"It's cruel," Stewart repeated, not as angrily this time. "We should tell Daven anyway."

The president smiled a little, but there was nothing sinister in it. "Stewart, let me cheer you up a little. I'm going to order a full investigation of Colbert. Do you really think Harmon will help us if we break the terms of that agreement within days of signing it? He would not."

Stewart's heart leaped a little, and he was much happier suddenly. "Help us? You think he would?"

"Considering he's the one who asked me to do it, what do you think?"

Now Stewart sat up very straight. "Oh, *fuck*. Sorry, sir, I mean...he...he *asked* you?"

Rickon nodded. "You want to take it on? You can have it, but you need to keep yourself together and be objective. Can I count on you to do that?"

"Yes, absolutely. A hundred percent. On what grounds does he base his suspicion?"

"Instinct, for now. I said it wasn't enough at first, but I've had a few days to think about it. Give yourself a week to get a plan together, and in the meantime I'll call him and let him know."

"Jesus Christ," Stewart murmured as he glanced at Salome again. Her eyes were wide, clearly she was hearing this all for the first time as well.

"Sir," Salome put in, "Are we going to tell Daven that we're investigating Colbert?"

"No-"

"We have to," Stewart said quickly. "He'll quit if we don't."

"No, he won't," Salome interjected quickly.

"With all due respect, he absolutely will. I don't trust him to stay quiet, confidentiality agreement or not. He's a martyr, just like Hank. Maybe worse, because he's the opposite of impulsive, and he's going to stew about this and eventually get himself thrown in jail on purpose just to bring attention to what's happened. We'll never see it coming. And that's going to destroy his chance to have custody of the Bancroft boys."

Rickon looked alarmed. "Are you certain of that?"

Stewart nodded. "I would bet my career on it. We need to tell him now."

"I completely disagree," Salome said politely.

"You've only met him once. I know him, and Hank warned me about it several times, too. He was extremely worried that Daven would fall on his own sword."

The president held a hand up. "As the FBI, your first duty is to the investigation. But as human beings, our first responsibility is to those boys. Stewart, you can tell him. But if he breathes a word of it to anyone else, I will put him away for a long time *and* cancel the investigation. Clear?"

"Yes, sir."

The president dismissed him, and Stewart had to fight his legs to go slowly and not carry him in a flat-out run to his office.

Stewart wasn't wrong about Daven at all, even though the man hadn't mentioned the H-word in days, and he was barely on speaking terms with Rupert over it. Their last conversation had ended in a bitter fight about how fast one should move on from such a tragedy.

Rupert had to bite his tongue as he walked down the hallway to his boss's office with a new article in hand. There was nothing more he wanted than to quit, and it pissed him off that Daven had so quickly introduced a contract for him to sign in order to keep him from doing it. If he had known his friend thought so little of Hank, or that they would be unable to get along for more than 30 seconds at a time, he would have never signed.

Knock, knock. "May I come in, boss?" he asked politely.

Daven was searching for something in his closet. "Come in," came the muffled reply. "Hold on, just looking for my phone charger."

Rupert waited by the desk with newspaper in hand like he was a soldier standing guard. Daven found the item in question and went to plug it in, making no effort to speed up the process or make any kind of greeting as he sat down.

"What is it?" he finally asked.

Rupert placed the newspaper in front of him. "I know I don't have permission to talk about Hank, but what about Floyd? Look at this. Someone took a photo of him and the caption says the police were after him. We're going to get a ton of questions about this."

Daven lifted the paper, feeling his stomach turn nastily as the sight of Floyd standing alone at a crosswalk in an obviously bad part of town, looking completely lost and scared.

"What the hell?"

"There's no context or date to it, and it's so blurry that this paper didn't confirm it's him. Obviously we know it is. What do you make of it?"

Daven studied it harder, having no earthly idea what it meant. He automatically reached over to his phone and dialed Stewart.

"Daven? Wow, I was just about to call you."

"Why? Is it about this photo?"

"What photo?"

Daven swallowed hard. "Where is Floyd?" he demanded. "This says the police were after him, and he's standing alone on a corner in the snow. It's an article in the Denver Post."

"Oh. Yes, Floyd ran off when he was in Philadelphia on Saturday. We found him, he's safe now. Look, I've got to tell you something."

"*Was* in Philadelphia? Where is he now?"

"Daven, he's fine. You're not to ask about him again. Remember our agreement?"

"I want proof he's safe, or I'm talking to the press and you'll have to arrest me. Call me back when you have it."

Daven hung up the phone angrily.

"What the fuck was that?" Rupert asked hotly. "What did he say? You know you can't talk!"

Stewart called back immediately, but Daven sent it to voicemail.

"Rupert, I-"

"Now he's calling me," Rupert blurted in a slight panic as he yanked his phone out of his pocket. "I can't ignore it, Dav."

Daven took the phone and answered it himself. "What do you want?"

"If you hang up on me again, we're going to have a serious problem. Do you understand me?"

"We already have one. I want this photo explained, and I want proof Floyd is safe. This says the police were looking for him."

"They were. They found him. He's *fine*. I can't tell you anymore than that, and you know I wouldn't lie to you, nor would the president."

"You, no. But I don't trust Rickon as far as I can throw him."

Long pause. "You need to pull it together, Daven. I have news on the Colbert front."

"What?"

"We're launching an investigation of him, right now, directed by the president. The same president you just disrespected so thoroughly. He approved it over Salome's repeated objections, all because I said *you* were totally convinced of Colbert's interference and could help me prove it."

Daven was frozen in his spot, hands and face tingling from anxiety. "I see."

Stewart was furious now. "Rickon is your boss now. Not Hank, and he's *not* the enemy. I expect you to act accordingly and treat him with respect at all times. Is that also understood?"

"Yes," Daven responded coolly. "My apologies."

"Thank you. Floyd is fine." Stewart was much calmer now. "He got over-emotional and left the hotel for a short time, and got lost, but we brought him back in time to say goodbye to Hank. There was no panic attack or anything, if that's what you're worried about."

"I was," Daven admitted quietly, greatly relieved to hear the story behind the picture.

"One last thing. You are not to breathe a single word of this investigation to a single soul. If you do, it will be canceled because then it's considered tainted. I'll update you as much as I can. Goodbye for now."

"Thank you," Daven said as he hung up the phone and handed it back to Rupert.

"What'd he say?"

Daven didn't answer; he simply reached into his desk and pulled out the original contract Rupert had signed. "I release you of this contract," he said simply as he ripped it in half, and then into quarters.

"Dav? What are you doing? Why?"

"Because I can no longer keep to my side of the agreement."

"Since when?"

Daven looked at the phone meaningfully. "You can draft your own severance package and I'll sign it without argument."

"I don't understand," Rupe prompted somberly.

"Our agreement said I have to keep you in the loop on everything. As of right now, I can no longer do that. You may leave whenever you wish."

Rupert paused, considering it, then discarded the idea as he clapped his friend on the shoulder. "Nope. You're stuck with me. Want to go get a beer?"

Daven covered Rupe's hand with his own, and then gently peeled it off. "You still don't understand. This is...I can either be your friend, or be your boss. I can't be both at the same time."

"Fine. Then you're my boss from 8am-6pm, and my friend from 6pm to 8am. Now they're not at the same time."

"You know that's not what I mean!"

Rupe spread his hands out in a 'no duh' gesture. "Yeah, I do. But don't take the coward's way out, Dav, and just kick me to the curb like this. You're better than that."

Daven considered this. "We're just not aligned at all, it's not going to work. I...my feelings about Hank are complicated. I'm angry at him, I'm sad, I'm everything in between...mostly angry. I just don't want to talk about him, or the boys. It doesn't mean I don't care. Can you accept that?"

Rupert nodded solemnly. "Yeah. I hear you."

"Then stop arguing with me every five seconds. I can't make a move without your disapproval, and it's driving me crazy."

"Oh, really? Have you noticed I can't even blink without you glaring at me? I'm not the one who did this to Hank, Dav. Don't take it out on me."

The two men stared at each other for a little while, then Daven backed down.

"Alright. Let's move on. Sorry, but I'll have to take a storm check for the beer."

"*Rain* check, Dav."

"And I'm going to take the rest of the week off. Unless you have any objection?"

"Of course not. I'm glad. Please get some rest."

"Call me if you need anything."

"You too, thanks."

TWO MONTHS LATER

Denver, Colorado

June 10

Harmon picked up the newspaper again and read the paragraph three times over:

In a shocking revelation brought forth by inside sources, it was discovered that the leaders of the Seditionists have collectively paid almost two million dollars out of their personal funds to cancel the deeds of 14 household servants. Additionally, all contracts the Seditionists held with the state to employ indentured labor on their campus grounds have been breached and paid off. What this means regarding the organization's stance on the Bonded Retainers Laws is unclear, but apparently we won't be seeing any more tightening of the leash under those articles. Sources say both men have now hired back several of those former servants and laborers for hourly pay and full benefits. We are working hard to confirm this and will report again tomorrow with any updates.

"Holy shit," Harmon breathed to himself quietly as he picked up the phone and dialed the leader of the Seditionists. As expected, Daven didn't pick up. In almost ten weeks he never had, nor had he answered any emails. It was almost as if the man refused to acknowledge that Harmon existed at all. Stewart hadn't interfered, either, and basically told Harmon to put on a pair of big boy pants and shut up about it.

He left another voicemail anyway.

"Daven, Harmon here. Still need to know if you want to work together on the July 1 vote. It has some measures in it related to the indentured servitude laws, as I'm sure you know. This is strictly business. Call me back when you have a moment."

Los Angeles, California

Seditionist Headquarters

Same day (June 10)

Daven was sitting at his desk alone, drinking green tea and tapping the desk incessantly with his silver pen as he read. The July 1 draft measures were out, and it was going to be a bold move to oppose them. His thoughts were interrupted by the face at the window, and he pressed the button on the desk to open the door.

"Hey. New office looks good on you," Rupert said with a small smile. Taylor slid into the office behind him.

"Thanks," Daven responded blandly. Moving into Hank's office had all but made him an emotional train wreck at first, but now he found it comforting.

"A courier was just here," Rupert said, changing the subject quickly, and he handed two envelopes to Daven. "I brought Taylor in because the first one concerns the July 1 measures. Harmon sent a handwritten note to request we cooperate with him. Says you aren't returning his calls and emails."

"Correct. But yes, we need to work with him. Taylor, let's talk later. I'll need you to lead this charge. Maybe 9am tomorrow, if that works."

Taylor nodded and left. When the door shut behind her, Daven looked at the other envelope.

"Rupert, I...I know what this is. And I don't want to open it."

"You have to."

"Open it for me?" Daven asked as he handed it back.

Rupert ripped it open. "It's a summons to report to Philadelphia to retrieve Hank's letter. You were expecting this."

"I know."

"You have to go."

"I can't. I'm going to ask Stewart to let you go get it for me. Are you okay with that?"

Rupert shook his head. "No, Dav. I think this is something you need to do yourself."

"I knew you were going to say that," Daven grumbled angrily.

"We haven't fought in two months, and I'm not going to fight you now. I'm *asking* you. Please go do this. It's what Hank wants. Maybe you'll even get a chance to talk to him and hash this out."

Daven rubbed his temples about a dozen times before responding. "Will you go with me?" he asked quietly. "Please?"

Rupe put the letter into Daven's hands, and nodded. His eyes were wet suddenly.

"Of course I'll go with you. I'll make the arrangements and coordinate with Stewart myself. Private plane?"

"Yes. Email Maurice, he'll handle it for us. I don't want anyone else to know."

"Okay. We'll get through this together, Dav."

"Thanks, Rupe. Wait…before you do anything, I think I'm going to take you up on that rain check I got back in April for a beer."

"Sounds good. I'll go pack up and pull the car around back."

CHAPTER TWO

Philadelphia

June 15

It had been four hours since Stewart quietly led Daven to his most private conference room and handed him the letter. Four hours...that's what it took for Daven to recover from his rage and let Stewart know he was ready to talk.

The man had led him into his office and sat Dav down gently, knowing this was going to be a horrifically ugly confrontation. And also knowing there was very little he could do to offer comfort.

"I'm so very sorry, Daven. There's nothing I can add to the letter. At least not while the investigation of Colbert is still ongoing. Once that's over, you'll get the uncensored version, and you'll know what I know about the boys."

"The investigation, that's right," Daven said flatly - sarcastically, rather - as he folded up the letter and put it into his inner coat pocket. "How is that going, by the way?"

Stewart cleared his throat. "I'm surprised you haven't asked me about it yet. It's been ongoing for about six weeks now. We don't have anything solid yet."

"You haven't asked for my help on anything," he responded bitterly. "I thought you said the president wanted you to work with me."

"Daven, *please* don't do this. Don't turn on me again. I'm overwhelmed as it is, and getting animosity from you won't help matters. I'm completely on my own. I can't even summon Harmon and ask for his help."

Daven didn't back down. "So...when it's discovered that Colbert was behind all this, who are you going to summon to bring Hank back from the dead?"

"That's totally unfair. He knew what he was doing, it was his choice."

"His *choice,* really? He was innocent!"

Stewart raised an eyebrow slightly. "Oh, come on. I know about those papers in his safe, which you certainly have found by now and haven't mentioned. That alone would have gotten him twenty years. So I'd tread very lightly if I were you."

"Is that a threat?" Dav bristled.

"Not at all. It's a reminder of who you worked for," Stewart answered calmly. "Hank was *far* from innocent."

"I disagree, but that's irrelevant now, isn't it? Nobody cares anyway. Tell me exactly why he gave up his kids to the state when he had the option to turn them over to me," Daven demanded.

Now it was Stewart's turn to dish out some bitter sarcasm. "Oh, I see. So this is personal. It isn't about justice. You just got your feelings hurt."

Daven shook his head in frustration. "No. You're hiding something, and I'm starting to think there's a major conspiracy going on, to be honest. This is about vengeance, not justice."

"Alright, that's it. You're done here." Stewart stood up abruptly. "I was hoping to help you understand, but it's like talking to a brick wall. You need to go before I throw you out."

Daven stood, too. "The public is going to demand answers I can't give them. I hope you're ready to be held responsible for my party's downfall."

"Me, personally? No. This is not my fault. You know what Hank's last words were to me?"

"What?"

"Stay true. You used to say that to him, he said."

Daven felt his eyes stinging. "Yes."

Stewart lowered his voice to an angry near-whisper. "I took his advice, and I trusted you. I could have been prosecuted myself for that little note I slipped you a few months ago. Never mind that - you know who I told about those papers in his safe? Nobody, because Harmon would have flipped out and stopped negotiating. Yet you still dare to stand in my office and accuse me of leading some kind of sinister conspiracy plot?"

"I didn't say you were *leading* it. Maybe you're just a pawn, too."

Stewart was red, but he kept his voice low. "Right. We're definitely done here. Go back to Los Angeles, and don't contact me again unless it's an emergency."

"You won't be hearing from me again, don't worry."

"If you're thinking of quitting, don't. You want some more bad PR? Because I can easily get an injunction that legally prohibits you from leaving. Push me any further and I'll do it right now."

Daven's nostrils flared. "I don't care. Do it, then."

"Consider it done. It'll be signed before you get on your plane. Any other insults or accusations you'd like to add before you go?"

Trust him, Dav. He's always been a friend to me.

Daven heard Hank's voice clearly in his head, as if they were standing in the same room. It startled him, and he jumped back a half-step in his dismay. The last thing he needed right now was hearing his dead friend give him unwanted advice.

"Are you alright?" Stewart asked a few moments later in true concern as he watched the blood drain from Daven's face.

"What?"

"Sit down for a minute," Stewart said as he pulled Daven's chair back out, then went to his little refrigerator under his desk. "I want you to drink some water."

Daven remained standing by the door. "I'm fine."

Stewart walked over and handed Daven the water after uncapping it. "Drink. You're white as a sheet."

"Please accept my apologies," Daven said abruptly. "I'm not being fair."

Stewart blinked in surprise. Once, then twice. "Okay. Well, that was the last thing I expected to hear. Hank told me this is how it would go and warned me to prepare for a huge fight. He definitely didn't predict an apology, though."

"I'm stressed. You don't know what it's been like for me, not knowing what happened to him."

"Really? You think Hank's only friends were you and Rupert? Maybe I wasn't as close, but I assure you this hasn't been easy for me, either."

Daven nodded. "I need to know, if...on the last day, when he was..."

"We were told it was painless and peaceful. I didn't witness it myself, thank god. But he was in good spirits that day, all things considered, if that helps you any."

"It does," Daven confirmed after a minute. "I just want to ask one more thing. It's genuine curiosity, nothing else. If you're so convinced Hank had this coming, why are you-"

"I never said he had it coming," Stewart corrected firmly. "Look, I have to stop talking now. I've already said way too much. I trust you not to make me regret it."

Daven lifted the water bottle to his lips and drank half of it in one gulp. "You won't. I'm sorry. I was being an unfair, colossal dick."

"I'm glad to see we're finally in agreement about something. But I forgive you, and I won't get that injunction if you just promise to hang in there a little longer. And to help me when I ask you, which will be soon."

"Agreed. May I let Rupert read this letter?"

"Yes. Almost forgot to mention that you and I need to talk tomorrow morning about the press statement. I'll call you at 8am your time."

"I...my apologies in advance if I'm not exactly receptive to whatever you want to say. I'll try my best not to be a dick about it, but..."

Stewart nodded sympathetically, then pushed the door open. Daven left without another word, feeling like he had just walked into someone else's life all of a sudden instead of his own.

Hank's life, actually. And it scared the hell out of him.

Daven returned to the hotel immediately, but wished he had held off. Rupert was waiting for him in the lobby, and he had no idea how he was going to break the news to him. Hadn't even thought about it, but he couldn't wait now. The sooner he got it over with, the better.

"Let's go upstairs, your room," he said darkly. Rupe nodded, but said nothing. The guards followed them, waiting a respectful distance down the hallway as the door to the room closed. Daven inhaled deeply as he took a few steps in.

"You should sit down," he said quietly, as he pulled out chairs for both of them from the dining area's table.

"Oh god," mumbled Rupert as he complied, hesitating at first to comply, but then sitting so close to Daven that their knees were touching slightly.

"I have terrible news," Daven began, his voice deeper and more enunciated that usual. "And I...honestly, I should have been spending all the time I had in the car thinking of how to break it to you, but I didn't, and that was selfish. I'm sorry, this is probably going to be...there's probably a better way I can say it...but..."

"Just tell me, Dav. It's alright."

Daven didn't look at Rupe. "Hank not only pled guilty, as we already know, he...he also chose execution instead of prison."

"Uhhh..." was all Rupert could manage for now.

"And even worse, it was carried out on March 31. He's gone, Rupe." Now Daven lifted his eyes and locked gazes with his shocked friend. "He's...it was actually his choice. I don't know why, but it's done."

Rupert swallowed a few times, but otherwise stayed calm. "Okay. Where's the letter?"

Daven wordlessly reached into his coat and handed it over, then got up to get Rupert a drink from the minibar. He thought about reaching for one of the beers, but then selected two water bottles instead and went to sit back down. Rupert took one but made no move to open it.

"They censored it," he said needlessly, pointing to the paragraph in question. "Something about the boys has been completely removed."

"Yes. I've been told I'll get the uncensored version when…" He didn't know when, so he let the sentence hang. Rupert didn't ask him to finish it.

"Right. Well, we aren't due to fly home for another three hours. Can we leave now?"

Daven nodded. "Yes, if you're feeling up for it."

"I am. Let me get my stuff together. I'll need about fifteen minutes."

Rupert didn't bring anything that would take fifteen minutes to pack, but Daven rose anyway and patted him on the shoulder, then slid quietly through the connecting door into his own suite and laid down.

His heart shattered a few minutes later when the sound of a loud sob broke into his thoughts, and he sat up and was puzzled to realize it was his own. He hadn't shed real tears yet, not even about losing the boys. The only time he'd come close to breaking was when Hank's office was unsealed a month ago and he made the mistake of going inside before it was cleared out.

But Hank's downfall hadn't been real, then. It was now.

The suite's inner door slid open from the other side as Rupert slipped in, sat down on the bed, and rested a hand on his friend's shoulder. Daven turned around and embraced him, and they held onto each other and cried for a little while.

CHAPTER THREE

Philadelphia

Rupert was absolutely dreading the plane ride home. He figured Dav would be silent, brooding, angry. Possibly even hostile. Not that he didn't have a right to be, but it was going to be a long six hours if he was any of the above.

Daven was equally dreading the trip, for different reasons. His guards Martinez and Toby were there, too, and the plane wasn't big enough to have any private conversation with Rupert. For two months - actually, almost three - Dav had remained completely silent in regards to Hank. Hadn't said a word about him, hadn't allowed anyone talk about the situation, and answered exactly zero questions publicly. Back in April the media had been in an uproar for weeks about the missing boys, but the FBI quashed that by explaining Hank had sent them to a boarding school before Daven could seek custody of them. End of story, and it blew over fairly quickly, all things considered.

Had Daven been any other man, he would have been embarrassed by that statement, possibly even self-conscious about what people would think of him. He didn't care, though. He wasn't Hank and never worried about being liked, and had no time or inclination to address it. So Rupert and Taylor forged ahead, kept in line, kept their mouths shut, and watched Daven out of the sides of their eyes while he waited impatiently for Stewart's next move.

Rupert knew something was up, of course. He never asked, but his instinct told him Colbert was being investigated. The fact that Daven couldn't tell him didn't bother him. That would have been too much of a distraction; it was better to move on, to focus on things that could be controlled, and work on getting the organization back together again.

The plane had barely leveled out at altitude before Dav turned his seat around and rested his eyes on his tired friend.

"What's the latest tally?" he asked matter-of-factly.

"53, including two more who resigned this morning," answered Rupert. That was how many people had left the organization after April's announcement that Hank wasn't coming back, and that Daven Johansson was interim CEO for a period of six months. After that, the president could approve him as a permanent replacement. The only person who knew he probably wouldn't was Daven himself, but he had never mentioned the possibility yet.

"Over ten percent now," Daven replied. "Can we run that lean?"

"Of course. We were always overstaffed anyway, you know Hank. Always paranoid about people working themselves to death, ironically enough."

Daven looked out the window and took a deep breath. It was time to tell Rupert his suspicions. "I doubt Rickon will confirm me on November 1."

"What? Why?"

"He hates me, for starters."

Rupert furrowed his eyebrows. "He does *not* hate you. Don't be overdramatic."

"Stewart said..." Daven glanced aside at the guards, who were obviously listening carefully while pretending to be totally disinterested. "Never mind. Martinez?"

The young man started, and turned with a slightly guilty expression.

"Yes, sir?"

"Have you heard from Avery? I was wondering what he's been up to."

"We went out the other night. He's with the LAPD again, working for my dad."

"Is he happy?" Daven asked mildly, and Rupert looked sideways at him in surprise. He had never heard Dav ask if *anyone* was happy, ever.

Martinez looked as if he was going to say yes just to avoid tension, but he didn't. "No, sir. He misses Hank and the boys very much. He mentioned that...."

"What?"

"He said he wanted to come see you, but he was afraid he wouldn't be welcome. He wanted to explain what happened in Philadelphia."

"Did he tell you?"

"No, sir. I'm...he wouldn't tell me a thing like that. He's very private."

Daven fell silent for a minute, then cleared his throat. "I see. Thank you for telling me. He's mistaken about not being welcome. I'll call him up when we get home."

Rupert stood up and went to flip on the television. "Let's all watch a movie. What do you feel up for, Dav?"

Daven replied glumly, "I hear they're making a film about the Titanic. It might be perfectly appropriate right now."

"Maybe so, but a tragedy is the last thing we need to watch." Rupe leaned over to examine the little cabinet full of VHS tapes and perused them carefully. "Maybe a comedy."

He finally pulled one out decisively.

"*Herbier Goes to Monte Carlo*?" Daven scoffed.

Rupert ignored him and handed the tape to the flight attendant, who cued it up for them on the player and doused the cabin lights. Daven felt rather than saw the guards watching, too, and was annoyed that they seemed delighted by the selection.

"Anthropomorphisation of cars is a silly premise for anything other than a kid's movie," Dav grumbled.

He only got a glare in return.

"Fine," Dav sighed. "Play it, then."

"This was one of Theo's favorites when he was really little. He always begged Millie put it on when she was babysitting the boys."

Daven shifted uncomfortably in his chair, feeling the eyes of the guards on him once again. He really didn't like Rupe speaking of the Bancroft sons in past tense, like they were dead, too, but there was nothing he could say about it.

"Oh. I didn't realize, sorry. I'll try to enjoy it, then."

"Thank you."

Daven didn't enjoy it, of course, and hardly paid any attention at all. He wanted so badly to take Hank's letter out of his coat and read it again. And again. And again. But he refrained, and didn't open until he got home. Then he put it in his safe and went to bed.

It would be weeks before he took it out again and noticed Hank's hastily scribbled note deep inside of the envelope, far away from the prying eyes of Stewart and Salome:

804-253-7894

It would be another two weeks before Daven saw it and called, and months before Lester would call back and agree to help him.

JUNE 30 - early morning

"Hello," said the voice on the other line. A few moments passed, then, "Hello?"

Daven cleared his throat and pitched it up a bit. "Who is this, please? Just want to make sure I have the right number."

"Nice try. Who are you?" the man demanded.

Another long pause. "I see we are at an impasse. Very well. I received your number from Hank Bancroft some time ago, but I was not in a position to call until now. Can you talk? It's important."

"I'm in a meeting. Let me take your number and call you back."

"Not possible. When is a good time to call you back?" he asked tersely.

There was a long pause.

"Okay, let me read that back to you," the man said, a note of amusement in his voice. "310-758-5100. Is that right?"

Daven's heart jolted painfully. His cell number. How the hell..? "No. I'm not sure who's number that is. When would be a good time to call you back?" he said again, trying to keep his voice steady and unconcerned.

"Actually, I'm not interested. Please remove my number from your database. Have a good day."

The angry man hung up. Daven called Taylor and Rupe to his office, brutishly admitted where he got the man's number from, and asked them to drop everything and find out who it belonged to. He dismissed Rupert's protests and sent them on their way.

Taylor came back less than an hour later, and Daven fully expected to hear it was untraceable. She dropped a sheet of paper triumphantly on his desk and crossed her arms, smiling from ear to ear.

"A certain Robert Boyd, boss. Chief Administrator of the Bonded Retainers Training School for Minors. Do you know him?"

Daven snatched the paper off the desk. Hank's old roommate and best friend. No wonder he had Daven's number. But the man was a fierce Urbane....what the hell was Hank up to now?

"Excellent work, Taylor. Where's Rupert?"

"In a PR meeting until 3pm. Do you want me to get him out?"

"No, thanks. I'll wait. Thanks. Lunch is on me today, whatever you want."

Same day - afternoon

It was the fourth time Daven had called, but the last two times he had said nothing.

"Jesus H Christ on a pogo stick. You again?" Lester scoffed. "Why don't you just talk to me? I don't bite. Not today, anyway."

Brief pause, then Daven finally spoke. "Are you the same Lester Boyd who was friends with Hank Bancroft for so long?"

"I'm going to hang up now. Goodbye."

"Just a moment, Mr. Boyd. I'm a friend of Hank's. I want the deeds to the Bancroft boys transferred to me, and I need your help to do it."

Holy shit, thought Lester, every drop of blood in his body turning to ice. He knew that voice.

"Absolutely not," he blurted harshly. "You really think I'm going to give them over to you assholes to brainwash for the next twenty years?"

"So they *are* there, then. Excellent."

Fuck ! Lester breathed under his breath, furious at himself for falling into such a simple trap. It took him a minute to collect himself; visions of losing his job and being blackmailed by the Seditionists were already filling up his darkest thoughts.

"Screw you, you stupid son of a bitch," Lester muttered angrily.

Daven was clearly unmoved by the insult. "Don't worry, I won't tell anyone you fell for that."

Lester slammed down the phone, which rang again less than a minute later. He picked up with shaking hands.

"You should seriously consider cooperating with me," Daven said politely. "Hank Bancroft was framed. We have proof now, and I'm going to submit it to the FBI soon. It's too late to save Harmon and Colbert, but not the boys."

"You've picked the wrong man to bully, idiot," Lester interrupted hotly, hating that he was so rattled he couldn't think of anything better to say. *Framed?* Not possible; the Seditionists were just getting desperate now and trying to mess with his head.

Daven retorted with a hint of regret in his tone, "As I said, I'm a friend in this particular discussion. To both you *and* the Bancrofts. Hank made it clear that you were a man who cares deeply about their welfare, if nothing else."

"What discussion? You can't have them, and you're nuts if you think I'm going to waste one more second on you. Lose my number, pal."

Daven replied casually, "No. I'm not giving up until they're safe with me, no matter what it takes."

"Don't you fucking threaten me," Lester warned. "I had nothing to do with any of this."

"I understand that. But I need your help. Please."

Complete silence from Lester's side invaded the line for at least a minute, then he finally said, "No. Hank was guilty as hell, and you know it. You're the one who turned him in!"

" *What?*" Daven was astonished. "I absolutely did not. Who told you that? Harmon? Colbert?"

"Oh come on, Johansson. Stop the bullshit. Don't ever call me again. Especially don't ever threaten me again."

There was a brief silence on the other end of the line, and then a slight huff. "You've completely misunderstood my intentions. I'm not threatening you."

"Could've fooled me!" Lester practically yelled.

"Mr. Boyd...I did not turn Hank in. He was framed. I don't know how much clearer I can be."

"Look, Johansson, you're in deep shit. I know you are breaching the plea bargain just by calling me, so you're headed for jail time, my man, as soon as I let Harmon know. Start packing."

"I'm perfectly aware of what they could do to me, and I'm willing to risk it because Hank said you could be trusted. If you tell Harmon, I won't deny anything. I'll go to jail for this. Hank gave me your number in his very last communication with me, and he *never* would have put either of us in danger for no reason. I don't know why. You do. Call me back when you're willing to talk about the future of Theo and Floyd."

The call terminated before Lester could get another word in.

Daven sucked in his breath and held it for a long time, toying with the notion that he'd just made a huge, life-changing mistake. Lester knew there was a plea bargain, and he apparently knew what the terms were. He *knew*, while he claimed to have nothing to do with it. Hank had either dug Daven's grave or Lester's with his little note. And Daven realized it was probably going to be his, if he couldn't get Lester to work with him, and fast.

Fuck...

CHAPTER FOUR

Richmond, Virginia

BRTSM

Lester Boyd had, of course, fallen in love with the boys again as soon as they'd arrived back in April. He was relieved neither one of them seemed to have inherited the worst of their father's characteristics. They hadn't exactly inherited the best ones, either. Theo was lazy, Floyd was meek, and both the boys together were not much of a force to be reckoned with at first.

At first.

Something had changed in Floyd a while back, almost immediately after Lester had first heard from the mysterious caller who later turned out to be Daven. Floyd had been standing in Lester's office when that call came through, so at first Lester thought maybe he had heard the voice through the phone and figured out who was calling. It quickly dawned on him that of course Floyd would have recognized the phone number that Lester was stupid enough to blurt out loud for all to hear.

If that was the case, though...why didn't the boy saying anything, and why did he lose his openness and sweetness so quickly? Lester had seen the change the very next day, and it was bothering him so much that he had to nearly physically hold himself back from asking what the hell was up. The way Floyd held himself straight as a ramrod, the way he physically but subtly blocked Theo protectively…even the new tension in response to all but the mildest questions. It was almost as if he was scared to death that Daven had called. No, not scared. Angry. It made no sense whatsoever; Hank had mentioned time and again how close the boys were to Johansson and how much being separated for a year would hurt them.

Lester had wanted to tell the boys, of course, that Daven would take them out if this awful situation in a year. But he couldn't, and he certainly wouldn't anyway now that he suspected Floyd hated the man.

So Lester was distracted. It had been five weeks since Daven called to tell him Hank was allegedly framed. Thirty-five long, stressful days since Lester learned exactly why the new leader of the Seditionists was infamous for being approximately as subtle as a machine gun. In that time, Lester had quietly read up about him and pored over dozens of videos and news clips. The amount of material on him was limited, but it was enough that he felt almost knew Johansson personally now, and it disturbed him that something wasn't adding up.

Johansson definitely didn't seem to have the imagination or balls required to make up wild, unprovable theories out of the blue for no reason. He was also strictly forbidden from trying to find out where the boys were. And yet, he had done just that, at the risk of certain jail time and public shame and infamy. Nobody would do that unless they were one hundred percent convinced they were absolutely right. Not to mention it was extremely odd that he apparently didn't know the boys were going to be his in one year.

But then again, Hank possessed a masterful ability to manipulate anyone into believing anything; it was part of the reason he was so successful in politics even when he was pushing back against popular opinion. This could all be a trick. Perhaps he'd even brainwashed Daven into believing there was some kind of conspiracy. But why? He was guilty, after all. He'd never said he wasn't...

The only thing holding back Lester from telling Colbert that Daven had called was the fact that he'd inadvertently given up the boys' location to him. That alone would cost him his job. Every day since then, Lester had discreetly kept a set of boxes nearby to be ready for filling when the time came that he was inevitably asked to leave.

Nothing had come of it, though. Strangely, there was no further contact from Daven, which only strengthened Lester's curiosity and doubts rather than quashing them.

But he did nothing about it. Yet.

"Theo."

"Mmmmummph."

"*Theo*. Move over."

Theo opened one eye and peered at his brother, barely visible in the gloom. "Nightmares again?" he asked sleepily as he backed up against the wall to make room.

"Not a nightmare," Floyd clarified as he slid in bed next to his brother and held on tightly to him to keep from falling out. "An idea."

"Shhhhh. Oh god. What? Your last idea got both of our butts blistered."

Floyd sighed. "I'm sorry, okay? I've said it like a million times. Can you stop bringing that up?"

"No."

"I'm going to tell Mr. Boyd we know who he is."

"What? Why?"

"Because maybe he'll give us some news on dad. If we befriend him, start reminiscing, you know…maybe we can win his confidence eventually. Or he'll feel sorry for us, or something. And help us."

"Help us *what?* Floyd, it's 3am. And you always told me he hated dad."

Just as he said that, the overhead light came on and blinded them both painfully.

"Ow," Floyd moaned as he hurriedly got on his feet and shaded his eyes to look at the culprit.

"Mr. Bancroft," said the night manager of the dorm, quietly. "Back to bed."

"Mr. Donatello-"

"Nope. Out you go."

Floyd's sighed and looked around the room as Theo's three roommates woke and grumbled at him, rubbing their eyes painfully. He patted Theo on the head and walked back to his room, which he shared with no one at the moment, and flopped onto his back in the creaky bed.

"Sir, can't I just...there are two empty beds in here. Why can't I share with Theo? He's my brother."

"You'll have to take that up with Mr. Boyd." The man paused, then seemed to have a sudden deep thought and walked in the room to sit down on the bed opposite Floyd. "I haven't heard anything about your father yet."

Floyd stared at the ceiling. "I know. I...I really appreciate you trying to find out for me. I know I say that all the time, but it really means a lot. Thank you."

"Happy to help, but you know what I would appreciate in return? For you to stop fucking around and putting you and your brother in danger. Next time this happens, I have report you. No choice. Understood?"

Floyd turned on his side to study the older man he had become so friendly with over the past few weeks. "Deal. I'm sorry. But he's my brother-"

"Yes, I know, but it's not fair to the other boys to keep giving you special treatment. I've said it before, and I really mean it this time."

"Do you know Daven Johansson?" Floyd blurted suddenly, without thinking.

"Not personally, of course. What's he like?"

"He's a dick," Floyd replied blandly. "And he's the reason me and Theody are here in the first place. Mr. Boyd said I could write a letter to him so I did, but I haven't asked him to send it yet."

Donatello crossed his arms. "Are you upset with him for not seeking custody of you and Theo?"

"No! I'm glad he didn't, oh my god. That would be horrible."

"So what did you put in the letter, then?"

Floyd sat up again and pulled the sheaf of paper out from between his mattresses. "I asked him why he...why he turned dad in. They were best friends. He was my uncle. In name, I mean, not blood. Then he called here to talk to Mr. Boyd, and-"

"He called *here*?" interrupted Donatello, shocked. "He knows you're here? Floyd, who else have you told about this?"

"Nobody," answered Floyd quickly, a little hurt at his new friend's harsh tone. "I mean, Theo knows, but-"

Donatello stood up abruptly. "Okay, Floyd. Keep it to yourself from now on. I'm sorry, but I can't continue this conversation, ever. Don't bring him up again, and don't tell anyone else he called. Goodnight."

"Sir, wait..." Floyd called as the man started to leave. Then he swallowed hard as the light was shut off and the door closed abruptly, leaving him alone once again. He laid back on the bed, his eyes stinging with tears, and lay awake until dawn, staring at the ceiling and feeling his heart harden just a little more towards the man he had once called Uncle Dav.

Of all the conversations Lester Boyd had dreaded in all his life, this one had to rank at the top of the list. He tensed as Floyd - who was in trouble yet *again* for mouthing off to his teachers - trudged in sleepily and flopped into a chair before being given permission.

"What's this all about?" Floyd blurted moodily. "It's fucking 7 o'clock in the morning."

Lester gulped and leaned over to pick up his short cane. "Stand up," he ordered briskly.

"No."

"I would comply if I were you, kiddo."

Floyd eyed him dangerously. "I'm not afraid of you anymore, *Uncle Lester*."

Lester paused, set the cane down and crossed in front of the desk, then leaned back against it. His heart was beating so hard that it was making him dizzy, and Floyd's ferocious glare wasn't helping matters.

"How long have you known?" Lester asked quietly, after taking a few moments to gather his wits.

Floyd said nothing. He just stared.

"I gather Theo doesn't remember."

Again, dead silence from the elder Bancroft boy.

Lester threw up his hands. "Alright. So you know. What now, you're going to be a little shit from now on just to get back at me for-"

"Why did Daven turn in my dad and send us here? Did he have some kind of agreement with you? Were you two secretly conspiring against him this entire time?"

"Lower your voice. I don't know what you're talking about."

Floyd laughed humorlessly. "I knew it. There's no other reason he would have called here, but you're not allowed to talk to him, are you? That's why Mr. Donatello freaked out when I mentioned it to him."

"You did *what?* Floyd, what the holy hell has gotten into you?" Lester blurted, his hands raised up in the pre-surrender stage. "I've been nothing but nice to you since the day you-"

"I want Theo assigned to my room. Just the two of us, for the rest of our time here. That's the price for my silence. Take it or leave it."

Lester stared at him for several long, tense moments. "You've got me wrong, kiddo. I don't know what you think is going on, but-"

"Don't lie! And don't call me that. My name is Floyd." Floyd started to choke up a little, and Lester subconsciously wrung his hands together in his anxiety.

"Okay," Lester said patiently, "you can room with Theo, but we're going to have a long talk first."

Floyd stood up quickly, his expression still dark and dangerous. "No. We're done here. Have a nice day."

Lester stared in amazement as Floyd confidently strode out and disappeared. That was the exact moment Lester realized he was wrong about Floyd not having inherited Hank's temperament and worst traits. Wrong about being grateful the kid had gone a different direction.

Well. Turned out Floyd was going to be *just* like Hank, if this was any indication. *Shit..*

Floyd never spoke to Lester again on his own accord. He politely answered yes or no questions, left it at that, and broke no more rules. He was polite and obedient to the point of near absurdity, although the deepset restlessness in his manner never wavered.

There was only one time Lester started to go after him; Floyd was being uncommonly hard on Theo for the tenth time in a week it seemed, but the teenager was clearly in "big brother

459

protective mode." It was working since Theo had started to finally fall in line, too, so Lester let it go with a few mild words of warning which Floyd clearly intended to ignore.

Then Daven called back, unexpectedly, on an otherwise sunny day when Lester was finally feeling at peace with himself and his role in Hank's death.

"Mr. Boyd."

"Yes?" Lester replied patiently, although his heart began galloping like a racehorse going downhill.

"The FBI has prematurely ended their involvement in the investigation of Colbert."

"I don't know what you're talking about," Lester lied. "Stop calling me-"

"The agent responsible for the work has been fired," Johansson replied flatly.

"How is that any of my business?"

"Because I learned something very interesting last week. You were Harmon's negotiator for the plea bargain. Yet, last time we talked, you claimed to know nothing and that you had nothing to do with any of this."

Oh, fuck.

"So," continued Daven, "the fact that you lied tells me my initial instincts were correct. You were conspiring with Colbert and Harmon to frame Hank. Perhaps to get back at him for the way your friendship ended eleven years ago. Or because Colbert tricked you into his scheme, which I find far more likely."

Lester quickly hung up the phone and unplugged it for safe measure. Then he went to the empty office next door and shakily dialed Colbert.

CHAPTER FIVE

Los Angeles, California

Seditionists HQ

On a normal day, it took quite a lot to get Daven irritated. On a stressful day, it took very little. But he had never before yelled at any employee, no matter what the impetus. In fact, sometimes he would get calmer and quieter in inverse proportion to how much a situation was blowing up out of control. Disarming people with his refusal to fight was one of his greatest talents.

Today was a new day. He had started off the morning with a full-fledged shouting match with Rupert, followed by a phone-shouting match with Salome Danby, followed by the reprise of another shouting match with Rupert just before 5pm. Half the office had heard them all and most of them looked about ready to vacate the premises, as if a bomb threat had been called in.

"Dav, for the last time, you *cannot* make that call," Rupert fumed as he slammed his hand down on the desk for the second time today. "Are you out of your fu...out of your mind?"

Daven set his pen down and glared across the table. "You were warned, Rupe. I told you that you wouldn't like what was going on, and you agreed to stay out of it as long as I kept you informed. I've kept you informed, so keep your end of the bargain and *stay out of it!*"

"Absolutely not. Fuck it all, Dav, you're just asking to get yourself thrown in jail. I can't run this goddamned loony bin by myself, so-"

"That's enough."

Rupert didn't relent. "So you just...you're just going to tell Salome you've been in contact with Lester Boyd. For months."

"Not months. Three calls, over three months."

"Same thing. Jesus Christ, you're just like Hank. You know that? Not a shred of common sense, and everything done out of some horribly skewed sense of duty and honor." Rupert had broken into a sweat, and he was angrier than Daven had ever seen him. "You always said Rickon wouldn't confirm you in November anyway. So I suppose you think you have nothing to lose now, is that it? Fuck it all?"

"Pretty much, yes," Daven admitted, which completely threw Rupert off guard.

"What...wait, no," he stuttered. "You're trying to confuse me."

"No, I'm trying to shut you up so I can make this call before Salome leaves the office."

Rupert reached out and snatched up Daven's cell phone. "I'm not giving this back to you until you agree to think about it over the weekend. If you're still intent on committing harakiri, at least do it Monday morning so you don't ruin her weekend. Or mine."

Daven bristled. "I am *not* like Hank, by the way. If you ever say that again, our friendship is over. I would have *never* given up my kids the way he did. Nor treated them the way he did. *Never*. He chose to give them to Harmon over me, and you dare to say I'm just like him?"

Rupert crossed his arms and took a step back. "I get it now. This is personal. You don't give a shit about our party anymore, do you? You're just pissed at Hank because you got your feelings hurt, and-"

"I have to do what's right, Rupert, and to be bluntly honest, your opinion of *why* I'm doing it doesn't matter. Especially when you don't know all the facts."

Rupe nodded, his anger leveling out somewhat. "Fair enough. So you're going to tell Salome how you've been investigating on your own against FBI mandates, and let her know that you've been interfering and working secretly with Stewart on the side. Is that all, or is there more? Oh, by the way...if you do that, I will quit on the spot."

Daven slowly walked over to Rupert and lowered his voice to a near-whisper.

"Fine, I'll tell you what's upsetting me. Stewart was fired this morning because he accidentally let it slip to me that Lester Boyd was Harmon's negotiator. The investigation is now over."

Rupert's jaw dropped. "Holy shit. Dav...I..."

Daven continued, "Obviously, that opens up an entirely new set of questions that will have to be answered. The reason I'm calling Salome now is take all the blame and offer to resign if she re-hires Stewart to continue the investigation, and start a new one on Lester Boyd. So, if you quit…"

Rupert nodded, then took a few minutes to stare out the window and gather his thoughts. He didn't move a muscle, and neither did Daven as he sat behind his desk, watching thoughtfully and feeling like he had just swallowed an anvil.

Rupert said eventually, very quietly, "I'm sorry, Dav. You have to do what you can live with. I won't quit."

"Thank you. If it's any consolation, she's not going to take the offer. But I have to ask."

"Hmmm. Wait…three calls to Lester Boyd now? Did you call him again, even though you swore to me you wouldn't?"

"Yesterday. It didn't go well. He hung up on me."

"You…you lied to me."

"I broke a promise, actually. Not the same thing, but you have a right to be angry about it if you need to."

Rupert turned around, walked slowly up to the desk, and didn't take his eyes off his friend. "I see. When you explain this to Salome, kindly confirm to her that I had nothing to do with any of this whatsoever, and that you're acting against my express wishes and advice."

"I will, of course. I may be a lost cause, but your standing in this organization is intact, and I intend to keep it that way."

Rupert was stone-faced. "Well, you're right about one thing. My standing is all we've got left now."

Daven eyed him worriedly, and started to reply, but he could thinking of nothing. Rupert turned and left the office, shutting the door quietly behind him.

Daven didn't call Salome. He snuck out after the conversation with Rupert and went home to think about it.

Hank's home, rather. He had sold his own in August, and Hank's old house was on the market now with several offers. The boat was gone, too, and all the cars except for the Thunderbird. Every dollar had gone towards the staggering bills he and Rupert had received from canceling the deeds to their household servants. The money for the second house would go straight into a irrevocable trust for the boys, Daven had already decided, so that their owner would have the money to cancel their deeds when they reached the halfway point. Floyd would be 26, and Theo would be 22.

For the hundredth time as he greeted his dog and his two fosters (it didn't feel right saying Starsky and Hutch were actually *his* now), he wondered how the boys were doing now, and what their future could possibly be like. They'd never see their dogs again if he didn't succeed in his mission to vindicate Hank. It almost didn't bear thinking about.

Maurice met him in the living room and took his coat and briefcase away.

"Thanks, Maurice. Sorry I didn't let you know I was coming home early. Any news on the real estate front?"

"No sale yet. The offers keep piling up, it's quite amazing. Everyone wants a piece of Hank's history, apparently."

"Well, he did live there for ten years. That's understandable."

Maurice was no longer servant and was a well-paid employee who considered Daven a friend, but old habits never died hard. He started to ask a question, gulped a little, then ignored his pounding heart as he forged on.

"Any news of Hank and the boys?" he asked, just the same way he did every single day, and had done so for months.

"I'm afraid not," Daven replied automatically as he sat down to untie his shoes. "If the bills are ready to sign, go ahead and head home early. I'll take care of the dogs."

Maurice hesitated. "I'm sorry to keep asking. Are we ever going to know what happened to him?"

Daven stopped what he was doing, and considered the guarded question. Maurice had loved Hank and the boys, and it was increasingly unfair to keep the poor man in the dark.

"I know that you're really asking me *when* I'm going to tell you what happened to him."

Maurice nodded slightly, his expression worried.

"I can't, by law," Daven admitted shortly. "Sorry for not saying it plainly before. When I can, you will be among the first to know."

"I understand, sir. Are the boys ever coming back?"

"Don't call me sir. No, they're not. I've explained this to you already. I didn't seek custody of them."

Maurice flushed. "Right, sorry. On another subject, I'm sure you already know but I just wanted to remind you that Avery is coming over for lunch tomorrow."

Daven had actually forgotten completely, and again he was reminded of the many times he'd scoffed when Hank had insisted he'd need to keep a secretary at home once he was leading the party. Of course, the man had been absolutely right, Daven conceded begrudgingly. His life would have fallen to pieces a dozen times over already without Maurice to manage his schedule.

"Thank you, I'd forgotten. What time?"

"12:30. Chef said he sent you an email asking about the menu but you never replied, so I told him to make chicken piccata."

Daven swallowed hard as he set his keys into the drawer of the side table. That had been Floyd's favorite meal.

"I'm sorry, he'll have to make something else. I'll go talk to him. See you tomorrow."

"I'm sorry. I thought that was one of your favorites. My apologies if-"

"No, no," Daven interrupted politely. "It is. But I've had it for lunch two days in a row."

Maurice smiled, relieved that he hadn't made another mistake. Daven could be impossible to read sometimes. "Oh, I understand. Tomorrow's Saturday, by the way. I'll see you Monday."

"Right, thanks. Goodnight."

Daven found Chef and requested he go out to buy a few nice steaks, then went into the guest bedroom (he couldn't bear to move to the master suite yet) and fell sound asleep for almost two hours. He dreamed about Hank and the boys, as usual.

Richmond, Virginia

Colbert hadn't picked up the phone. Lester wasn't sure whether to be relieved or upset; he wasn't sure he'd find the courage to dial those numbers again. He certainly knew he wouldn't have the courage (or stupidity) to ever dial Daven back. Besides, what on earth would he tell him?

Friday nights at BRTSM were no fun for the school's 200 boys. It was always the most rigid formal dinner training, when they practiced serving and waiting. Like stuffy British footmen of old, outdated and relics, Lester always said to himself. But that was what the clients demanded, and so the school provided. The food was too rich, the service too formal, the conversation too stifled. He much preferred the staff dining room.

He dressed up every week, however, and put his best face forward as he walked into one of the fake-gilded dining rooms that served well for training. He had a one-in-five chance of being seated at the table where the Bancrofts were assigned, and to his dismay, found that he'd indeed beaten the odds. Floyd was stationed directly behind his chair, looking sharp but remarkably sullen in his dress uniform. Lester half expected to be garroted before dessert, he realized wryly. Theo was across the table, but he had a different expression altogether; it was more of a sad resignation and acceptance.

Lester looked up and down the table of 20, ten people to each side. All of them except himself were teachers eager to show off their new charges to the assistant dean; the same one who wanted to be anywhere else but here. He sat back as Floyd unfolded the napkin and laid it deftly over his lap.

"Thank you," he said automatically as he reached for his water. This was the second-most advanced table for training, the boys having already graduated from serving 7-course meals and were now trying out a 9-course meal for the first time. Their next move would be to the 12-course meal table, but that wouldn't be for at least four or five weeks. They had to master this first.

Lester didn't taste the first five courses. He was hyper-aware of Floyd's presence, made worse by the fact that he couldn't see his face 99% of the time. The elder Bancroft was perfection, however, and spilled nothing and made no mistakes. Theo, on the other hand, was a nervous wreck and couldn't seem to get anything right. He was soon removed from the table by the butler, and was seen no more. Lester wasn't worried; the boy would get some refresher lessons to give him a boost of confidence and be back next week.

Lester finally caught Floyd's eye as he set down the main course.

"You're doing well, son," he murmured quietly, approvingly.

Floyd froze. "I'm not your son," he replied sharply, a little too loudly. Lester's dining table neighbors looked up in horror as Floyd stepped back and reached for the next plate.

"I haven't had lamb in ages," Lester announced with a fake-plastered grin to those who were watching him. "Looking forward to this one."

He didn't taste the lamb, either. When the next course was placed in front of him, he carefully avoided making eye contact with his angry server. It took him a few seconds to realize it wasn't Floyd at all, and he looked up in surprise at the Butler, who saw his confusion and rushed over to his side.

"Something wrong, sir?" the coat-tailed man asked very discreetly as he bent over to speak directly into Lester's ear.

"Where did Floyd go?" Lester whispered neutrally. "He was doing a really good job."

The butler looked amazed. "Sir? I...he was taken away for discipline, of course."

"That's not necessary, Paul. Bring him back, please."

"But, I...it's already...we've already sent him off, sir. My apologies."

Lester nodded and let it go. He had never known a dessert and mignardise to last so long in his life. It felt as though three hours had passed before the interminable meal ended and he could get back to his office. Floyd was outside the door, of course, waiting obediently in the "chair of doom" that he had been getting to know all too well lately.

Lester walked up carefully and then sat down on the bench next to him, not even remotely upset that the teenager wouldn't meet his eye. It was understandable.

"I shouldn't have called you son. Next time I'll be more careful."

Floyd looked aside at him with red-rimmed eyes. "You could have told the head butler that before he...before he.."

Lester glanced down at Floyd's welted palms and felt a surge of anger, but it would be inappropriate to sympathize right now. He hardened his voice instead. "He did his job when you messed up yours. You knew better. Got to control those impulses. Alright, you're forgiven. Just so you know, Theo isn't in trouble. Just had a bit of a bad night, it happens."

"Oh, right. So he can have one, but I can't?"

"You know it's not the same thing. I have some Advil in my office, if you want it. Will take the edge off the sting."

"No."

Lester shrugged. "Alright, well...you did a really good job tonight, otherwise. I was impressed."

Floyd said nothing; he was thinking about the servants who used to serve him and Theo.

Lester decided to take the plunge while Floyd was here and pretty much his captive audience. He might not have a chance otherwise.

"Floyd," he said quietly. Gently. "Your dad sent you here because he knew I'd look after you and take good care of you. I'm really trying my best, kiddo. I had nothing to do with the crimes he was charged with. None whatsoever. I need you to hang in there and get past this."

"Then why was Daven calling you and why is it all a secret," Floyd asked flatly, not even phrasing it as a question. He was already convinced of his conspiracy theory and didn't need an explanation.

"Your dad left him my number so he could call and check up on you guys. I didn't know that when he first called, I mean...when you boys were standing in my office. He and I were never friends, let's just put it that way. He's the last person I wanted to talk to at the time."

Floyd turned to look at Lester now. "To check up on us? Why? He doesn't give a shit about us. I hate him. Tell him we're dead."

Lester shook his head in confusion. "I don't know why you would say that. Your dad told me you treated Daven like an uncle, and vice versa. What on earth happened to make you hate him?"

"He turned dad in and made us slaves, maybe? No big deal," Floyd jeered, and Lester sat up a little bit taller.

"Floyd...who told you that?"

"Hailey Hendricks."

"The shit reporter? *Hailey?* You listened to *her*?" Lester was shocked. He didn't follow politics anymore, but even he knew Hailey was trash.

"It was...it was on the news," Floyd said, faltering a little.

"Look," Lester said with a sigh, "you're sixteen years old. Almost seventeen. I'm not going to talk to you like you're a child anymore, okay? Do you want to speak as adults?"

"Yes," Floyd replied after a moment, looking as scared as a toddler all of a sudden.

"Reporters lie sometimes. They work for network brass who get paid to pay other people to say what they think people want to hear. Hailey is the worst of the worst, downright corrupt, and she was lying. I can tell you that with a hundred percent certainty."

Floyd seemed amazed and confused. "What?"

"I'm also going to tell you - adult to adult - that I'm putting my job on the line by telling you all this. I work for the Urbanes.

Do you think they'd want me telling you their reporters are liars?"

"No. I mean, I knew anyway, kind of. That's why my dad would never let me watch the news."

"Smart man."

Floyd sat up straight. "Alright, then I just have one more question."

"Sure."

"Daven was me and Theo's guardian. So why did our dad choose to have us enslaved rather than sent to his house to live, if he was such a good guy?"

The hair on Lester's neck raised up a little at that question, and his stomach churned uncomfortably. He was suddenly ill-at-ease again over his part in the negotiation.

"I don't know, Floyd. I really don't. If I had been a fly on the wall at the FBI, I could tell you."

"Well, I don't believe you. If you'd seen how he was acting, and the way he refused to defend dad...."

Lester shrugged again, but his throat was tight. "Well, I'm telling the truth. Not much else I can say about it."

"I eavesdropped on one of his calls with Daven once, just before he left," Floyd said quietly. "It was an accident. He didn't know I was under his desk. I'd been playing hide and seek with Theo and dad came in talking on his cell phone. We weren't allowed in his study."

"Did he find you?"

"No. He was really angry already, and I didn't want to make him madder, so I just stayed there. He told Uncle Dav that Colbert was going to keep his promise to him, as he always knew he would even after ten years."

"Promise to what?"

"To visit him in jail. I never knew they were friends after everything that happened during the Revolution. Thought they were enemies, but Dad never really told me anything about work. I just...sometimes I feel like I don't know him at all."

The hair on Lester's neck raised even higher. "Wait. He said that ten years ago Colbert made a promise to visit your dad in jail?"

"Yes."

"That's...are you sure that's what he said?"

Floyd nodded, then wiped his nose with the back of one hand. "I'm sorry, I really miss...I just...I want to go home."

Now Lester's eyes were moist, too. "I know. I'm sorry."

"I never thought I would miss him this much. He can be so mean to me and Theo sometimes." He looked down at his welted hands in disgust. "But at least he never does *this*."

"Yeah...that's something, at least," Lester agreed helplessly. "You can go back to your room now."

After Floyd left, Lester went into his office and sat down hard, trying not to think of the poor kid bursting into tears. He was already distracted anyway by something Colbert had said long ago - during their first meeting about the trial - suddenly tugged at the edges of his consciousness, but never quite fully formed itself. Like trying to remember the voice of someone long dead, he mused grimly. He tried hard to remember, then gave up, laid his head on his arms, and began dozing on the edges of a dream.

A few minutes later he awakened abruptly, the stark memory of the only words Colbert had ever said about his Seditionists informant suddenly ringing clear in his head like a church bell:

The man talks like a goat with a banana stuck in his throat, but he has all the right access to get shit done.

The right access to get shit done. That didn't mean what he thought it meant...did it?

If there was even a possibility it did, though...

It was a few minutes before midnight when Lester drove into town with a long coat over his suit, praying the entire time that he wasn't losing his fucking mind by jumping to the crazy conclusions he was currently coming to. He spotted a gas station far from his usual haunts and pulled over. Nobody would recognize him here, and there were no cameras.

It was 12:35am. He took a deep breath, cursed under his breath for a little while, then picked up the pay phone and dialed Daven. He was so nervous it took him three tries to get the number in correctly.

Los Angeles

Rupert Aster house, 9:50pm

Daven strode up the front stairs two by two just as the front door opened. As usual, he didn't think to call first, but the Johansson guards had given the Aster guards a heads-up that the boss was on the way over, and Rupert had hastily gotten dressed and ran down to intercept him just in time.

"Everything okay, Dav?" Rupe asked fearfully as his friend reached him and grabbed his arm in a tight grip. He noticed his guards jump and move slightly towards him, but he quickly warned them off with a slight shake of his head.

Daven was almost breathless. "Who do we know that talks like *a goat with a banana stuck in his throat?*"

Rupert stared at him in shock. "What the....?"

"It's a serious question, Rupe. Think on it," Daven urged. "Quickly."

Rupe shook his head like a dog. "Alright. Uh. There's...that strange fellow in accounting, you mean?"

"Exactly. Yannick. He's been working with Harmon and Colbert this whole time. Probably still is."

"Holy shit," Rupe whispered back fiercely. "That fucker!"

"Come with me to the office. I'll have Taylor and Shane meet us there."

"Yeah, of course. Give me a couple minutes, got to finish dressing and tell Millie."

"I'll tell her. Where is she?"

"Uh, in the tub."

Daven blushed instantly. "Never mind, I'll wait in the car. Hurry."

CHAPTER SIX

Los Angeles

"I think I scared your guards," Daven observed nonchalantly on the way to the office.

"You did. They'll get over it." Rupe was a nervous wreck. Vance was driving them in the truck, which didn't have privacy glass, so Daven hadn't explained anything yet.

"This traffic," Rupert complained a few minutes later - again - unable to keep his silence for more than a minute at a time. He knew he was getting on Daven's nerves, but he couldn't help it. "10 o'clock at night. Don't these people have to work tomorrow? We've gone less than a mile."

Vance replied quickly, "Going as fast as I can, sir. Santa Monica Boulevard down to 10th Street is closed for a film shoot."

"Oh. Thanks. That wasn't a criticism, by the way," he added belatedly. Vance said nothing.

Daven glanced meaningfully at Rupe; it was one of his many trademark looks that needed no words. This one in particular was the ' *calm down before you give yourself a stroke'* version.

"It's Friday night, in Los Angeles. Of course there's traffic."

"Why didn't we take the Escalade?" Rupert complained. "You're killing me here."

"Rupert," Dav mumbled warningly as he looked up again from scrolling through emails on his phone.

"You know, our party's own policies forbid you from using personal vehicles while conducting company business. It's not safe."

Daven bristled a little. "Not safe for me, or for you?"

Rupert rolled his eyes. "Fine. Sorry. I'll shut up."

"Thank you. I took this car to try to keep the press from tailing us. No use getting them worked up into a frenzy about why we're going to the office on a Friday night."

"Oh. You could have just said that."

"I would think it was obvious," Daven shot back.

Vance cleared his throat and glanced backwards at them through the mirror. "Sorry to eavesdrop. We're being followed by at least 3 cars I recognize."

Daven resisted the urge to look backwards. "No need to apologize. Thank you. Please go to Taylor's instead of the office. Rupe, call her and let her know we're coming. I'll call Shane."

They both whipped out their phones and ten minutes later the car pulled into Taylor's condo building in Brentwood. The press cars veered off in surrender at that point, and Daven grunted in satisfaction. Since Taylor was on the way to the office, she wasn't there, but she gave them the numeric code to get in the apartment. As they entered, Rupe discreetly made eye contact with Vance and Martinez, who took the hint and went back out to the foyer and closed the door.

"So," Rupert said with a tense grin as they settled on the couch, "I really thought you were just coming over to tell me the world's worst dad joke back at the house. *A goat with a banana down his throat?*"

Daven cocked his head quizzically. "Dad joke?"

"It's...never mind. Would you kindly let me know what the hell is going on now? Please?"

"Yes. Lester Boyd called me out of the blue. That description...it was something Colbert said to him a long time ago about his informant. I knew right away who he meant, of course."

"Boyd couldn't have told you this earlier? Like months ago? Jesus."

"Apparently not. I don't know what happened to make him change his mind and call me."

"How do you know this isn't a trick? What motivation did he have to call you?" Rupert asked with great reluctance. He hated even mentioning the possibility, but they had to consider it.

"I don't know if it's a trick, and I don't know why he called."

Rupe shook his head. "If it's true...well, I thought Yannick was one of our best. Damn. Did he say anything else?"

"Yes, and this strictly stays between you and me. I mean it. You cannot tell a single soul. Promise me."

"I promise," Rupert gulped.

Daven stood and took his coat off, then folded it over the arm of the chair and sat back down.

"Turns out the reason Hank agreed to execution was because Harmon agreed to turn the boys over to me after one year if he pled guilty and died for it. Otherwise, he was going to drag out the trial forever. It's clear the boys would have ended up indentured for life if so, considering what we've learned since then."

"What the...so, Harmon basically extorted him."

"Yes. I'm assuming the FBI wasn't aware of that detail, because it's incredibly illegal, needless to say. Either that, or...."

"Or what?"

Daven took his time answering, knowing his very words were treasonous to the core. "Or the FBI was complicit in this scheme all along. Possibly even the president, too."

"What the fuck?" exclaimed Rupert as he leaped to his feet. "Wait, this is too much. I need time to process."

"I know. Regardless whether I'm right or not, if I take Harmon down, he loses control of the deeds. They'll be transferred to the state automatically, not to me."

Rupert went deathly pale. "Shit. You're right. What are you going to do if we can't vindicate Hank, then?" he asked hoarsely.

"I don't know. And without Stewart..." He didn't need to say the rest.

"Jesus, Dav. Do you think Lester Boyd was in on it, too?"

Daven nodded. "That was my first thought the moment I heard he was the negotiator. You know who his boss is now? Colbert. You know who his boss used to be during the revolution? Colbert. Then Hank changed sides and they all threatened to kill each other. It all seems very conveniently lined up to settle some scores, doesn't it?"

Rupe thought about it for a few minutes while they sat together in silence. "Look, that's honestly, that is just an insane theory. Maybe some things line up, yes, but the more you look at it, there more problems there are with it. Stewart and Hank were friends, and...no, I just can't-"

They both jumped as the door from the foyer into the living room opened and Shane and Taylor came in together.

"Something going on, boss?"

Rupert and Daven exchanged knowing looks with each other.

"Yes," Daven replied calmly. "Quite the emergency. Sorry to pull you away on a Friday night."

Taylor dropped her bag next to the side table and headed toward the kitchen. "Alright then. I'd better grab us a few beers before we get started."

Rupert looked at Daven again. "Can I speak to you alone, please? Sorry Shane, we'll be right back."

They both stood up and went into Taylor's bedroom and shut the door.

"Dav, you know I would never say you're wrong unless I'm one hundred percent sure you're wrong. So that's not what I'm saying, But I have a different theory that you need to hear before we progress."

"What?"

"I think...look, I know Colbert. You don't. We worked together in-"

"Yes, yes, I know. What's your theory?" Daven urged his confidante impatiently.

Rupert took a deep breath. "It's possible Harmon was trying to *save* the boys with his offer. He was the one who wanted to trial to end so quickly. You know I hate him, but this...it's not him. Everything you've told me has Colbert written all over it, Dav. I saw firsthand what he was capable of during the revolution. You didn't come into the picture until after he fell. I was *there* working with him every single day until then. I'm telling you, it wouldn't surprise me at all if Harmon and

Stewart end up being the good guys in this mess and had no knowledge of Colbert's hand in it."

Dav stared at him. "That would explain why Stewart kept quiet about the documents in the safe. It would have prolonged the trial."

"It could explain a lot of things if we just take the time to sit down and think about it a little longer before jumping to conclusions. It's possibly even Lester was involved at first but changed sides, or maybe he was just as reeled in as Harmon and only recently started to realize things aren't adding up. Maybe that's why he called you. I don't know."

"Alright. That's a second possibility. The third is that Boyd is lying. Stewart told me he was not as deeply involved as I thought."

"So...a fourth scenario is that Stewart was lying," breathed Rupert shakily.

Daven was looking straight at Rupert now. "Maybe they're both lying. Number five."

Rupe took a deep breath. "Fuck, well..well, let's look at possibility six. We also have to consider...you're not going to like this one at all."

"What could possibly be a worse suggestion than what we already have?" Daven said with a shrug. "Let's hear it before I go jump off the balcony and put myself out of my misery."

Rupert suddenly had tears in his eyes now, which astonished his friend.

"Rupe? What…"

"Don't say that again, please."

Daven took a step closer to his friend, looking contrite and embarrassed. "I'm sorry. I didn't mean it, Rupe. Just frustrated. What's the sixth scenario, please?"

Rupert cleared his throat. "Not a scenario. An option. We have to consider waiting until after April 1 to make any move at all."

"That's…" Dav did the math in his head. "More than six months away."

"Yes," Rupert said shakily. "We wait until you have the boys in your custody. Play it safe. And then…if we have anything a hundred percent solid, we pounce and take Colbert down. Or Harmon, or the whole FBI or whatever. Who knows right now. But if we *don't* get the proof…"

"We let it go," Daven finished for him. "And Floyd and Theo remain Bonded Retainers in my house for 19 years."

"Yes."

"No."

Rupert nodded and wiped his eyes. "Just…promise me you'll seriously think about it. We don't have Stewart's support anymore. Salome and Rickon aren't your friends. So if we jump the gun and we're *right* , and Harmon loses those deeds…hell, even if we're wrong he could refuse to turn them over if he thinks you're after him. Let's just say that I very much doubt this alleged agreement exists anywhere in writing.

If all we have to do is wait another six months before we make our move, isn't that worth it? The boys are at a boarding school with Lester Boyd, they'll be alright."

Daven turned away and rubbed his temples hard. "I don't know what to do. Do you suggest we stop investigating Yannick until I decide, then?"

"Not at all. If you decide to wait, I say we lay him off with a nice severance package so he can't do any more damage, or get suspicious, and then we take our time backtracking through everything he's ever said and done while he was with us."

"We can't just lay him off and keep everyone else. Talk about creating suspicion."

"We'd have to reorganize the entire department, then."

Dav sighed. "Another cover-up to cover another cover-up. Great."

"Basically, yes. Remember who we're doing this for. Two innocent teenagers who probably don't even know their dad is dead right now."

Daven said nothing for a long time. He just stared at a painting on the bedroom wall. Through it, rather.

Rupe prompted eventually, "Taylor and Shane are waiting for us."

"I know. Hank would know exactly what to do already. He'd be planning every step. I'm not him. I'm...not sure what to do." He sighed heavily.

"He would have already gone in with guns blazing, making some stupid impetuous decision that got us all dug in deeper shit than we started with. So yeah, thank god you're not him."

Daven finally looked at Rupe. "He wasn't *always* like that."

"Yes, he was. You were his voice of reason, and I have always trusted you to do the right thing. You always have. So whatever you decide, I'm all in."

Daven nodded, a bit overcome by emotion for a few seconds, then went back to staring at the painting. All he could think about were the times when he *hadn't* done the right thing. The receipts he'd held onto, for starters.

Rupert cleared his throat roughly. "Time to make a decision, Dav."

Daven shuddered a little. "We're going to wait. Let's tell Shane and Taylor it was a false alarm. Go ahead and send them home."

"You're...this is Taylor's house, so we're the ones who need to go home," Rupert said gently, without any snark. "Are you sure you want to make a decision this quickly? Maybe you should think on it some more."

"No. If the FBI couldn't pin down Colbert's involvement in six months, it's arrogant to think I'll be able to do so on my own."

"But we have Yannick now."

"It's not worth the risk. We'll do the reorganization and get rid of him that way. After I get the boys, we look into his actions. Not before then."

"Dav, I respect your decision and won't say anything more as long as you can assure me you are okay with potentially letting Colbert get away with framing Hank and-"

"Hank's dead, Rupert!" Daven replied hotly. "Forget him now. We can't risk giving Harmon a reason to change his mind about handing those deeds over. If we expose Yannick, we endanger Harmon. Not worth it. Period."

Rupe nodded approvingly. "My thoughts exactly. Just wanted to make sure we were on the same page."

"Oh...that's why you were arguing against your own idea."

"Devil's advocate and all. Someone's got to play the part. I told you I'd be all in, and I am."

"Alright. Let's go home, Rupe."

CHAPTER SEVEN

Los Angeles

"Well you asked me to talk, so now I'm talking."

Harmon closed his eyes in pain and shifted the phone to his other ear. "I've changed my mind. I want you to stop."

"Why?" Daven asked nonchalantly. "You are the one who said I can't ignore you forever."

"On policy matters, yes. You're basically just antagonizing me for the fun of it right now, which I really don't appreciate."

"I have an idea, then."

"What?"

Daven smiled to himself. "Maybe if you take your tiny little hands off your tiny little dick, you can use them to cover your ears so you can't hear me anymore."

"Fuck you, Daven. You're never getting the deeds now."

BEEEEEP. BEEEEEEP. BEEEEEP. BEEEEEEP.

Daven groggily reached over to slam his hand down on his alarm clock for the second time. For several long moments he wasn't sure where he was, until the rapidly increasing movement of Shannon's ticklish tail against his feet caught his attention and eventually brought him back home.

"Hey sweetie," Dav said with a dry grumble as he reached over and scratched her head, then cracked one eye open. She inched up closer to him on her belly - like a soldier crawling under a barbed wire obstacle course, Daven mused idly - and lay alongside him with wide eyes. Time for breakfast, or perhaps she really needed to poop. Both, most likely.

He felt the bed bounce once, and then twice, as the other two dogs jumped up and joined in the plea for their human to rise. Daven closed his eyes again, but he was wide awake already. Today was the day he had agreed to finally speak with Harmon after eight months of avoiding any kind of contact with the Urbanes, and to say he wasn't looking forward to it was a massive understatement. He reached over for his cell phone and dialed Rupert.

"Hey, boss. Did you finally get some sleep, I hope?"

"Yeah."

"Today's the day," Rupe reminded him unnecessarily.

"I know. I was just dreaming about how badly the conversation might go. Rupe..."

"Don't chicken out, Dav. You got this. You've been rehearsing for weeks."

Daven looked at his three dogs. No...his dog, and Floyd and Theo's two dogs. The latter two's happiness depended on every move he made next.

"Listen, I have to tell you something important. Are you alone?"

"Yes."

Daven took a deep breath. "I got a hold of Stewart last night. Finally."

There was a long pause on the other end. "You agreed not to drag him back into-"

"I know. Just listen. He confirmed the deal was legit, that the boys are mine again on April 1. I just...I wanted to thank you, Rupe. For convincing me to wait. You were right. But now I have a favor to ask you, and you're not going to like it."

Rupert took a deep breath, then picked his coffee back up. "Is this request going to result in an argument, by chance?"

"Yes."

"Fuck. Not sure I've had enough coffee yet."

Daven ignored that. "If Rickon doesn't confirm me tomorrow as new leader of the party, I want you to start the proceedings to take over."

"No."

"Rupe-"

"I said no, Dav, and that's the end of it." Rupert went to the other end of his office and shut the door hard. "You go, I go. End of story. Besides, he has no reason not to confirm you."

"Even if he does, I'm not sure I even want to bring the boys back into this life. You know what it's like, Rupe. I work 14 hours a day. It's not fair to them. Hank was...he was so absent from their lives, and never knew most of the time where they were or what they were up to. I can't do that to them. I should quit."

"Under different circumstances, yes. But you've forgotten one thing."

"What?"

Rupert took another deep breath. "Don't hate me for saying it, Dav. But it's got to be said. They're not your sons."

"I'm aware of that."

"They'll be your servants."

"Yes," Daven huffed. "As if I could possibly need another reminder. What's your point?"

"You know what my point is. They have to live by certain guidelines, or you're going to be in serious shit. You can't take them out sailing, or to museums, or what have you. Exactly what kind of quality time do you plan on having?"

"I'm not going to get into that right now," Daven replied calmly. "It's putting the cart before the bridge."

"Horse, Dav. What else did Stewart say?"

"The horse before the bridge, then. You know what I mean."

"It's *cart* before the *horse* . Are you going to tell me what else he said, or are we going to debate metaphors all day?"

"It's an idiom, not a metaphor. He also said he was fined an enormous amount by the FBI for his role in the ending the Colbert investigation prematurely."

"As we figured. Damn. Did you tell him about Yannick?"

"No, that was all. He hung up on me after saying he was going to block my number. That was literally our entire conversation, unfortunately. But what he did tell me was huge, and makes me feel a lot better about dealing with Harmon now."

Daven paused as he heard the incoming call beep on his phone. Speak of the devil.

"What the hell?" he wondered aloud. "He's calling me now."

"Did you have the time wrong? Forget to account for time zones, or whatever?"

"No. Hold on."

Daven clicked over to the other line.

"Johansson."

"Daven, sorry to call earlier than scheduled. I was hoping we can meet in person instead of over the phone."

"Um. When?"

"Today. I'm in San Diego and can send my jet up for you."

And crash it into the side of a mountain just for kicks. "No, thank you. Phone is fine."

"It's incredibly important, and for your ears only," Harmon urged. "But I can't come up to Los Angeles, for the same reasons you won't go to Denver."

"I'm not going to San Diego, either."

There was a sigh on the other line. "Fine. Palm Springs?"

"No. I will consider Temecula. There's a vineyard there with private space. The manager is a good friend of mine and very discreet. That's your only option. Take it or leave it."

"I'll take it. 2pm?"

"That's fine. I'll email you with details."

"No. Call me back. Put nothing in writing to me or to your friend. What's the name of the vineyard?"

"Ponte Inn. May I ask, why do you-"

The line went dead, and Daven held the phone and stared at it like it was made of lava. "What the..." Then he remembered Rupert was still on the other line, and he clicked back over.

"Sorry, Rupert. He just wanted to reconfirm the time of our meeting." Daven flushed a little; he hated lying to his friend but he wasn't quite sure yet what had just happened, and wasn't willing to admit he'd made a rash decision to meet his rival in person. Secretly, no less.

"Did you manage to do that without pissing him off?"

"Of course. I'd better go. Lots to prepare, and I haven't read over the policy documents enough to memorize the big points. I'll do the call from home."

"I think that's for the best," agreed Rupert. "No chance of anyone overhearing anything. But please do call me right after and tell me everything."

"I will, of course."

Seditionists HQ - Los Angeles

1pm

Rupert sighed for what seemed like the hundredth time today as he pored over more newspaper articles relating to the rumors that Hank was no longer among the living. The FBI had of course said nothing, and neither had the Seditionists. Daven had a brief call with Salome to discuss, but she was certain that it was all idle speculation and not an information leak. Rupert wasn't so sure, but so far, nobody seemed to be taking it very seriously. That made him feel a little better, but not much.

His concentration was suddenly broken by a knock on his door, and he hit the button on his desk that unlocked it remotely. "Yes? Come in."

His assistant came in and handed him a packet. "Courier just came by and dropped this off for you and Daven."

"Thank you." Rupert waited until she was gone and then ripped the packet open, and then picked up the phone to call Dav, who didn't answer.

"Dav, we just got something at the office you need to see for your call with...for your 2pm call, rather. The updated measures for December, and it's way too big to fax over. Looks like quite a few changes in verbiage you two will need to discuss. Call me back."

Rupert rang for Taylor, who came immediately. "Sorry to turn you into an errand girl, but I need you to take this over to Daven's house immediately. He'll need it for a 2pm conference call he's taking from home. Use my driver. Thanks, love."

Rupert went back to his coffee and articles, and thought nothing else of it until Taylor called him 45 minutes later.

"Hey Taylor, everything okay?"

"No," Taylor replied, a little bewildered. "He's not home."

Rupert looked at his watch; it was nearly time for the call. "What? Are you sure?"

"I'm certain. He has one guard on watch, but the car and other two guards are gone. Toby said he was too busy for visitors, but he's obviously not there. I'm waiting outside just in case he shows up. If he doesn't, what do you want me to do with this?"

"I'll call you right back."

Rupe called Dav at the house and on his cell, but only got the option to leave a voicemail. Then he tried Martinez, and

Vance. Both went straight to voicemail. Now he was alarmed, and made the decision to call Shane in telecommunications for assistance.

"Yes, boss?"

"Sorry to bother you, Shane. I can't get a hold of Daven and it's critical. Can you let me know if his phone is turned on?"

"Sure. One moment."

Rupert swallowed hard; it wasn't odd for Dav to ignore everyone and disappear off the radar when he got overly focused on a task. But him not being home for such a crucial phone call, not to mention both his guards unreachable as well? That was another story...

"Sir?" Shane sounded concerned.

"Yeswhatisit?" Rupert blurted quickly.

"I'm showing his phone is not turned off, physically, but it doesn't have a signal. He's out of range."

"What? *Out of range?* Where was it last located?"

"I can't...you know it's against policy for me to tell you that, sir."

Rupert smiled a little; he was the one who had written the policy. "It's a matter of his personal safety, Shane. I take complete responsibility and will report it to Daven myself. Where was the phone last detected?"

There was a telling pause. "Can you send an authorization email first, please?"

"Of course." Rupert reached over to his laptop and yanked up the lid, then banged out a quick message to both men explaining what he had just asked Shane to do, taking great care to emphasize that Shane had first refused exactly as protocol demanded.

"Sent. Tell me when you receive it."

"Received, thank you. I'm showing that phone last pinged a cell tower in Temecula 17 minutes ago. Let me check the address....that tower is located at the intersection of Meadows Parkway and Rancho California Road. That doesn't mean it's exactly where he was, he could be anywhere within a few miles of it."

Rupert knew exactly where he was, cell phone tower be damned. He was meeting with Harmon in person at Ponte Inn...in secret, for some reason. As if that wasn't bad enough, he would learn afterwards that Rupert was spying on him and it wasn't really a secret at all.

Fuck. I'll be lucky to have a job at all after today, never mind what Rickon says...

"Alright, thanks Shane. That explains what I needed to know. Appreciate it," Rupert finally said in a strangled tone. "Have a nice afternoon."

Temecula, 2pm

Daven set down his briefcase as he entered the small boardroom, where he found Harmon awaiting him. The man looked incredibly nervous for a change, and Dav wasn't sure what to make of it. His own heart started beating overly fast in response.

"Good day," he said politely as he took off his coat and sat down. He wanted to ask what the hell was so important about the December measures that required a last-second, in-person meeting, but he refrained with some difficulty.

"Good afternoon," responded Harmon. "Is this room bugged, or do you have any recording devices on you?"

"No to both questions. Are *you* recording us?"

"No."

Daven didn't touch the papers he had brought along. "I take it we're not going to be discussing the December measures."

"I don't know if we'll have time."

"You're nervous," Daven observed calmly. "Why?"

Harmon shifted in his chair, then picked up a pen and started tapping it on the table. "I know you hate me, Daven. For what happened to Hank, and all that. Can't say I blame you."

"*All that?*" Dav echoed mockingly. "Bit of an understatement, don't you think?"

"Perhaps, yes. I think that the way everything went down was tragic, but for the best. Just my opinion, with which you obviously disagree."

Daven didn't take his eyes off his enemy. "I'm curious. What gave you the idea that your *opinion* matters to me?"

Harmon laughed nervously, then set his pen down. "Alright. I can see Hank rubbed off on you more than I thought. I'm not going to fight with you. I...what I'm about to tell you is going to cost both of us our jobs, most likely. If you don't want to hear it, you should leave now."

Now it was Daven's turn to squirm in his chair. "I'm listening."

"Alright. I was in a meeting with Colbert yesterday, and he left his cell phone behind. I was taking it to him when it rang."

"Okay."

"And because I was a little distracted, I picked it up, thinking it was my own."

"Who was it?"

Harmon swallowed hard. "One of my former operatives whom Colbert had assured me we were no longer in contact with. I mean, for like...ten months. Asking for payment from me for his latest services to the Urbanes that I supposedly authorized."

Daven stared the man down hard. "You told the FBI and Hank that you had no more double agents. In fact, you used that claim to force us to disband our own counter-intelligence operations.”

“Now we get down to why I’m so nervous. This proves, as I suspected months ago, that Colbert is running his own operation without my knowledge. It goes without saying that Stewart leaving the FBI was the fatal blow in my attempt to prove it.”

“I see. A minute ago you said that this information would cost both of us our jobs. You, yes, but I don’t see what I have to do with it.”

“Right. Well, that’s where the next part comes in. I know you’ve been in contact with Lester Boyd, contrary to the terms of the confidentiality agreement you signed with the FBI. Simply put, I won’t hesitate to blow the whistle on you if you don’t answer my next question truthfully.”

Daven sat up straighter in his chair, his chest tight with anxiety and impending sense of doom. He couldn’t even say anything back, he was *that* flabbergasted.

Harmon continued calmly, “I want to know exactly why this man was laid off. My suspicion is that you somehow became aware of his activities, or at least suspected him of being a mole.”

“I want to know how *you know* he was laid off, since you claim to not be in contact with him anymore.”

"Colbert told me some time ago when I asked if we could possibly use the man's services again. I asked only to see what he'd say, and had no intention of actually carrying it through."

Daven desperately wanted to flee the room. It was getting hot.

"I don't know what you want," he said finally.

"To bring down Colbert. You have at least some kind of proof of the scheme, and you know what that could mean. I'll give you a few minutes to think about it anyway," Harmon said dangerously, in control again. He was always a hundred times more intimidating when the ball was in his court.

"Answer me first," Daven responded, his tone edgy and hard. "What *services* did he want payment for, exactly?"

"I don't know, and that's the truth. From what little he said, it's clear he genuinely thinks I'm in on the whole thing. I'm not, needless to say, but I played along long enough to allay his suspicion. So why did you separate him from your company? Did you get an inkling of what he was doing?"

Daven raised an eyebrow. "Let's get one thing clear first, Harmon. I'm not impressed by your threats. I have no interest in what blackmail designs you have in mind. What I want to do is bring down Colbert, and if I can help you do that, I'm all in. But you need to give me something, first. Otherwise I can't trust you with a single word out of my mouth."

Harmon looked at him out of the sides of his eyes. "What could you possibly want more than my silence?"

"The deeds to Theo and Floyd. *Now*, not on April 1. I'll pay the penalty for early transfer, whatever it is, I don't care. Just see it done and I'll give you all the information you want."

"No. They'll be the only leverage I have left if this goes south."

"Leverage? They're *kids!*"

Harmon scoffed. "Oh come on, you're just as guilty as I am trying to use them as a bargaining chip. Didn't you literally just ask me to trade them over in exchange for information?"

Daven rolled his eyes, knowing he was defeated on that point. Then he ripped a piece of paper from his notebook and tore it in half, giving one to Harmon.

"You're right. But let's get started off correctly. We don't even know if we're talking about the same person. Write down this alleged mole's name. I'll do the same. Then we exchange papers and open them at the same time. If the names are different, I leave now and we'll never speak of this again. If they're the same, I'll cooperate with you. Agreed?"

Harmon nodded. "You do realize that if the names are different, you'll end up with the knowledge of two possible moles, and I'll have absolutely nothing?"

"Nothing? You mean, like what I'm getting out of this if the names are the same? Write it down."

Harmon obliged grudgingly, then passed his folded up paper over to Daven at the same time he received one.

Daven looked down at what was handed to him, and his heart flipped as he read it:

Yannick

He looked across the table to Harmon, who un-folded his own paper and looked down at it. He seemed stunned as he set it face down on the table, very slowly.

"Alright. It seems I owe you an apology," he said quietly. "Bringing you out here for nothing. But at least you know you had two moles now, and who they are. I have no fucking clue how to proceed now."

Daven stood up and started to put his coat on. "Well, I suppose I should thank you for trying. At least we agree on one thing. Colbert is a dangerous, manipulative liar."

"He's not the only one. Takes one to know one, am I right?"

Dav paused, one arm in and one arm out of his coat. "What's that supposed to mean?"

"Oh, nothing. It's just...the name I gave you? It's real. The one you gave me is fake, isn't it? Andrew P., really? Generic much?"

Oh, shit. "What makes you think it's fake?" Daven scoffed offhandedly, although his cheeks started to flush as Harmon sat back with a smug expression and crossed his arms.

"Is it for real?"

"Yes, that's him. Obviously I didn't give the last name for privacy's sake."

"Hmm. Funny thing. I didn't think it was fake at first, actually. Just thought I'd throw it out there to see what happens. Did you know you blush like a little girl when you lie?"

Daven did know that, actually. It had caused much embarrassment in the past. "I'm not lying."

"Another lie, and you're getting even darker. Look, Daven, I get it. You don't trust me, and I don't blame you. But there's one thing I want you to know before you go."

"What?"

Harmon uncrossed his arms and laid his hands flat on the table. "I may be an insufferable, annoying, smug piece of shit to you. But I saved those boys from a *lifetime* of servitude, and that's the truth. You know who condemned them first, though? It wasn't Colbert, and it certainly wasn't me."

He meant Hank, of course. Daven nodded. "I know that Hank...did some things," he admitted.

"Yes, he did. But what compelled him to do those things in the first place?"

Daven looked at the floor and thought about it. "Colbert, I suppose, when it all boils down to it. Goes way back."

"Correct. Chicken and the egg, Daven. They were each other's own worst enemies."

"Don't lecture me."

"The cycle was broken when Hank paid the price, but I'm not going to let Colbert get away with it. Especially since what he's done is going to be the end of me, too. I know that prospect cheers you. So I'm going to ask again...why did you suspect Yannick was working with him?"

Daven continued staring at the floor for a minute, then slowly removed his coat and sat back down into the chair. After a moment, he pulled the desk phone over and positioned it exactly in between both of them.

"If we're doing this, we're doing it properly and calling Salome together. Right now. The first thing you're going to tell her is that you're signing the deeds over to Rupert today."

"Rupert? Not you?"

"Correct. I'll have to tell her about my involvement with Lester Boyd in order to explain how I got the intel on Yannick. But I'd rather go to jail than keep those boys in servitude for one more day in an Urbanes indoctrination center. Understood?"

Harmon looked aghast. "That's not what it is. Wait a minute...just a second. *Lester Boyd* told you it was Yannick?"

"Not directly. I'll explain it to her. Are we proceeding, or not?"

Harmon inhaled sharply, realizing that Daven had no idea Lester held the deeds to the boys. If they got Boyd in trouble...well, shit. Then he may not release the deeds out of spite, or even lose them outright. But if Daven knew that, he would never in a million years cooperate at this point. All he had to do was wait until April 1, after all, and the boys were his. Harmon held out his hand and decided not to mention that little detail.

"Yes. I've got your back, and I expect you to have mine. If you can agree to that, then let's do it."

Daven shook it after significant hesitation. Then Harmon started dialing Salome while Dav did everything in his power not to vomit all over the table.

THREE HOURS LATER

Daven looked at his phone's emails for the first time when they were almost near the house, and he practically exploded when he saw that Rupert had been tracking his location.

"You've got to be kidding me," he muttered angrily, and Martinez looked back at him over the headrest.

"Sorry, sir?"

Daven put down his phone. "Nothing. Did you have any missed calls from Rupert today?"

"Yes, sir. There was no signal at the meeting complex."

"Okay. Let's swing by his house, please. I'll only need a minute, so wait in the car."

"Shall we alert his guards that you're coming?"

"Yes, please." Daven had the habit of springing up on people unexpectedly, although he didn't intend to. He just assumed the other person would know, naturally.

Rupert was waiting at the front door when they pulled up, and he silently led Daven to his study. Both men were bursting at the seams with anger and confusion.

"Don't ever track me again," Daven began, then held up a hand when Rupert started to protest. "That's the end of it. No need to explain, no need to apologize. Just don't repeat the mistake."

"Fine. Do you care to explain why you ran off and secretly met with Harmon in a non-secure location? This is bullshit, Dav, you can't do that to me. I'm supposed to know everything."

"Calm down. You're officially on the know-nothing list as of right now. My meeting with Harmon wasn't about the measures, that's all I'm going to say."

"What the-"

"Quiet, please. There's something I have to tell you. It couldn't wait until morning."

Rupert did calm down, although, he hated to be told to calm down. That only made things worse, but something in Daven's bearing stopped him from blowing up any further.

"What's wrong?" he asked in genuine concern, and not a little fear.

"I'm sorry to do this to you, Rupert, I really am."

"Are you…are you *firing* me, Dav?"

Daven looked askance at him. "What? No. God, I wish it was just that."

"*Just that?* Okay, what the hell is going on?"

"Is your basement still equipped for servant's quarters?"

"Uh…we haven't gotten around to remodeling the rooms, but they're being used as storage for the moment. Why would you ask such a thing?"

Daven reached into his jacket and started to hand over a poor copy of a fax that had already been almost unreadable to start with.

"What is this? I can't make it out."

"Deeds. I'll have to explain later, but the boys belong to you now. Floyd and Theo, I mean. Can you put the rooms back in order for them? They should arrive within 48 hours, but I don't have their flight information yet. When I do, I'll pass it along."

Rupert didn't take the paper. He was white as a ghost.

"Dav…what in the holy fuck is going on. Tell me right now."

Daven looked him in the eyes and said matter-of-factly, "I can't. Please just take good care of them until I get things all sorted out. I'm flying to Richmond tonight to collect them in the morning and see them off, then I'll be in Philadelphia for the rest of the week."

"Are you...holy shit, did you get arrested?"

"Not yet, but the possibility is there until I can get some things cleared up. That's why I didn't have the deeds transferred to me."

Rupert was astonished to see Daven actually smiling a little. He was...was he *happy*? Happy about *what?*

"Have you been drinking, Dav?"

"No." His smile fell off abruptly. "Rupert, I need help with something else. I'm going to have to tell them about Hank before they find out on their own. If you have any ideas...I have no idea what to say."

Rupert shook his head. "Regardless, you can't just drop a bomb like that and then put them on a plane by themselves. I'm coming with you and we'll talk about it on the way over, and I'll fly back with them. What time are you leaving?"

"In two hours. We'll pick you up, of course. Are you sure?"

"Yes. Let me get packed and tell Millie what's happening. Call me when you're about ten minutes away."

"I will. Thanks, Rupe," Daven said warmly, and they gave each other a small but manly hug.

"Sorry for my initial response, but it was quite the shock. Of course we're thrilled to have Theo and Floyd back. It's going to be strange, though...wow. Servants. I can't wrap my brain around it."

"Me either. See you in two hours."

"Dav?" Rupe called as his friend started to walk away.

"Yes?"

"We're taking a private plane, I'm guessing?"

Daven nodded.

"You should bring the dogs," Rupe said firmly. "They're the best kind of therapy."

"Good idea. Thanks. See you soon."

The Curtain Call

Beyond the Stars

CHAPTER ONE

Los Angeles - same evening

"I'm on the way. Please bring your checkbook."

Rupert refrained from groaning; he knew Daven would pay him back without being asked. "Oh god, the early transfer fees. How much is the damage this time?"

"Three hundred thousand. Needless to say-"

"I know."

Daven paused. "That's per deed, by the way."

"Of course it is." Rupert tried not to grimace at his wife, who was standing a few feet away after having zipped up her husband's little suitcase.

"We're coming up the driveway, now," Daven grunted.

"Be right there. Thanks."

Rupert hung up and turned to his wife. "I'm so sorry about this, Millie."

"It's alright," she said quickly. "I've already said a hundred times that I'm glad the boys are coming."

Rupert noticed her eyes were wet and red all of a sudden, and he quickly wiped away the emerging tears and hugged her tight. "I'll call our movers first thing in the morning to clear out the basement and set those rooms to rights again. Don't worry, you won't have to do a thing except let them in and point the way-"

"That's not what I'm upset about. You know we have three empty bedrooms upstairs, right?"

"Please don't start, Millie. I don't like it either, but they have to live downstairs. That's the law."

She pulled away abruptly. "I wonder who's fault *that* is."

"You're not being fair. Sweetheart, can you go get the checkbook while I take this suitcase outside? Please?"

"I'm not letting them live in the basement, Rupe. It's cold, and dark. They're Hank's kids, not some old luggage we can just leave in a corner and forget about until they're needed."

Rupert almost retorted something bitter about her not feeling the same about their previous servants, but instead, he stepped forward to gently wipe her hair off her face and lay his hands on her shoulders. "Sweetie, you know we can't have them living upstairs. I'm not going to fight you about it. Their rooms will be in the basement, and that's final."

"Final for you, maybe. Not for me. You know Theo's afraid of the dark. He wouldn't even go into the basement of his own house in broad daylight. Hank's going to be pissed when he hears about this, law or not. You're his best friend, and those are your godsons!"

Rupert ignored the sudden lump in his throat and let a dark edge creep into his tone. "I have to go. The basement needs to be ready for them by the time I get back. If it's not, they'll be sleeping on boxes and luggage until it is, and I'll lock them down there if necessary. Are we clear?"

Millie eyed her husband curiously, and her expression softened. "From your reaction to me mentioning Hank, I'm guessing the rumors are true."

"What rumors?" he asked needlessly, and that was all the answer she needed. Her eyes glistened again.

"Oh god. Do they know?"

Rupert hesitated, but ultimately declined to answer outright. "Babe, you know I love Floyd and Theo as much as I love our own kids. That's exactly why I'm insisting we follow the law. They could be taken away if we don't. Not worth the risk."

"Fine. Basement it is. But we're taking their dogs in, too," she replied with steely determination.

"Of course." He leaned over and kissed her on forehead. "Seriously, I've got to go. Love you."

Richmond, Virginia

Floyd had tossed and turned all night long, more restless than he'd been in months. When his alarm went off at 6am, he couldn't believe that he'd only gotten about an hour of sleep while his brother had slept soundly and peacefully for at least 7 hours straight.

"Theo," he called, their usual morning ritual starting a bit early; usually Floyd was only coherent after hitting the snooze button half a dozen times.

"*Theo* . Theody. Samantha. Theo I am. I am Theo. Am I Theo?"

"*Shut up, Floyd.*"

Floyd started to sing his usual morning song - something from Sesame Street he'd heard ages ago, but with some variation of "Theo" substituting every word - when the shadow of someone walking up and standing in front of the door stopped him in his tracks. He laid back down and covered himself up entirely, just in time. The door shuddered opened with a squeal, and then slowly the room became brighter and brighter.

"Floyd. I know you're awake. Get dressed and come with me, kiddo."

Floyd pulled the blanket down just enough to peek out. He hadn't been in trouble in weeks, but that tone of voice indicated otherwise, and he started to tremble.

"What did I do?" he asked nervously. There was no reply; the door shut again and the shadow stayed put. He looked over at his brother.

"What did you do?" Theo asked fearfully.

"Nothing." He got up anyway, and quickly threw on his clothes and shoes, and also a jacket so that he could pretend the cold was causing shivers instead of anxiety.

"Floyd..."

"It's okay, Theody. I got this." Floyd was far more nervous than he would admit as he pulled open the door. Lester Boyd was still waiting on the other side, looking grim.

"You're not in trouble, but you're not going to like what's next, either. You got to promise me you'll keep your mouth shut until it's over. I want absolute silence, or else. Got me?"

Floyd stared at him in dismay. "Is that, like...a threat?"

"If it has to be. Follow me."

He led the bewildered teenager to a building on the far edge of campus, way past the point Floyd was allowed to go, and yes - it was damned cold. Now he was shaking from anxiety *and* the chill. The sun was turning the sky purple above the tree line.

"You're freaking me out, Lester," he finally said. "I mean, Mr. Boyd. Sorry."

Lester turned towards him at the door of the plain building, which clearly housed some kind of administrative function. "I'm dead serious, Floyd. Silence unless you are asked to speak directly, in which case it will probably be yes or no questions. And you're going to stick to yes or no. Clear?"

"Wait, can't you just give-"

"Floyd."

Floyd put his hands in his pockets and shivered. "Yes. It's clear."

"Thank you. Hands out of your pockets, stand up straight. Let's go."

They forged ahead and quickly turned into a room which could only belong to someone very high up in the hierarchy of the school, because the room made Lester Boyd's office look like a dilapidated shack.

Before Floyd could fully take in his surroundings, a heavy door on the far side opened with a loud click. When Rupert and Daven walked through, Floyd nearly pissed himself in surprise. He was vaguely aware of Lester tightly squeezing his arm to keep him in place as a third man emerged after Rupert, but Floyd didn't know him.

"Quiet, Floyd," Lester grumbled warningly. "Stay still."

The third man came forward and stood in front of Floyd. "I'm Mr. Sebastian, the president of this school. We haven't had the pleasure of meeting yet."

"Pleasure?" Floyd blurted hotly, and Lester squeezed his arm painfully, but subtly enough that the other men in the room didn't notice. Then he let go, and Floyd felt himself wishing he hadn't, because he didn't know if he could resist the urge to flee from the room as quickly as possible.

Floyd didn't look at his two "uncles," but he had turned bright red at the first sight of them. Daven had noticed it, of course, and didn't approach him as planned. Lester realized Daven had expected a much happier welcome, but he was about to be sorely disappointed.

Mr. Sebastian looked at Lester and nodded, then back to Floyd. "Floyd, the deeds to you and Theo have been transferred to Rupert Aster. You'll both be leaving our school today to travel back to Los Angeles with him and take up residence in his home. How long do you think you'll need to pack?"

So much for those yes or no questions, Floyd thought idly. He forced himself to remain polite. "I want to stay here. Theo will as well, so no need to ask him. Thank you, though."

The room went dead silent, except for Rupert's sharp intake of breath, and Lester felt rather than saw the hot glare from Daven directed at him specifically.

Sebastian gathered his wits and then spoke again. "I'm afraid you don't have any say in the matter. Return to your room and pack, please. As quickly as you can manage. Thank you, Mr. Boyd."

Daven stepped forward. "Just a minute, please. I want to talk to Floyd before he goes."

Sebastian hesitated. "Rupert is his deed holder, so technically you need his permi-"

"He can talk to him," Rupe interrupted firmly. "Got a room they can use?"

Daven stood a respectful distance away from Hank's oldest son and tried not to let his own disappointment and surprise dictate what he said next.

"Floyd, please explain why you would want to stay here. I'm not understanding why you would say such a hurtful thing. We've all but moved heaven and earth to get you back."

Floyd stared at him stonily, all defiance and stubbornness. "I refuse to believe you're that stupid," he nearly spit out. "You know why!"

Daven held his hands out in a *what the hell are you talking about* gesture. "No, I don't. Why don't you tell me?"

"Go fuck yourself. You act like we'd be going home, like you're doing us a favor...but you want us to be *Rupert's servants!*"

"You're going to be servants no matter what, Floyd. Might as well be with someone you trust, and who loves you. You're extremely lucky it all worked out this way."

Floyd laughed a little. "Lucky. Yeah. I *don't* trust him, and I definitely don't trust you. I repeat: go fuck yourself. How much did you pay for us, anyway?"

"Three hundred thousand dollars. Each. But Rupert and I would have spent every last penny, and begged and borrowed if we had to, in order to get you out of here. Your dad, by the way, wanted exactly this. So don't tell me you aren't coming. I won't accept it, because it dishonors his efforts and sacrifice."

Floyd seemed truly taken aback by that - deeply stunned, actually - and had no immediate reply.

"Listen, Floyd," Daven said quietly, in desperate surrender. "Whatever's happened, we can talk about it later. I've got a plane waiting on the tarmac for you at Richmond Airport.

Your dogs are inside, waiting for you boys. I'm not going to let them be disappointed."

Daven was inexpressibly relieved to see Floyd visibly calm down at that. "My...my dogs?"

"Yes. Starsky and Hutch are not even 20 miles away. I had to leave Shannon at home, but she's waiting for you, too. I know you have questions about your dad, and I'll answer them. But not here. I want to get you the hell out of here as quickly as possible, before Lester can change his mind."

Again, Floyd was stunned. "What does Lester have to do with this?"

Daven replied calmly, "He owns your deeds. I've already given over the check to pay for them, and Rupert's got provisional custody...but until you sign the transfer, he can change his mind. Which he might do, by the way, if you continue to behave like this."

It was obvious Floyd had no idea Lester held his deed, and - exactly as Daven hoped - the knowledge quickly obliterated Floyd's warm feelings towards the man.

"You mean he didn't ever bother to tell us that he *owned* us? This whole time? What the fuck! That's sick."

"Language, Floyd, please. He didn't bother to tell me, either. I just found out today. All Bonded Retainers have the right to refuse transfer, or request one, if they feel their personal safety is in peril. It's one of the many laws put in place for your protection. You and Theo will have to sign the new deeds and approve your own transfer. I'm asking you to please do that, and not fight about it."

"I'm not signing anything until you tell me where my dad is and what happened to him," Floyd decided firmly. "Right now, in this room. Not later."

Daven had gone over this exact scenario with Rupert on the plane. He knew that was going to be Floyd's reaction all along, and was prepared. But that still didn't make it any easier. He swallowed a few times and then took a deep breath.

"No. Not here."

The door open and Mr. Sebastian stepped in. "Gentlemen, time to wrap it up. Floyd, out."

Floyd went instantly and without argument, to Daven's surprise and relief.

"Mr. Johansson, I hope you convinced the boy this is for the best."

"I don't know. I hope."

They went back into the office, where Floyd took the new deed from Lester and read over it a few times. Then he looked back up - pointedly aiming a question directly at Rupert, not Daven.

"Where are my dogs?"

Rupert answered nervously, having just heard a brief explanation from Lester in the meantime exactly what the hell was going on between Floyd and Daven. "Your very bad dogs are on the plane at Richmond Airfield. They made a nice snack out of the new upholstery somewhere over Kansas when we weren't looking, but I know you'll ensure they behave on the way back."

He thought that would cheer Floyd up, but it did nothing. He was as determined and steely-eyed as he'd ever been.

"Haven't agreed to go back yet. I have conditions. I understand we have to live in the basement, technically, but Theo gets a room to sleep in upstairs at night."

Rupert started a little, then nodded. "Agreed."

"Rupe-" interrupted Dav.

"No, it's fine. Theo sleeps upstairs when we don't have guests, and the pool house if we do. Any other conditions?"

"He starts homeschooling again."

"No, Floyd." That was from Daven. "Absolutely not. There are laws Rupert has to follow in order to keep custody of you boys. We can bend some to your needs, but this isn't one of them."

Floyd nodded. "Fine. No corporal punishment for him, then."

Rupert nodded readily. "Or you, Floyd. You have my word. If that's all, please go ahead and sign so we can get the hell out of here."

"It's not all. You're going to tell me and Theo what happened with dad. Not him." Floyd threw a glare at Daven, then back to Rupert. "That brings me to my last condition. You will never ask me to assist Daven in any way, or even speak to him. At the dinner table, at functions, whatever. I won't do it. After today, the bastard doesn't exist as far as I'm concerned."

"A moment, gentlemen, please," said Lester as he stepped into the tense little circle and took Floyd's arm, then pulled him into the same room where he'd spoken with Daven earlier and slammed the door behind them.

"Owners aren't allowed to touch their servants without their consent, Mr. Boyd," Floyd warned as he jerked his elbow away.

Lester froze. This was the exact reason he'd never told the boys he had their deeds.

"Floyd, calm down. I've told you before, Daven doesn't deserve to be treated that way. If you only knew the shit he's been through in the past eight months trying to get you freed, you'd be kissing his ass. Get back in there and apologize before I cane the crap out of you as a parting gift."

"Do it," Floyd challenged. "I'm not apologizing."

The door opened again and Daven pushed in impatiently. "Let him go, Mr. Boyd. It's alright. I agreed to those terms. Floyd, it's time to make a decision. Come on. Out, both of you."

With a final glare at Lester, Floyd strode from the room. "I'm not signing until Theo does. Mr. Sebastian, will you kindly walk me back to my room? I don't know how to get there from here."

"Mr. Boyd will walk you back."

"I'm not going anywhere with him."

"Mr. Boyd will walk you back," Mr. Sebastian repeated patiently. "Mr. Johansson and Mr. Aster will depart for the airport now and wait for you there. You never told me how long it will take you to pack."

"Half an hour, at the most. If we decide to leave, that is."

"Very well. I'll remain here with the deeds. Good day, gentlemen."

ONE HOUR LATER

Floyd had already known, of course, that Theo would instantly capitulate, no matter how his big brother felt about Daven. He hated being trained as a house servant, and was happy and energetic as the car pulled up to take them and Lester Boyd to Richmond Airfield, with the few belongings they still had between in one bag and the new deeds in a sealed envelope in the other.

After a few minutes, Theo spoke up. "Aren't you happy, Floyd? Oh my god. We're going home."

"You mean to Rupert's house. As his servants."

"Servants, students, whatever. Same thing. We practically grew up there. It's like home." Floyd fell silent while Theo leaned up against him. "Uncle Dav made this happen, Floyd."

Lester watched the elder Bancroft through the rearview mirror. He didn't like what he saw as Floyd slouched back further, the look in his eyes increasingly dark and lifeless by the second.

"You're right about that, Theo. We can thank Daven for all of this."

CHAPTER TWO

Richmond, Virginia

7:00am

Daven didn't feel anything as he and Rupert were escorted from the BRTSM's administration building to the airport. Perhaps it was numbness, or weariness, or he had exhausted his bank of emotions for the month…or, he knew, he felt too much and simply couldn't process it all. Not that it was a huge surprise, really. He knew Floyd was upset with him long before this, considering how the teenager had acted towards him back in late March, but it was the unexpected depth of the hostility that had shocked him to the core.

Rupert was shocked too; perhaps even more so. He'd had no idea Floyd harbored any ill-will towards Daven at all. He wanted to ask about it as they drove to the airport, but Dav wasn't ready, if the expression on his face was any judge of things. The man was clearly still wondering how the older boy had ended up telling him to go fuck himself with no apparent provocation.

So they rode in silence for a while, until Daven suddenly decided to open up.

"Rupe…it's a good thing the deeds went to you. I can't even fathom what would be happening right now if they had gone to me. Floyd would've refused to leave."

"Sure seems like it. While you were talking to him, Lester whispered to me that Floyd thinks you turned Hank in. Did you know that?"

Daven turned and stared at Rupe for a moment. "No. I knew he was upset that I didn't defend Hank after he was arrested, but...what the hell gave him the idea I turned him in?"

"I think it's pretty clear that Lester Boyd brainwashed him. Probably got to Theo, too."

Daven thought about what he had heard behind the door a few minutes ago: Lester telling Floyd he should be grateful to Daven for trying to save them. Trying to make him apologize. The man definitely didn't do this.

"It wasn't Lester. Had to be something he heard on the news. Remember Hailey dropped that alleged report that I was behind all this back in March? Floyd might have caught wind of it."

"Oh...shit. Well, you can easily disprove that now. Show Floyd all the lawsuits for slander she's been hit with in the last few years. Can't believe it took that long for her to lose her license."

"Hmm. Yes. Just so you know, I've asked Lester Boyd to move to Los Angeles and work for us. He turned it down right away, but I know he'll change his mind in a few weeks. We need to start thinking of a position for him."

Rupert's jaw dropped. "I'm sorry, I thought I heard you say you *asked Lester Boyd to move to Los Angeles to work for us.* Come again?"

Daven nodded, but he didn't look at Rupe. His thoughts were far away, on another planet almost. "I can't tell you why, but he knows."

"I can't accept that, Dav," Rupert said sternly.

"You'll have to, I'm afraid. I'll explain when I can. It might be a while. First things first. I was planning to tell the boys about Hank, but looks like you agreed to be the messenger for that. What are you going to say?"

Rupert rapped on the privacy glass in the car, and it rolled down a few inches. "Martinez. Have the driver pull up at the Waffle House off the next exit. You guys can go get a bite and leave us alone in the car for a bit."

"Yes, sir. Call me when you want us back in."

"I will."

The glass rolled back up as they pulled into the restaurant. Once the men had left the car, Rupert turned back around to glare at Daven.

"Okay, Dav. We need to have a serious come-to-Jesus. Look, I didn't say anything when you suddenly foisted the boys upon me as servants, even though I already have three kids. Now I'm going to have five, and four dogs. I wrote that $600,000 check without blinking-"

"I'm paying you back when we get to the airport."

"-after I barely whimpered when you met secretly with Harmon without informing me. I fought with my wife over this, for you and those boys. And yes, I'll take the last-second responsibility of telling them about Hank even though I'm not prepared, because you never bothered to tell me Floyd was pissed at you. What I won't do is sit back and let you treat me like I'm some kind of untrustworthy blabbermouth. I'm flying home in an hour with two traumatized teenagers who think their Uncle Dav just had their dad executed by their own government, while you get to disappear off the radar for a week and let me and my family deal with the nuclear fallout that these poor boys are about to experience. Do you realize what a massive PR nightmare this is all going to be? And you want Lester Boyd there now, too, whom Floyd *also* hates? I deserve to know what's going on, and you have no longer have any right to keep it from me. So start talking."

Daven's expression never changed during this tirade, which only made it worse for Rupert.

"No," Dav answered calmly, folding his hands in his lap and cocking his head slightly at his right hand man.

Rupert was appalled. "No? Did you just say...no?"

"Correct. But perhaps what I should've said is *not right now.* Maybe you'll figure it out on your own, if you calm down and think hard enough about what's going on and why I would do all these things. Take your time, we don't have to be at the airport for a while."

"I don't understand you. I don't understand any of this. Jesus Christ. All this subterfuge. You're Hank, reincarnated." Rupert shook his head and fell silent, wondering if his anger could possibly set the car on fire in its intensity. He refused to think about the situation at first, preferring to silently fume and think about how to write his resignation letter. He had just composed it all inside his head when the unexpected occurred.

"Holy shit." He sat straight up in his seat. "Lester is cooperating with the FBI. You knew he was going to turn against Colbert. You said so months ago."

"Hmm. I do recall saying that, come to think of it." There was a slight sparkle in his eye now, and he totally unconscious of it, but Rupert knew that look like he knew two plus two equals four.

"Is it really necessary to ask him to come to Los Angeles?"

"Silly question. Come on, Rupe, you're smarter than that."

Because Lester would never be able to find a job again in Urbanes territory after this, Rupert realized. He pulled his mind away from the topic for a moment and studied their driver and Martinez through the windows of the Waffle House; they appeared to have just received their bill. Rupert picked up his phone and quickly dialed Daven's guard.

"Come to the car, please. Just you, only for a moment, thanks."

Daven looked sideways at him. "What are you doing?"

Rupert dug out his wallet. "Paying their bill, of course. Want anything to go?" He took out two twenty dollar bills and handed them to Martinez, asked him to grab them some food, then turned and smiled sadly at Daven when they were alone again.

"Alright, so I get it. You know what? You've learned a lot from Hank about strategy. I'm impressed. But I'm also worried as shit, you must know that."

"Of course. I have no intention of getting myself executed, though."

"Well, it's a pretty strange state of affairs when I can say something like that is the best news I've heard all day. Thank you."

Daven chuckled a little. "I wonder what Hank would think of us right now if he could hear us. Probably shaking his head and muttering *amateurs*. He would have solved this whole crisis months ago under different circumstances, without breaking a sweat."

Rupert looked at him in disbelief. "You think too highly of him, Dav. Always have. I loved him too, but *solved* this? Really? No, he *caused* this. Don't forget that."

Daven was quiet again, and Rupert broke the silence a minute later. "So, when I tell the boys...I think Floyd won't want you there at all. Or maybe there, just not saying anything."

"I don't know. Ask him. We should go."

Rupert picked up his phone again, but paused halfway through dialing Martinez's number. "So, one more question. While I'm going back to H.A., you're heading to Philadelphia. Are you getting arrested, or not? Tell me honestly."

"That's up to the president. You already know I breached the confidentiality agreement. Technically, they can charge me with conspiracy. But I don't think they will."

"You don't think? That doesn't make me feel better."

Dav shrugged, so Rupert went back to his phone and finished dialing the number.

Lester looked back at Floyd again through the rearview mirror. Theo was now sound asleep on his brother's shoulder, mouth open and breathing heavily. Floyd was wide awake, and he looked right back at Lester.

"About five minutes away, Floyd. You okay?"

Floyd ignored him and turned to stare out the window.

"I can tell you on the plane why I kept that secret, if you're willing to listen," Lester said quietly, although he doubted he could wake Theo even if he shouted it at the top of his lungs.

Nothing from Floyd. Lester sighed and looked up to watch a large cargo jet coming down the glide slope just overhead. It seemed like the landing gear could have thumped the top of the car if the pilot had dipped down just a few feet lower. Less than two minutes later they pulled into the private hangar, and the driver got out and shut the door. Lester turned all the way around in his seat.

"Floyd. Harmon was supposed to get your deeds. Your dad insisted that I get them instead so I could turn them over to Daven after a year, because he was convinced Harmon would be in jail by now."

"Is he?"

"No. Why you're going to Rupert instead, five months early, I don't know, but I have an idea and you should be damned grateful about it."

Floyd shrugged. "Don't care. Doesn't explain why you kept it a secret."

"Your dad insisted on it. He thought you wouldn't trust me if you knew. He was right, of course, as you've just proven. He knew you too well to risk it."

Floyd shrugged again. "Like I said, I don't care. Wait...what do you mean, *knew* me?"

"What?"

"*Knew me* . Past tense. Why did you say it like that?" Floyd's voice was suddenly pitched an octave higher, and when Lester didn't immediately respond, he grabbed the door handle and bolted out of the car towards the plane.

Lester followed in a panic, but he was too late, and he arrived to all kinds of yelling inside the cabin. He poked his head around the bulkhead and saw that Daven had his hands out in a defensive gesture, while Rupert was holding Floyd's arms in a bear hug from behind.

"Calm down, Floyd. Hey, calm down," Rupert said soothingly, over and over.

Daven glared at Lester. "What the hell did you say to him?"

"Where's my dad, you traitorous fuck?" Floyd nearly spit at Daven.

Daven didn't look at him. "Mr. Boyd, go get Theo, please. Bring him up so we can talk." Then he gestured to his guards and the stunned pilots. "All of you need to leave, please. Right now. We've got this."

Lester went back to the car with a sickly-pounding heart and woke up Theo. "Hey, kiddo. Up and at 'em. You've got to get on the plane to help calm your brother. Come on."

"What? Is he having a panic attack?"

"Not yet, but sure looks like he's on the way. Come on and let's try to help him out of it."

Too late. Floyd was already lying on the floor, heaving in fruitless deep breaths, eyes wild. Theo went immediately to his side and pushed his hood back and out of his face.

"Do we need to call medics?" asked Rupert quickly. He was scared, not having seen Floyd before in this state, although he'd heard about it.

"No," Daven responded, going down on a knee on the side of Floyd opposite Theo and putting a hand on the boy's chest. "He'll be okay. You remember how to breathe, Floyd. Come on, start counting."

"Get off me," Floyd growled, and Daven stood back up quickly.

Theo looked around the cabin. "Can you guys leave us alone, please? I've got this. He just needs some breathing room."

They didn't move, then Theo asked again, not as politely, but more pleadingly.

"Come on," Daven finally said to his little entourage. "Off the plane. Let's go."

"You okay now?" Theo asked some time later, when it was obvious Floyd was perfectly fine. Physically, anyway.

"Yeah. Thanks for your help, Theody." Floyd started to sit up, then laid back down again. "Can you go get Lester?"

Theo stood up and did as asked; Floyd was upright and in a chair by the time they returned, looking grim.

"Can you sit, please?" Floyd asked Lester, very politely.

"Of course. You look a hell of a lot better than you did twenty minutes ago. Thank god."

"I understand now why you didn't tell us about the deeds. I'm sorry I freaked out on you."

"You are literally the last person in the universe who needs to apologize for anything, Floyd."

Floyd took a bottle of water from the little table off to the side, and drank a few gulps. "Please tell us what happened to our dad. Theody, sit down."

Lester's heart lurched a little. "Yeah, you'd better sit. Thanks. I'm sorry, boys. Your dad is...he passed away in April. While he was in jail."

Theo stopped breathing for a few moments, then whined a little, but Floyd had no visible reaction. "How long have you known?"

"I just found out yesterday." Lester's voice broke, and he started to tear up. "That's why Daven and Rupert came to get you. They also found out yesterday, by the way."

Floyd gestured to Theo, who got up and sat in his lap, looking stunned and red-faced. Floyd put his arms around his little brother protectively and held on tightly.

"Did he get sick?" Floyd queried, his voice a bit muffled through Theo's mop of hair.

"Not sick. You remember he had a heart attack about six years ago?"

"Of course."

"That was a minor one. He had another one and this time, a big one, he couldn't be saved. Everybody tried, but...they really tried. They couldn't save him. I'm told he felt no pain at all and wasn't even aware of it. Happened in his sleep. He was...you may not believe it now, but it probably was for the best, because he was going to be in jail for a long time. And he would have been so desperately unhappy there.”

”So he was found guilty.”

”He admitted to his guilt, actually. So...do you understand what I mean by this maybe being for the best?”

Floyd nodded again, and went white as a sheet when Theo wailed a little.

“Thank you. Can you leave us alone, please?”

Lester got up, squeezed Floyd’s shoulder, then patted Theo on the head and left the plane. Daven and Rupert were waiting expectantly, shivering at the foot of the stairs.

“Both of you, in the car,” Lester ordered sternly. “We need to talk.”

“You okay, Theody?”

Theo nodded. He was in shock, and quiet as a mouse for the past few minutes. “You always said he’d work himself to death, Floyd. Guess you were right.”

“Yeah.” Floyd was in shock, too. He hugged his brother a little tighter. “I feel like...I think I’m going to throw up?”

“Me, too.”

Neither one of them did, though. They just held each other tightly, willing tears to come that stubbornly refused to emerge for now...the eye before the storm, as it were.

Daven burst out of the car, in total disbelief of what Lester had just done. It would be many hours before he realized it was the right thing, but right now? Nothing but fury. He turned around as Rupert got out of the car and slowly approached him.

"Calm down, Dav."

"You can't *possibly* agree with this bullshit?" Daven hissed.

"Keep your voice down."

"He actually had the nerve to blackmail me, and you're okay with it."

Rupert pulled his coat tighter around him and zipped it up. The day seemed to be getting colder as the sun rose, not warmer. "Not blackmail, Dav. A bargain."

"He said...he said he'd refuse to corroborate my testimony if I don't go along with this! It's unconscionable! Oh my god, you do agree with him. I can't believe it."

Rupe nodded. "Yeah, I do. I mean, I definitely thought he was completely insane at first, but if you think about it...what do the boys gain from knowing the truth? Nobody knows but us, and Harmon and literally all of three people in the government. I don't know if you remember, but Hank's death certificate does say heart attack."

Daven was nearly in a rage, his coat blowing around in the wind like dancing flames on the tarmac. "How the *hell* am I going to explain this to Salome and President Rickon?"

"You don't. They have no intention of ever letting the boys know the truth anyway. Why do you think there's no written record of anything that happened, hm? Especially if it's discovered that Colbert was the one who caused all this. Can you imagine how much that would damage them, and not to mention, Floyd and Theo?"

"I can't lie to them. I won't."

"You don't have to. Lester already did it for us."

"Did you put him up to this?" Daven asked accusingly.

"No! Are you fucking kidding me?" Rupert responded hotly, completely astonished. "How and when would I have possibly done that? I can't believe you would even say such a thing."

Daven shook his head, then surrendered. "Fine. I'm going to say goodbye to them, then I'm heading up to Philadelphia. We'll talk when I get back to Los Angeles. Don't even think of trying to contact me before that, and consider yourself lucky that I'm not firing you right here and now."

Daven stalked away and climbed the stairs to the plane, forcing himself to slow his breathing and his pace. It would do no good whatsoever to show the boys his current state of mind.

Floyd didn't look up as he came in, but Theo and the dogs did. Starsky was curled up in Theo's lap, while Hutch was shoved in next to Floyd on his seat, half-hanging over the side, tail wagging wildly as his human absently scratched his neck.

Daven kept a respectful distance, again, while keeping his tone gentle and reassuring. "Floyd. I just learned that you think I turned your dad in. My guess is you heard that on the news, or read something Hailey wrote. That explains why you're so upset with me. If it were true, I wouldn't blame you a bit. But it's not. We'll talk when I get back to Los Angeles on Saturday. My deepest condolences for the loss of your father. He was my best friend, and I swore to him that I would protect you and Theo for the rest of your lives if something happened to him."

Now Floyd spoke up, but his tone was hard. "So why does Rupert own our deeds, then?"

Daven pinched the bridge of his nose, and then took a step closer. "Because I'm not ready to be a father to you boys. I work too much, sleep too much, don't understand teenagers...there's a whole list of reasons why Rupert and Millie were a much better choice. Hank would have agreed, by the way. But my mission to protect you doesn't change because of that. I'm going to Philadelphia now for a few days, and the only thing I'll be working on is trying to cancel your servitude and free you completely. I'm dedicated to doing that at any cost, if it's possible."

Theo sat up, deeply interested now. "Is it possible?"

"I hope so, Theo. I really do. It's going to take a long time to work out, maybe months. In the meantime, you're going home with Rupert and the dogs to rest for a while, and then…well, we'll see. Be really nice to him, and be good. He loves you. So do I, by the way."

"Thank you, Uncle Dav," said Theo. Daven felt his heart glow a little, but it was tamped down again when he glanced at Floyd, who was still glowering and obviously felt no such gratitude for his father's best friend.

"See you soon, boys."

Daven left the plane and looked around for Rupert, who had gotten back in the car to get out of the cold. He beckoned him out with his finger. Rupert got back out, and stood in front of his boss, looking sullen and hurt.

"Yes, sir?"

"Don't call me that. Sorry I went off on you. I don't want to fire you. I just…this is a nightmare. Safe travels home. Oh, wait! The check."

Daven went to the trunk and opened his briefcase, and then wrote the check for $600,000 and quickly handed it over.

"Thanks, Dav. I was thinking that perhaps you should tell Salome that you didn't tell the boys about the execution, of course. They'll be grateful to hear it, and that might help you."

"Well, I need all the help I can get, so that's good advice. I still don't agree with it, though."

"You don't have to. Just accept it. Remember the boys gain nothing by the truth on this one."

"They don't gain anything, no, but I feel like we've lost our souls by doing it."

Rupert shrugged. "Maybe we have. I'm fine with it, for one. I suppose this means you're going to retract that job offer to Lester?"

"Obviously."

"Of course. Well. Good luck in Philadelphia."

Rupe opened the door and Daven got back in his own car; thankfully his driver had waited in order to prevent him and Lester from having to ride together. That would have been a veritable bloodbath.

As they both were driven away, Rupert heard a few barks emerging from the plane, followed by a loud thump and some stifled laughter. He smiled to himself, then walked into the hangar office where the flight crew was waiting.

"I think we're good to go, gentlemen and ladies. Sorry for the delay."

CHAPTER THREE

Los Angeles - 10 days later

"No, it's not like that," Rupert clarified, shifting his phone to the other ear. "Sorry, let me explain. Floyd's not defiant at all. He does everything we ask. Sometimes resentfully, but he always does it. I was referring to the way he protects his brother. I had to scold Theo for playing around with the gas stove, and Floyd came running in from god knows where, hellbent on starting World War 3 about it. He acted like I was murdering Theo, when I was only trying to prevent him from blowing up the house."

"What did you do?" Daven asked with a huge yawn as he stretched and tried to wake up fully from having slept in so late. Again. The hotel's bed was way too comfortable for anything else.

"I sent him back to his room to calm down, and he cussed up a shitstorm the whole way down. You should have seen me trying not to laugh. The next morning he strode into the living room and announced that I must never raise my voice again to his brother, then proceeded to make us all an amazing breakfast and was perfectly polite. Never said a word the rest of the day. He might be the death of me before the new year, Dav. I can't figure him out. He goes from being pitifully subservient one moment to blowing up at me the next, and it's not always about Theo. Speaking of which, the day *that* little brat takes an order without arguing, I'll be king of England

and you'll be my queen. Floyd's spoiling him is only making it worse. Have to admit I cringe thinking back about how upset I'd get at Hank whenever he took his belt to them, but now I get it."

"No, you don't. This behavior is new. They never acted like that at my house, or at their own as far as I know. In all the days they spent with me I only had to make them stand in the corner a handful of times for fighting, but they were really little back then. They're such good kids otherwise. Hank was way too hard on them. I would even go so far as to say borderline abusive at times."

Rupert agreed with a harrumph. "Yeah. I wasn't going to say it, but...anyway, Millie swears they never did this in home school, either. So I thought of giving Floyd a lot more to do, too, since he seems to like being busy. I might put him on a much tighter schedule. Give him some goals and rewards. That would give him less time to think up new reasons to be mad at me."

"That sounds like a good plan. Have you tried talking to him about Hank?"

"*Tried* being the operative word. Yes. Twice. There won't be a third time. Learned my lesson. He was very grateful to us for letting Theo sleep upstairs, though, and that's helped a lot."

"Be careful with that."

"We are. Listen, I wanted to ask you about one more thing. I know it's a delicate subject but ignoring it isn't going to help. Lester said the plea bargain states that the boys have to go to you on April 1."

Daven braced himself. "I know, and I've been putting off mentioning it to you because I'd rather talk about it in person. Turns out that particular agreement was in writing after all. I saw it with my own eyes on Friday."

"Oh, shit. So we waited all that time for nothing. Doing nothing. I'm so sorry, Dav."

"Not your fault. Besides, neither of us knew Lester Boyd held the deeds, remember? I already asked Salome to override it, but the president said no. It's binding, Hank made sure of it. He couldn't have foreseen Floyd's objection to me. I'm appealing anyway, but it will fail and on April 1 they're mine for 19 years. I'm sorry, Rupe."

Rupert wasn't sure whether to be happy or sad about this news. "Okay, well...then we have about five months to change Floyd's mind about you."

"I'll be home Wednesday night, I think. On Saturday I'll tell him. No use keeping it from him and making him distrust me even more. That way he has those five months to come to terms with it."

"I think I should tell him."

"Why?"

"I just do. I'd rather him be mad at me about it than you."

"You have to live with him. Are you sure that's wise?"

"Trust me, Dav, please. I understand teenage boys about a million times better than you do at the moment. Let me tell him."

"When?"

"Now. He's out mowing the lawn. When he's done, I'll tell him we just got off the phone and that was the decision, and hope it instills a little trust that I'm keeping him updated every step of the way."

"Alright. If you're sure. Good luck."

Rupert didn't wait until Floyd was finished; instead he walked outside immediately after hanging up the phone and signaled him with a big wave to turn off the machine. Floyd set it to "quiet idle" instead, since it was a pain in the ass to restart, and waited for Rupert to reach him.

"Hey, Floyd. I just got off the phone with Daven. We need to talk. Or I need to tell you something, rather. You don't have to say anything if you don't want to. Will you come with me to the pool house, please?"

Floyd set the mower into an upright position and turned it completely off. "Funny how you act like I have a choice," he replied calmly, and started to walk towards the pool house.

Rupert froze in his tracks, his heart racing a little. Practically every encounter with one of the Bancroft sons was making a new grey hair sprout on his head, and it was wearing him out.

They were so much like their father, although each in different ways.

"Floyd, come back here," he called in his normal tone.

Floyd stopped, a little confused, and walked back to Rupert with a quizzical expression.

"Let's try that again. Floyd, I have some news I'd like to tell you. Will you come to the pool house with me, please?"

Floyd said nothing, just stared at him blankly and crossed his arms.

"Okay," Rupert said after waiting a few long moments in vain. "You've been here ten days, and I've never ordered you to do anything once. I always ask. Always. Why are you suddenly treating me like some kind of evil dictator?"

"Because you keep framing your orders as a question in order to pretend I still have free will. But we both know I don't, so you acting like you're giving me a choice is just pissing me off."

Rupert swallowed hard. "I see. Thank you for being honest and giving us the chance to improve our communication. Go to the pool house, Floyd."

"Yes, sir."

"Thank you."

Floyd took the news completely stone-faced, which Rupert was actually thankful for since it was far better than almost any alternative.

"So...does this mean he can't free us?"

"I didn't say that. This is the contingency plan in case he can't. He's coming back to Los Angeles on Wednesday and will want to talk to you and Theo about the situation on Saturday."

"If he does free us, what then? We're still minors. Who will we live with? Will we have a choice?" Floyd's eyes were moist, and Rupert's eyes watered a little in response.

"Honestly, I haven't even thought about it. You'll have to ask Daven. One thing I do know is that my family is your family now, and if you have a choice, you can choose us."

"I don't want to choose! I just want my dad back."

That marked the immediate end of Rupert's fortitude; he started to cry silently and couldn't say anything more. Floyd watched him for a little while and felt his own heart seize up in response. Eventually he spoke up again.

"Sir...may I go now?"

Rupert wiped his eyes, taking a few moments to gather all his strength to get his shit back together before making a reply.

"In a minute. Floyd, you and I haven't talked about Daven at all. I promised I wouldn't make you talk to him, and I won't.

But whatever I have to do to convince you he wasn't behind your dad's downfall, I will do it. I'll get the damned president on the phone if I have to. Just tell me what you need to help you get past this."

Floyd looked up, his eyes dry again. "I want to talk to Hailey Hendricks."

Rupert was startled into near speechlessness. "Hailey? Floyd, for god's sake. She's the one who caused this whole mess. No. Out of the question."

"You just said you'd do whatever I wanted. Do you have her number?"

"Yes, but....no, Floyd. Absolutely not. Don't ask me again. And while we're at it, I'm going to give you another order. Don't call me sir again. I'm Rupert. I'll tell Theo as well."

"Yes, sir. Rupert, I mean. I want to talk to Hailey. Right now."

"No. Go finish the mowing, and don't ask me again."

"No."

"No..?"

"I'm going to my room," Floyd declared firmly as he got up from the chaise lounge.

So much for that lack of defiance Rupe mentioned to Dav. He stood up now, too, and he was pissed. "Floyd, if you were one of my sons I'd already be getting the paddle out. Stop taking advantage of my promise not to, and do what I say. Outside. Now."

"Or else what?"

"That's not fair. You know I'm not going to do a damned thing, that's what. This situation is so fucked up, I'm the bad guy no matter what I do. Even when I'm trying to help you...it just...I can't understand." Rupert threw up his hands in surrender. "Do what you want, Floyd. But you're not talking to Hailey, ever, and that's final. It's for your own good."

Rupert left the pool house feeling like he was going to have a stroke from all the stress. He went to his master suite on the third floor and ran himself a painfully hot bath, hoping that Millie and the kids stayed out on their shopping trip for another hour or so.

When he heard them returning about 50 minutes later he pulled himself out of the bath - and out of his daydreams of being back in Maui with Dav and Hank - and hurried downstairs to see what help Chef needed with dinner, since he was certain Floyd wouldn't be showing up again.

He was surprised to find Floyd in the kitchen, quietly slicing potatoes and keeping a watchful eye on Theo's clumsy efforts to get all the right pots and pans heated up. Chef made his way over to Rupert.

"How are they doing, Chef?"

"Floyd might steal my job someday soon. Theo, not so much, since he doesn't try half as hard."

"That's alright, he's young. What are you guys making tonight?"

"Floyd asked to make beef wellington and cheddar potatoes au gratin. Is that okay?"

"Of course. You know that's my favorite meal. It was his idea?"

"Yes, he even had the nerve to insist on it." Chef chuckled a little. "Cheeky brat."

"Okay. That's good. Thanks."

Rupert went outside to put the mower away before the rain came. But it wasn't anywhere in sight, and all of the grass was cut.

He went into the garage instead, and sat down on a stool next to the mower and quietly "talked" to Hank about his boys. He might have cursed at him a little, too, for the hundredth time.

The days steadily improved as Rupert adjusted his style to try to keep Floyd happy. He gave the teenager a busier schedule, clear choices when he could, and clear orders when he couldn't. Even Theo was better and had started doing his chores without complaining. Most of the time, anyway.

That wasn't to say there weren't some tough issues to handle. Floyd had asked about Hailey twice more, and Rupert had calmly refused to discuss it. Each time, Floyd retreated into himself entirely, refusing to work until he snapped out of it many hours later. On one occasion, almost a full day. Rupert let him get away with it, much to Millie's dismay. She felt Floyd needed a firmer hand and that her husband was coddling the teenager, and she was right. But Rupert was tired of fighting with him.

He was also dreading the day that Daven would finally request to speak to the boys. He had been stuck in Philadelphia for another week, so there was no opportunity to try and get an in-person meeting together. Rupert knew he was dreading it more than anyone else; possibly including Floyd himself.

CHAPTER FOUR

One Sunday, between breakfast and lunch, the house phone rang and Floyd picked it up automatically as he was walking from the dining room into the kitchen.

"Aster residence.......hello?"

"Um. Hello Floyd, this is Daven. I need to speak to Rupert, but he's not answering his cell."

Floyd turned and eyed the cell phone that Rupert had uncharacteristically left lying out on the side table by the front door when he came home from church. It must be completely dead, Floyd figured.

"I'll go get him. Please hold."

"Thank-"

Floyd set the receiver down on the counter, then went to retrieve the cell phone so he could return it to Rupert for charging. He was surprised to see it wasn't dead, just on silent. He looked around furtively; no one was watching. So he slipped it into his pocket, then ran upstairs to find Rupert.

Floyd had sent Theody upstairs to play with the dogs, then locked himself in the basement bathroom, where he now sat on the closed toilet. His hand, which held Rupert's phone, was shaking violently. He had guessed the unlock code on the first try (the anniversary date, 12/31…so 1231). Now he just had to scroll through the contacts to find Hailey's number, and he hadn't yet found the courage to do it.

But when he finally did…there it was. Hailey Hendricks. Two phone numbers. Floyd called the first one; it was a disconnected line. He waited a minute to try the second one, feeling like he was going to vomit.

This one rang. And rang. And rang.

No answer after fifty rings.

Floyd scrolled back up and felt his heart stop again at the sight of Harmon's name. Without thinking, he hit "dial" and held his breath.

"Hello, Rupert. Thought we had an agreement not to call each other. Like, ever?"

Floyd felt like he'd been punched in the gut. He started to breathe fast. Too fast. Shit.

"Rupert?"

Floyd hung up and scrambled off the toilet. The phone lit up brightly, the screen showing "Incoming: Home." He quickly realized that Rupert was calling his own cell in an effort to find it within the house, and a few seconds after that call went to missed, the screen lit up again.

Incoming: Hailey Hendricks

In a panic Floyd hit the button to send the call to voicemail, cleared the call logs, and fled the bathroom to go back upstairs to replace the phone before Rupert could discover what was up.

Then the worst case scenario happened. Rupert was already in the living room, looking around in confusion, and he happened to turn just as Floyd came creeping through the door. Floyd froze as Rupert's eyes traveled down to his hand and widened in stunned comprehension.

"I'm sorry," Floyd said quickly, shakily, and he hurried over and handed him the phone. Unfortunately, Hailey Hendricks was calling back again.

"Interesting. Hailey is calling me. Did you talk to her?"

"N-no. I dialed her, b-but I chickened out."

"Wait for me in my office," Rupert ordered sharply, then he picked up the call. "Hello, Hailey. Yeah, sorry, butt dial."

"I'm sorry," Floyd mouthed before he turned away, petrified at Rupert's livid expression.

He slipped into Rupert's office, barely able to breathe. How stupid he had been! He couldn't believe himself. The man would have every right to say what he wanted now, or do what he wanted, and Floyd wouldn't even be mad. He deserved whatever was coming next, he knew without a doubt.

Rupert slipped into the office about fifteen seconds behind him, shutting the door quietly, but Floyd jumped at the clicking lock as if a gunshot had rang out.

"You called Harmon too, huh? Why?"

"I don't know. I chickened out with him also."

Rupert looked like he was going to slam the phone down on the table, but he collected himself just in time and laid it gently onto his big desk calendar.

"This is completely unacceptable, Floyd. It crosses a line I never thought you'd even consider, or be capable of."

"I know. I'm sorry."

"What do you think I should do about it?"

Rupert's face was like the worst thunderstorm imaginable, and Floyd shivered. He was suddenly ice cold.

"I think...I think you should..." He swallowed hard and composed himself, then felt his own anger building up quickly. "Whatever you do, it doesn't matter. I memorized Hailey's number, and I will call her when I have a chance, unless you chop off my hands and make it impossible. Then I'll just ask Theody to call her. Either way I'm getting an answer from her, whether you like it or not."

Rupert looked about to implode, but instead he took a few deep breaths and then sat down to think. Floyd watched him mull over the situation for a while, and was surprised when Rupert pulled his desk phone over to him, and calmly asked Floyd to sit down.

"Are you...are you calling her?"

"Yes. Afterwards, we'll discuss your punishment." Rupert punched the numbers quickly, and Hailey picked up on the first ring. Floyd's heart nearly stopped when he heard the voice. That same voice that had so confidently accused Daven of the ultimate treason.

"Is this a joke?" she responded without saying hello.

"No. This time, I really need to talk to you. I want you to tell me what proof you had in regards to your claim that Daven turned in Hank Bancroft. The story that you ran back on March…I guess around March 20."

"Oh, go fuck yourself. Lose my number, asshole."

She hung up, and Rupert raised an eyebrow at Floyd.

"That's Hailey for you. See why I didn't want you to call her?"

Floyd nodded. He was green. "Call her back. I'll talk to her directly."

"Are you sure?"

Floyd nodded again. Now he was white. "Do it. Please."

Rupert dialed back with a suppressed sigh.

"What the fuck, Aster? You suddenly got the hots for me, or what?"

Floyd swallowed hard and closed his eyes. "Ms. Hendricks? This is Floyd Bancroft."

There was silence, and it appeared Hailey had hung up. But then Floyd heard a car horn honking in the background, so he gathered his courage again.

"Ms. Hendricks, do you remember me from that day? When you gave me so much encouragement about my driving test?"

"Yeah. Yes, I do."

"Well, I never got to thank you. I passed it, you know, because you gave me the confidence to go through with it. So, thank you."

"Um. You're welcome? That's what you called me about?"

"No ma'am. I know you've heard the reports that I'm living with Rupert as his servant." Floyd's voice was hoarse. "I've been pissed off at Daven for months because I thought he turned my dad in. Because of your report, I mean. Now I'm being told he didn't, and it's making me a basket case. I just...I just want to know the truth. He used to be like a second father to me. I'm not mad at you or anything. Can you tell me if that report was true? Just a yes or no, and I'll never bother you again."

Silence. Rupert wiped his eyes with the back of his hand. Floyd had broken his heart so many times, it was a wonder it could still beat on its own.

"Ms. Hendricks?" Floyd said eventually. "You still there?"

"Yes. Didn't you get to read the FBI statement? Your dad allegedly turned himself in."

"I did read it." Floyd hated that his voice was shaking a little. "But I don't trust the FBI. And Daven didn't defend him at all. So I thought they were lying."

"Yeah, we all did, honey. We still do. Everyone who reported this story lost their journalism license, including me, because we were supposedly all wrong about Daven. There was no proof. But he did it, you just got to connect the dots and it all comes together clear as day. Rupert knows this already. Hell, everyone knows. You *should* be pissed at Daven. I would be if I were you."

Floyd looked at Rupert, stricken, then back at the phone. "Okay. I just wanted to hear it from you directly. You were so nice to me that day, and I guess I knew you wouldn't lie to me. Thank you for your time."

He reached over and hung up the phone, then sat back and glared at Rupert. "You should have let me call her way back when I first asked! Why didn't you?"

"Because she's a pathological liar, Floyd! The only honest thing I've ever heard her say in ten years was the part where she told you there was no proof that Daven turned Hank in."

"Yeah, I got that. I'm not a little kid, I know when someone's lying. You should have let me call her earlier. That was fucked up, man."

Rupert was confused now, and it took him a while to grasp what Floyd was saying.

"Wait, so...you *didn't* believe her just now?"

"No, of course not. For one thing, I started by asking her if she remembered encouraging me to take my driving test. She said yes, but that never happened. Jesus, how gullible do you think I am?"

"I never said you were gullible, Floyd. Mind your tone, please."

Floyd huffed. "*Everyone* lies to me. Everyone. The only person who has ever told me the truth all the time is my dad. I've become an expert bullshit detector in the past 8 months."

Rupert held his tongue with effort; he knew full well Hank had been dishonest with his sons on many occasions. Mostly to protect them, but also to prevent fights.

"I haven't lied to you, Floyd."

Floyd smiled without humor. "Yes, you have. You and Daven have known dad was dead for months. Know how I know? The night we arrived, your wife gave me her condolences, and said it had been a hard secret for you to hold in for so long. That you'd been working so hard to honor his legacy."

Oh, fuck....

"Floyd, I'm sorry," Rupert said quietly. "I can't defend that."

"No, you can't. And neither can Daven. So when you wonder why I have trust issues-"

"No, you're wrong about Dav," Rupert said quickly. "He never told you that. Lester and I did, without his knowledge. He nearly fired me over it, and he's still super pissed off at me. Ask him directly, he'll tell you the truth."

"Why did *you* lie, then?"

Rupert sighed, feeling completely foolish. "Ironically enough, it was to gain your trust."

"Nice job. Call Daven, please. I'll ask him. If he lies to me, I'm done with both of you forever."

Rupert held his breath as he dialed and hit the speakerphone function.

"Not a good time, Rupert," Daven answered tersely.

"Uh, make it a good time. I've got Floyd here with a question."

"How long have you known my dad was dead?" Floyd blurted impatiently.

They heard Daven excusing himself and a female voice answered; apparently he was in a meeting with Salome.

"Floyd?"

"Yes. Answer the question, please."

"I found out on...June 15."

"How long has Rupert known?"

There was a pause. "The same day. He was in Philadelphia with me when the FBI broke the news, and I told him when I got back to the hotel."

"And Lester? When did he find out?"

Now there was an even longer pause.

"Tell him, Dav," Rupert said quietly.

"Yes, trying to. I'm thinking. I honestly don't know if it was on April 1 or April 2. But one of those days. I'm sorry, Floyd. They shouldn't have lied to you. I don't support it, and I'm still really angry. It's one of the many things I wanted to tell you when we see each other again."

Then Floyd steeled himself and proposed the question Rupert was most afraid of, the one that could spin the poor kid into a nervous breakdown he might never recover from.

"Alright. So…I'm guessing he didn't die of a heart attack, either."

"Rupe, take Floyd over the house right now and give him Hank's death certificate. The real one, not the photocopy. The combination to his safe is 120949."

Rupert snatched up a pen. "Wait, say that again, sorry."

"120949."

"Okay, we'll head over. Any other questions, Floyd?"

"No. Wait, yes. Have you figured out if you can free us, yet?"

"Not yet. I'm in a meeting right now to discuss getting your dad's conviction overturned as a first step, but we haven't progressed very far. The fact that he pled guilty is causing huge issues that frankly, I'm not sure we will be able to overcome."

Floyd looked hopeful, regardless of that glumly doubtful answer. "Okay…well, good luck."

"Thanks, Floyd. I understand Rupert has told you the other news, about April 1."

"Yes."

"I know you're not happy about it, not that he even needed to tell me. I'm still trying to get that overturned as well so that you can stay with him. We'll talk soon."

"Okay. Thank you. Bye."

Floyd looked at Rupert as he hung up the phone, his expression stricken again. "I don't want to go to the house."

"You don't have to. I'll go get the thing and bring it back for you, okay?"

"No. I want to see it come out of the safe for myself."

Clearly Floyd's distrust of Rupert had grown exponentially in the past few minutes, not that he could blame him.

"Well, the safe is bolted into the wall. You either come with me, or I bring the papers to you, no other choice."

Floyd nodded. "Okay. Let's go."

Floyd completely fell apart as they pulled into the driveway, as Rupert feared he might. Toby, the current guard on duty, ran into the house and came out with Kleenex and a bottle of apple juice. Floyd went through an entire box of tissues and was just starting on a second one when the sky suddenly broke open and started drenching landscape. Rupert was glad for the roofed porte cochere that extended over the driveway and covered the car.

"Thanks, Toby. Help me get him inside."

"No, I'm fine," Floyd insisted as he sniffled. "Please, let's just get this over with. Hi, Toby. It's nice to see you again."

"You too, Floyd. Been a long time." Toby was red-eyed, too.

Floyd got out of the car and asked to open the safe himself. He didn't need to look at the paper as he punched in the number and swung the door wide open.

"I don't know where it is," he mumbled.

"I don't either."

Floyd pulled out a few large envelopes, reading the titles and then carefully setting them down on the desk as he reached in for more. He took out a powder blue one, about half the size of the others, and froze at what it said on the front.

"This is it," he said, sounding a little strangled. He didn't hesitate to break the seal and pull out the little certificate, but his hands were shaking. He scanned it for a while, then put it back in and replaced all the other envelopes on top of it and shut the door.

"I don't know how to lock this back up again."

"Want me to do it?"

"Yes, please."

Rupert went over and fussed with the door for a bit, not being familiar with the mechanism either. When he turned around, Floyd was gone, and Rupe found him standing in the middle of the living room.

"The house looks exactly the same," he said, sounding a little bewildered.

"Yes. Daven wanted to make sure you boys came home to how you left it. He didn't bring any of his own furniture or decor. Sold it all. Your rooms are as they were, too."

"It must be so weird for him to sleep in dad's bed."

"He doesn't. I doubt if he's been on the third floor even once since you left. He sleeps in the guest bedroom, or on the couch."

Floyd turned around to look at Rupert. "He sold everything else, though?"

"Yes. The other house, the boat, and the two SUVs. That's how he was able to afford freeing all of Hank's servants and paying the transfer fee for your deeds a couple weeks ago."

Floyd nodded again, clearly overcome but still managing to stay stoic, somehow.

"Did he sell Thunderbird?"

"No, he'd never do that. It's in the garage. Do you want to see it?"

"No. Let's go, please."

They drove back to the house in dead silence, but when they were parked, Floyd didn't move.

"What's on your mind?" Rupert asked.

"I was just thinking. I said earlier that everyone lies to me. That my dad was the only person who never lied to me."

"I'm so sorry, Floyd. I don't know how to make it up to you."

Floyd shrugged. "You can't. I was wrong, anyway. Dad did lie to us. He told us he was innocent. And he died in jail after admitting he was guilty. How long was his sentence? You never told me. Don't lie again, please."

"His record was sealed so we honestly don't know, Floyd," Rupert fudged. Better him than Daven, since he was already a lost cause in Floyd's eyes. "When they seal records like that, it's a life sentence 99% of the time. That's why Lester told you his passing was a mercy."

"The death certificate said heart attack, by the way. I'm sorry for not believing it."

"Don't ever apologize for any of this."

"Trust me, I won't. But I shouldn't have taken your phone. What's my punishment?"

"Nothing."

"Don't baby me. I fucked up, I can take it."

Rupert shook his head slightly. "I forgive you. Don't ever do it again, though. It would be nice if you stopped swearing so much, too."

"Okay." Floyd reached out for the door handle and started to tug it open, but stopped again.

"Rupert, don't take this the wrong way. You're my owner, so I have to treat you respectfully. But you should know that I really don't trust or respect you anymore. I don't want to be part of your family, and I actually want you to treat me like just a servant, as crazy as that sounds. So please leave me alone. If I need someone to talk to, I've got Theo."

Rupert felt his heart fall down to somewhere around his knees. "I hear you. It's not crazy, it's you setting your boundaries and I completely respect that. Let me be blunt for a moment, too: as long as you behave in a civil manner, we'll have no further problems. I can't, and won't, put up with all the attitude you've been giving me lately. I will start handing down discipline if necessary, because we can't continue like this. It's not healthy for you, and it's all been a terrible influence on your brother."

Floyd paused uncomfortably. "What kind of discipline?"

"I don't know," Rupert replied truthfully. "Let's not cross that bridge before we come to it. Even better, how about we avoid that bridge altogether?"

"Fine. Then I want to keep calling you sir. I'm not comfortable with anything else."

"If you insist."

"Thank you. One last thing. May I please stay in the car for a minute and borrow your cell phone?"

Rupert wanted so badly to ask who he was going to call. He feared the worst, naturally. Hailey. Or Harmon. Lester, maybe, although his number wasn't in the phone.

He didn't ask, however. He wanted to trust Floyd again, and had to start somewhere. Might as well be now. He took his phone from his back pocket and handed it over, then got out of the car.

"Rupert, *please*. I'm really busy. What now?"

"It's Floyd. I'm alone. Sorry to interrupt your meet-"

"Hang on."

"Okay."

Floyd's heart was pounding a little, and he almost hung up while waiting for Daven to come back on the line. It seemed to take forever and a day.

"Sorry, Floyd. Please continue."

"Um, hi. I just...you said you're trying to get the thing overturned. The April 1 thing, I mean."

"Yes, I made a little headway on it already. It's not as high of a priority as the other goal, to be honest, but it's far less complex. A matter of one simple legality to overturn, rather than a few dozen."

Floyd took a deep breath and smiled a little to himself. One thing he had forgotten that he really liked about Daven was that the man was incapable of being condescending and therefore treated everyone as intellectual equals, which always made Floyd feel a lot smarter and more worldly than he really was.

"Yeah, about that. I actually wanted to ask you to, um…to stop trying."

There was a puzzled pause on the other line. "You mean stop trying to overturn the April 1 decree?"

"Yeah. I meant that." Floyd suddenly felt ridiculously shy and awkward. "If it's okay with you, of course, and not too much trouble."

"If I remove it from the docket, I can't put it back again."

"That's fine."

Another pause, shorter this time. "Floyd, that means you and Theo will be transferred to my custody on April 1. I know you understand that, but please confirm this is really what you want before I proceed."

"Confirmed."

"Okay. Consider it done. Anything else?"

"No."

"Alright. One of us has to tell Rupert about this. I'll do it if you don't feel comfortable."

Floyd couldn't have been more grateful for that offer, and knew then he'd made the right decision. "Yeah, please tell him. He'll understand. When are you coming back to Los Angeles?"

"I wish I knew. It could be as early as Wednesday, but probably Friday. I'm afraid Shannon is going to forget who I am in the meantime."

"She won't. Starsky and Hutch didn't forget me and Theo and all, and that was like seven months."

Daven chuckled a little, which surprised Floyd slightly.

"That's good to hear. Alright, well, I'd better get back to it. Lots of ground to cover still, and it's getting late."

"Okay."

"Oh, and Floyd? I don't know what changed your mind, and won't ask. But I'm really happy that you did, all the same."

"Me, too. See you soon, Uncle Dav."

CHAPTER FIVE

Daven had never been more exhausted in his life as he climbed aboard his chartered jet for the flight back to Los Angeles. Three weeks of meetings in Philadelphia had steadily sapped every iota of energy he had left, which wasn't much to start with. Now he had a bad cold and a boat load of bad news to take home with him.

He felt guilty for not having kept in touch with Rupert at all, not even having called him for five days, but there wasn't much he could say about the FBI's stubborn and inexplicable reluctance to move on Yannick and Colbert. The only good news he really had was that he was merely fined for breaking the confidentiality agreement, and it was a fairly small amount considering the offense. There was no mention of any legal trouble, and he was stunned to find that he actually could get along with the president really well; he had shown himself to be a surprisingly forgiving man.

The caveat for this forgiveness, however, was that Daven was required to stay on as leader as the Seditionists for two more years in order to avoid destabilizing the nation's political world if the Urbanes went down. He'd accepted readily, pretending to care deeply about such stability. In reality, he just knew that if he left the party now - when he was *finally* being listened to by the president - his influence in Colbert's investigation would plummet to exactly zero.

Rupert would be thrilled, of course. That's exactly why Daven hadn't told him yet, because he didn't want to hear what great news it supposedly was. There were the boys to think about now; he was going to need to find ways to cut his workload dramatically in order to avoid following Hank's footsteps as an absent father.

No. *Owner.* Not father.

"Sir?"

Daven looked up from his seat, then dutifully buckled his seatbelt. "Sorry. I need a drink before we take off, please. Something strong."

"We have Jameson Irish Whiskey onboard, and Grey Goose."

Daven's brain jolted a little, the coincidence making the hair on his arms stand at attention. Both of those drinks had been Hank's adult beverages of choice on the rare occasions he indulged. *Overindulged* , rather - Hank never did anything halfway, and his resulting hangovers had been truly spectacular to witness.

"Actually, I'll just take some water. Sparkling if you have it."

Daven pulled out his phone as she walked away to call Rupert, but there was no answer. So he dialed Hank's cell phone, which had never been disconnected for some reason, just to listen to his voicemail message again. He wasn't sure why he did that every few days, and had been determined to stop, but he couldn't help himself.

"Dav. Wake up!" a deep voice urged.

"What?"

"We're crashing. Got your seatbelt on? We're going down."

"Hank?! What the hell? How...HOW are you here?"

Hank shrugged. "I don't know. But we're going to crash if you don't level out."

"Level out? What do you mean?" Daven asked coolly. "Wait. I'm dreaming, aren't I?"

"Yeah." Hank smiled. "You got me. I was just testing you. You believed we were crashing, didn't you? And you were actually glad. Relieved, even."

Daven gulped audibly. "So...we're not crashing?"

"Nope. Disappointed?"

"Yes. Wait, no...I don't know. That's strange, isn't it?"

"Hm. How about if I tell you we're not the only ones on this plane?"

He jerked a thumb behind him, and Daven turned around to see Floyd and Theo standing in the aisle, looking petrified.

"You go down, they go down, Dav," Hank said sternly. "You got to level out and get some altitude. Mountains ahead. Brace yourself."

Daven jerked upright with a gasp, suddenly fully awake, his neck aching from leaning up against the window for so long in the cold airplane cabin.

Rupert Aster was having a horrifically bad day at the office. Not only had the news of the boys being servants at his house gotten out - for which he wanted to blame Hailey even though there were dozens of other people who knew - but somehow word had leaked that Colbert was under investigation. Rupe had all but flipped his lid when he found out at breakfast, scaring the boys with his rare temper (all of them, including his own) and setting his poor wife on edge yet again. To make matters worse, Daven was completely unreachable due to his travels back home, and Salome was refusing to take his call.

In short, Rupe was ready to quit and go hide under a rock for the rest of his life. It certainly didn't help that it was Employee Appreciation Day at the office, which provided unnecessary distraction and sucked up all the time he could have been using to field dozens upon dozens of media inquiries.

And now, just as he was making headway on a media statement, his wife was calling to let him know that Floyd had disappeared. Rupert immediately raced home in a panic.

"Floyd, this is it. This is the last straw. I told you there was going to be discipline from now on, so here we are." Rupert's voice was at normal volume, but he was pissed and there was a significantly dangerous edge to it.

“I was only gone for like twenty minutes!” Floyd argued, not listening to a word.

“Forty-three minutes exactly. Where were you?”

“I went for a walk. The gardeners left the side gate open. Nobody saw me!”

“In the corner, Floyd. Forty-three minutes, same amount of time you were gone; or until you decide to tell me what the hell you were thinking. Your choice.”

“Rupert-”

“Oh, *now* it’s Rupert? Go. I’ll be sitting right here, working on the project I had to abandon in order to race home to find you.”

Floyd went. He only lasted four minutes before he turned around and quietly asked to speak.

“Yes, *please*,” Rupert huffed. “Anything is better than the silent treatment you’ve been giving me all week.”

Floyd didn’t look straight at Rupert; just slightly off to the left. “I’m sixteen years old. Almost seventeen.”

“Okay. You’re upset at getting a little kid’s punishment, I understand. Since you know you best, how do you suggest we handle this?”

Floyd swallowed down the lumps in his throat. “No, that’s not...I wasn’t trying to get out of it. I’m *sixteen*. I should be in high school right now, kissing girls and giving you headaches for reasons other than just going for a walk. Smoking marijuana, ditching class, whatever. I'm going crazy being locked up here. This is so fucked up!"

"I know, but-"

"You know what's even worse?" Floyd continued quietly, but his voice was now tinted heavily with anger and accusation. "This law that put me and Theo here as your slaves? It's *your* fault for promoting it in the first place. And Daven's. So don't expect me to be grateful to either of you for anything. *Ever.*"

Rupert felt himself rapidly getting smaller as his indignation deflated, while also taking note of the fact that Floyd apparently didn't include his own dad in the reasons for his hostility. Rupe didn't really trust himself to reply for a few moments without his voice cracking, but Floyd was waiting expectantly, and this was the first time he'd been open about his feelings.

Say something, you idiot. And don't cry.

"You're not my slaves," he replied carefully. "And you *know* Daven is doing everything in his power to change the situation. You have every right in the world to be angry, but I'm begging you to be patient."

"He won't be able to do a damned thing."

"Not for lack of trying. I want to remind you, Floyd, like it or not, that despite my position you'll get arrested for being unaccompanied in public. That means transfer to state custody and manual labor. So you *will* stay on these grounds at all times, end of story. And I *will* reinforce that rule with whatever means necessary if you so much as set a toe outside the gates again without a pass. Is that understood?"

Rupert had harshly barked out this last part, and was satisfied to see Floyd react in an appropriately chastened fashion to the veiled threat. The teenager breathed deeply to himself as he crossed his arms, nodded, and stared at the floor silently.

"I'm sorry, Floyd. I hate yelling, and I really don't want to break the promise I made to you back at the school, but it was incredibly selfish to leave like that. Think of your brother. Do something stupid else stupid and you'll get separated, and I won't be able to do a damned thing about it. Is that what you want?"

"No," Floyd replied quickly, without hostility.

"Okay, then. Let's put this behind us and move on. Listen, Dav is flying home right now. If you'd like, I'll invite him over tomorrow and you two can go out to the pool house and talk. As long as you need. Would you like that? I assume you'd prefer that over going back to your own house."

Floyd nodded again, his heart warming by a few degrees at the pointed reference to *his* house.

"Okay. I'll arrange it with him. Look, no matter what you say, you're part of my family. I love you, and I want you to be safe and as comfortable as possible. The security at this house is for my protection, not your imprisonment, but if–"

"I'm not going anywhere as long as Theo is still here," Floyd interrupted hoarsely.

"Good to know."

"May I go back to the corner now?" Floyd was done talking; his fists balled back up and his expression hardened again. But it had been a good start, Rupert knew.

"Wait. I just realized the dogs haven't been out to play today at all. Are we just going to keep neglecting them like that on a beautiful afternoon like this?"

"Beautiful? It's been raining sideways."

"Eh, just a few sprinkles now."

Floyd glanced outside. "Yeah, but the sky is *black*."

"Light grey. Don't exaggerate."

Floyd gave in now, realizing what Rupert was up to. The barest hit of a smile played on his mouth. For a fraction of a second only, yes, but it was definitely there.

"Should I take the dogs out to play now, before the storm starts up again?"

"What an excellent idea, thank you. Yes. I'm going back to work. I think I'd like bacon cheeseburgers for dinner, can you arrange that with Chef?"

There was a tentative knock on the airplane's lavatory door, and then Martinez's muffled voice.

Daven gathered himself quickly and exited, his face still glistening because he had run out of paper towels to wipe the water away. "Yes. I'm fine."

"I'm sorry, sir, I didn't mean to intrude. I was concerned-"

"Where are we?"

"I guess over Palm Springs somewhere. We're starting the descent. That's why I came back to-"

"Yes, thank you."

"Alright." Martinez shifted on his feet and looked a little sideways at him. "If you're going to be okay, I'll go back up front."

Daven walked back into the main cabin and looked at the seat next to his. "Sit down, if you don't mind. Right here. Please."

Martinez sat, looking more concerned than even a few minutes ago, but he said nothing and relaxed a little into the softness of the swivel seat. It was the same chair that Starsky and/or Hutch had chewed up, but since repaired, the leather seat now a slightly different color than the back and arm rests.

Daven took another long drink of water. "Look, I, uh...we were in Philadelphia for a long time. I think I maybe said fifty words to you altogether."

"I think closer to a hundred would be a fair guess," Martinez responded lightly. In truth, it really was closer to fifty. Maybe forty, all of which were probably *'let's go'* at the end of each day.

"I'm sorry." He really meant it, too, which surprised both of them. "Listen, I've been meaning to tell you something for a while. But I wasn't allowed to. The FBI is making a statement tomorrow regarding the status of Hank Bancroft. I know you were friends, and that he was close to your dad."

"Yes." Martinez nodded sagely; in truth, the only reason he had stayed to protect Daven - a man he secretly disliked - was because he promised Hank he would. This chat was the longest they'd ever had in one sitting already, and nothing much had even been said yet.

Daven took a deep breath. "I'm afraid I have some very bad news to tell you, and there's no use trying to soften it. Hank passed away. It's being made public in the morning. I'm sorry to break it to you this way, but I didn't want to...are you okay?"

Martinez wiped his eyes with his sleeve. "Uh, yeah."

"I'm sorry."

"No, it's good. I knew, anyway. I'm good, really...it's kind of a relief to just hear you confirm it, one way or the other."

"You *knew*?"

"Not hard to figure out when you guys are always talking about him in past tense."

"Oh." Daven was embarrassed, but it passed quickly. "I'm truly sorry you and I started off on the wrong foot and still haven't quite learned to walk yet. I appreciate your efforts more than I could ever express. And I mean that literally; I'm really, *really* bad at telling people how I feel about them. Thank you for staying with me even though I've given you exactly zero reasons to do so. I'm not a nice person, unfortunately."

Martinez couldn't really argue with that, considering the offhanded and aloof way Daven had treated him for months, so he didn't.

"Alright, so…where do we go from here? I don't mean you and me, I mean just everything in general. The party, and the kids. What happens to them?"

"I've accepted formal leadership of the party. As for the rest of it, I can't tell you, and it won't be included in the FBI release. On an unrelated note, I'm going to ask Avery to come back and work for Rupert and help take care of the boys now that their introductory period is almost over and they can start going out in public again. I've been trying to set up a conversation with him for a couple weeks, but he never responds."

Martinez was still wiping his eyes, but he was totally composed otherwise. "He's on vacation, so don't take it personally. Went on some backpacking trip for like three weeks. He'll be back today, I think. Or tomorrow. He always asks about you, you know. Always tells me to say hello."

Daven nodded, feel greatly relieved but also confused. He thought Avery hated him for some unknown reason, especially because the man had bowed out of two lunches they'd arranged, with little explanation. Daven hadn't invited him again.

"Great. Thank you. I'll call him in a few days and set up a luncheon meeting at his favorite restaurant. I'd be very pleased if you would join us. At the table and in conversation, I mean."

Martinez blinked in surprise. "I...are you sure?"

"Yes. No obligation, of course. I wouldn't blame you for declining, considering...well, everything." Daven waved his hands around vaguely, then stared out the window, already lost in thought again. "No need to answer now," he added absently.

The guard wasn't sure what his answer would be, but his heart glowed a little at the invitation anyway. He kept silent and thought about Hank for a while, and once again mourned the loss of the man who had singlehandedly reunited the Martinez family by taking him in as a new guard without hesitation after their first meeting. It was so hard to understand why he was gone.

CHAPTER SIX

"Sorry I missed you earlier, Dav, what's up?"

With all the background music it sounded like Rupert was at a party, and Daven glanced at his watch. It was 3:30pm here in Los Angeles, on a Friday.

"I'm on my way home from the airport. What's all that noise?"

There was a slight pause. "Happy hour."

"Oh...okay."

"Been a bit of a week. You sound horrible. Are you sick?"

Daven grunted. "As a dog. I hate that saying, though. It makes no sense. I've never seen a dog with a bad cold."

"You know," Rupert said, ignoring the observation, "I've been waiting three freaking weeks for you to tell me what's going on. You've said nothing. Are you leaving us, or what? I don't even know if I can wait even one more minute until home you, get you...get home. I mean."

"Are you...are you *drunk?*"

"Had a few, yeah. It's been a bit of a week."

Daven sighed. "So I've heard. No, I'm not leaving the party. I was confirmed. There's literally nothing to tell you. The president can't make a fucking decision either way."

"Oh. Swearing. Yikes. Dav, um..."

"What?"

"The boys. I think we'll have to put Floyd in therapy again."

Daven nodded. "Sorry to hear. I'll pay for it, of course."

"You haven't asked about them lately. Like, at all. Not checked in once all week. Hank never asked about them either when he was away and that used to drive you crazy."

Pause. "He was their *father*. We'll talk when you're sober again. Who's with you?"

Rupert rattled off a list of about 19 people, and Daven closed his eyes in pain. All those colleagues, seeing Rupe drunk like that. It didn't bear thinking about.

"You should go home. It's not proper to...you know what, never mind."

"Mmmhmm. Hey, can you come over tomorrow and talk to Floyd."

"Actually, I was hoping I could come over now. Maybe since you're not home that might be an even better option."

"Yeah," Rupert said after thinking about it. "Call Millie and have her ask Floyd. I don't know if he's ready. He had a hell of a day."

"Oh. I'm afraid to ask."

"Probably best if you don't."

"Alright. Don't do anything tonight that's going to land you in the papers on Monday."

He hung up, then dialed Millie. Floyd wasn't ready, she confirmed after briefly consulting with the teenager. Maybe tomorrow.

So Daven went home and laid awake all night long.

Saturday Afternoon, 3pm

Daven said nothing much until he and Floyd were in the pool house with a couple of bottles of soda and a box of Kleenex. Theo had been happy to see him, of course, but despite his last heartwarming conversation with Floyd, it was abundantly clear that the teenager wasn't exactly thrilled with his return yet.

"It's good to see you again," Dav began as Floyd made himself comfortable on one of the big patio chairs that had been pulled inside the pool house for winter. "So sorry for being late. I've been on the phone with the FBI for hours today. I have a lot to tell you, but first things first. I haven't secured your freedom yet."

Floyd didn't seem surprised. "Okay."

"The good news on that front is that the answer wasn't no."

"I don't understand why you're even bothering. Dad was guilty, and this was our sentence. Why would they ever consider just suddenly letting us off the hook?"

Daven took a deep breath. Here goes. "I'm going to be honest with you Floyd. Now, and forever. The reasons behind that possibility are so unbelievable, that frankly, I can't even process it. If I can't, neither can you."

Floyd sat up a little, looking offended. "Oh."

"Secondly…Rupert knows you've been watching the news, but he doesn't say anything because he doesn't want to fight with you. I want you to stop. Promise me you will."

"Why?"

"Because a lot of stuff about your dad is going to get out soon, and most of it will be twisted into lies and be very disturbing to you. Rupert and I will keep you updated on the actual truth."

"I know about Colbert already. Saw it this morning."

"You know nothing about it from just that little blurb. Rupert told me about your call with Hailey."

Floyd flushed hotly, but said nothing.

"Things are about to get even crazier," Daven continued coolly, "and you only heard one piece of a moving machine of a thousand pieces we've been working on. Promise me you'll stop sneaking in to the TV room."

Floyd hesitated, then shook his head no.

Daven sighed, disappointed but not surprised. "Alright. Then let's move on. This next part is going to be very hard to hear, but I need you to be strong. If you're not ready, tell me."

Floyd glanced at the Kleenex box, then back to Daven. "Um. Will I ever be ready? Go ahead."

"Your dad didn't get a prison term. He was headed that direction, at least twenty years. Then something happened and he...he was sentenced to death."

"Okay. That makes sense," Floyd said calmly, his shaking voice betraying his placid expression and thudding heartbeat. "He said..."

Daven didn't prompt him, despite his immediate, keen interest in what Hank had said. Something changed the teenager's mind, though, and he waved his hand dismissively.

"I'm sorry, Uncle Dav. Go ahead."

Damn. "Alright, well, this is the worst part. I can't even fathom how I could possibly soften the news. Your dad, he really did have a heart attack. That was the legal cause of his death, and what they had to put on the certificate. But it was...it wasn't natural. It was artificially induced. By lethal injection."

"Uhhh." Floyd broke into a heavy sweat now, too, and his face was bright red.

"Do you understand what I'm saying?" Daven asked needlessly.

"Yeah. You know what, maybe I wasn't ready for this news after all."

"You're taking it very well, considering."

"Not really. Um...did you ever consider that maybe this was something you could have kept from me, that I would have actually been fine with *not knowing?*"

Daven shook his head. "No. I never considered that. No one on earth deserves the truth more than you. I will let you decide when we should tell Theo, if ever. Lester and Rupert know, but I basically told them I would kill them both if they didn't let me tell you myself. So don't blame them. If you're going to be mad at someone for that, it should be me."

"I'm not mad. But all that crap they said about him dying in his sleep, and no pain-"

"It was true. They fully sedated him first. He felt nothing, and I'm told he was in good spirits before that. Joking around, and not concerned about dying, at all. Which is, of course, so typically Hank."

It was, too. Floyd could picture the scene easily. He looked at his hands, then wiped his eyes with his sleeves again, but said nothing. Asked nothing.

Daven waited a while, then gently probed. "You mentioned a few moments ago that your dad said something to you. What was it, exactly? It might help me."

*

I chose this, Floyd. Don't blame anyone else. I'm content. Take care of your brother, and be really good for Dav. I love you. We'll be together again someday, and none of this will matter.

*

Floyd had thought he meant it literally - as in, *we'll be together again in maybe ten or twenty years and move to a cabin off the grid in Yosemite,* or similar. The idea that he meant another thing entirely - something otherworldly - had never occurred to the teenager. Not even *once,* until this very moment.

The words were meant for him alone, and no one else. Gently murmured into his ear within sight of the FBI, but not within hearing. Their lives had been so public, so exposed, so open for interpretation by strangers, that this parting reassurance was the only secret they had left to share between the two of them.

And it was going to stay that way.

"No," Floyd replied to Daven in a near-whisper, multiple streams of tears now trickling down his face. "It won't help you. But it helped me."

Daven handed Floyd the box of Kleenex. "I feel like I should leave you alone, even though I don't want to. Is that what you want?"

Floyd nodded and sniffled, then looked up at the sound of something suddenly raking against glass. He peered around Dav to the pool house door, where a familiar face was staring at him intently, paw pressed flat against the screen.

"Shannon's here!" he yelped, a little startled.

"Yes, I asked Rupert to go get her. Want me to let her in?"

"Of course!"

Daven squeezed him on the shoulder and got up to open the door. Shannon came bursting in, sliding a little on the tile, and nearly knocked Floyd to the ground in all her unabashedly canine exuberance.

Daven shut the door and went back in the house, where Rupert was waiting in the kitchen impatiently, and angrily, for any kind of news from his boss.

"I told him about the execution," Dav said flatly as he picked up an orange from the fruit basket and stopped at the island to peel it.

"Oh. Shit. You didn't tell me you were going to-"

"Well, I did. So that's over with. Don't mention it to him, obviously, best to leave it alone."

"You *think?*" Rupert was stunned. "Alright. Change of topic, then. Colbert was arrested last night."

"I know," Dav replied calmly. "We should go into your office."

"Of course you know," Rupert continued without a pause as walked them down the hall and opened the heavy door for them both. "And then Harmon sent out that incredible statement this morning. What in the holy hell went down in Philadelphia? You said yesterday afternoon nothing was moving along, next thing I know I'm waking up to a freakin' overnight political apocalypse. You've got one a hell of a poker face, Dav."

"Thank you, I think. But I wasn't lying. They were all at a stalemate when I left, so I'm just as surprised as everyone else. The president couldn't make a decision on anything, and I was about to stroke out from the stress, so I insisted they let me go home for a few days to catch up on work, since you've been the running the place by yourself. Thank you for that, by the way. But then…"

Daven told the story of everything that happened after that, all occurring within the past 18 hours. Rupert couldn't believe it, but then he could…and then he couldn't again. Turned out Harmon himself had finally lost his patience with the pace of the investigation, threw up two middle fingers to the president, and took matters into his own hands.

Even more noteworthy, he had done it *publicly*. He started with a damning press release and media statement at 4pm on Friday, shortly after which Colbert was taken into custody in front of his entire staff. Harmon, of course, was immediately relieved of his leadership position by the president himself for interfering in an official investigation, but he had planned for that.

So now Colbert was in jail, long before his time was due (or well after, depending on one's point of view), a fact which, on the surface, seemed destined to derail the investigation so thoroughly that all the evidence tracks carefully laid down would be completely obliterated, a smoking trail of wreckage left strewn along them. Harmon had planned for that too, of course. He had learned a lot from Hank without even meaning to.

"*Witness tampering?* Are you fucking kidding me?" Rupert exclaimed as he stormed around his home office in a fit of enraged disbelief. He was exhausted already, and it had only been about ten minutes since the conversation started. "That's all they can pin on him? After everything he did?"

Daven stood placidly by the credenza, carefully peeling a second orange. "Calm down. Al Capone went down on tax evasion charges when they couldn't nail him on anything else. I'll take what we can get."

"Jesus Christ. Colbert will *maybe* get a few years in jail. Which witness is claiming it?"

Daven smiled beatifically and popped a wedge of orange in his mouth. "That's the best part. Harmon is claiming Colbert tampered with *him* and induced him to file false charges."

"Jesus Christ," Rupert repeated, stunned. "How the hell are you so calm right now?"

Daven shrugged. "Because it gets even better. Turns out Harmon was in cahoots with Yannick the entire time I was in Philadelphia. Before that, actually. Ever since we met in Temecula when I confirmed he was our mole."

"Oh, wow. Wait....you did *what* in Temecula??"

"Never mind. Anyway, Harmon got a hold of him and tipped him off, without the FBI knowing. Told him Colbert had done him dirty, and apparently befriended him instead of threatening him. I'm not sure of the details on that yet. So Yannick agreed to reconnect with Colbert and start recording the conversations. When they had enough to go on, Harmon pulled the fire alarm. Now the FBI can't possibly stall or hide the investigation any longer."

"Shit. They must be pissed."

"Let's just say today's calls contained more obscenities than I've ever heard in my life, on all occasions combined. Even Hank would have blushed."

Rupert was speechless when Daven smiled again. *Smiled.* Genuinely. *Twice in one day.*

"Alright. So...what do we do now?" Rupe asked, shaking his head in amazement.

"Nothing. These oranges are amazing, by the way. Where'd you buy them?"

The weekend was a veritable bloodbath for the Urbanes. The Seditionists said nothing, responded to zero requests for statements, and Daven made the decision to close the office for the upcoming week. Then he actually shut off his phone and his computer, and stayed in bed with Shannon for two days straight. Thanks to all the Nyquil he needed to fight his cold, he slept fairly peacefully through the entire ordeal.

This was contrary to Rupert, of course, who monitored every word said or written about the affair and drank a entire six-pack of Red Bulls in 36 hours to keep him going.

Seven weeks after the fracas began, it was over as suddenly as it had begun. Yannick had somehow gained immunity for his testimony and would get off scot-free, a fact which pissed off Rupert, Daven, and Harmon to no end. But they all knew that the man simply wouldn't have cooperated with the FBI otherwise, and they'd be back at square one without him. So they each quietly resolved to find peace within themselves for the compromise. Some things you just couldn't fight.

Harmon received a two-year sentence in a minimum security facility for his part in the affair, which basically amounted to gross negligence and violation of public trust for being totally oblivious in regards to the actions of his right hand man. He would have received more if he'd been implicated in Janet's murder, but nobody was. There simply wasn't enough proof of anything, and Colbert had at least been smart enough to not be recorded talking about it. But the Urbanes Organization was found culpable anyway in a separate civil lawsuit Daven had quietly filed on the side, and eventually were ordered to pay multi-million dollar settlements to both Janet's family and the Bancroft sons' trust funds.

Colbert got 3 years in a nasty federal prison for witness tampering after the hung jury argued for three weeks over the other alleged crimes, the charges for which were eventually dismissed. They simply couldn't buy all of Yannick's claims after multiple witnesses had thrown reasonable doubt upon his integrity and motives. And they weren't wrong.

It didn't matter in the end, though. Colbert was brutally shanked in prison six days into his sentence by another inmate, and was left to die alone, gasping and panicking, his hands cupped full and overflowing with his own blood and vomit.

Harmon had planned for that, too.

EPILOGUE

March 2, 2019

Johansson House

"Floyd?" Daven poked patiently at the teenager in his bed for the third time, then shook him a little. Nothing. He waited a moment longer, and then pulled the covers off without mercy once he remembered Hank's stories of what it took to get the kid up.

"Mmmphhm," he mumbled as he turned around and cracked open one eye.

"Hi," Daven said gently. "Do you know what day it is?"

Floyd startled a little, then sat up quickly, rubbing his bleary eyes. "Yes. Sorry, I'm up."

"Can you be ready in fifteen minutes?"

"Yes, sir."

"Please don't call me sir anymore. We talked about this."

"I know, sorry. I'm up."

"Okay. See you in the garage in 16 minutes."

Daven smiled, then went downstairs to find Theo, who was putting the collars on the dogs and refilling their water bowls. He was ready to go, of course, so Dav turned and headed down the stairs and into Avery's office. He and Brittany were there, chatting happily and sharing cinnamon banana bread that Floyd had made the night before.

"Hey boss."

"Ready to go, Avery? Big day."

"Been ready for about a year. Let's do it."

The quartet gathered in the garage, where Floyd was trembling slightly from nerves. The 17-year old pulled his hoodie tighter around him, and wolfed down another bite of the bacon breakfast burrito Chef had made especially for him.

"You ready, Floyd?" Daven asked quietly. "Theo?"

They nodded, so Daven closed the door and locked it behind him using the new fingerprint panels he'd insisted be installed on every door to keep Hank's sons extra safe.

"Okay, Avery. Let's get this little parade started, then. Boys, into the car."

Avery grinned, then went out to meet up with Martinez to get the SUVs positioned in the driveway.

Daven put the key into the ignition, then turned and regarded his best friend's sons fondly. "Happy Freedom Day. Today is going to be a bit of a circus, I'm afraid. But you already know that."

Floyd smiled a little, his eyes slightly moist. "Yeah. I don't think I'm going to mind all the cameras for a change. Let them look!"

"Don't go and become a ham on me, now," Dav joked as he backed the car out and waited for his guards to position their SUVs in front and in back of them.

Twenty minutes later the little procession - at first surrounded by news vans from every TV station within 200 miles - pulled by itself into a parking lot which had been closed and cleared out for the morning just for them, even screened from view of the street with black netting similar to the kind used for film shoots. Daven pulled through into that private area, closest to the building, then he and Theo got out.

Floyd swallowed down the last of his burrito, slid over to get behind the wheel, and poked his head out the window.

"Okay, guys. Here I go. Wish me luck."

"You don't need luck. You've had enough practice. Just remember to take it easy with those brakes, you were still too hard on them yesterday. What did I tell you is most important to watch out for?"

Floyd sighed a little, but it was all in good humor. "Pedestrians and bicycles. I know. Got it."

"Good. Alright then."

Daven walked away to greet the DMV manager to chat with him for a moment and give him a check. Then the man got into the car with Floyd and buckled in. Daven, Theody and

Martinez all stood back to wave him off and shout good luck, despite Daven's claim that he didn't need it, while Avery climbed back into the SUV.

Floyd grinned, then turned his attention into the car and keyed the ignition.

That rumble.

Oh my god. Dad...I wish you were here to see this.

He got sad for a moment until he remembered his dad *had* been here to see this. It had been one of the man's proudest moments. And now Floyd would have the memory of Daven here to see it, too.

In reality, Dav could have easily turned in the paperwork for Floyd's old license to be reinstated, which would have taken all of three minutes, but he'd insisted on a new test to make sure Floyd was ready. Again. But Floyd didn't mind; he was pretty sure Dav also just wanted to be here for this event and make a memory of his own, on this first day as a second father and freshly retired former leader of the Seditionists.

"Okay," the instructor began. "Take a right out of the parking lot, Floyd. We'll go about half a mile and turn left."

Floyd's heart glowed as he pressed the accelerator just the right amount in order to pull out of the parking lot without lurching, and drove carefully down Santa Monica Boulevard, tailed closely by Avery's huge black Escalade...which in turn was quickly followed by overly-eager news vans.

Floyd ignored them all and sucked in a surprised breath at the sight before him. The ocean seemed an impossible shade of blue today, and somehow stretching into the sky farther than the horizon should allow. The trees whizzed by three times greener and brighter than he remembered, the pedestrians all absurdly radiant in their colorful spring attire.

It was utterly dazzling.

"I'm going to pretend you didn't just roll through that stop sign," the instructor said quietly. "Turn left at the second light."

Floyd quickly wiped his eyes as he flipped on his turn signal, then hesitated.

"I'm sorry, sir," he said quietly. "For the stop sign, too, but...can we go straight for a little while longer?"

To the ocean, he meant. As far away as he could get right now from what lay behind him. The instructor smiled a little; Daven had quietly asked him to give Floyd some leeway from the normal test route, within reason of course.

"Sure. Just mind the signs and keep up with the traffic. Going a bit too slow at the moment."

Floyd smiled now too as the light turned green and he undid the turn signal and pressed the accelerator again; more firmly this time. *There. That's better.* The Thunderbird purred contentedly at the faster speed, and Floyd's eyes glistened again as he patted her gearshift lovingly. He changed lanes once, then again, then confidently ramped up to meet the speed limit.

"You seem a lot more comfortable already. That's good," the instructor declared happily. "I think you're going to be fine, Floyd. You've got this. Just pay attention, keep your eyes on the road."

Floyd was starting to grin broadly, and he nodded in response, but he didn't actually hear the man's words at all.

"Yeah, I've got you," he was gently murmuring into the steering wheel. "I've got you. We've got this. We're going to have so much fun. Just you wait…"